Disney Fairies

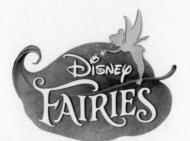

Vidia and the Fairy Crown

By Haruhi Kato

TOKYOPOP®

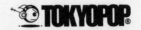

HAMBURG // HONG KONG // LOS ANGELES // TOKYO

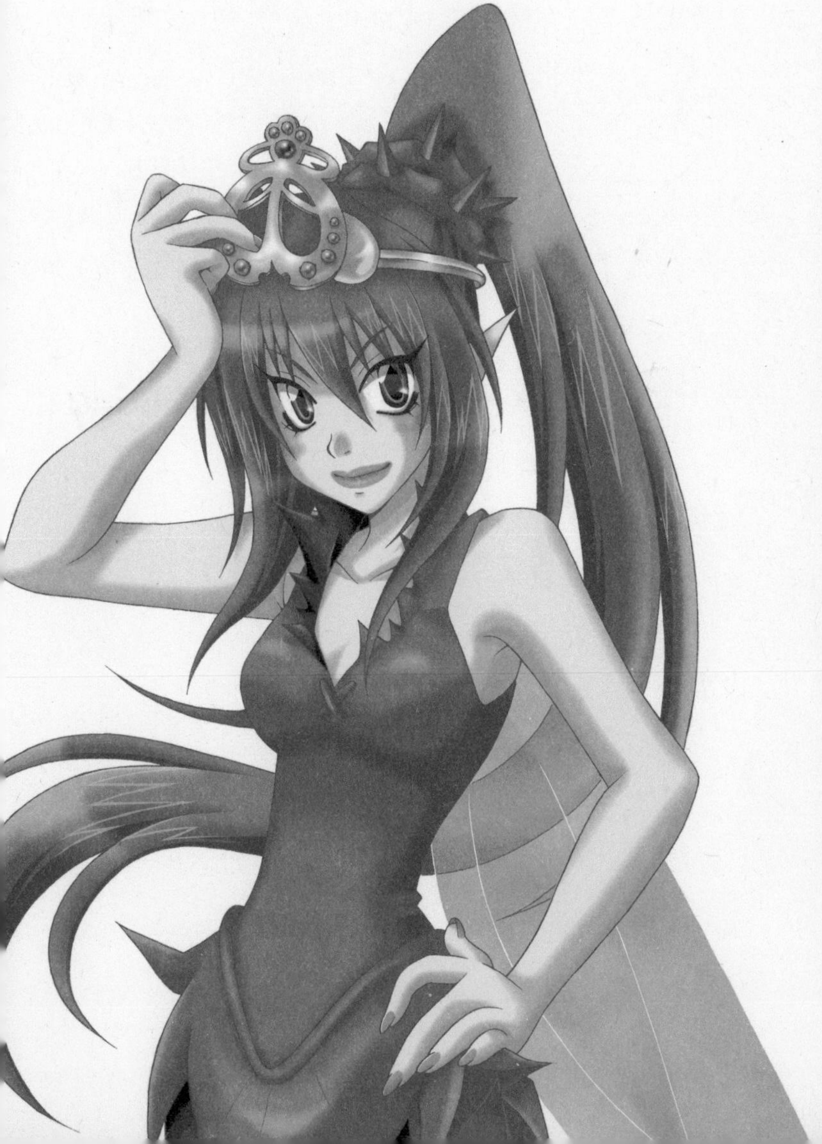

Believing is just the beginning

All About Fairies

IF YOU HEAD TOWARD THE SECOND STAR TO YOUR RIGHT AND FLY STRAIGHT ON 'TIL MORNING, YOU'LL COME TO NEVERLAND, A MAGICAL ISLAND WHERE MERMAIDS PLAY AND CHILDREN NEVER GROW UP.

WHEN YOU ARRIVE, YOU MIGHT HEAR SOMETHING LIKE THE TINKLING OF LITTLE BELLS. FOLLOW THAT SOUND AND YOU'LL FIND PIXIE HOLLOW, THE SECRET HEART OF NEVERLAND. A GREAT OLD MAPLE TREE GROWS IN PIXIE HOLLOW, AND IN IT LIVES HUNDREDS OF FAIRIES AND SPARROW MEN.

SOME OF THEM CAN DO WATER MAGIC, OTHERS CAN FLY LIKE THE WIND, AND STILL OTHERS CAN SPEAK TO ANIMALS. YOU SEE, PIXIE HOLLOW IS THE NEVER FAIRIES' KINGDOM, AND EACH FAIRY WHO LIVES THERE HAS A SPECIAL, EXTRAORDINARY TALENT.

NOT FAR FROM THE HOME TREE, NESTLED IN THE BRANCHES OF A HAWTHORN, IS MOTHER DOVE, THE MOST MAGICAL CREATURE OF ALL.

SHE SITS ON HER EGG, WATCHING OVER THE FAIRIES, WHO IN TURN WATCH OVER HER. FOR AS LONG AS MOTHER DOVE'S EGG STAYS WELL AND WHOLE, NO ONE IN NEVERLAND WILL EVER GROW OLD. ONCE, MOTHER DOVE'S EGG WAS BROKEN. BUT WE ARE NOT TELLING THE STORY OF THE EGG HERE. NOW, IT IS TIME FOR VIDIA'S TALE...

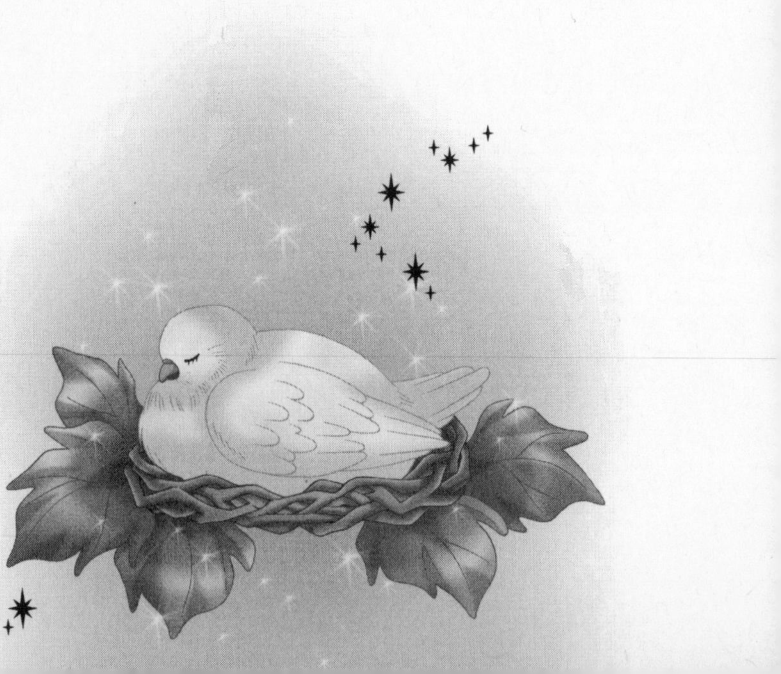

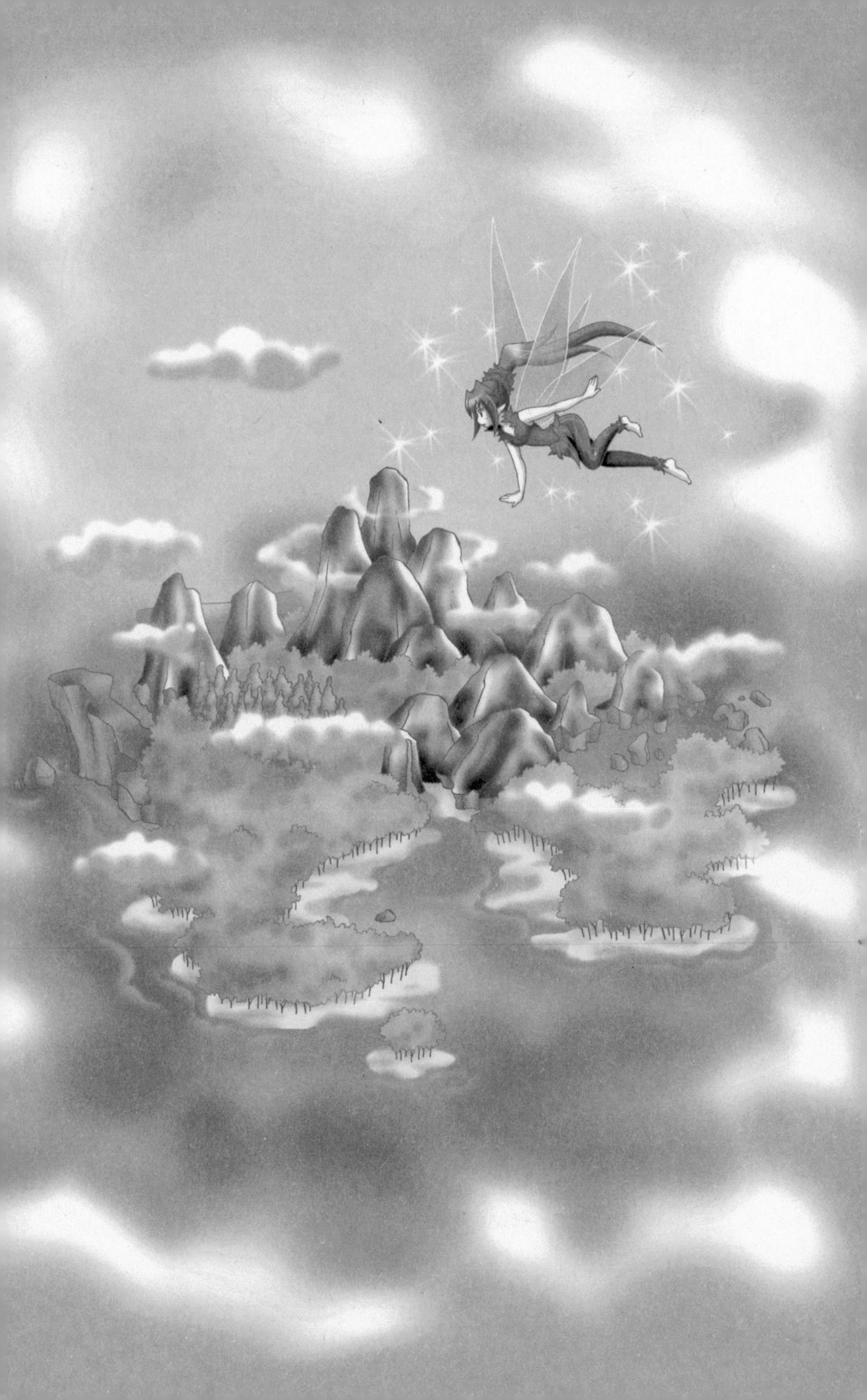

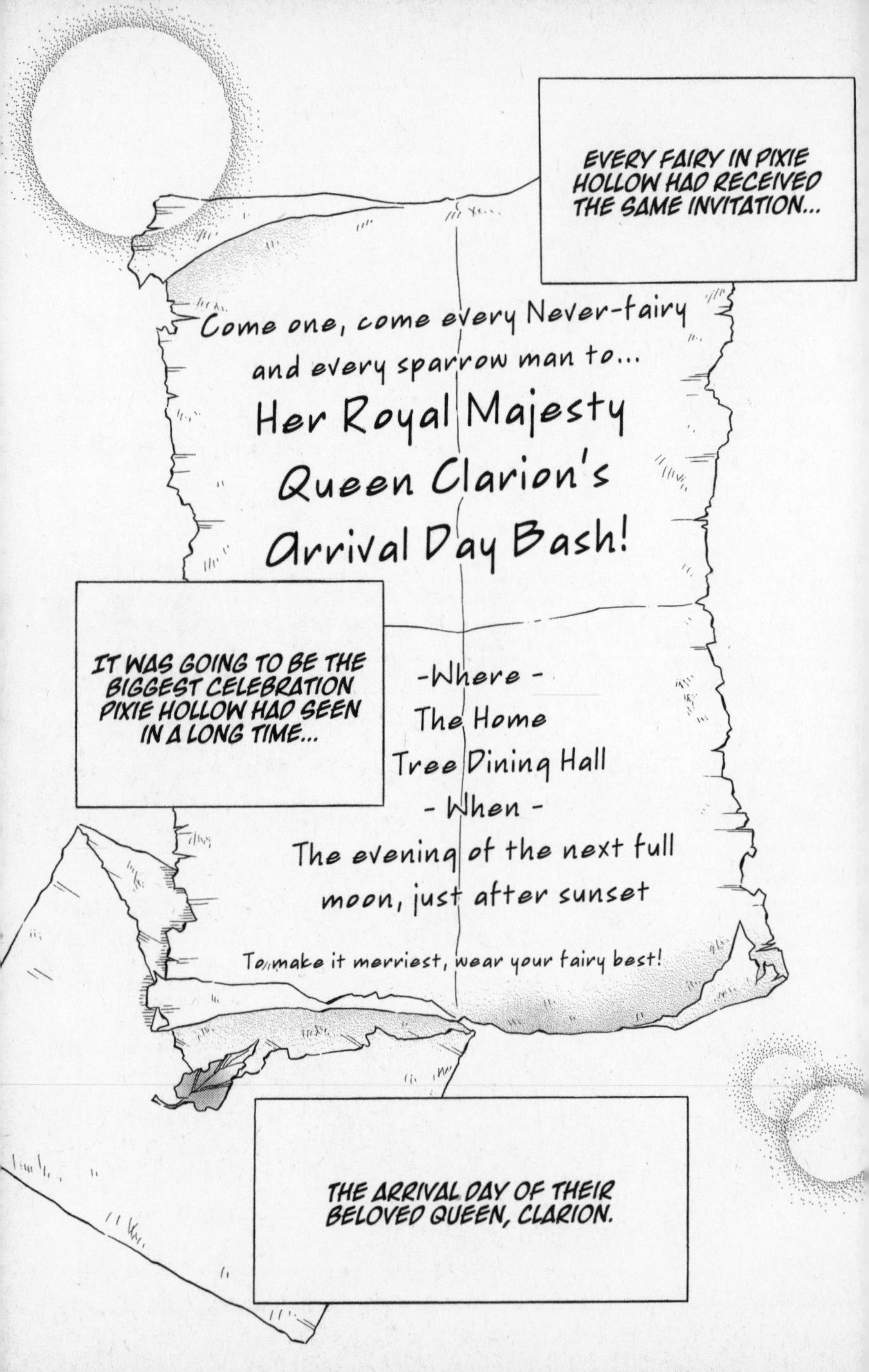

Come one, come every Never-fairy
and every sparrow man to...

Her Royal Majesty
Queen Clarion's
Arrival Day Bash!

-Where-
The Home
Tree Dining Hall
- When -
The evening of the next full
moon, just after sunset

To make it merriest, wear your fairy best!

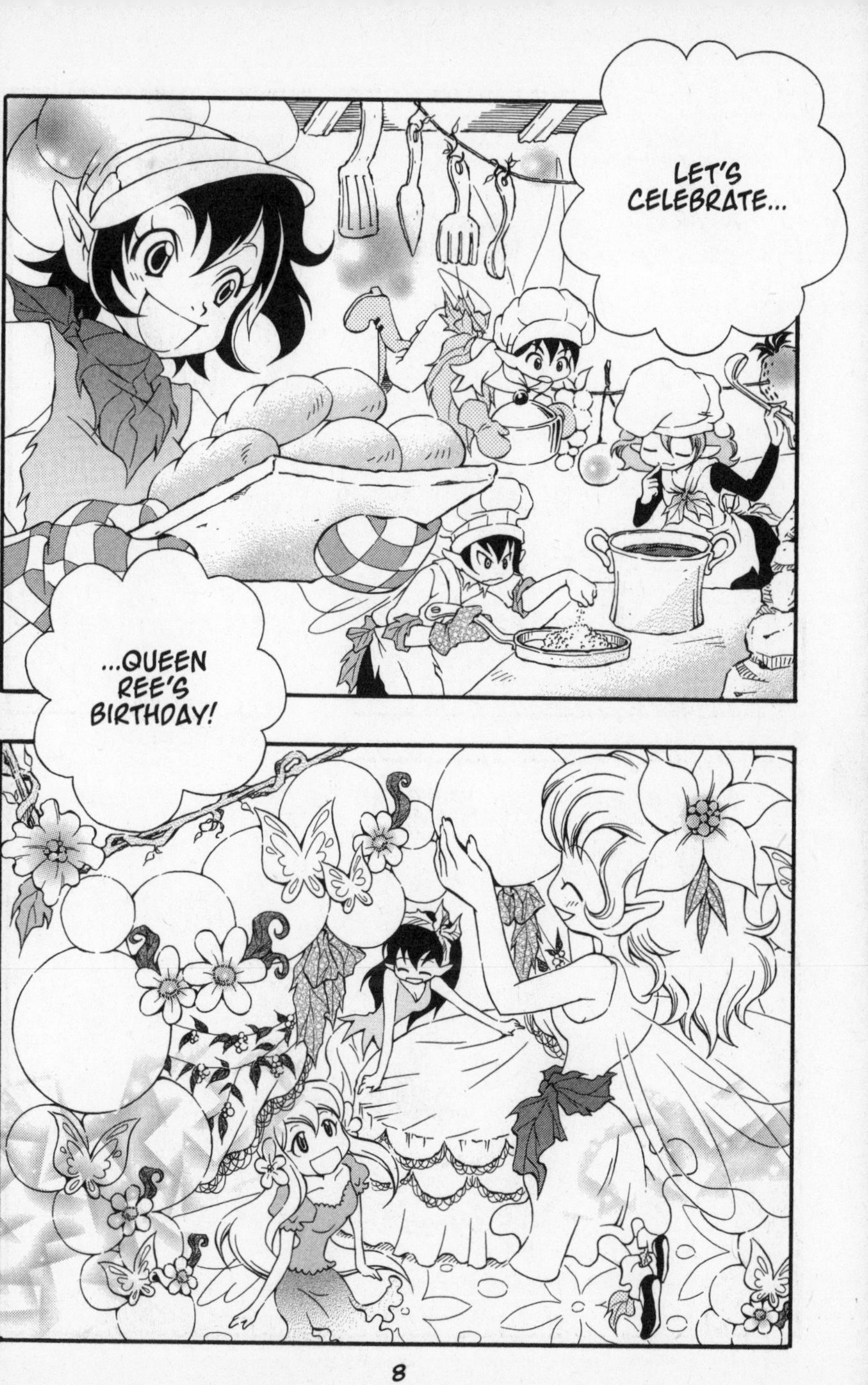
LET'S CELEBRATE...
...QUEEN REE'S BIRTHDAY!

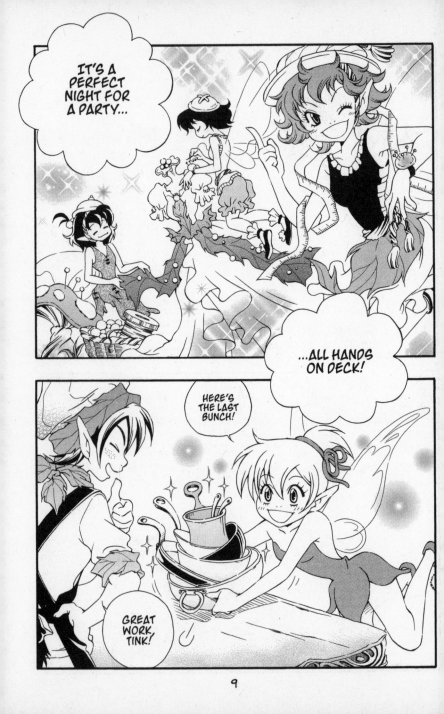

9

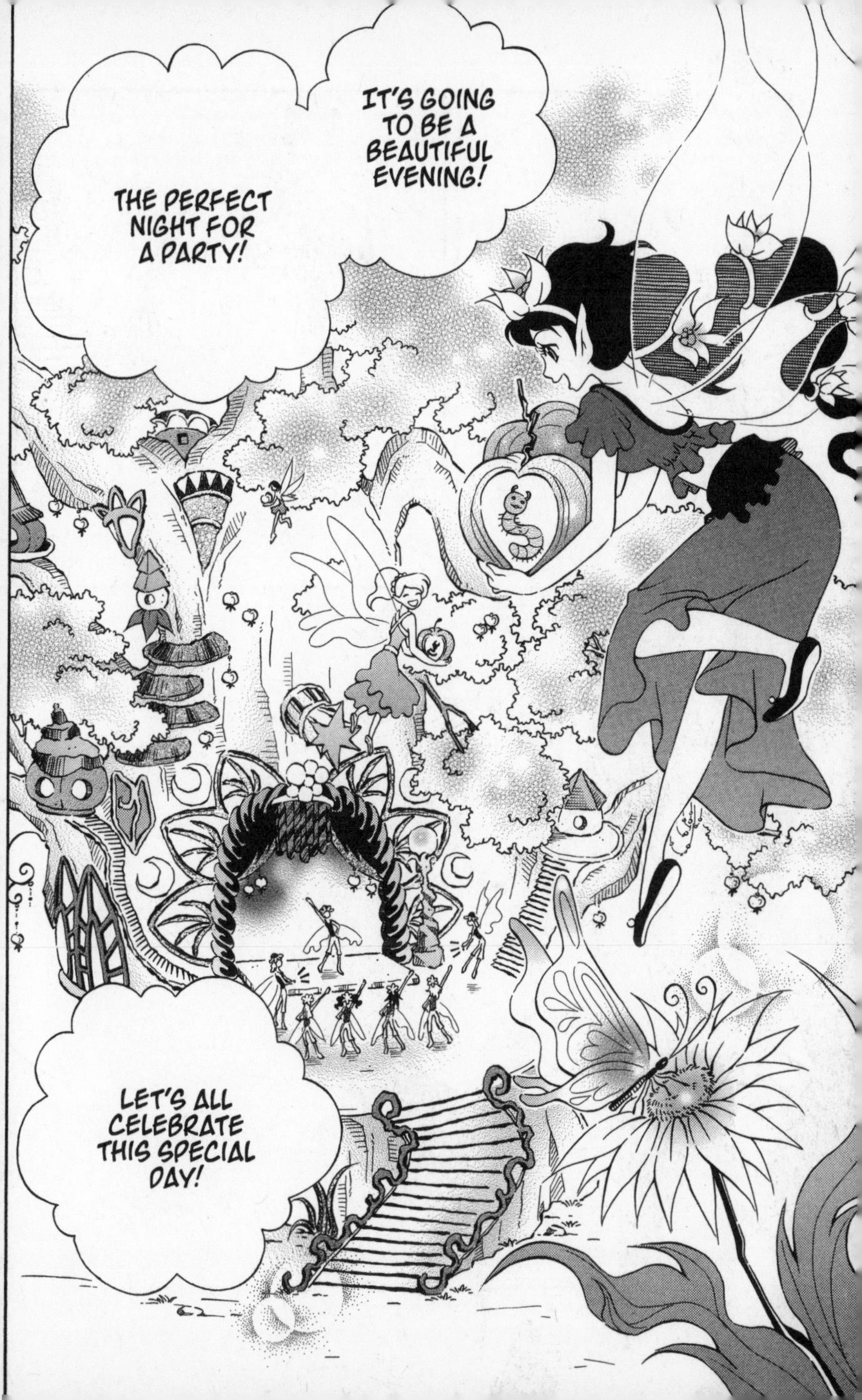
IT'S GOING TO BE A BEAUTIFUL EVENING!
THE PERFECT NIGHT FOR A PARTY!
LET'S ALL CELEBRATE THIS SPECIAL DAY!

READ THIS WAY

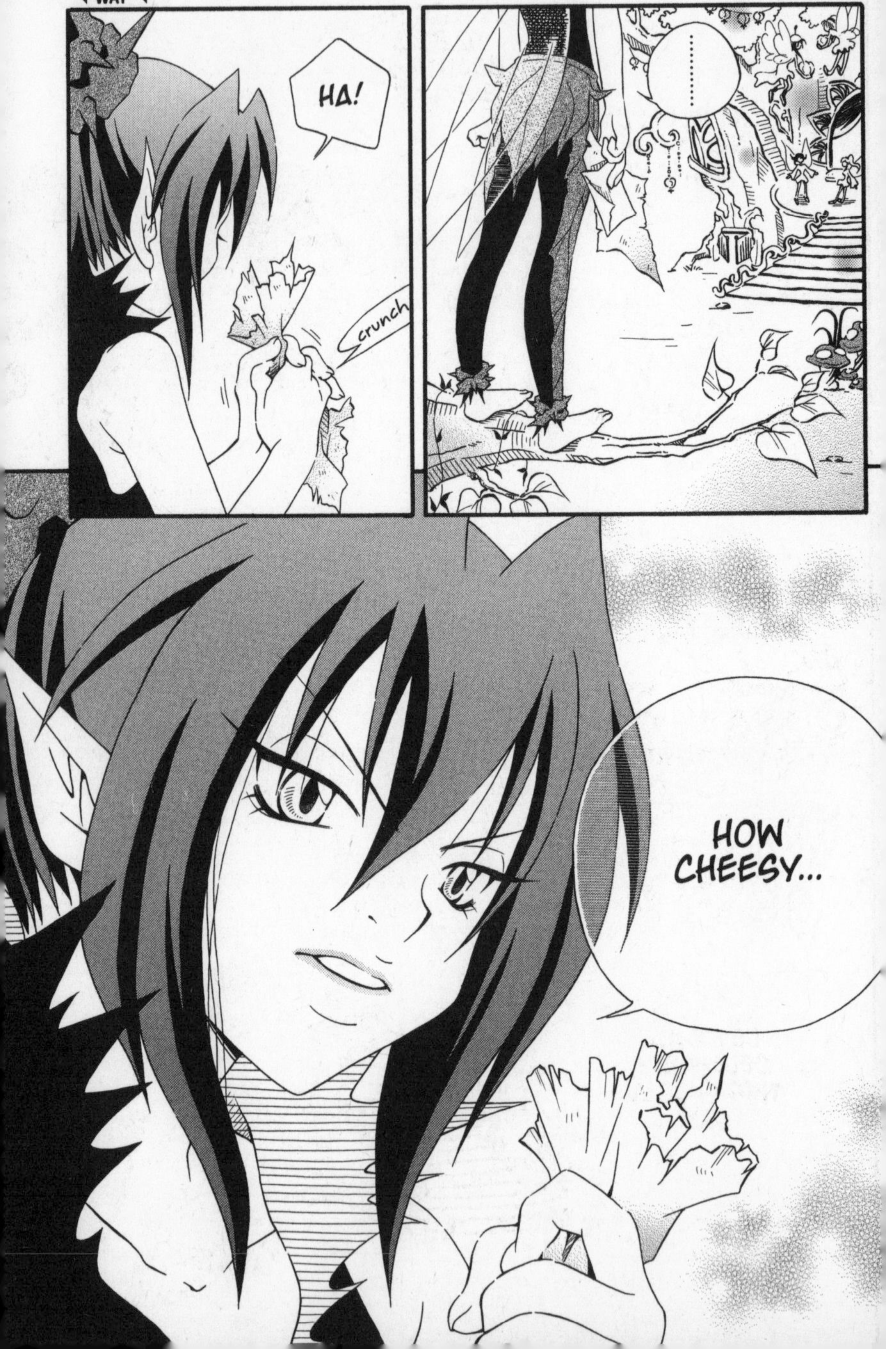
......
HA!
crunch
HOW CHEESY...

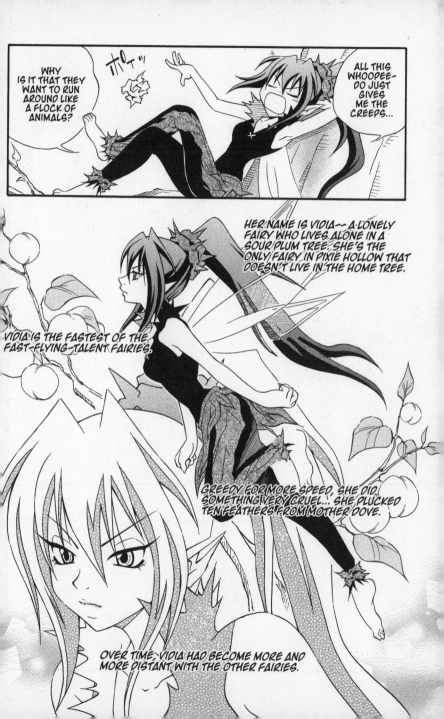

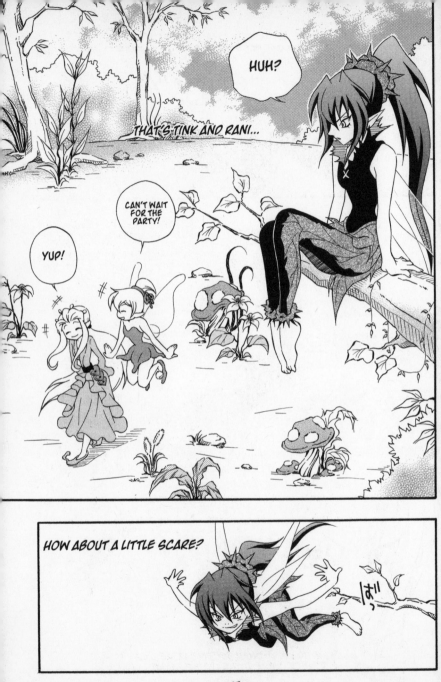

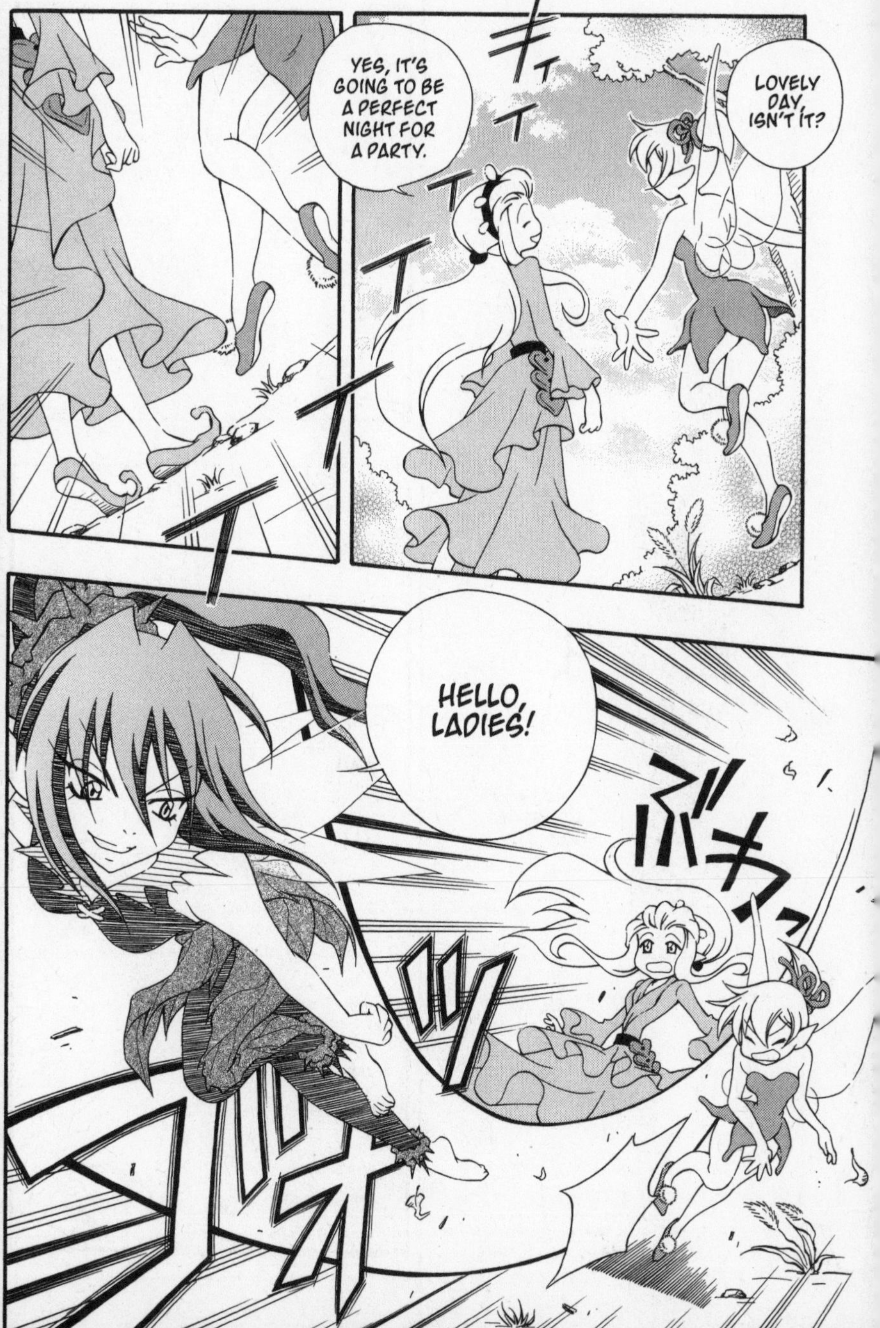
LOVELY DAY, ISN'T IT?
YES, IT'S GOING TO BE A PERFECT NIGHT FOR A PARTY.
HELLO, LADIES!

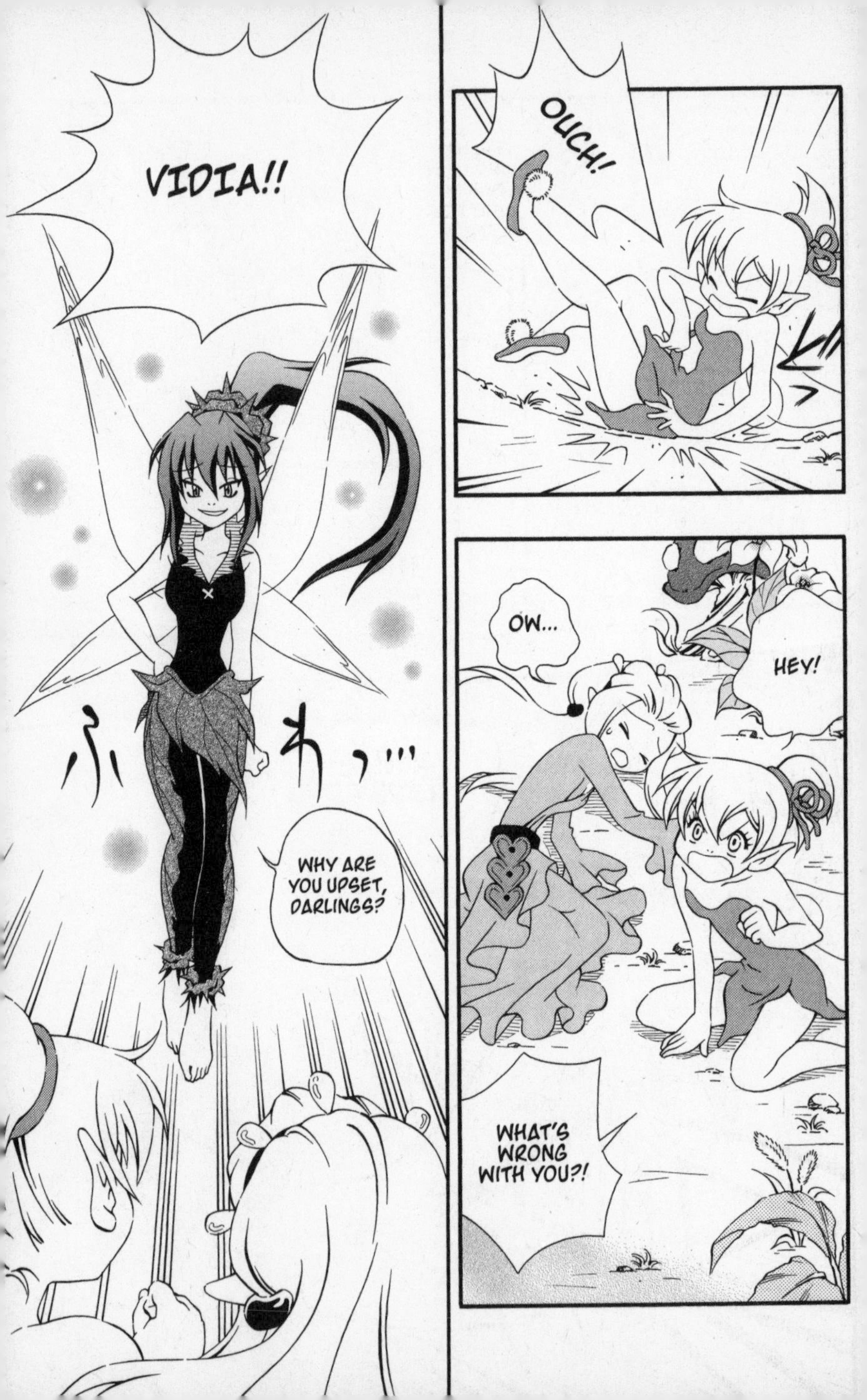
OUCH!
OW...
HEY!
WHAT'S WRONG WITH YOU?!
VIDIA!!
ふわ…
WHY ARE YOU UPSET, DARLINGS?

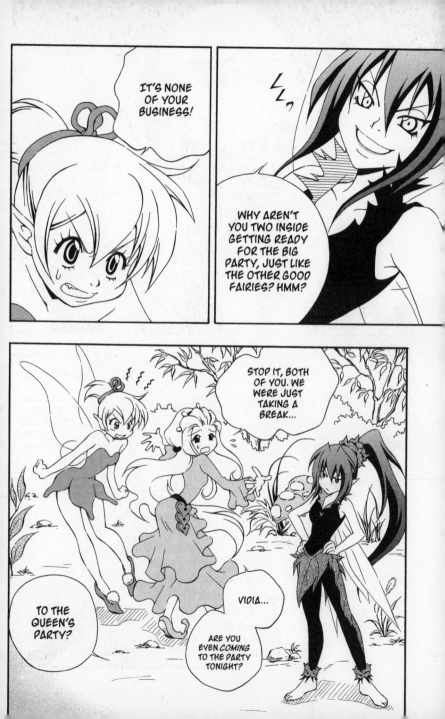

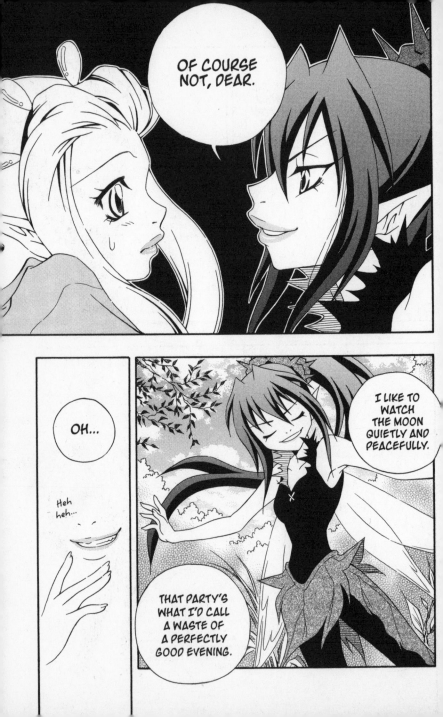

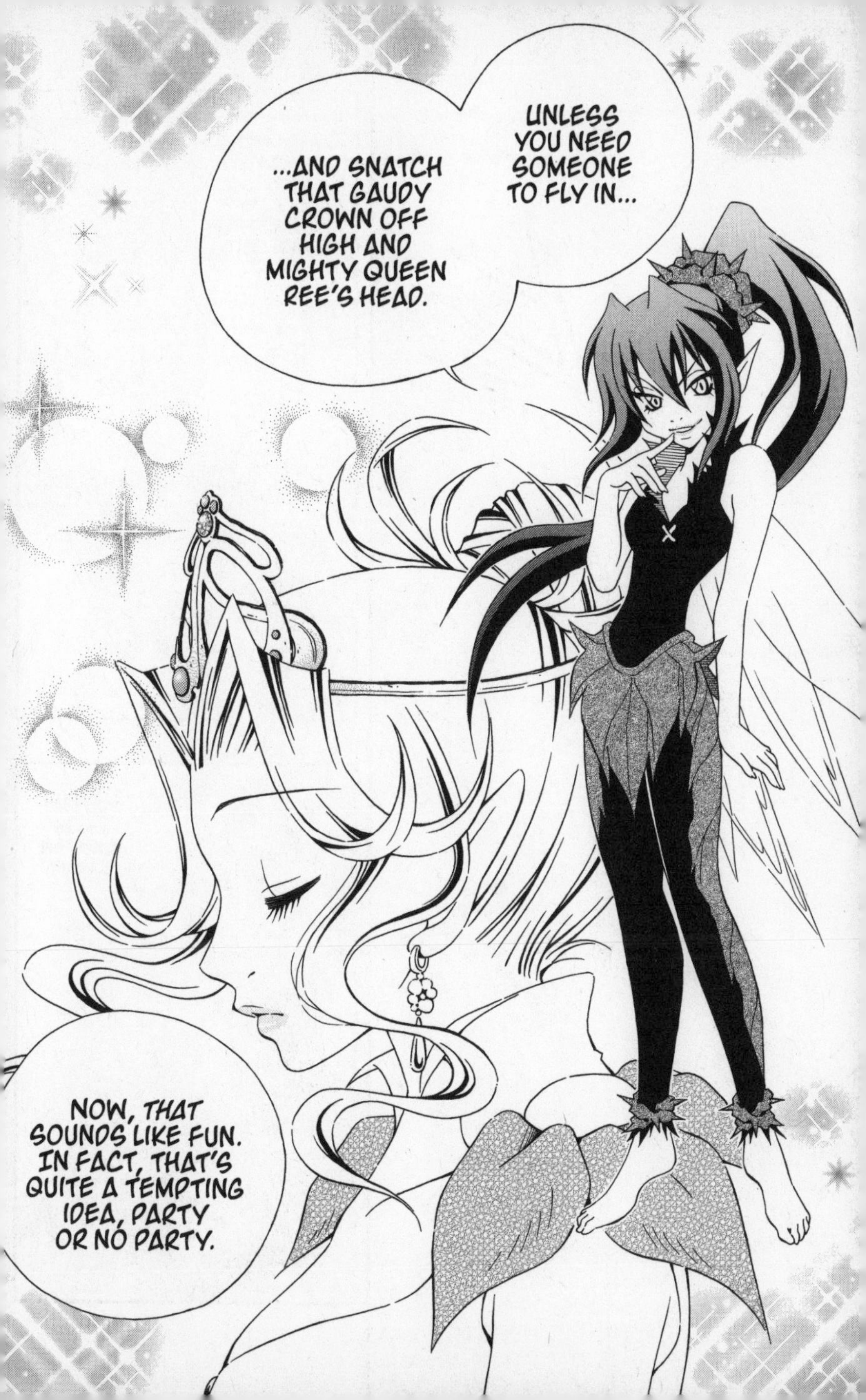
UNLESS YOU NEED SOMEONE TO FLY IN...
...AND SNATCH THAT GAUDY CROWN OFF HIGH AND MIGHTY QUEEN REE'S HEAD.
NOW, THAT SOUNDS LIKE FUN. IN FACT, THAT'S QUITE A TEMPTING IDEA, PARTY OR NO PARTY.

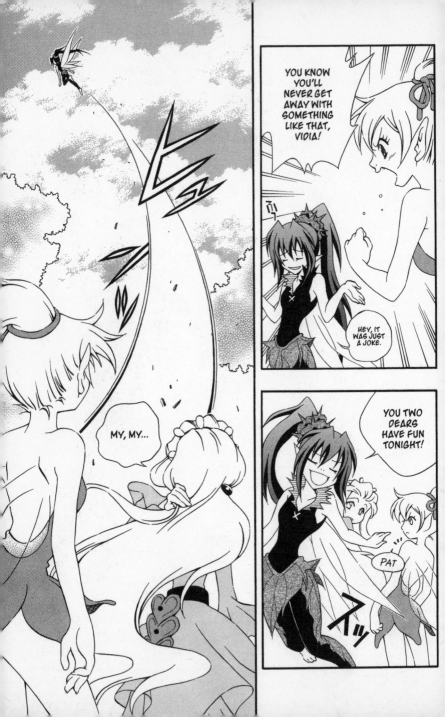

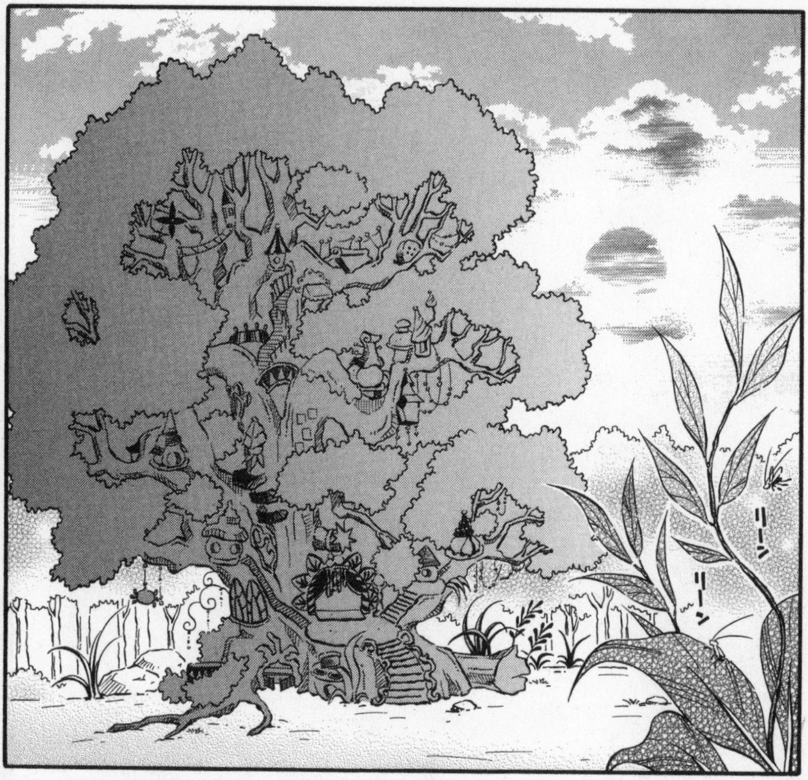
リーン
リーン

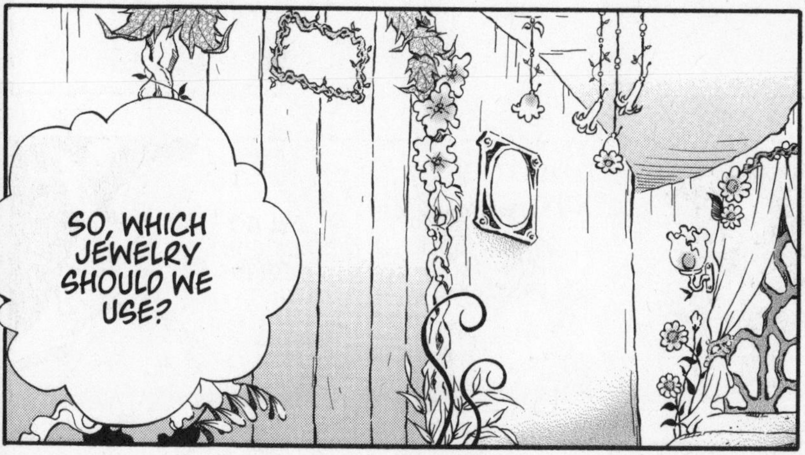
SO, WHICH JEWELRY SHOULD WE USE?

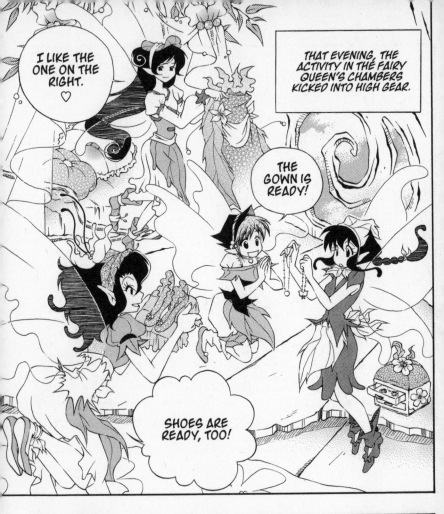

I LIKE THE ONE ON THE RIGHT. ♥

THAT EVENING, THE ACTIVITY IN THE FAIRY QUEEN'S CHAMBERS KICKED INTO HIGH GEAR.

THE GOWN IS READY!

SHOES ARE READY, TOO!

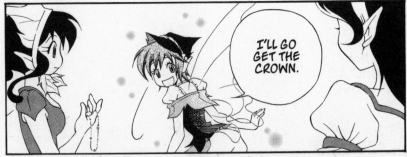

I'LL GO GET THE CROWN.

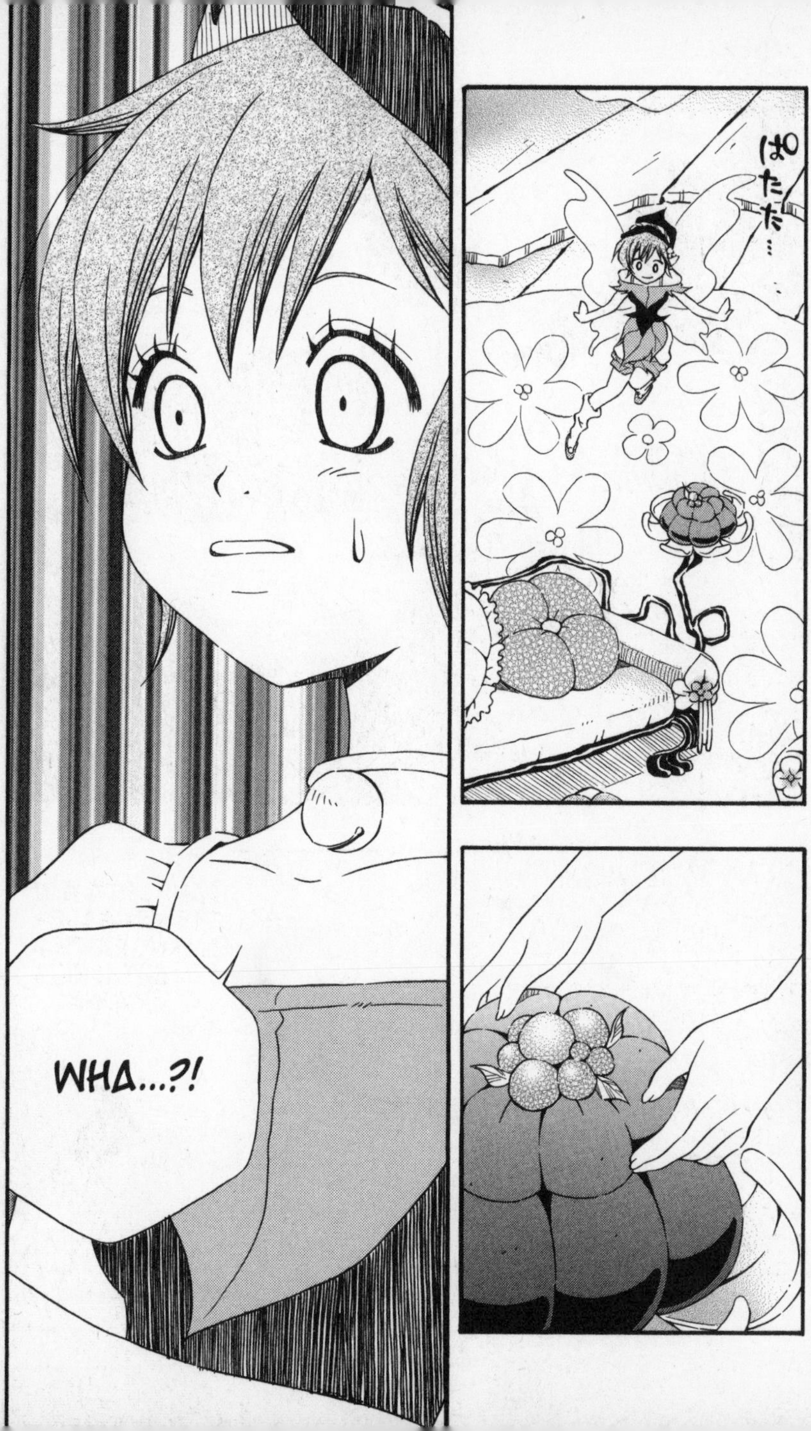
ぱたた…
WHA...?!

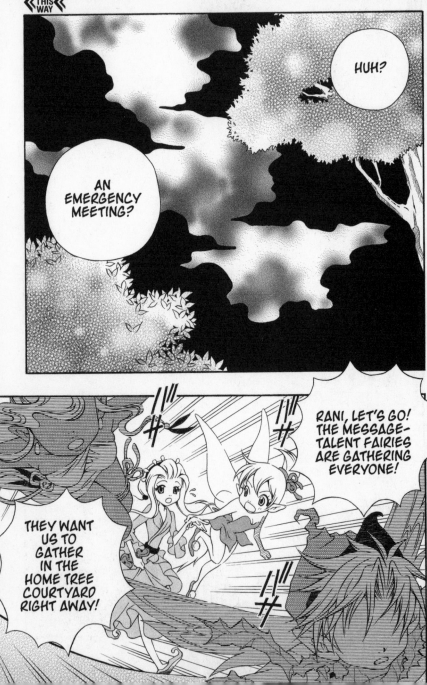

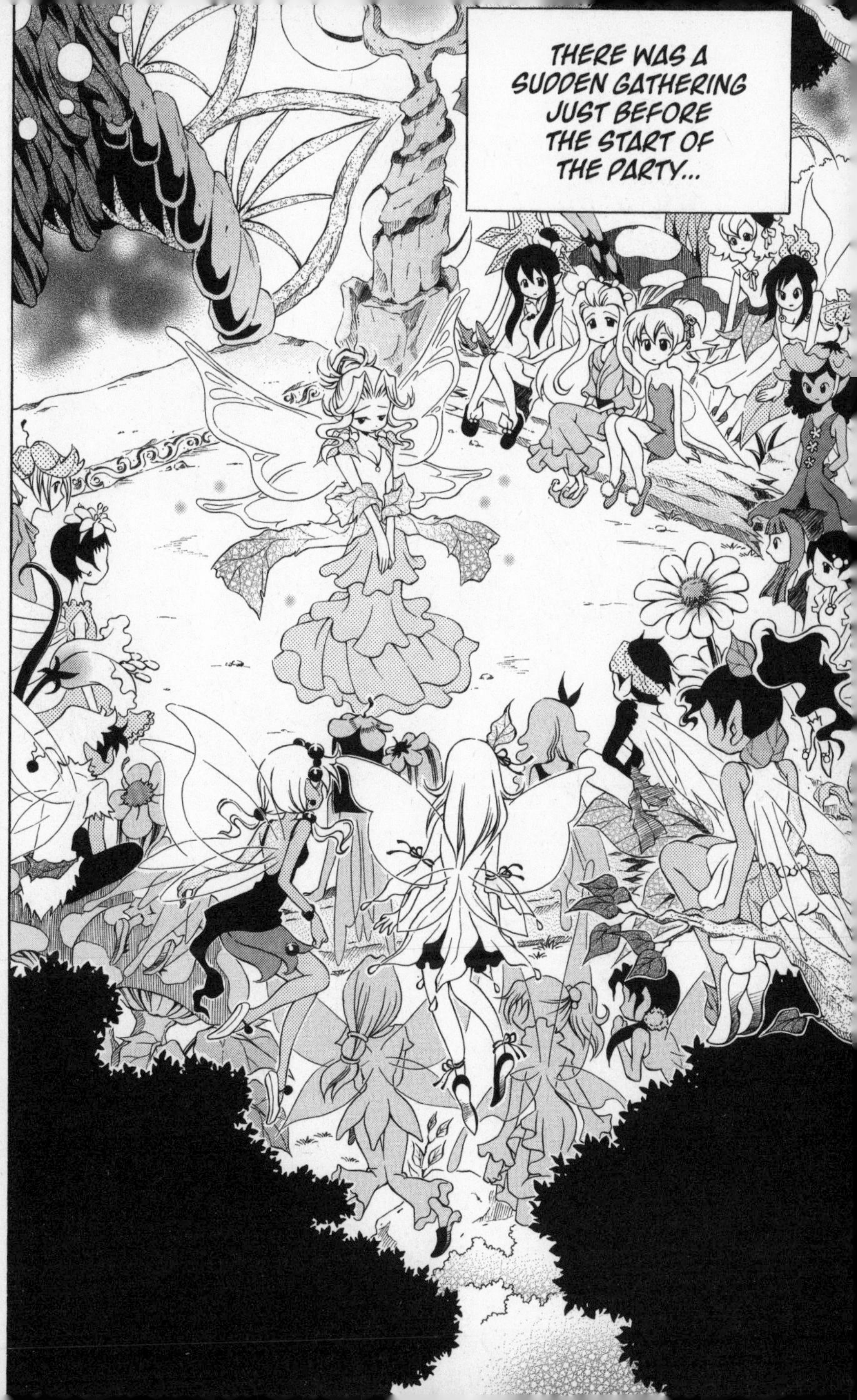
THERE WAS A SUDDEN GATHERING JUST BEFORE THE START OF THE PARTY...

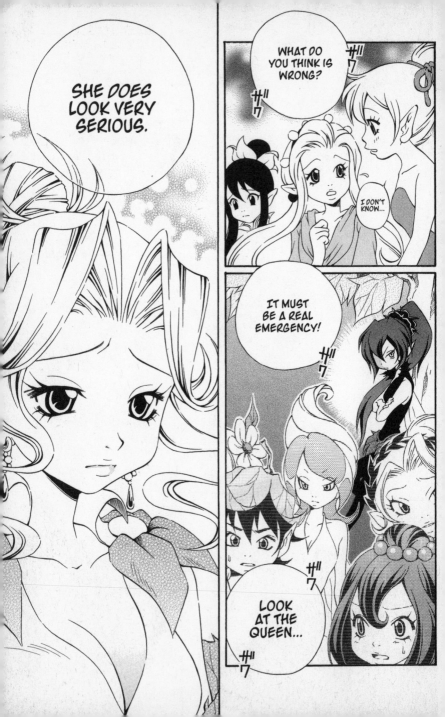

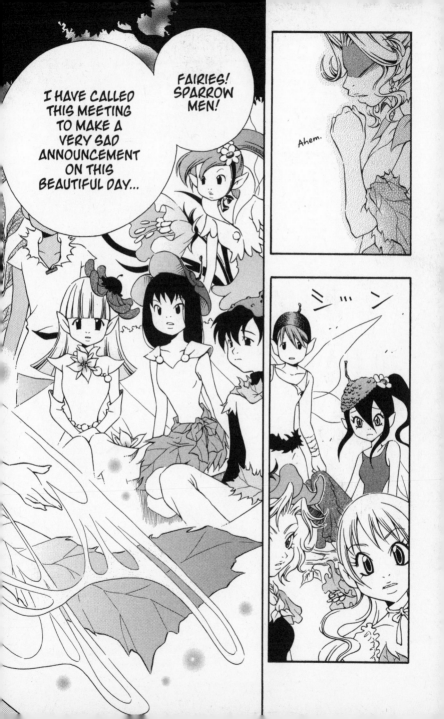

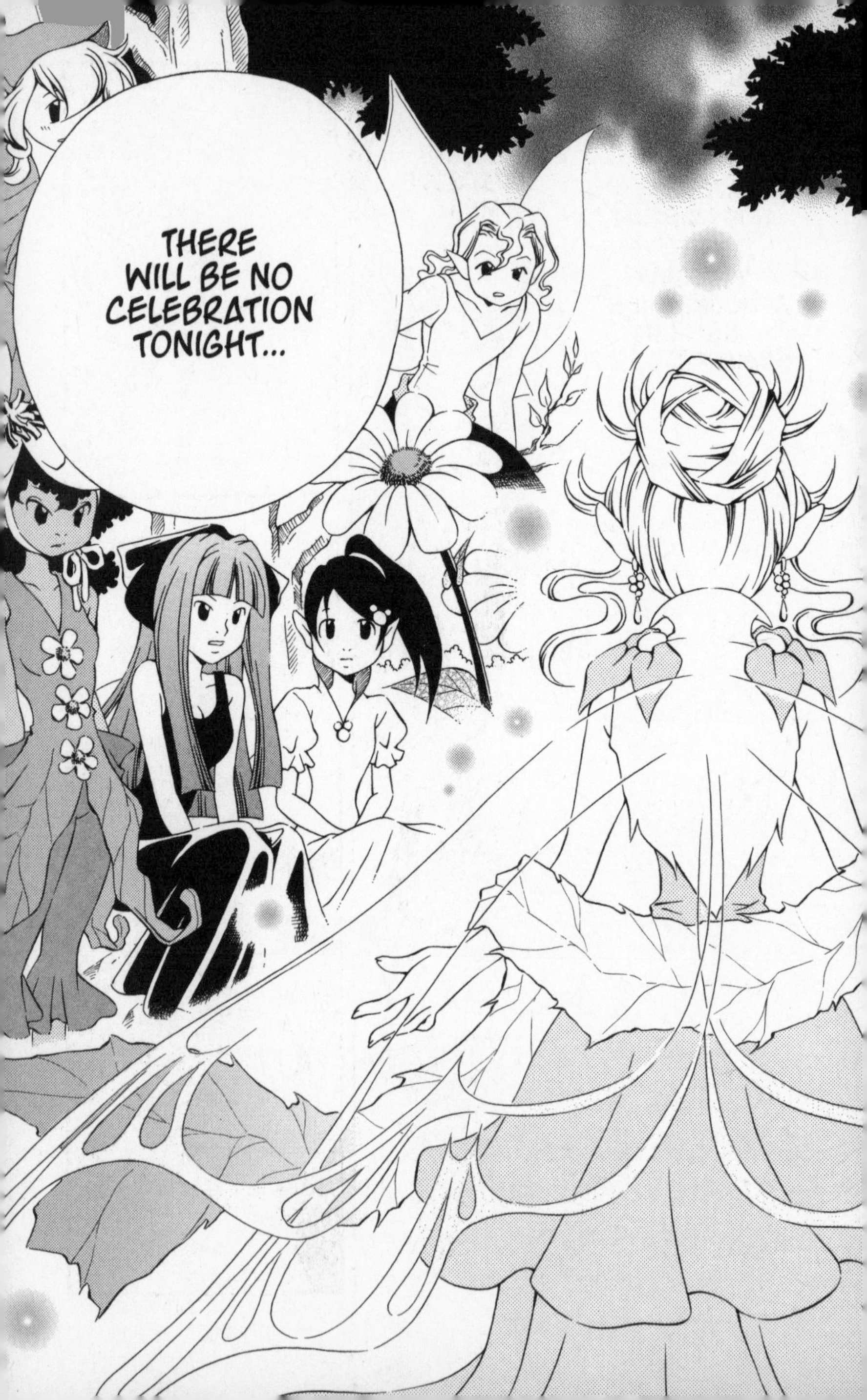
THERE WILL BE NO CELEBRATION TONIGHT...

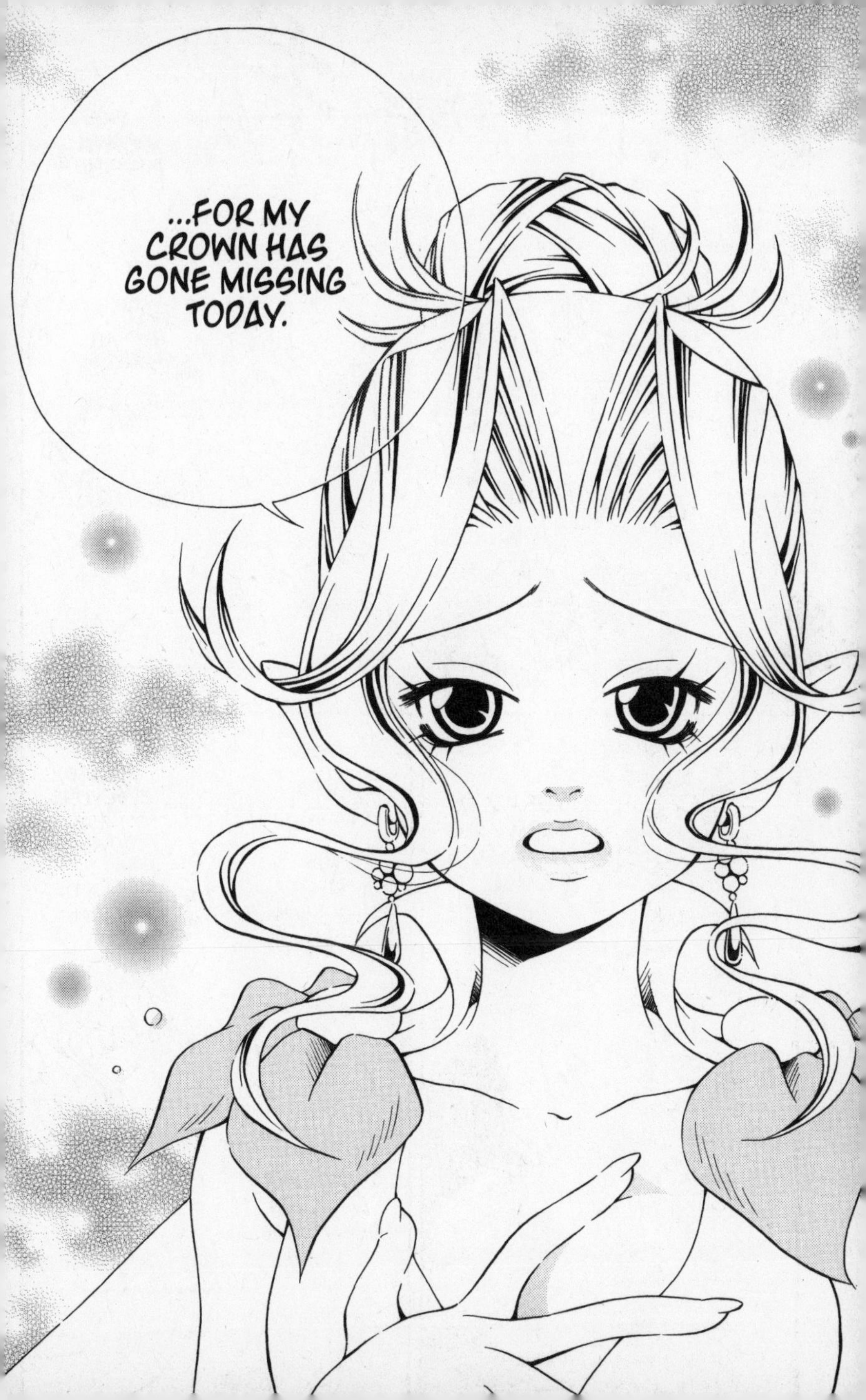
...FOR MY CROWN HAS GONE MISSING TODAY.

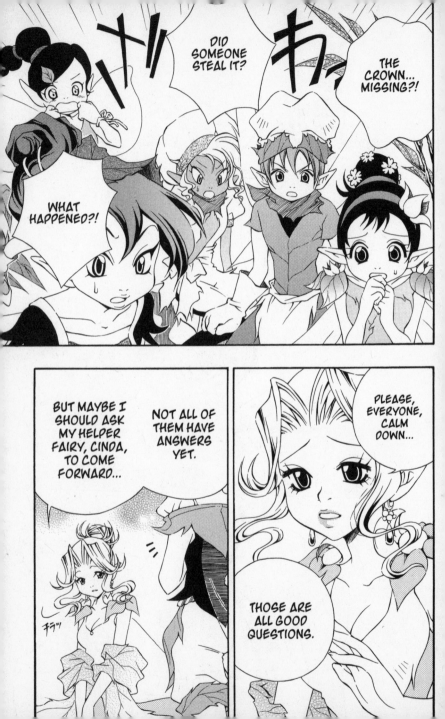

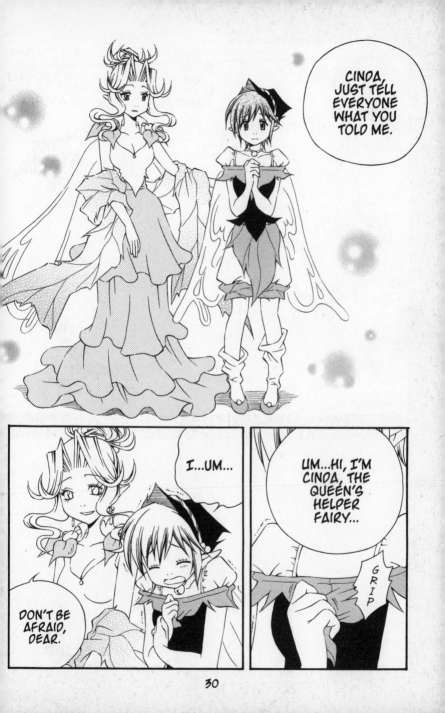

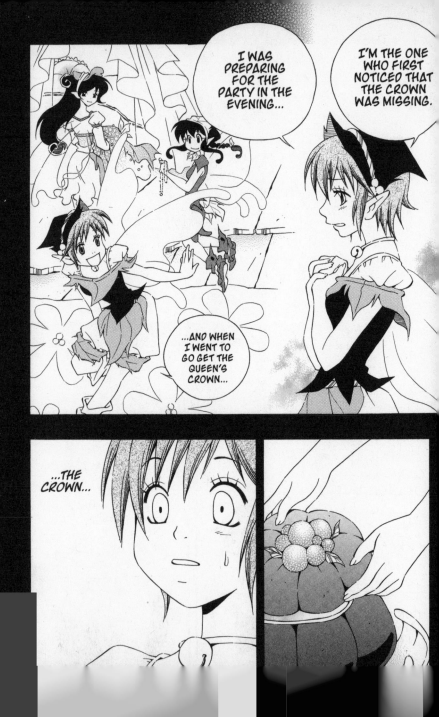

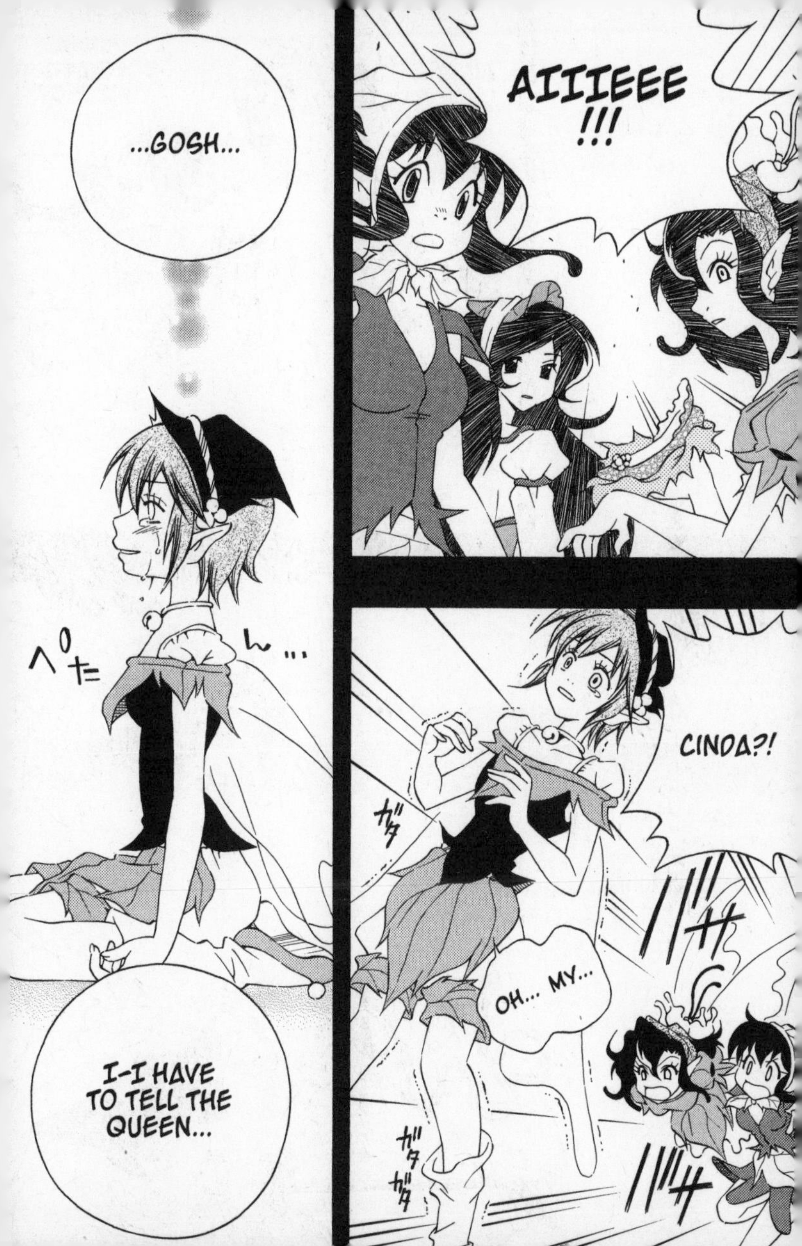
AIIIEEE !!!
CINDA?!
ガタ
OH... MY...
ガタガタ
...GOSH...
へたん...
I-I HAVE TO TELL THE QUEEN...

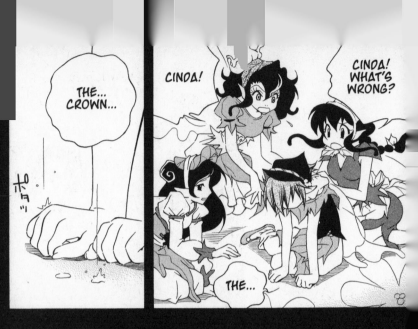

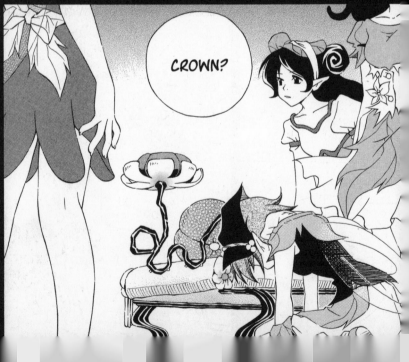

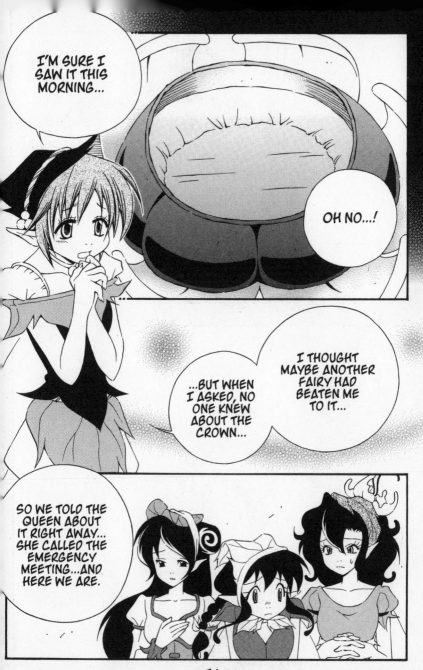

I'M SURE I SAW IT THIS MORNING...

OH NO...!

...BUT WHEN I ASKED, NO ONE KNEW ABOUT THE CROWN...

I THOUGHT MAYBE ANOTHER FAIRY HAD BEATEN ME TO IT...

SO WE TOLD THE QUEEN ABOUT IT RIGHT AWAY... SHE CALLED THE EMERGENCY MEETING...AND HERE WE ARE.

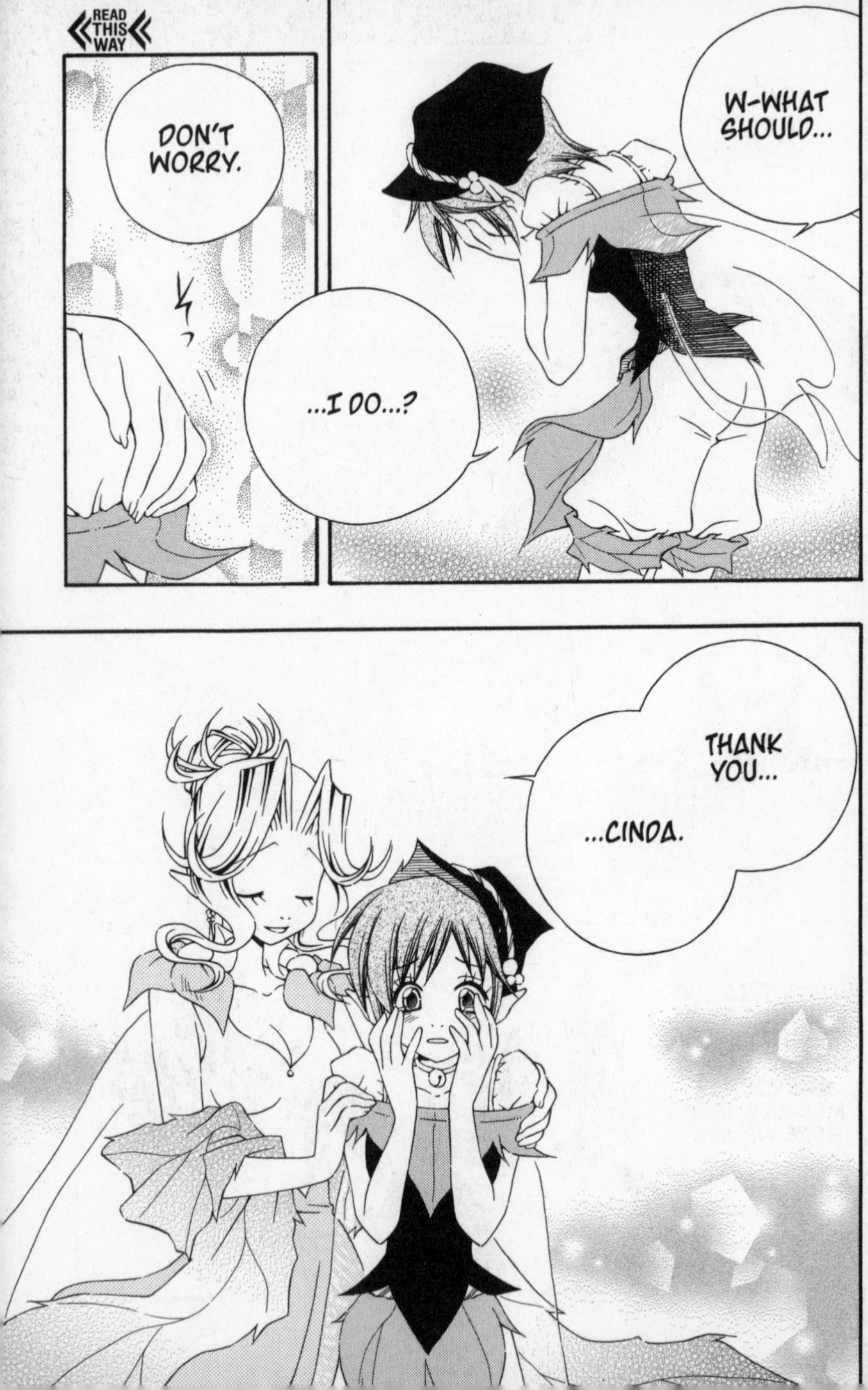
READ THIS WAY
W-WHAT SHOULD...
...I DO...?
DON'T WORRY.
THANK YOU...
...CINDA.

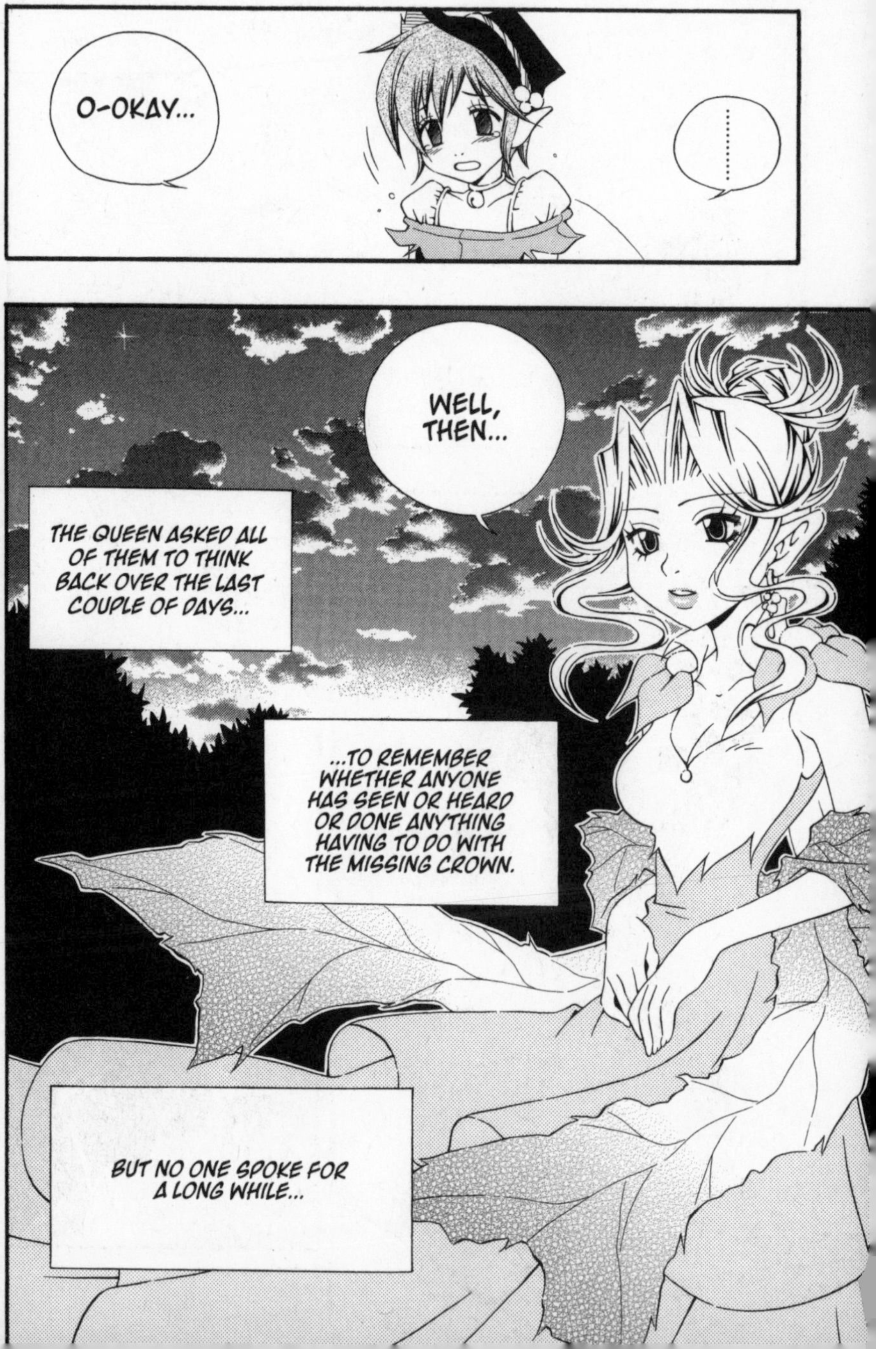
......
O-OKAY...
WELL, THEN...
THE QUEEN ASKED ALL OF THEM TO THINK BACK OVER THE LAST COUPLE OF DAYS...
...TO REMEMBER WHETHER ANYONE HAS SEEN OR HEARD OR DONE ANYTHING HAVING TO DO WITH THE MISSING CROWN.
BUT NO ONE SPOKE FOR A LONG WHILE...

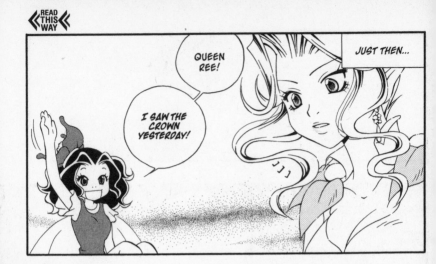

JUST THEN...

QUEEN REE!

I SAW THE CROWN YESTERDAY!

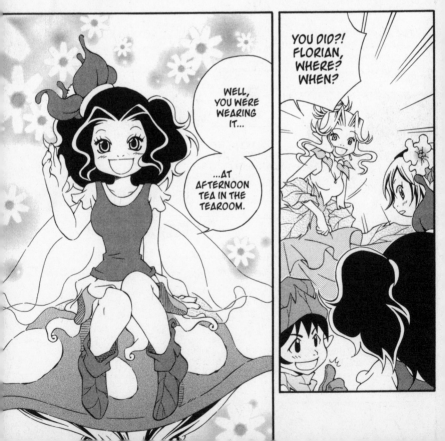

WELL, YOU WERE WEARING IT...

...AT AFTERNOON TEA IN THE TEAROOM.

YOU DID?! FLORIAN, WHERE? WHEN?

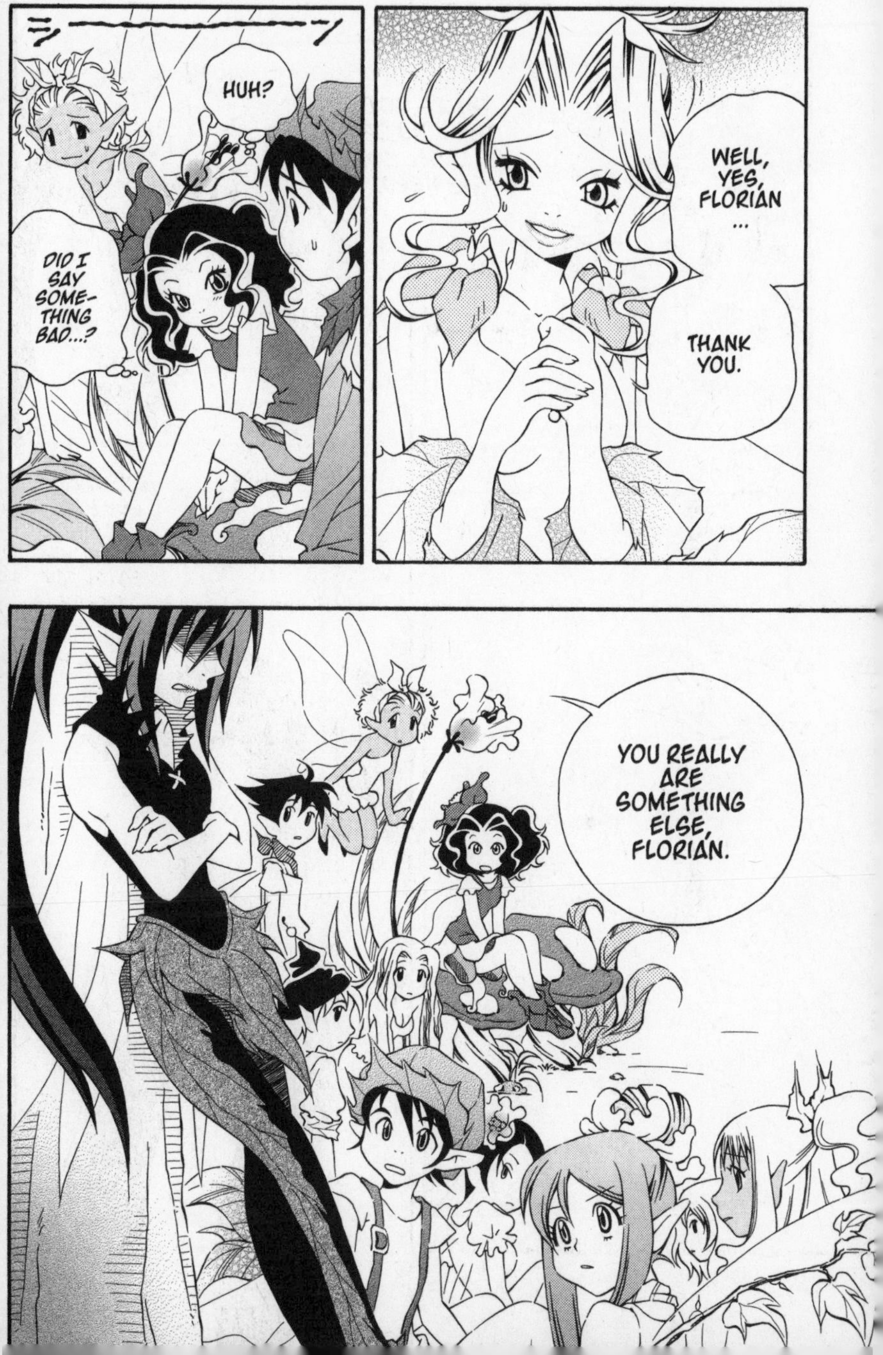
WELL, YES, FLORIAN ...
THANK YOU.
HUH?
DID I SAY SOME-THING BAD...?
YOU REALLY ARE SOMETHING ELSE, FLORIAN.

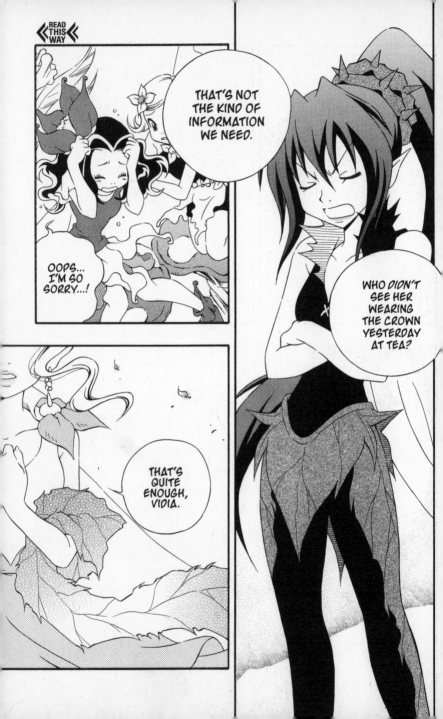

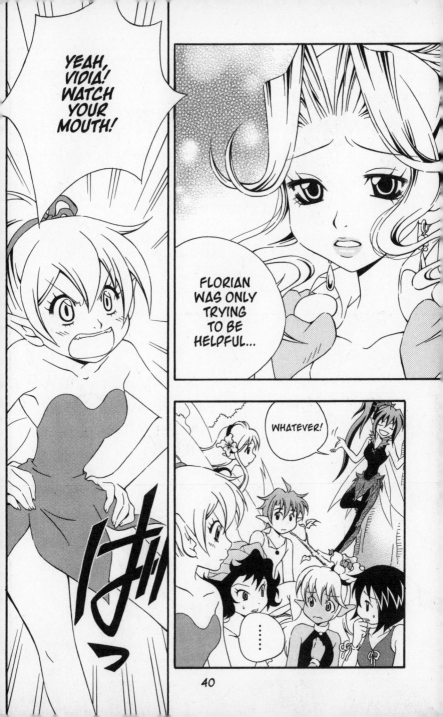

YEAH, VIDIA! WATCH YOUR MOUTH!

FLORIAN WAS ONLY TRYING TO BE HELPFUL...

WHATEVER!

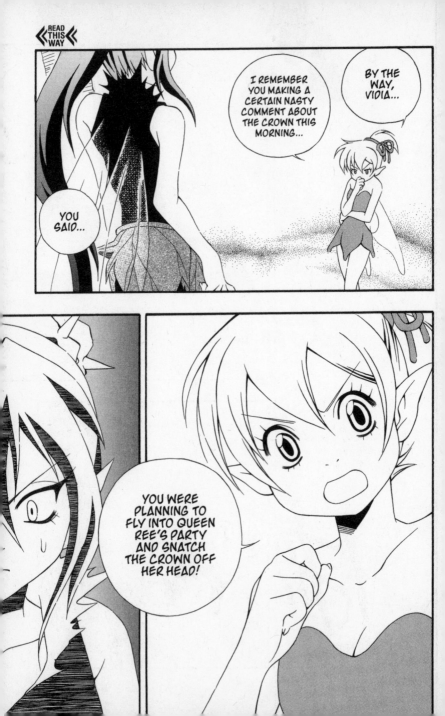

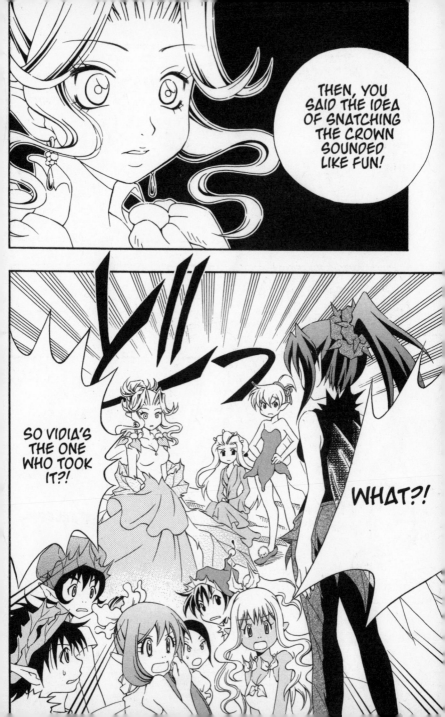

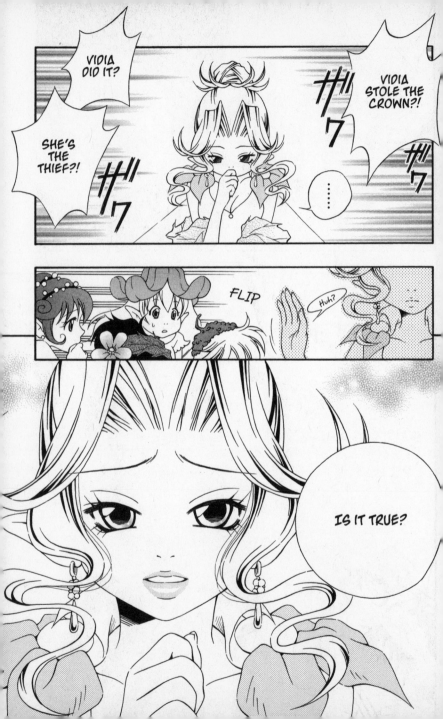

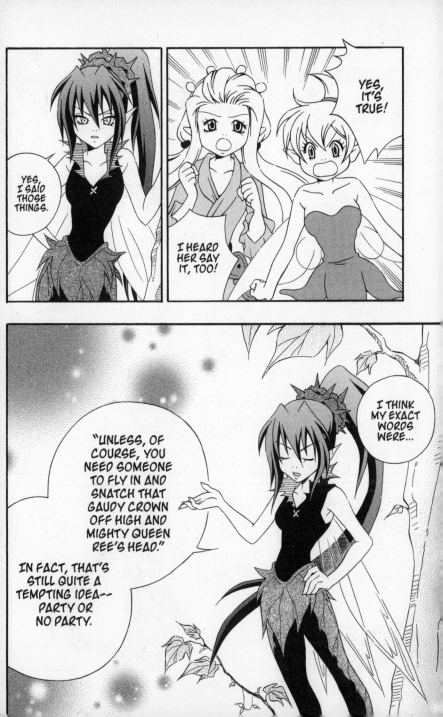

YES, I SAID THOSE THINGS.

YES, IT'S TRUE!

I HEARD HER SAY IT, TOO!

I THINK MY EXACT WORDS WERE...

"UNLESS, OF COURSE, YOU NEED SOMEONE TO FLY IN AND SNATCH THAT GAUDY CROWN OFF HIGH AND MIGHTY QUEEN REE'S HEAD."

IN FACT, THAT'S STILL QUITE A TEMPTING IDEA-- PARTY OR NO PARTY.

READ THIS WAY

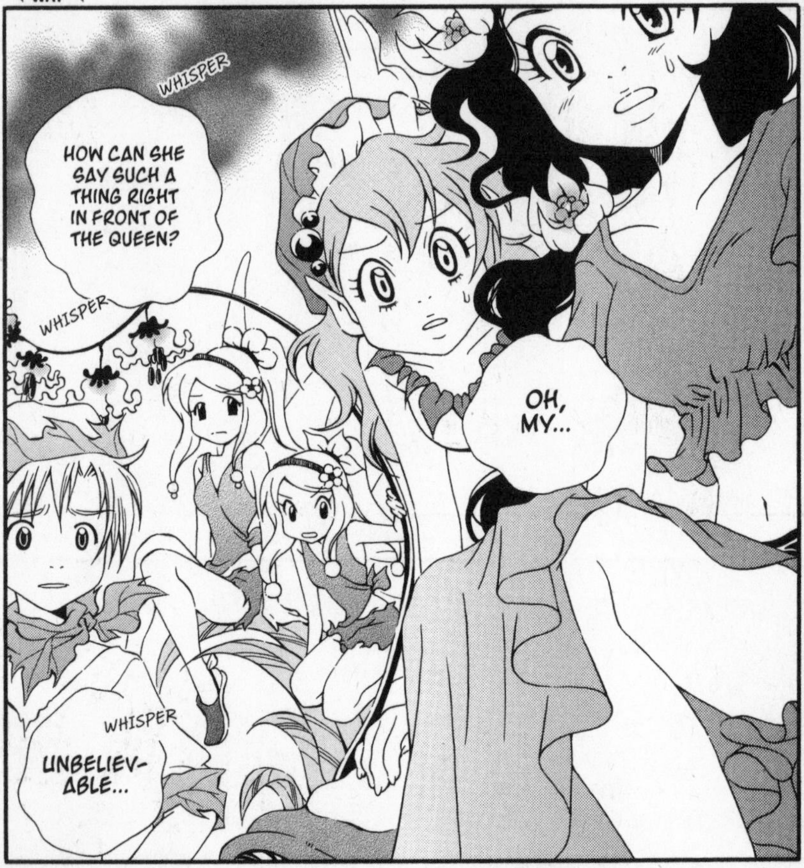
WHISPER
HOW CAN SHE SAY SUCH A THING RIGHT IN FRONT OF THE QUEEN?
OH, MY...
WHISPER
WHISPER
UNBELIEV-ABLE...

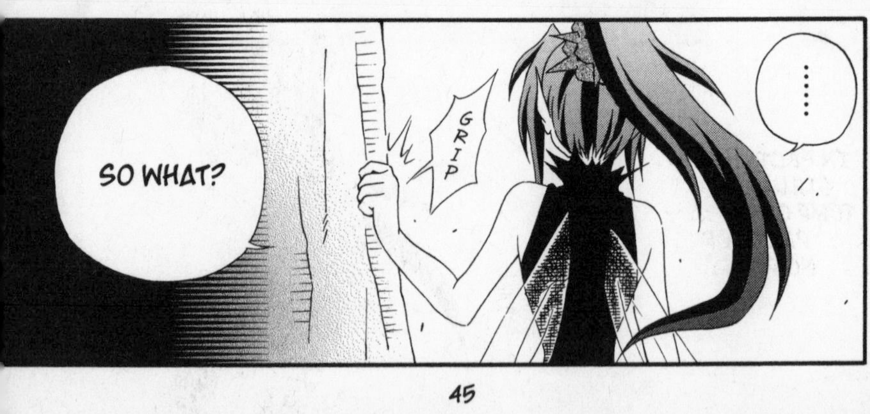
......
GRIP
SO WHAT?

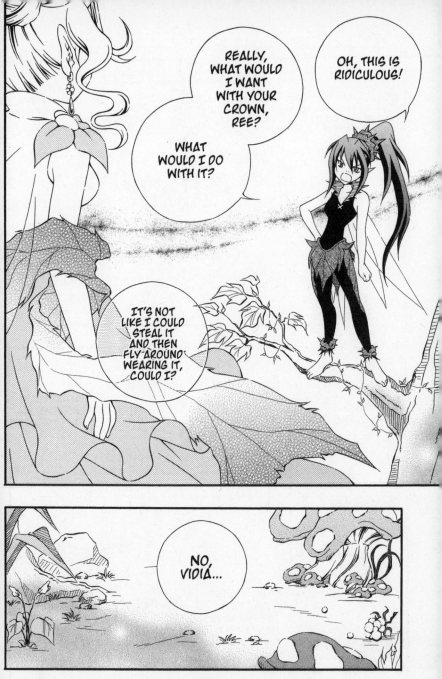

REALLY, WHAT WOULD I WANT WITH YOUR CROWN, REE?

WHAT WOULD I DO WITH IT?

OH, THIS IS RIDICULOUS!

IT'S NOT LIKE I COULD STEAL IT AND THEN FLY AROUND WEARING IT, COULD I?

NO, VIDIA...

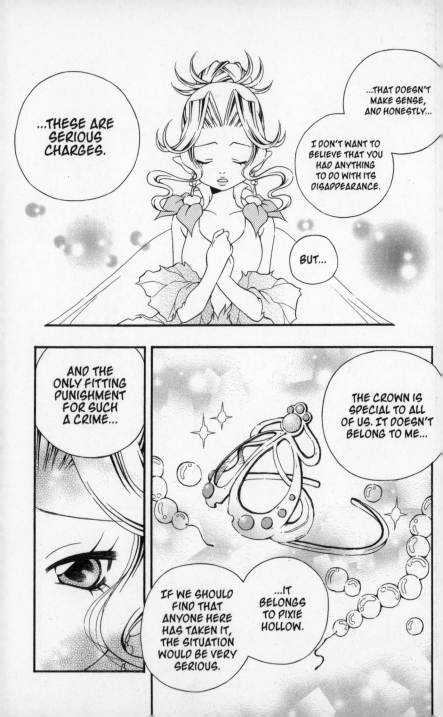

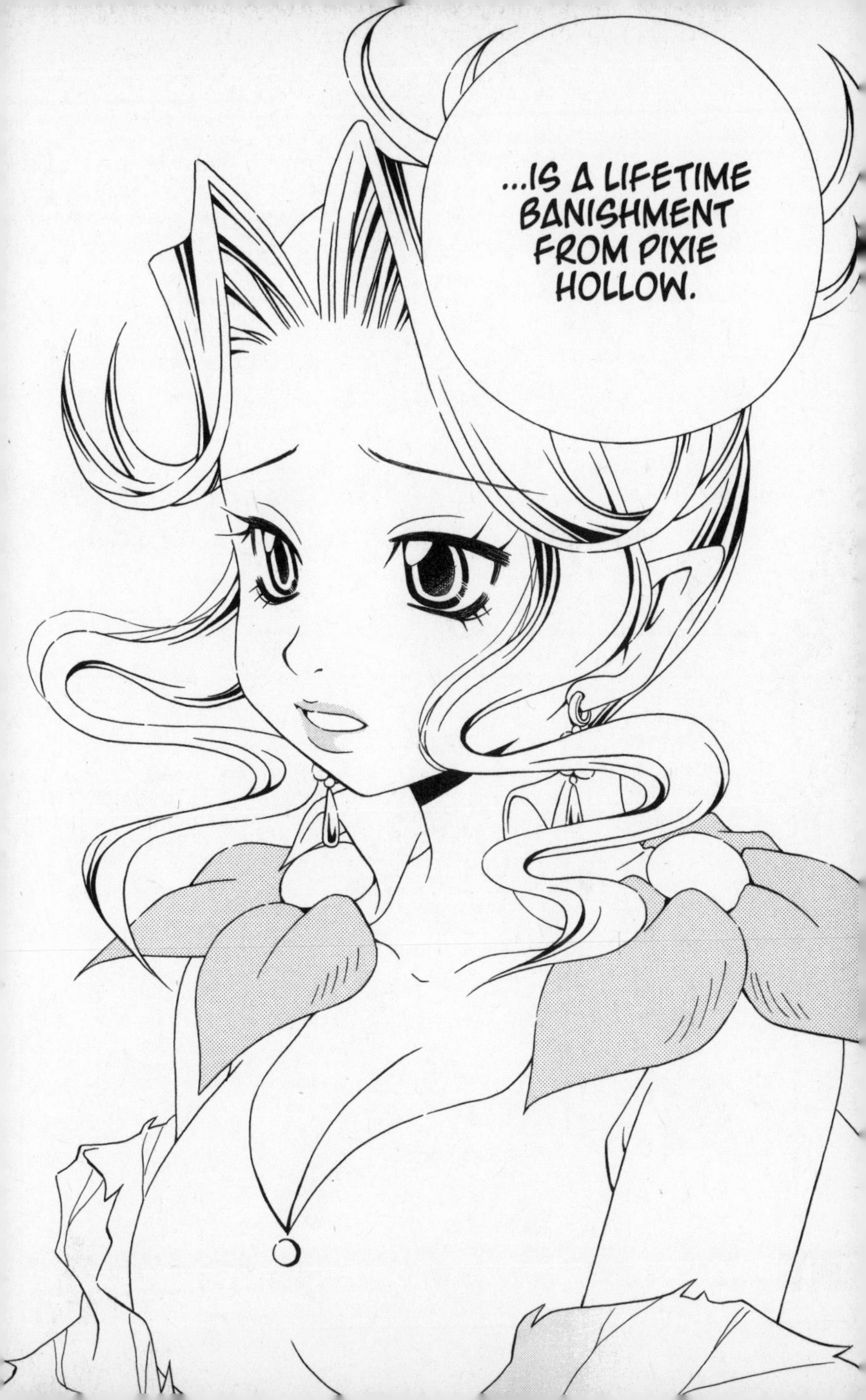
...IS A LIFETIME BANISHMENT FROM PIXIE HOLLOW.

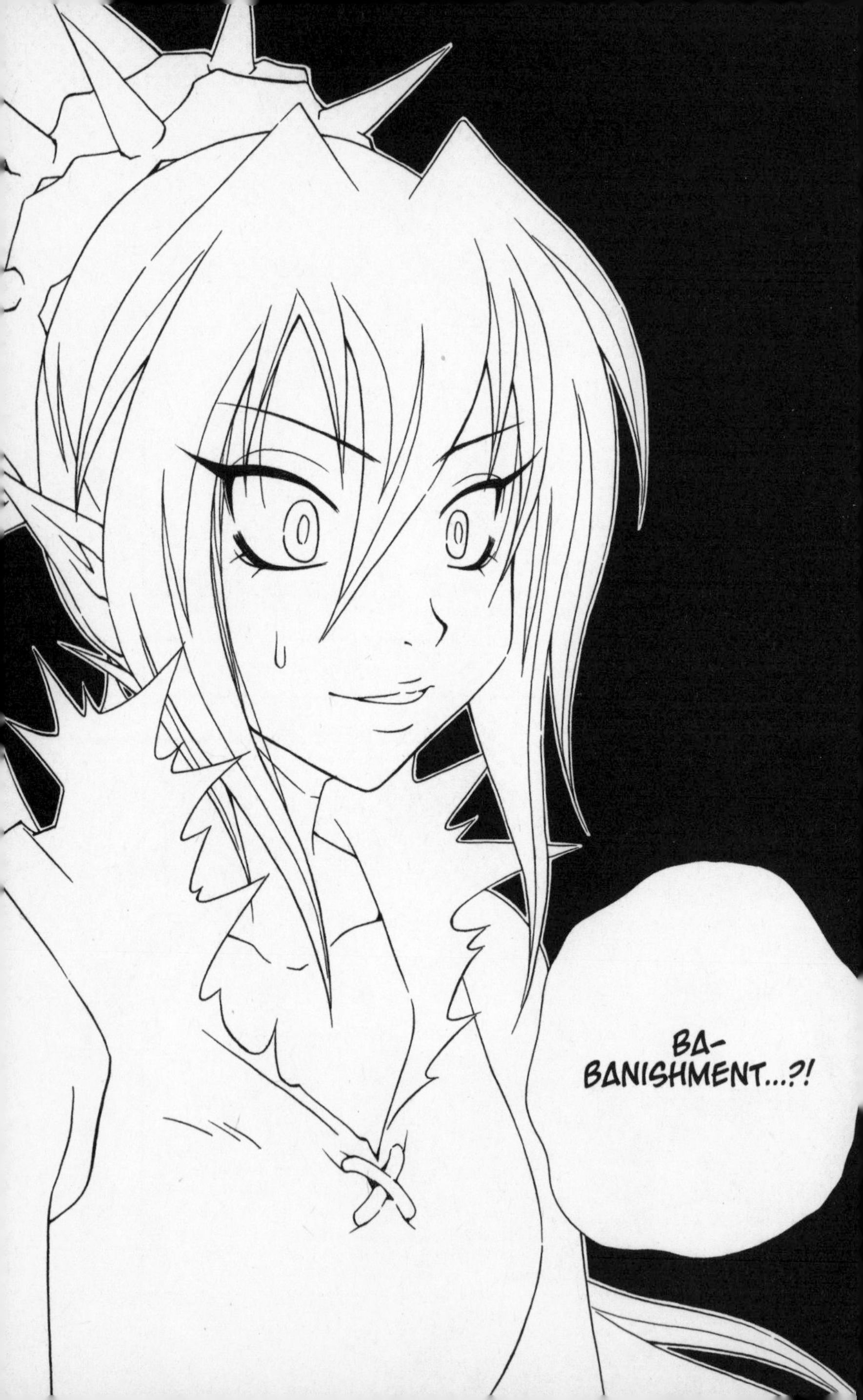
BA-BANISHMENT...?!

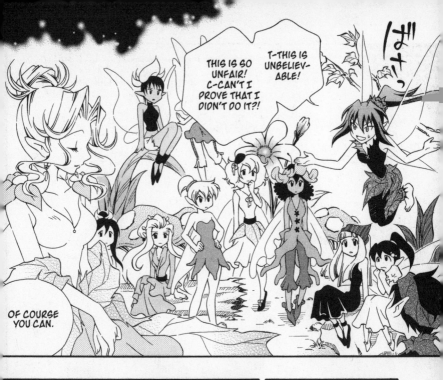

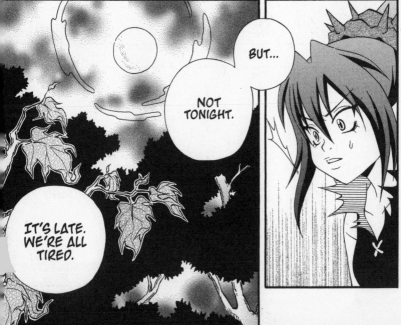

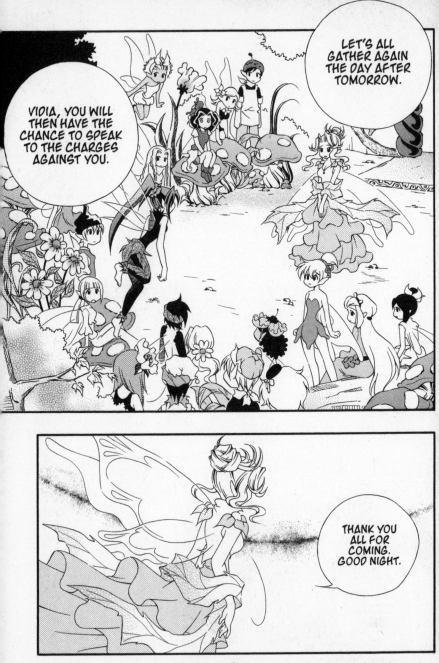

51

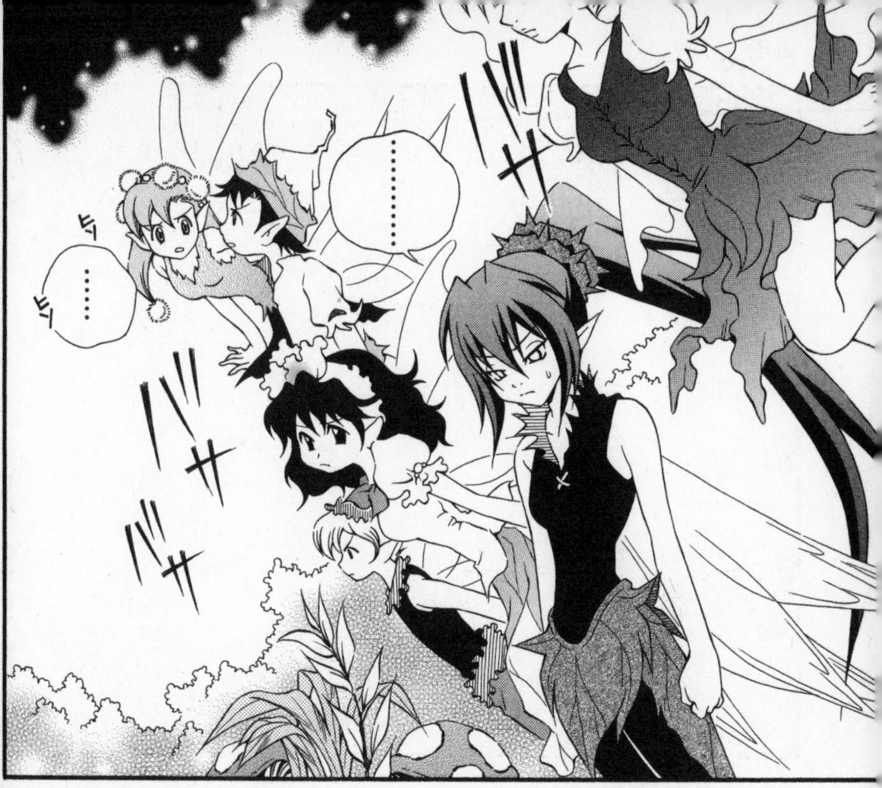
バサ
……
ヒソ
ヒソ
……
バサ
バサ
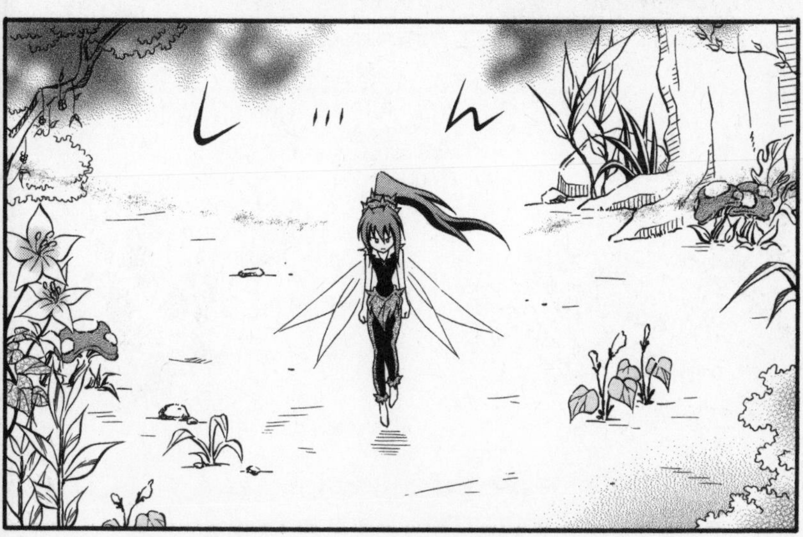
し…ん

READ THIS WAY

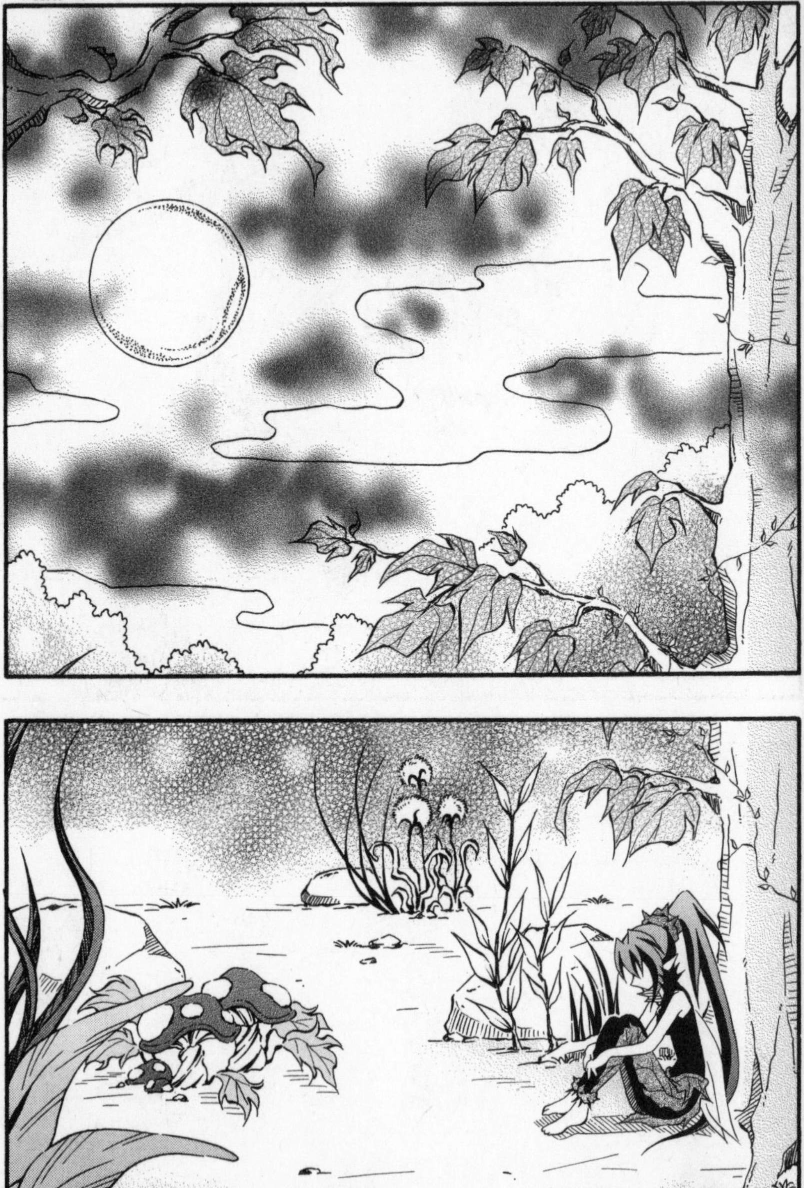

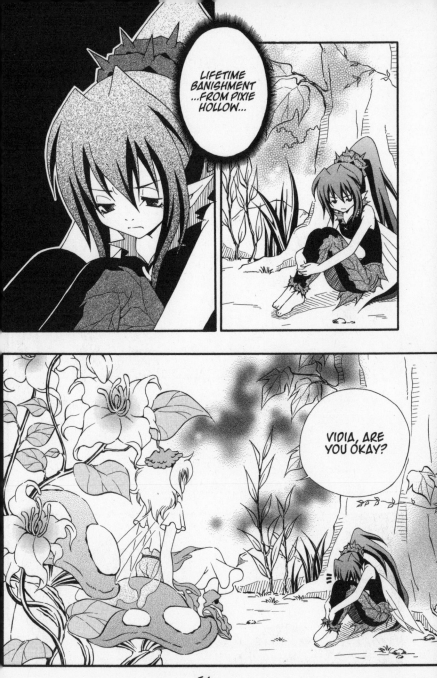

54

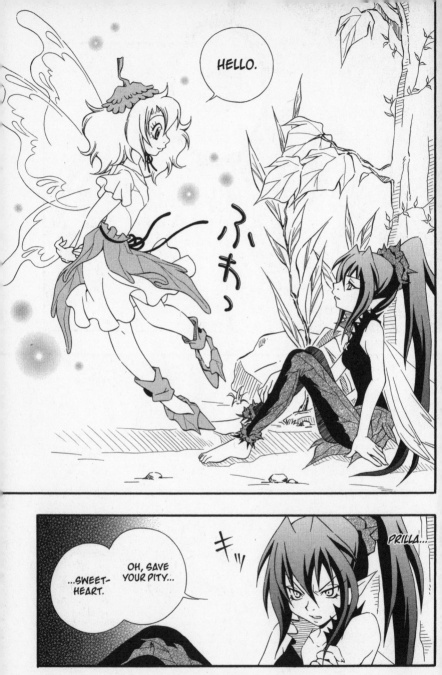

55

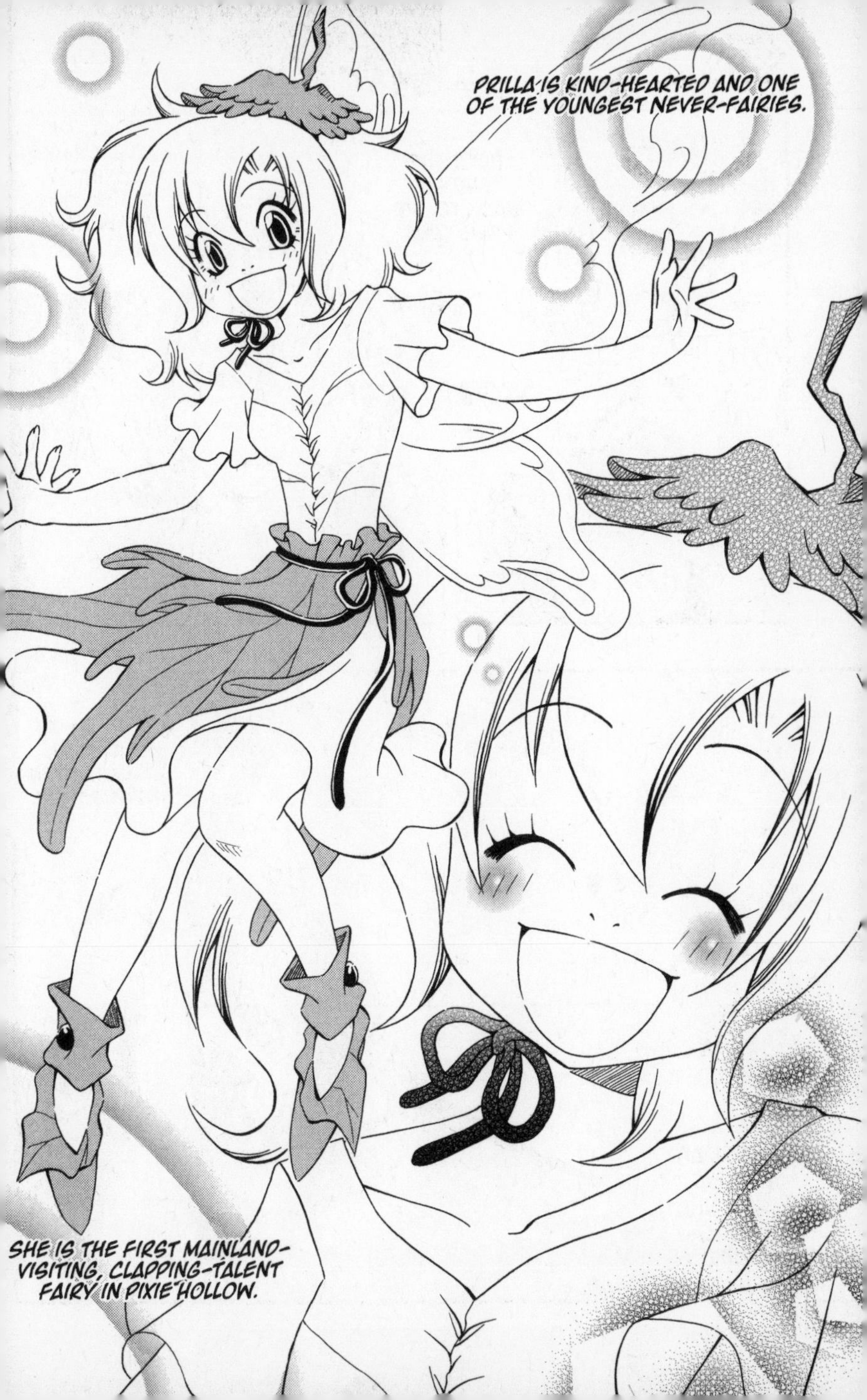
PRILLA IS KIND-HEARTED AND ONE OF THE YOUNGEST NEVER-FAIRIES.
SHE IS THE FIRST MAINLAND-VISITING, CLAPPING-TALENT FAIRY IN PIXIE HOLLOW.

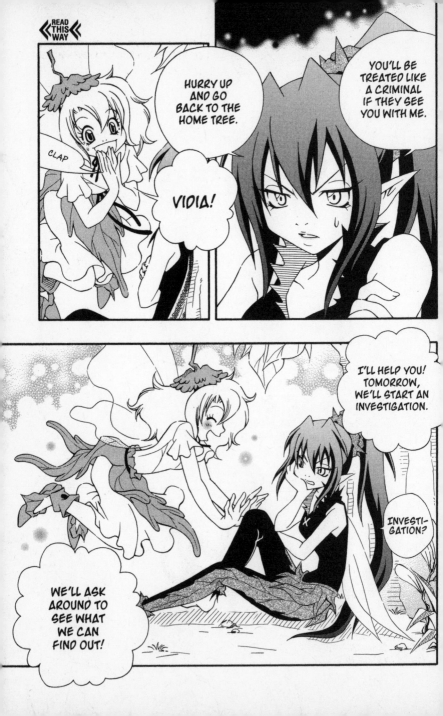

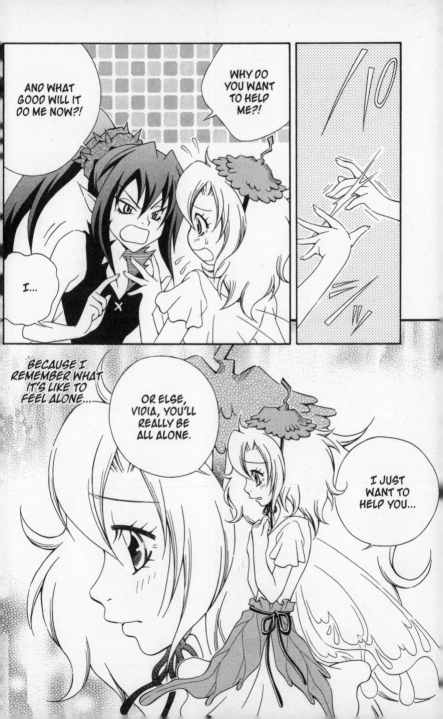

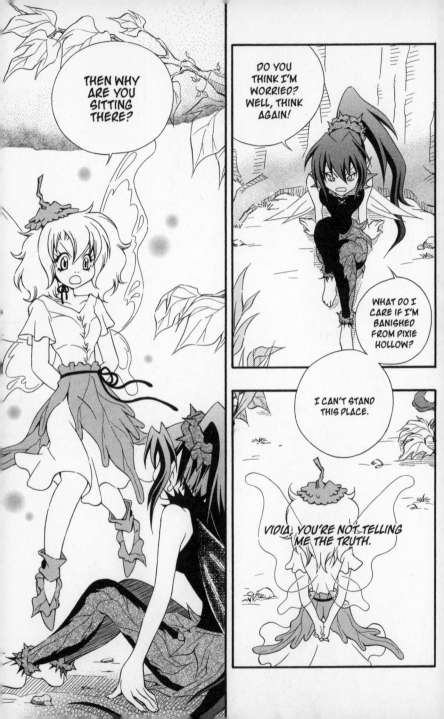

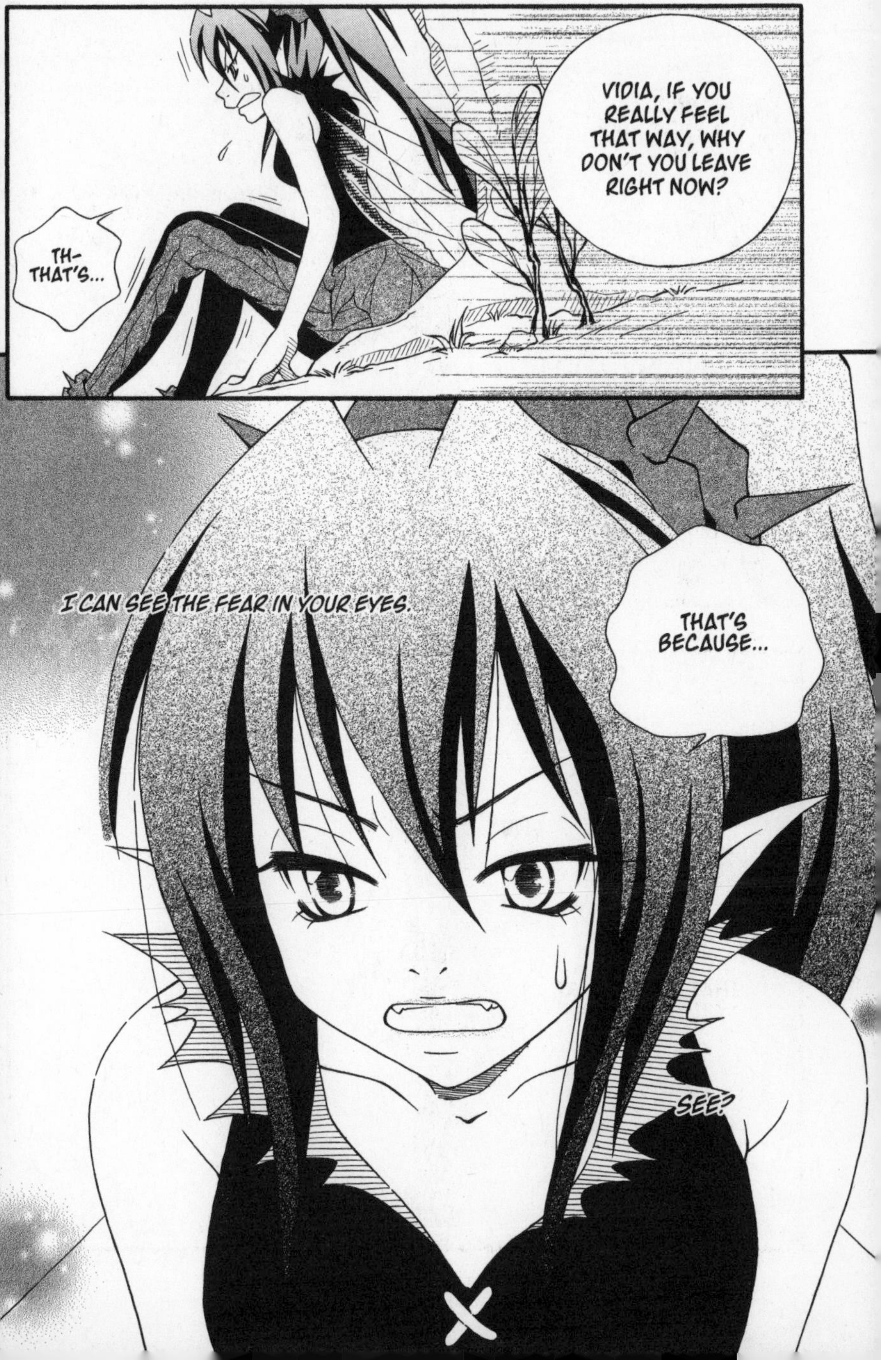
VIDIA, IF YOU REALLY FEEL THAT WAY, WHY DON'T YOU LEAVE RIGHT NOW?
TH- THAT'S...
THAT'S BECAUSE...
I CAN SEE THE FEAR IN YOUR EYES.
SEE?

READ THIS WAY

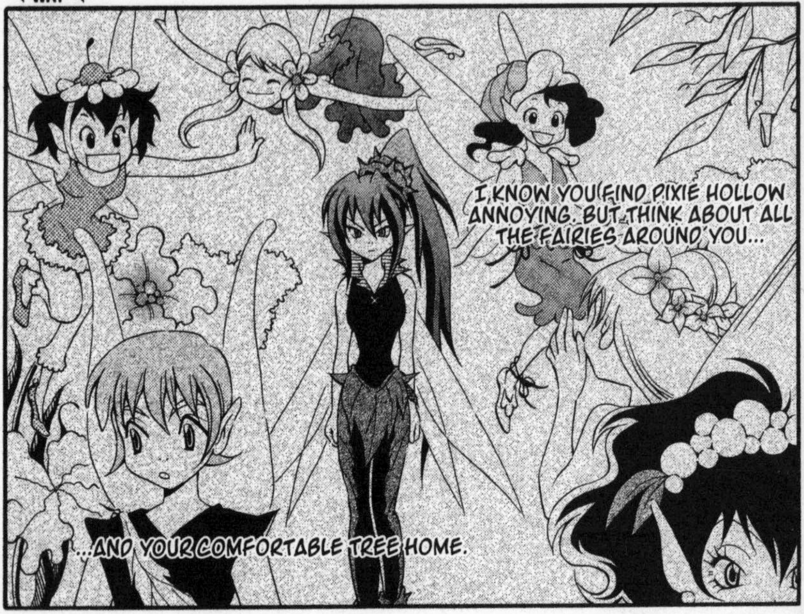
I KNOW YOU FIND PIXIE HOLLOW ANNOYING. BUT THINK ABOUT ALL THE FAIRIES AROUND YOU...
...AND YOUR COMFORTABLE TREE HOME.

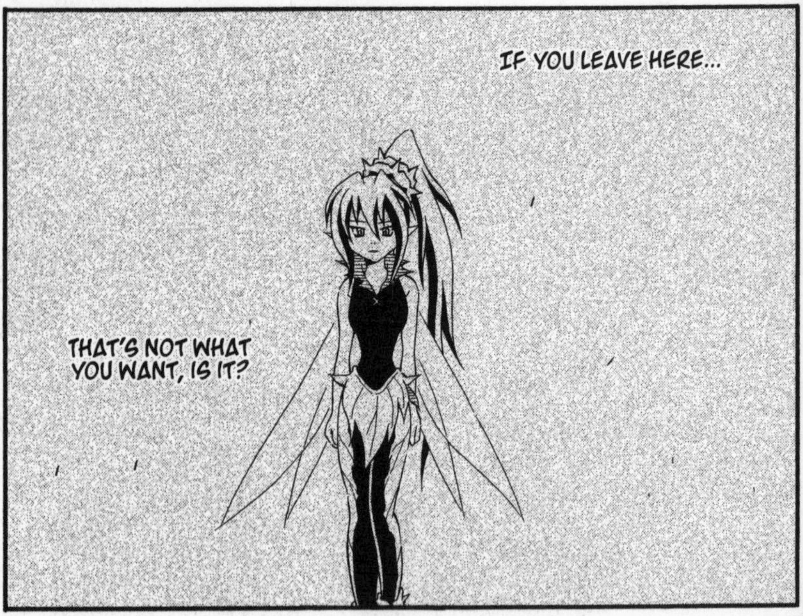
IF YOU LEAVE HERE...
THAT'S NOT WHAT YOU WANT, IS IT?

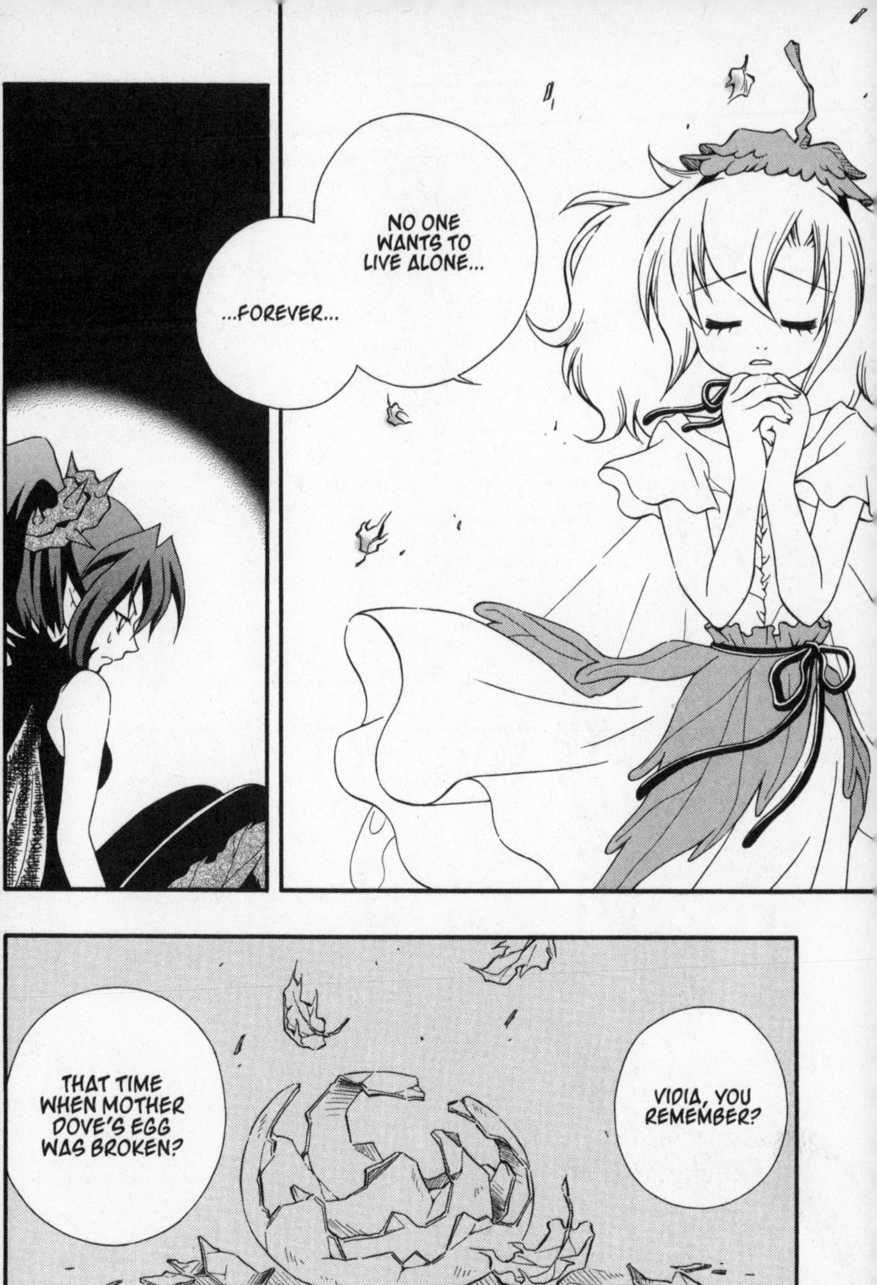
NO ONE WANTS TO LIVE ALONE...
...FOREVER...
VIDIA, YOU REMEMBER?
THAT TIME WHEN MOTHER DOVE'S EGG WAS BROKEN?

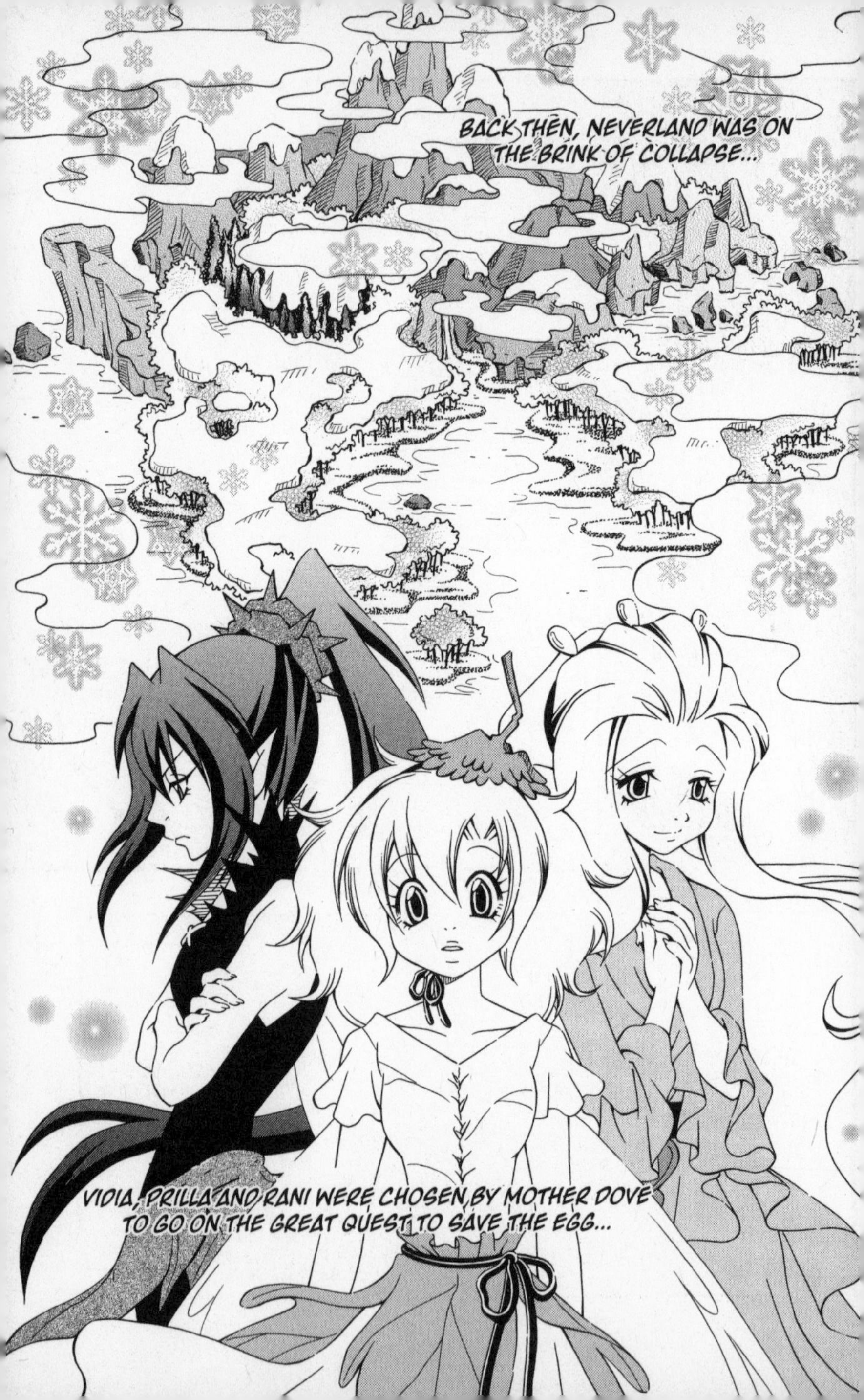
BACK THEN, NEVERLAND WAS ON THE BRINK OF COLLAPSE...
VIDIA, PRILLA AND RANI WERE CHOSEN BY MOTHER DOVE TO GO ON THE GREAT QUEST TO SAVE THE EGG...

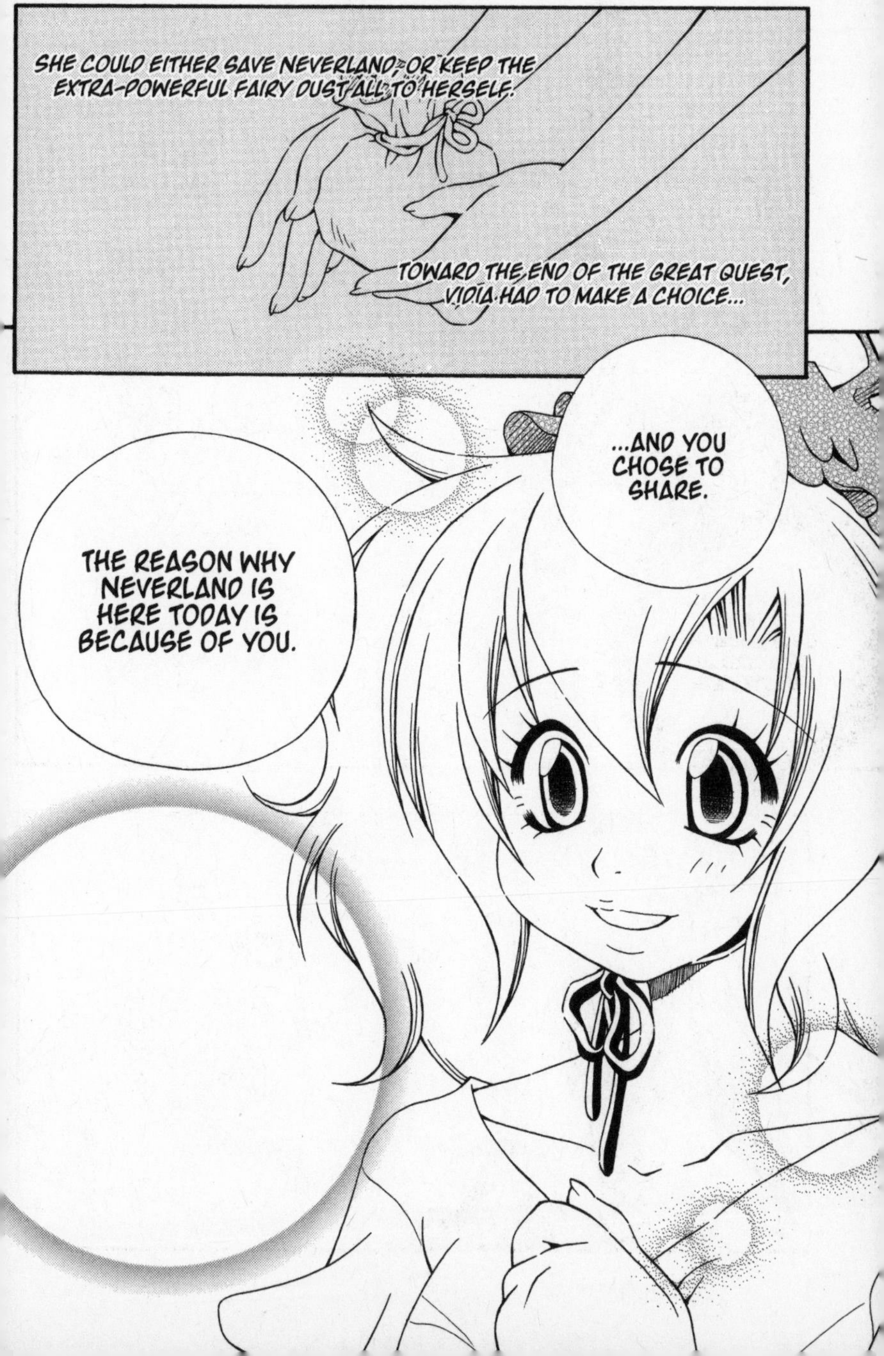
SHE COULD EITHER SAVE NEVERLAND, OR KEEP THE EXTRA-POWERFUL FAIRY DUST ALL TO HERSELF.
TOWARD THE END OF THE GREAT QUEST, VIDIA HAD TO MAKE A CHOICE...
...AND YOU CHOSE TO SHARE.
THE REASON WHY NEVERLAND IS HERE TODAY IS BECAUSE OF YOU.

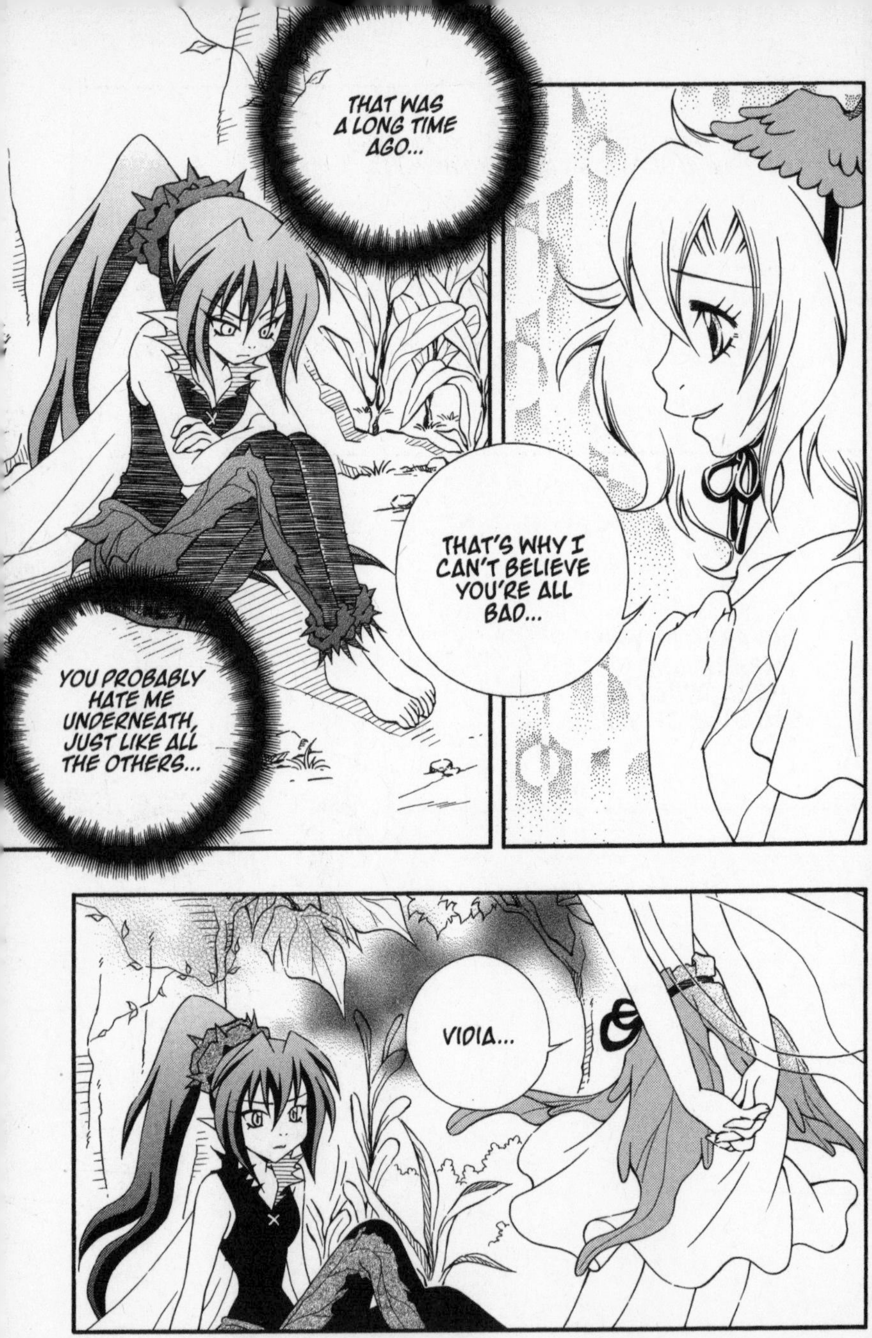
THAT'S WHY I CAN'T BELIEVE YOU'RE ALL BAD...
THAT WAS A LONG TIME AGO...
YOU PROBABLY HATE ME UNDERNEATH, JUST LIKE ALL THE OTHERS...
VIDIA...

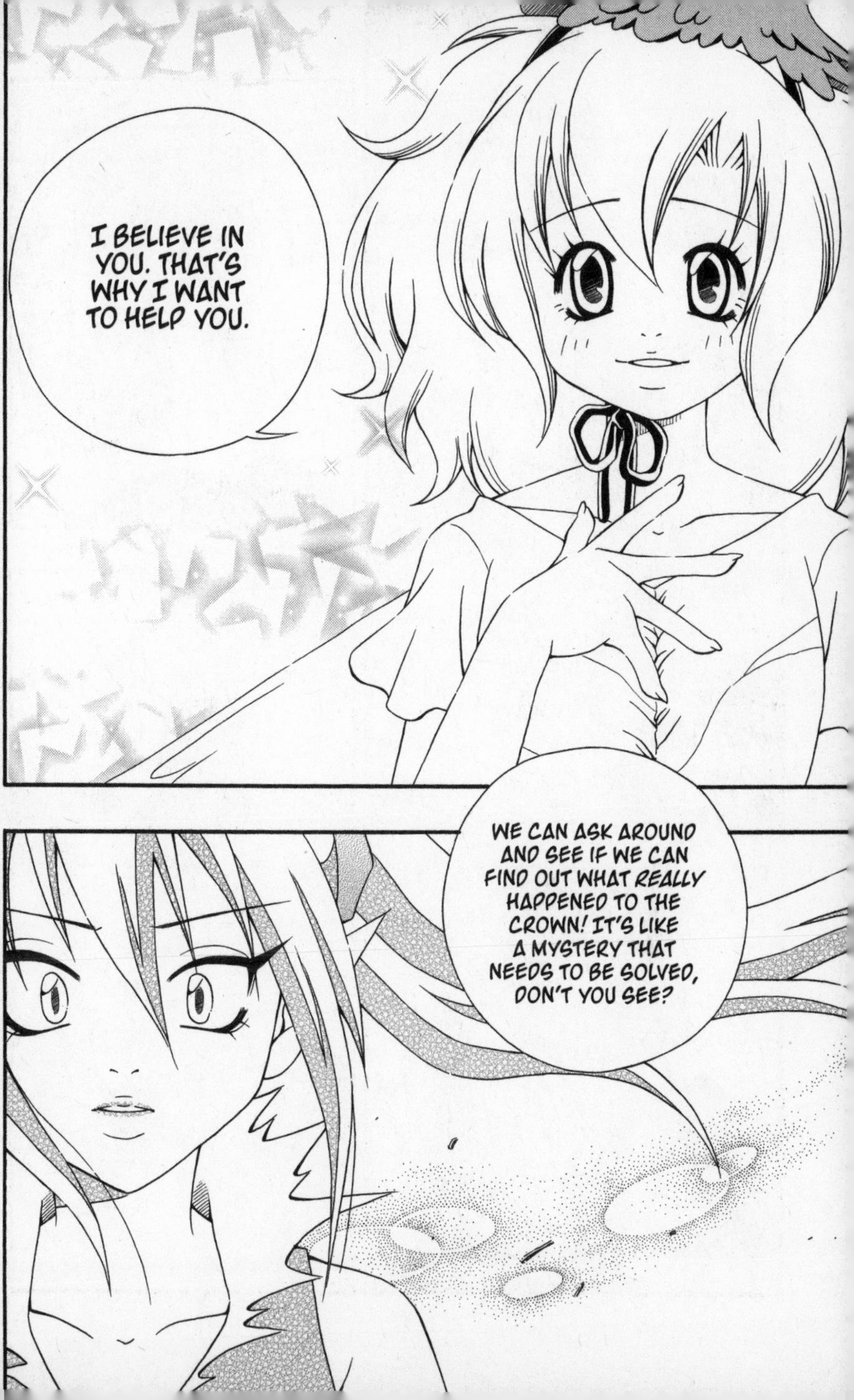
I BELIEVE IN YOU. THAT'S WHY I WANT TO HELP YOU.
WE CAN ASK AROUND AND SEE IF WE CAN FIND OUT WHAT REALLY HAPPENED TO THE CROWN! IT'S LIKE A MYSTERY THAT NEEDS TO BE SOLVED, DON'T YOU SEE?

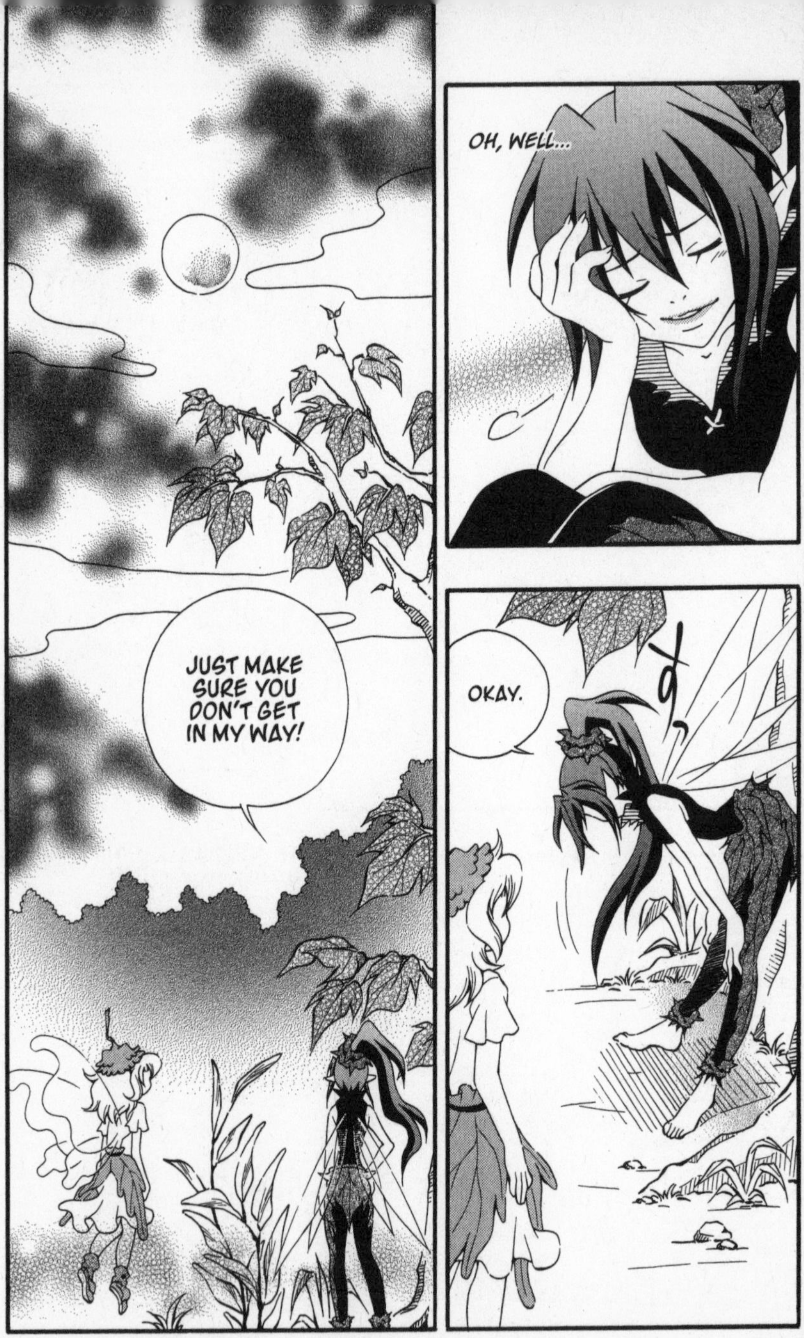
OH, WELL...
OKAY.
JUST MAKE SURE YOU DON'T GET IN MY WAY!

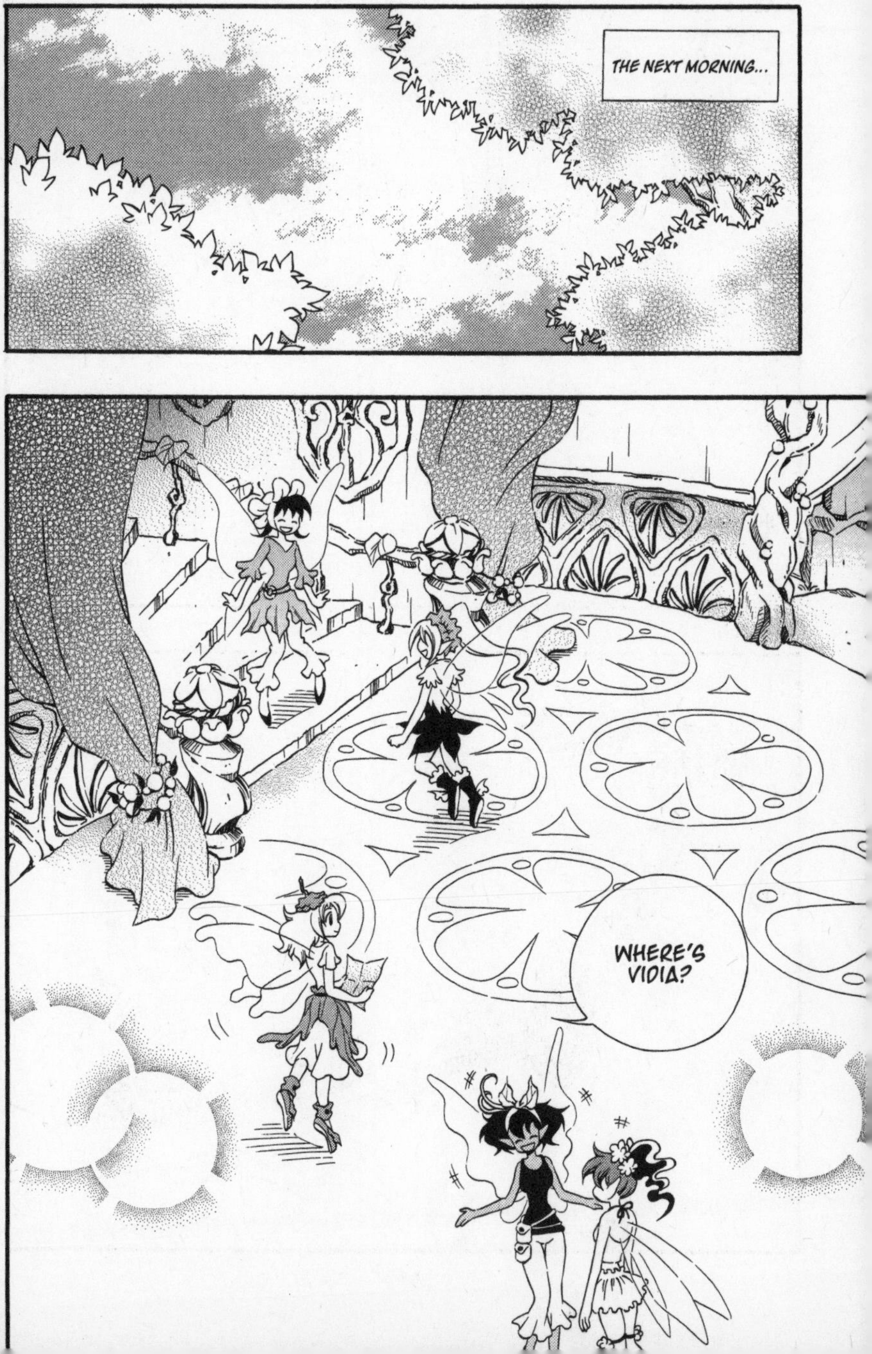
THE NEXT MORNING...
WHERE'S VIDIA?

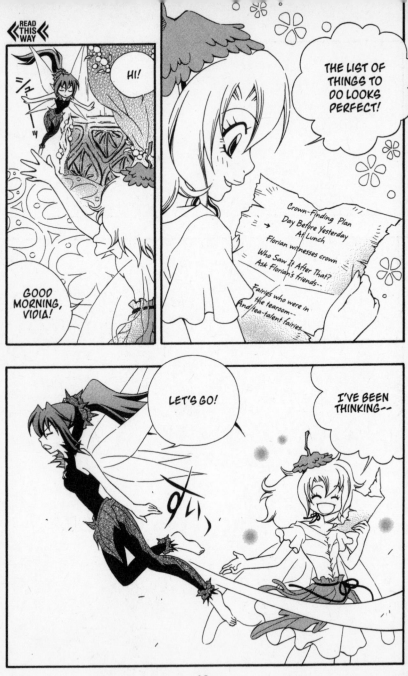

HI!

GOOD MORNING, VIDIA!

THE LIST OF THINGS TO DO LOOKS PERFECT!

Crown-Finding Plan

Day Before Yesterday
→ At Lunch

Florian witnesses crown

Who Saw It After That?
Ask Florian's friends--

Fairies who were in
the tearoom--
And tea-talent fairies

LET'S GO!

I'VE BEEN THINKING--

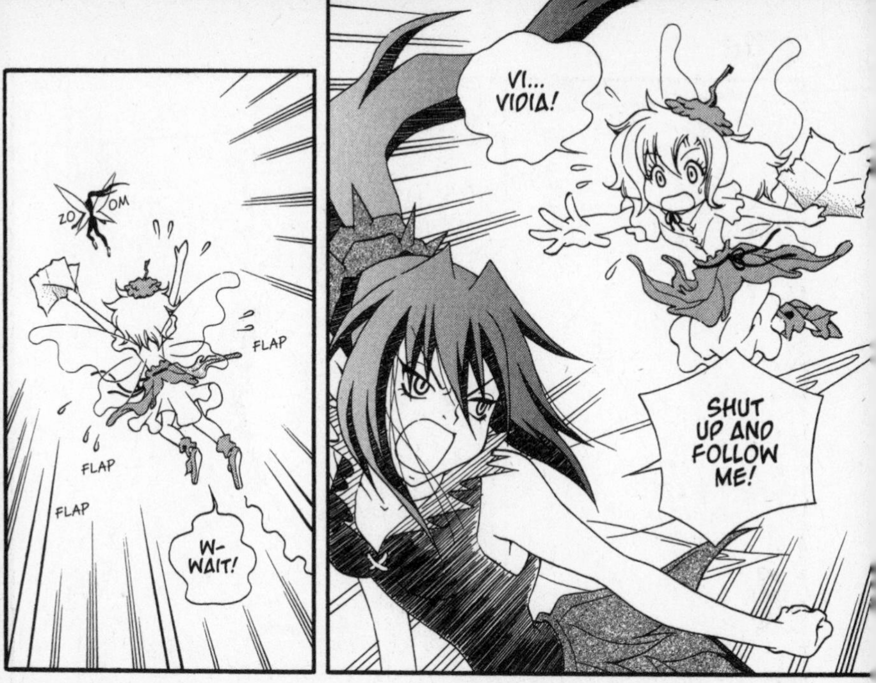
VI... VIDIA!
SHUT UP AND FOLLOW ME!
ZOOM
FLAP
FLAP
FLAP
W-WAIT!

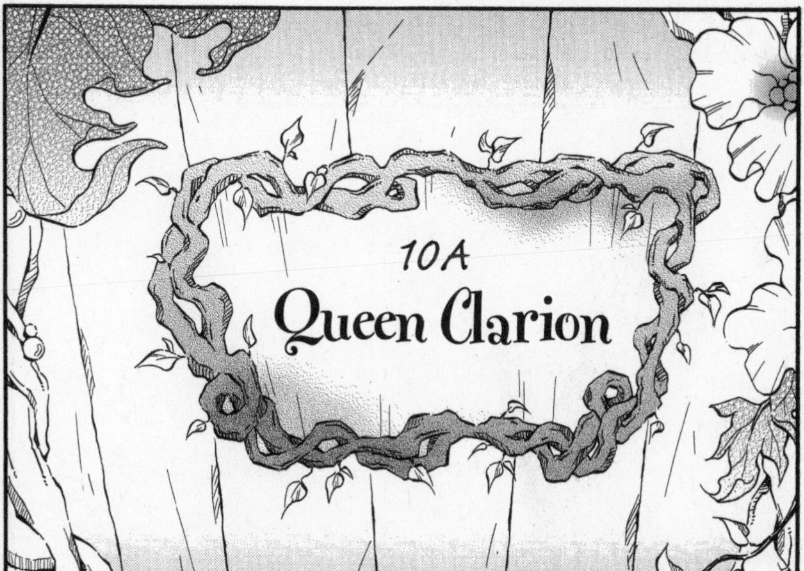
10A
Queen Clarion

READ THIS WAY

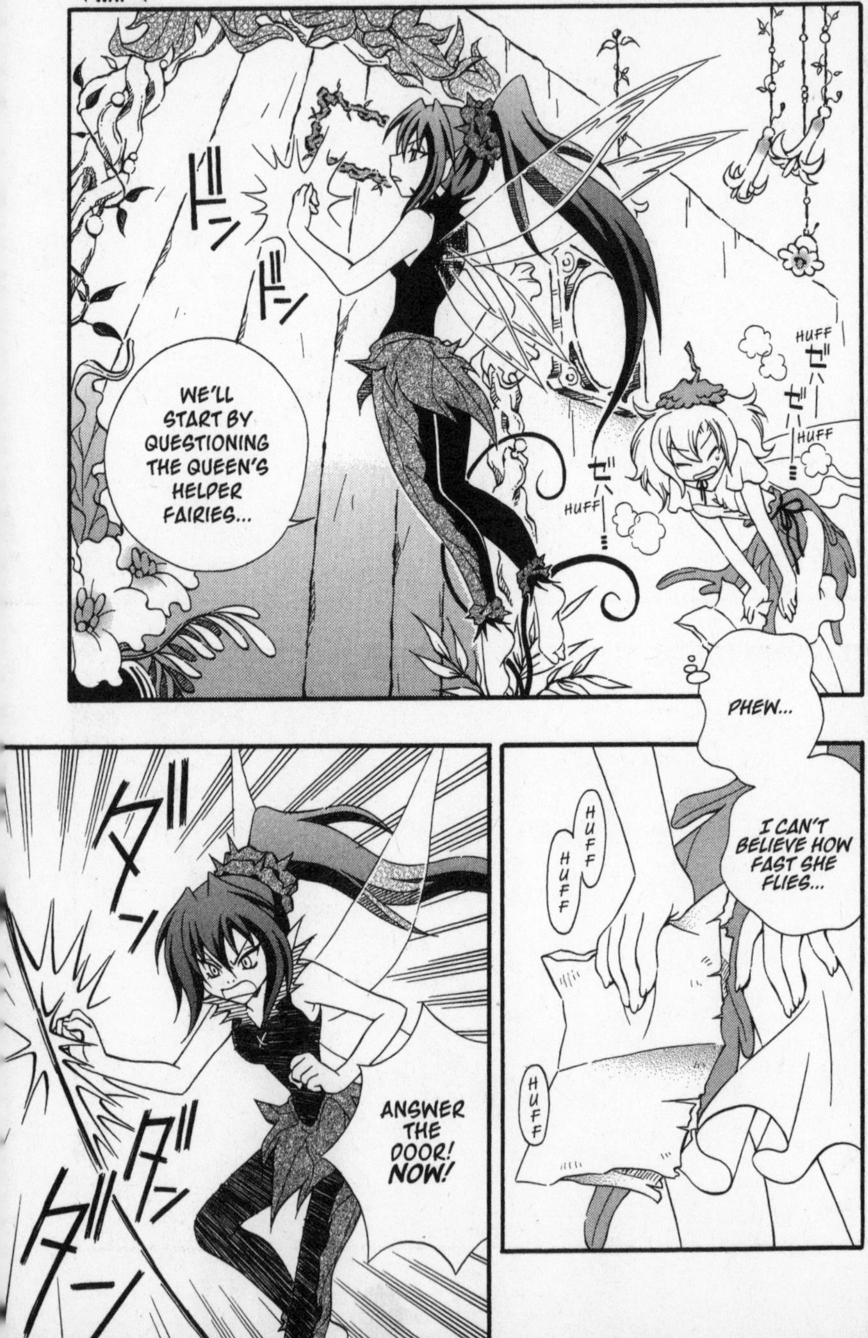

ドン
ドン
WE'LL START BY QUESTIONING THE QUEEN'S HELPER FAIRIES...
HUFF ゼハ
ゼハ HUFF
ゼハ HUFF
PHEW...
HUFF HUFF
I CAN'T BELIEVE HOW FAST SHE FLIES...
HUFF
ダーン
ANSWER THE DOOR! NOW!
ダン
ダーン

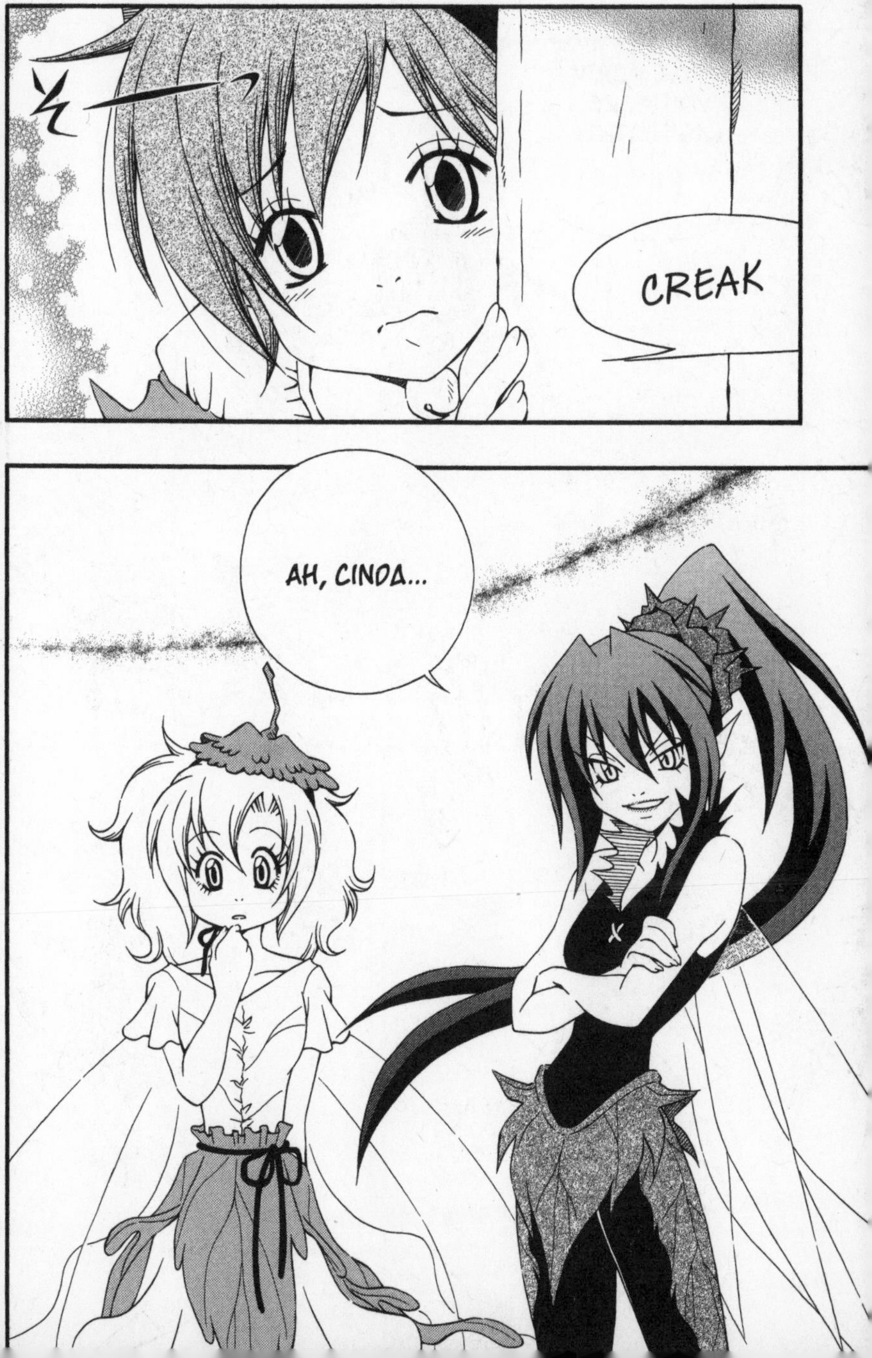
CREAK
AH, CINDA...

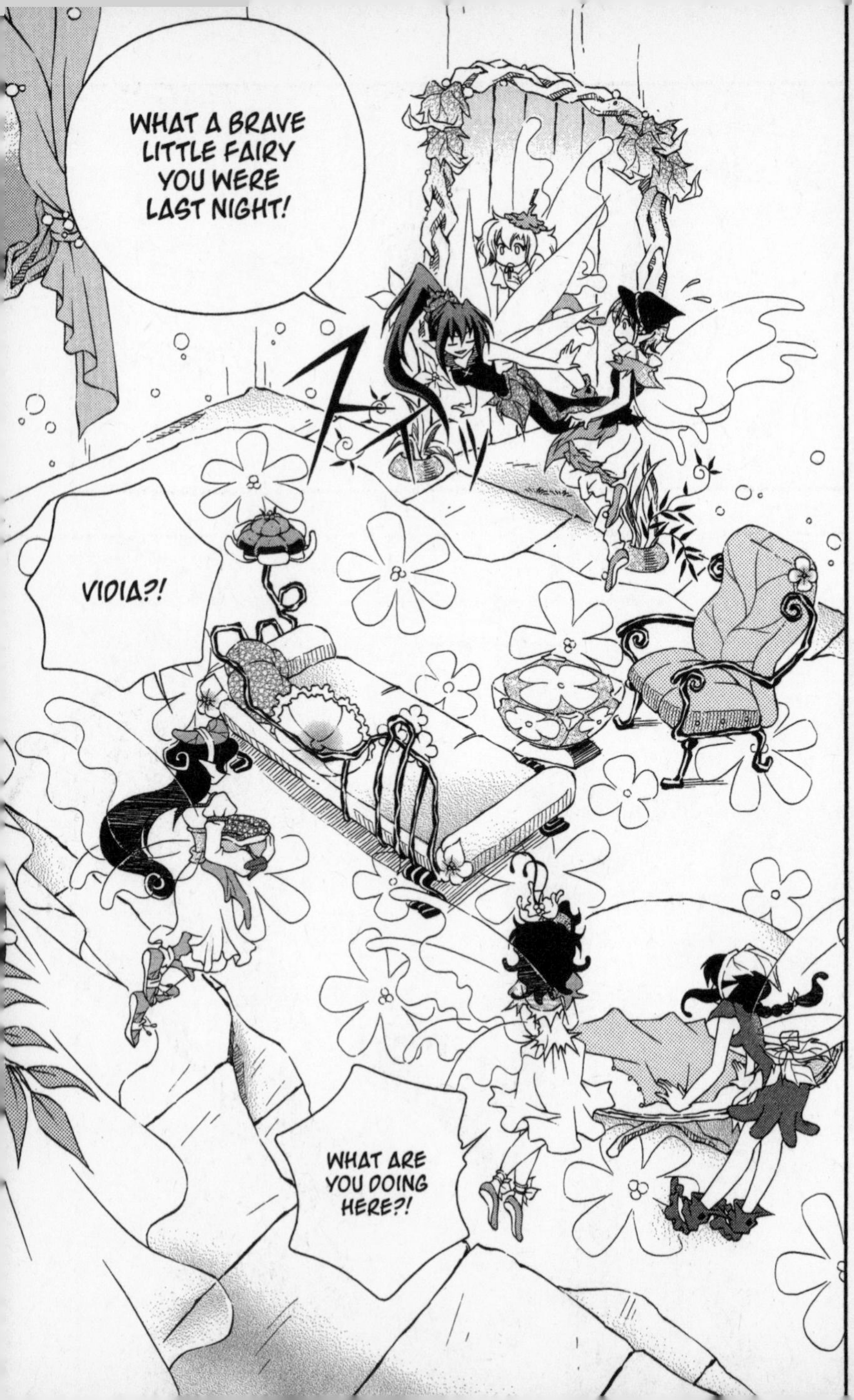
WHAT A BRAVE LITTLE FAIRY YOU WERE LAST NIGHT!
VIDIA?!
WHAT ARE YOU DOING HERE?!

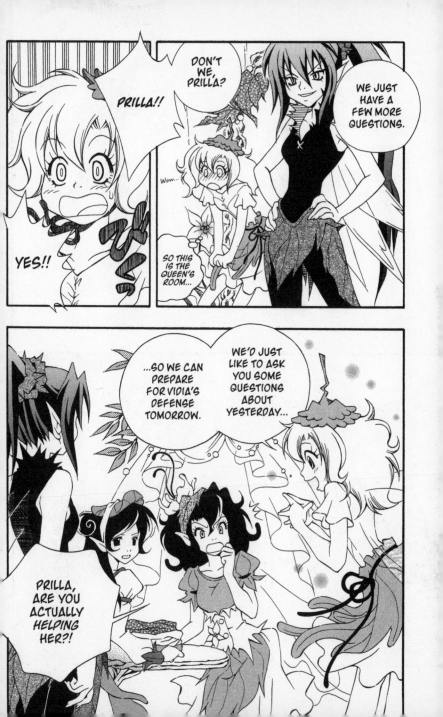

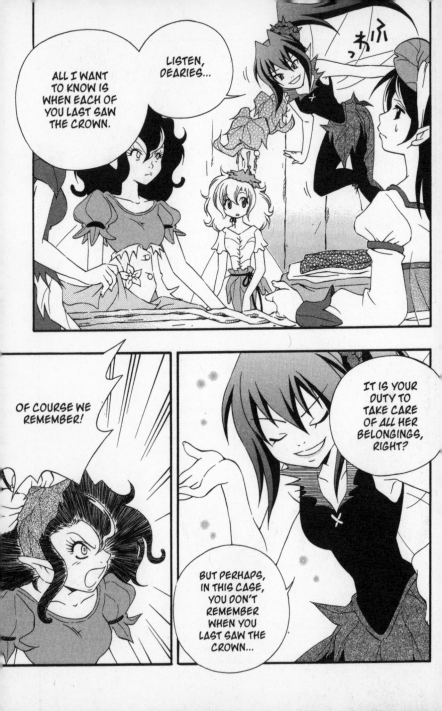

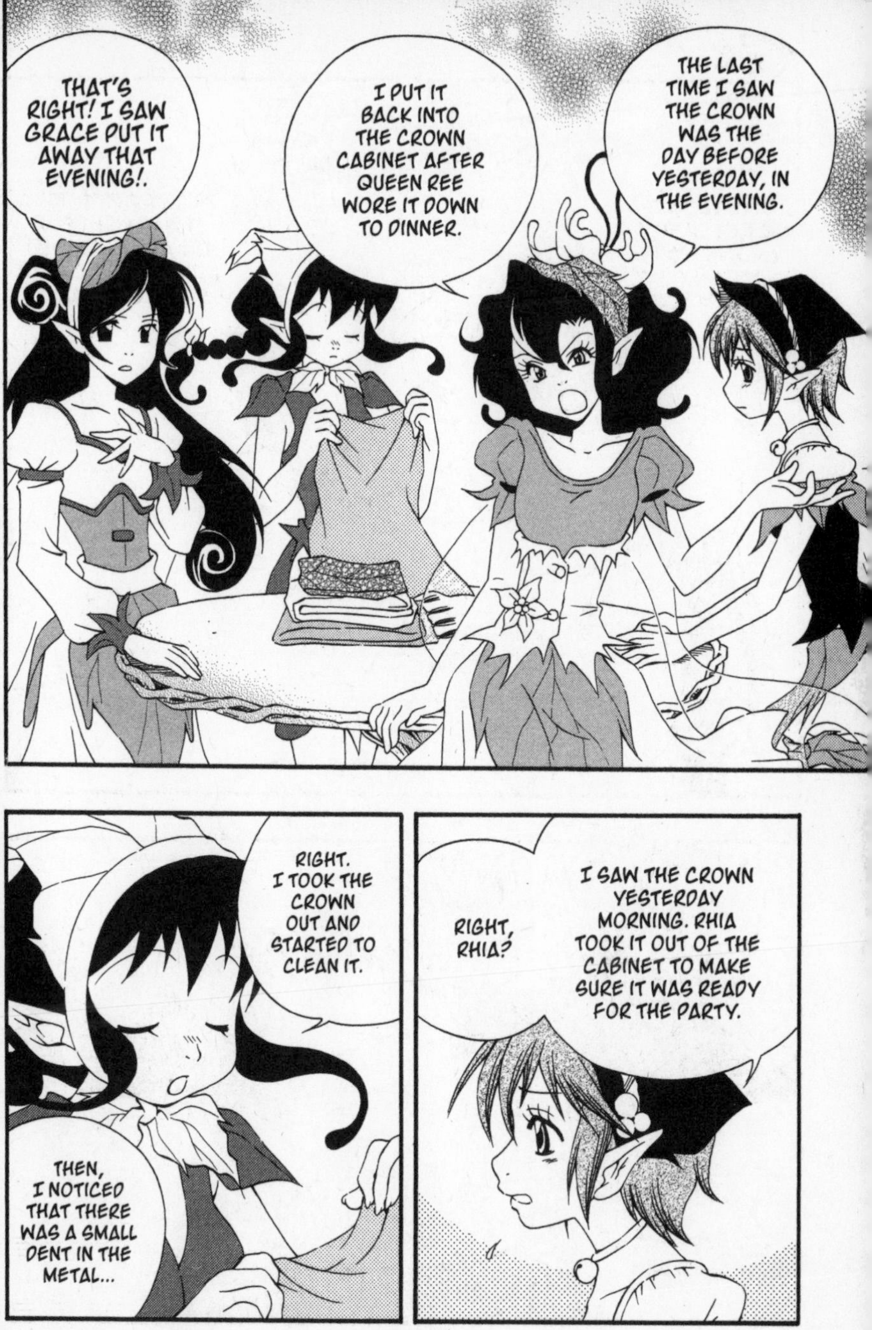
THE LAST TIME I SAW THE CROWN WAS THE DAY BEFORE YESTERDAY, IN THE EVENING.
I PUT IT BACK INTO THE CROWN CABINET AFTER QUEEN REE WORE IT DOWN TO DINNER.
THAT'S RIGHT! I SAW GRACE PUT IT AWAY THAT EVENING!.
I SAW THE CROWN YESTERDAY MORNING. RHIA TOOK IT OUT OF THE CABINET TO MAKE SURE IT WAS READY FOR THE PARTY.
RIGHT, RHIA?
RIGHT. I TOOK THE CROWN OUT AND STARTED TO CLEAN IT.
THEN, I NOTICED THAT THERE WAS A SMALL DENT IN THE METAL...

READ THIS WAY

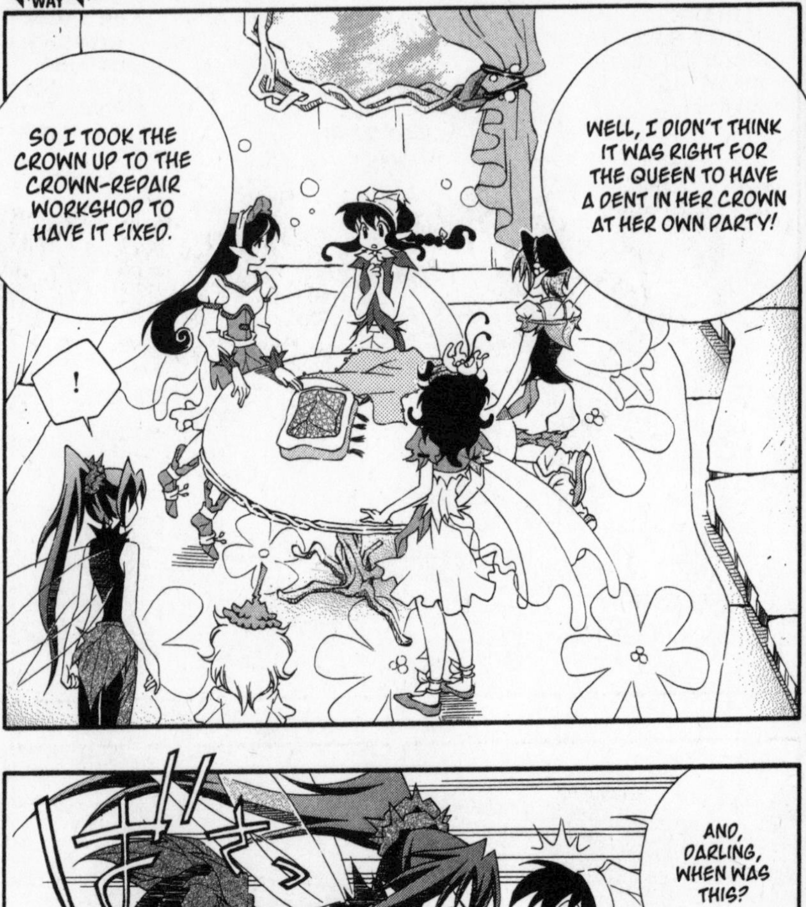

WELL, I DIDN'T THINK IT WAS RIGHT FOR THE QUEEN TO HAVE A DENT IN HER CROWN AT HER OWN PARTY!
SO I TOOK THE CROWN UP TO THE CROWN-REPAIR WORKSHOP TO HAVE IT FIXED.
!
AND, DARLING, WHEN WAS THIS?
Y-YESTERDAY MORNING...!

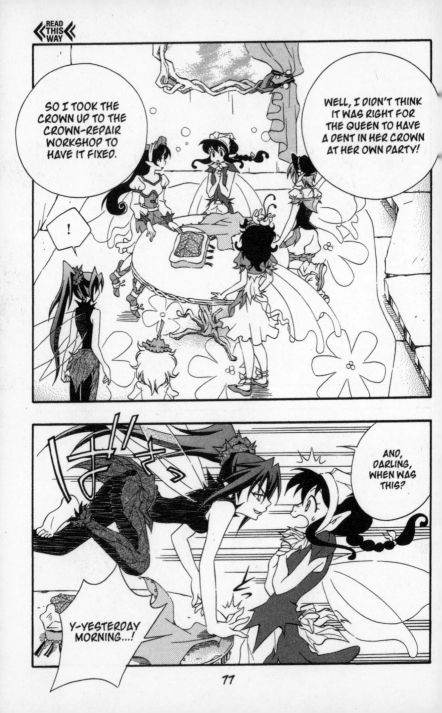

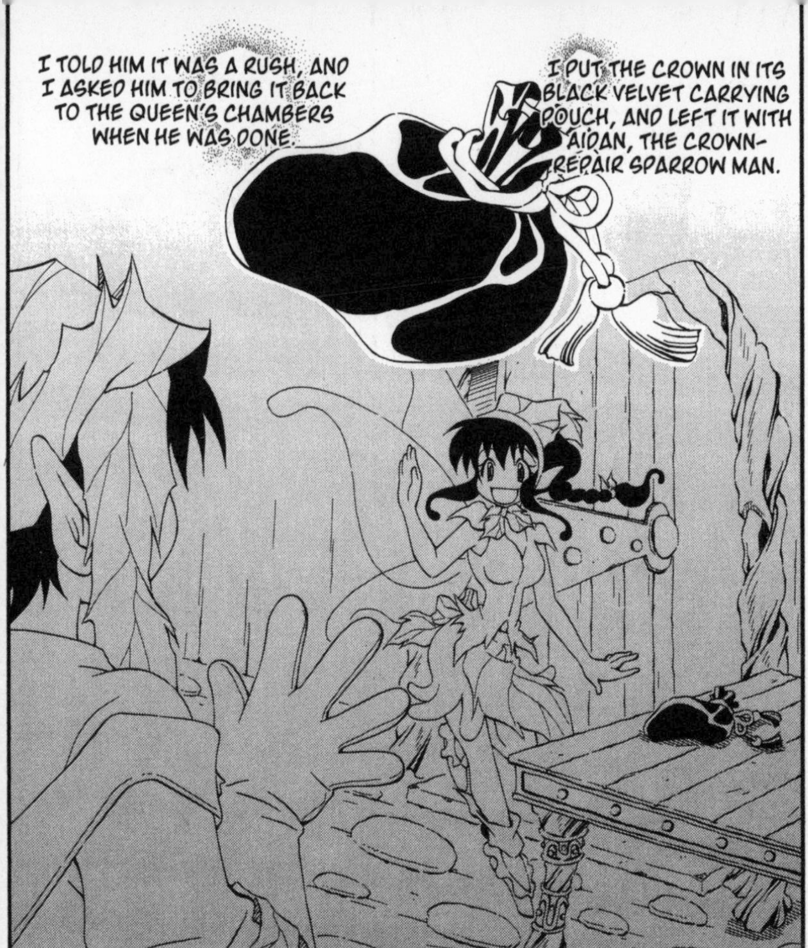
I PUT THE CROWN IN ITS BLACK VELVET CARRYING POUCH, AND LEFT IT WITH AIDAN, THE CROWN-REPAIR SPARROW MAN.
I TOLD HIM IT WAS A RUSH, AND I ASKED HIM TO BRING IT BACK TO THE QUEEN'S CHAMBERS WHEN HE WAS DONE.
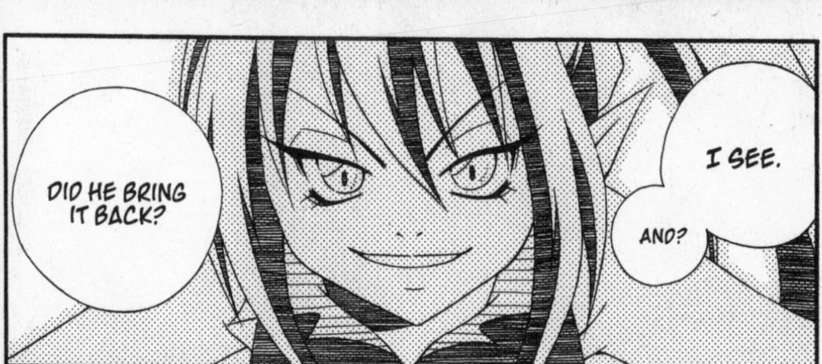
I SEE.
AND?
DID HE BRING IT BACK?

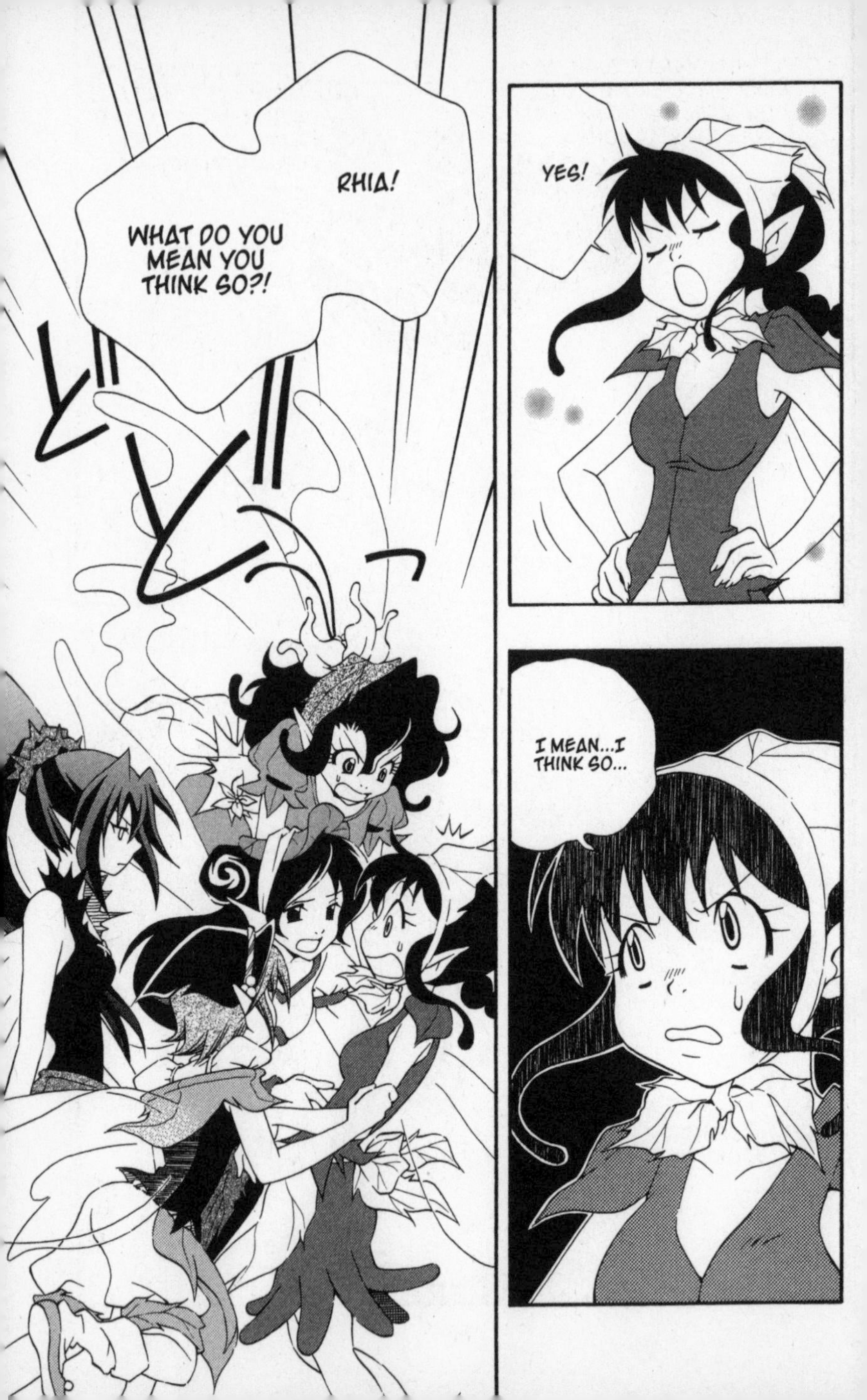
YES!
I MEAN...I THINK SO...
RHIA!
WHAT DO YOU MEAN YOU THINK SO?!

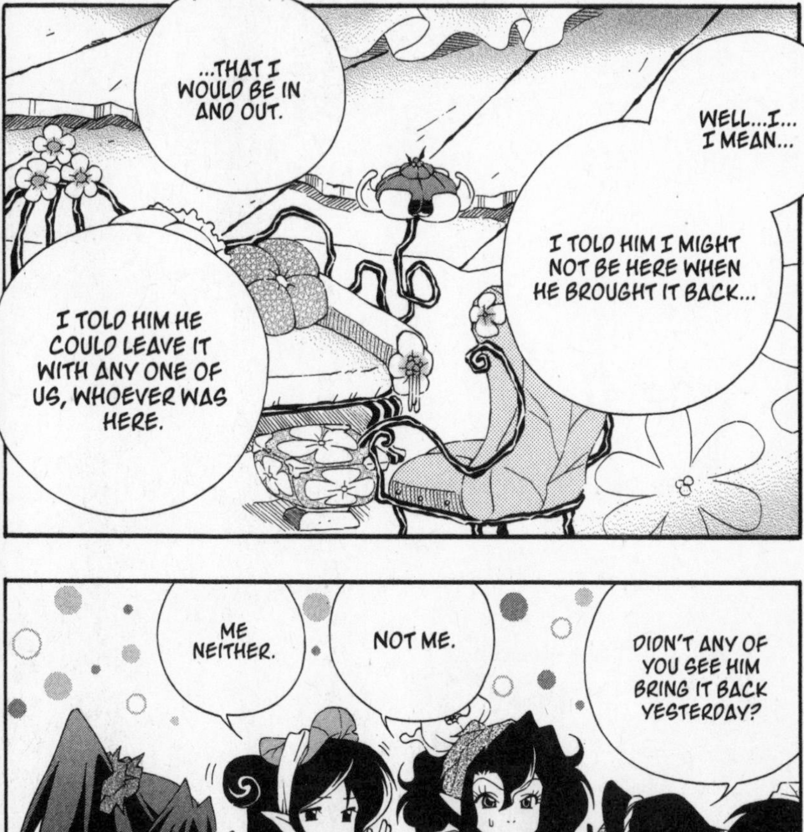
WELL...I... I MEAN...
I TOLD HIM I MIGHT NOT BE HERE WHEN HE BROUGHT IT BACK...
...THAT I WOULD BE IN AND OUT.
I TOLD HIM HE COULD LEAVE IT WITH ANY ONE OF US, WHOEVER WAS HERE.
DIDN'T ANY OF YOU SEE HIM BRING IT BACK YESTERDAY?
NOT ME.
ME NEITHER.

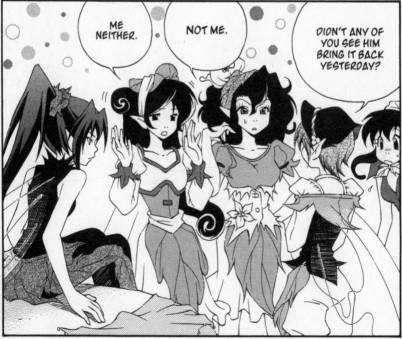

READ THIS WAY

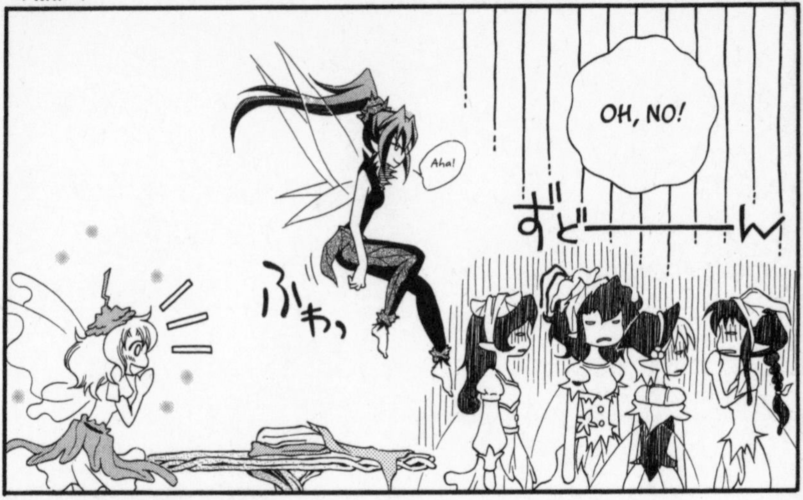
OH, NO!
ずど——ん
Aha!
ふわっ

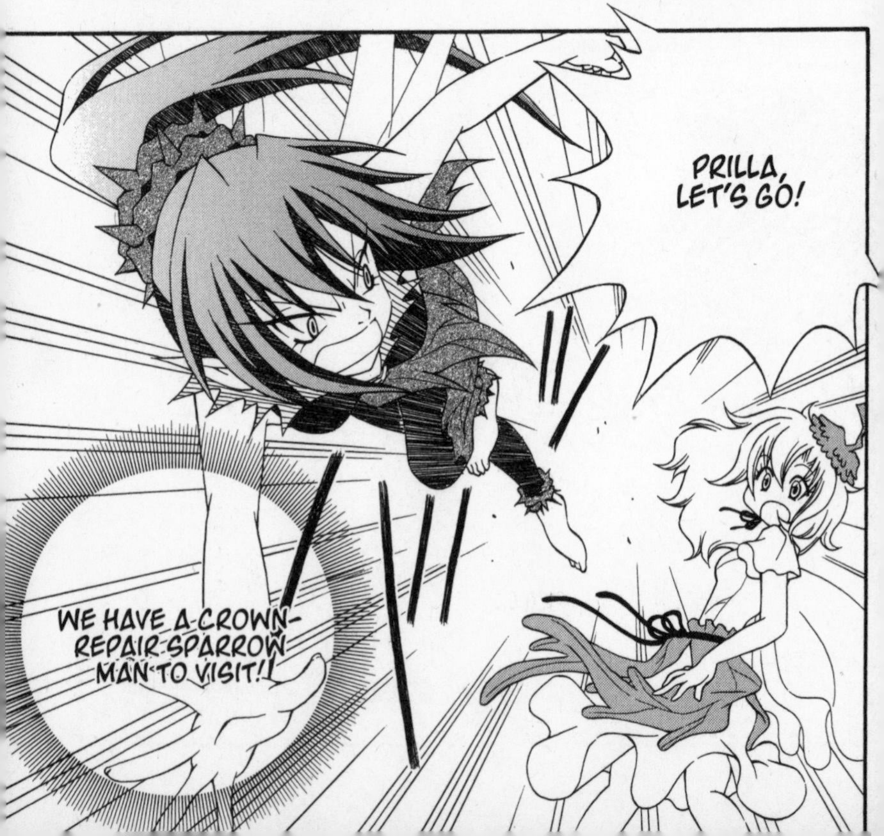
PRILLA, LET'S GO!
WE HAVE A CROWN-REPAIR SPARROW MAN TO VISIT!

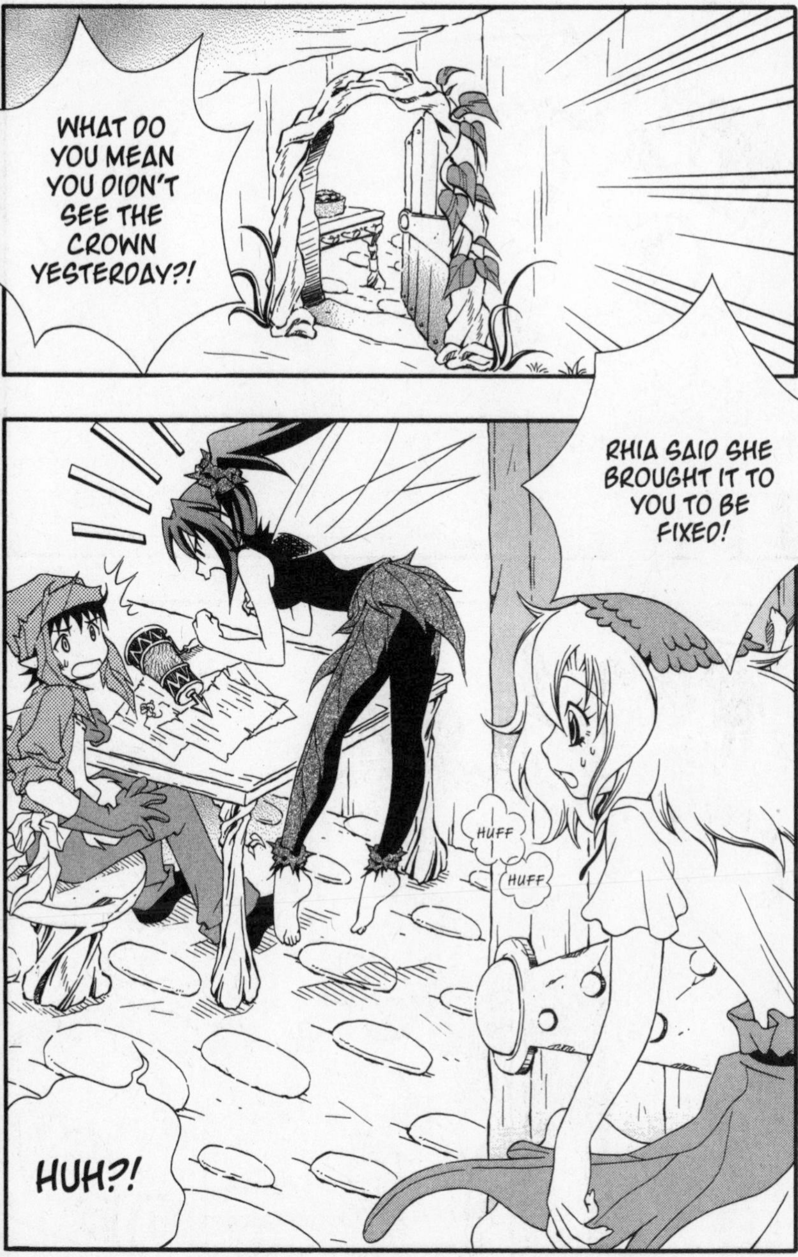
WHAT DO YOU MEAN YOU DIDN'T SEE THE CROWN YESTERDAY?!
RHIA SAID SHE BROUGHT IT TO YOU TO BE FIXED!
HUFF
HUFF
HUH?!

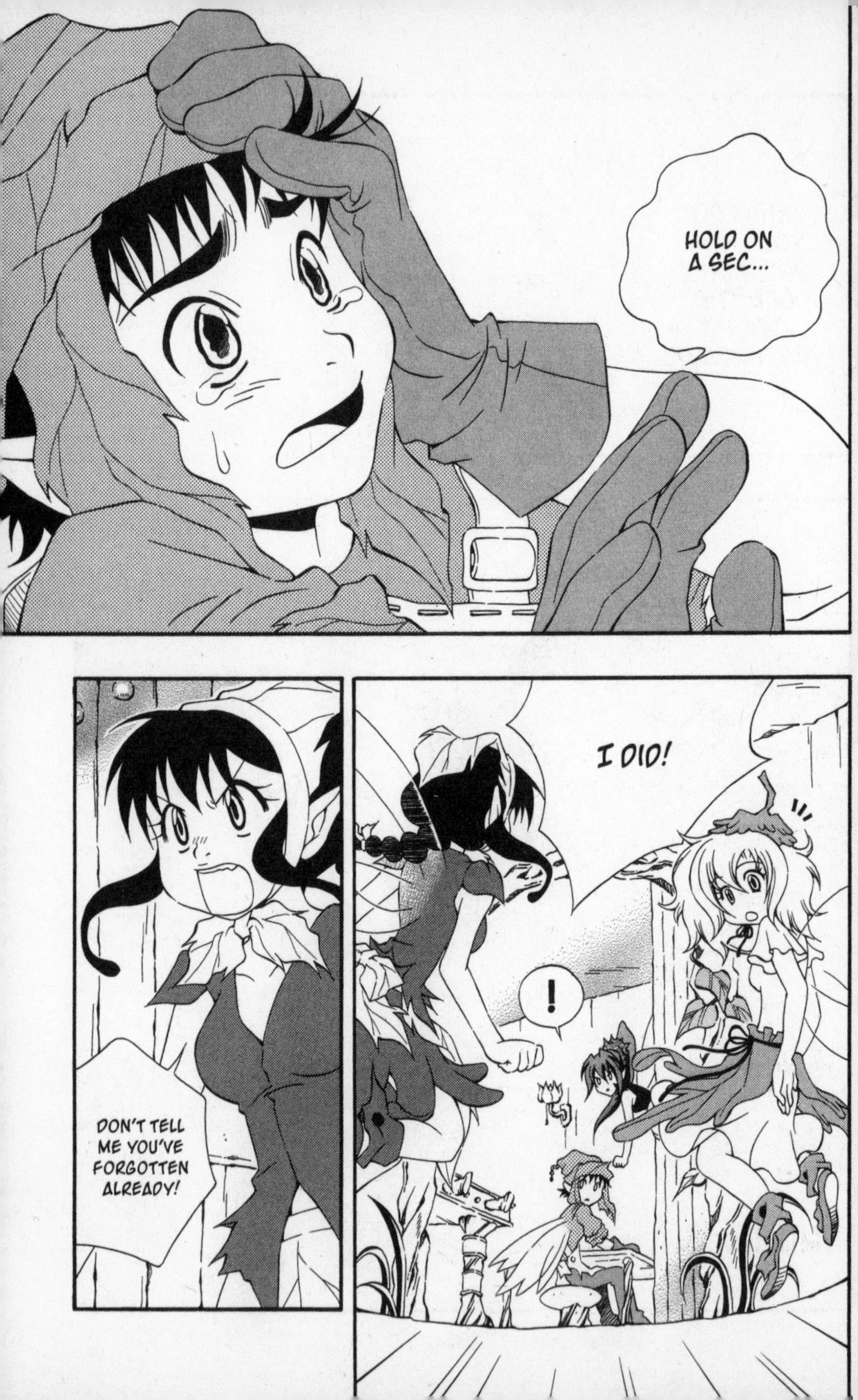
HOLD ON A SEC...
I DID!
!
DON'T TELL ME YOU'VE FORGOTTEN ALREADY!

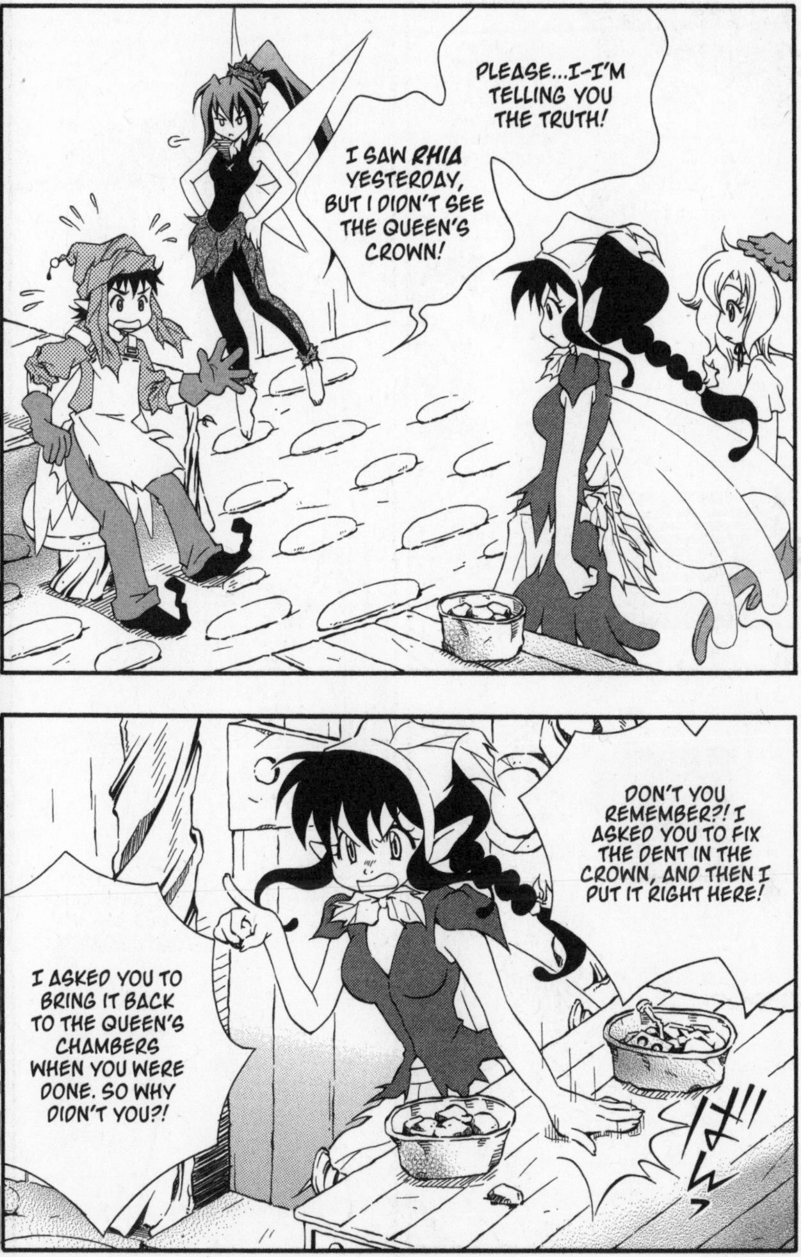
PLEASE...I-I'M TELLING YOU THE TRUTH!
I SAW RHIA YESTERDAY, BUT I DIDN'T SEE THE QUEEN'S CROWN!
DON'T YOU REMEMBER?! I ASKED YOU TO FIX THE DENT IN THE CROWN, AND THEN I PUT IT RIGHT HERE!
ばんっ
I ASKED YOU TO BRING IT BACK TO THE QUEEN'S CHAMBERS WHEN YOU WERE DONE. SO WHY DIDN'T YOU?!

READ THIS WAY

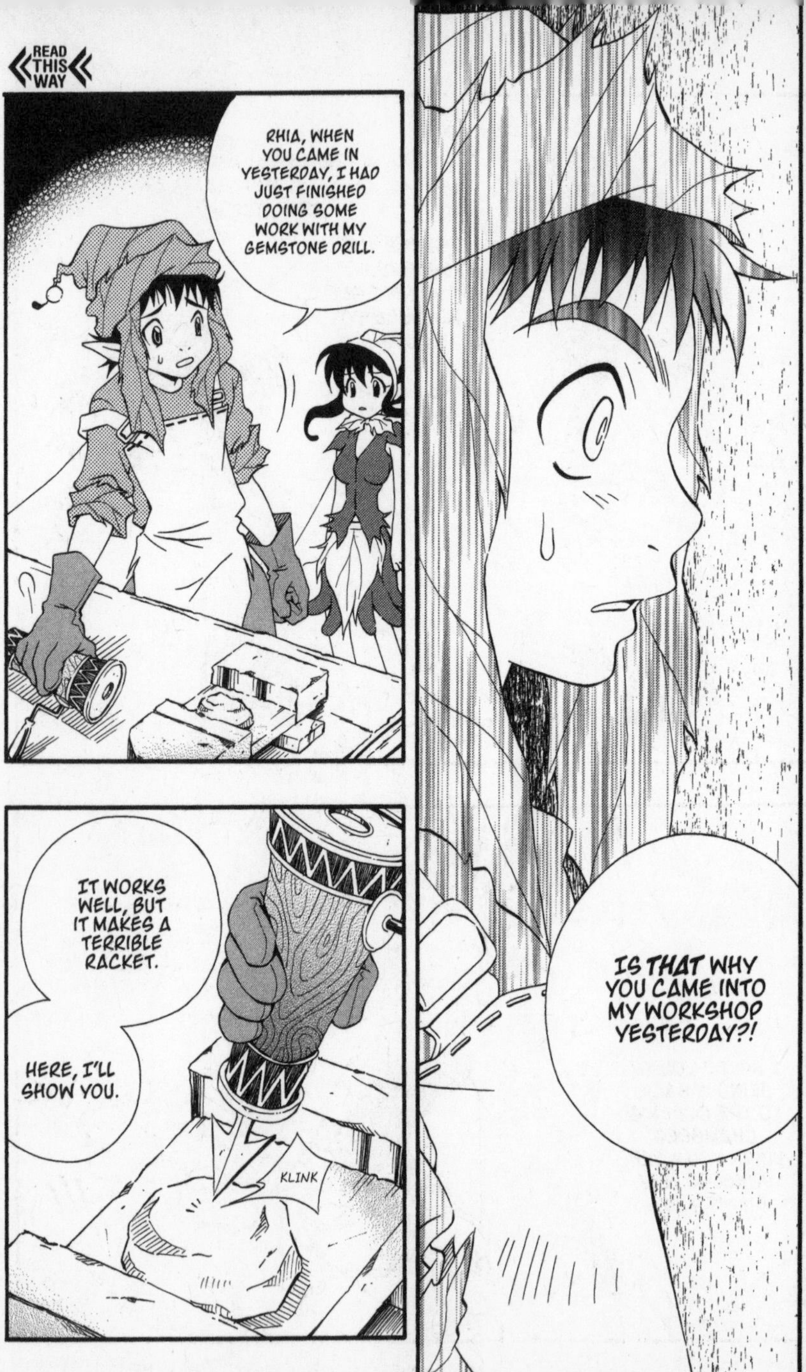
IS THAT WHY YOU CAME INTO MY WORKSHOP YESTERDAY?!
RHIA, WHEN YOU CAME IN YESTERDAY, I HAD JUST FINISHED DOING SOME WORK WITH MY GEMSTONE DRILL.
IT WORKS WELL, BUT IT MAKES A TERRIBLE RACKET.
HERE, I'LL SHOW YOU.
KLINK

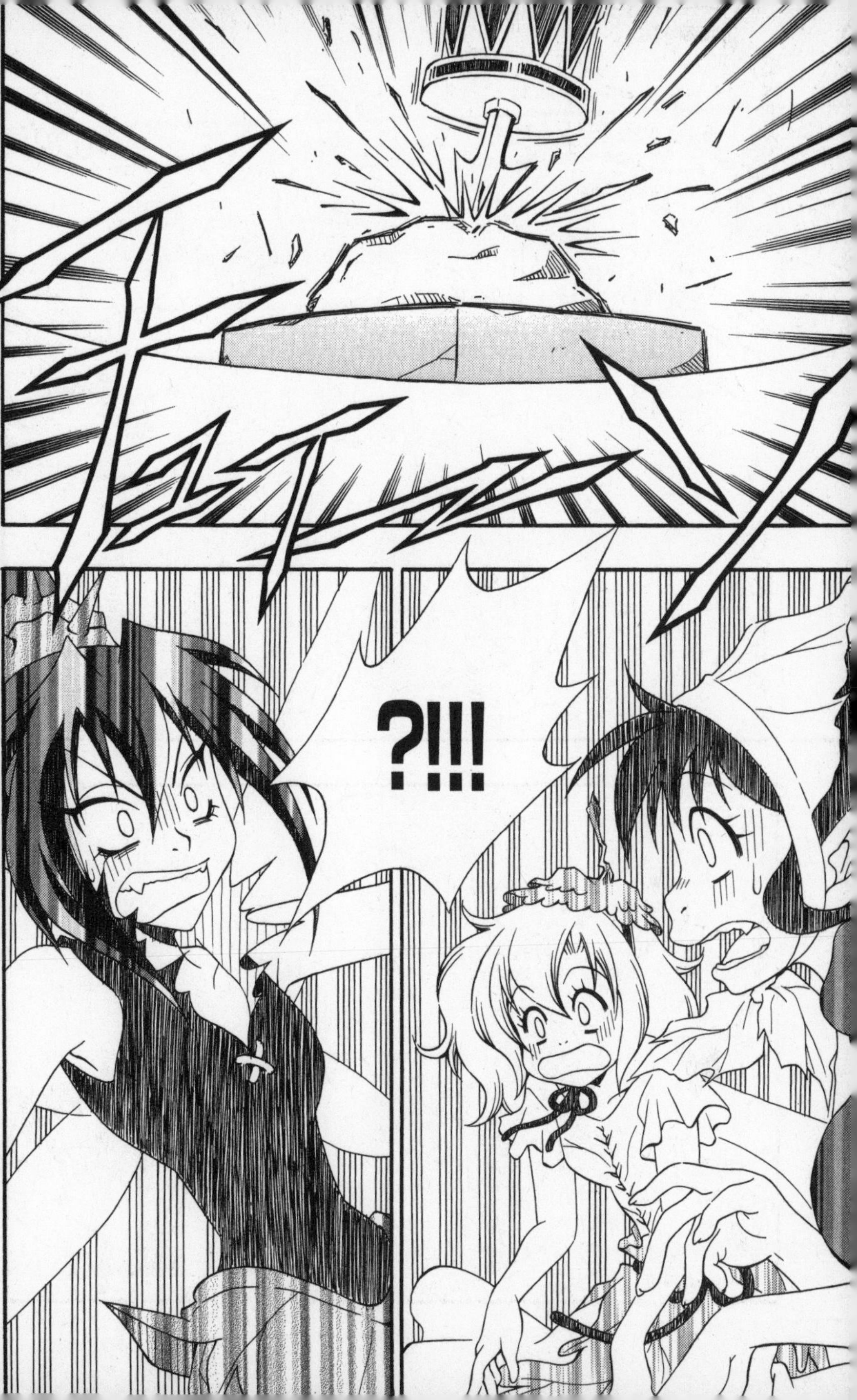
?!!!

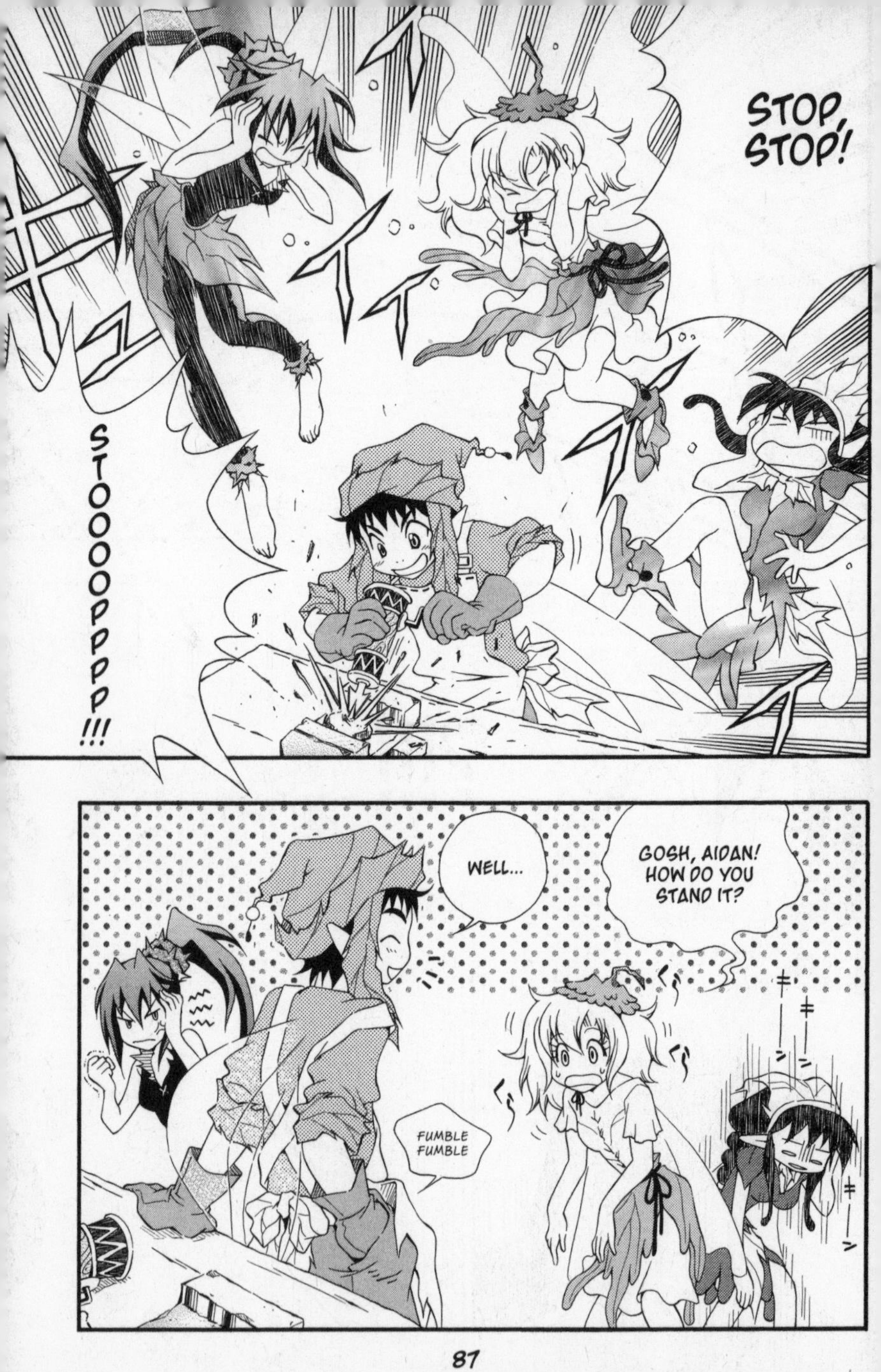
STOP, STOP!
STOOOOPPPPP!!!
GOSH, AIDAN! HOW DO YOU STAND IT?
WELL...
FUMBLE FUMBLE

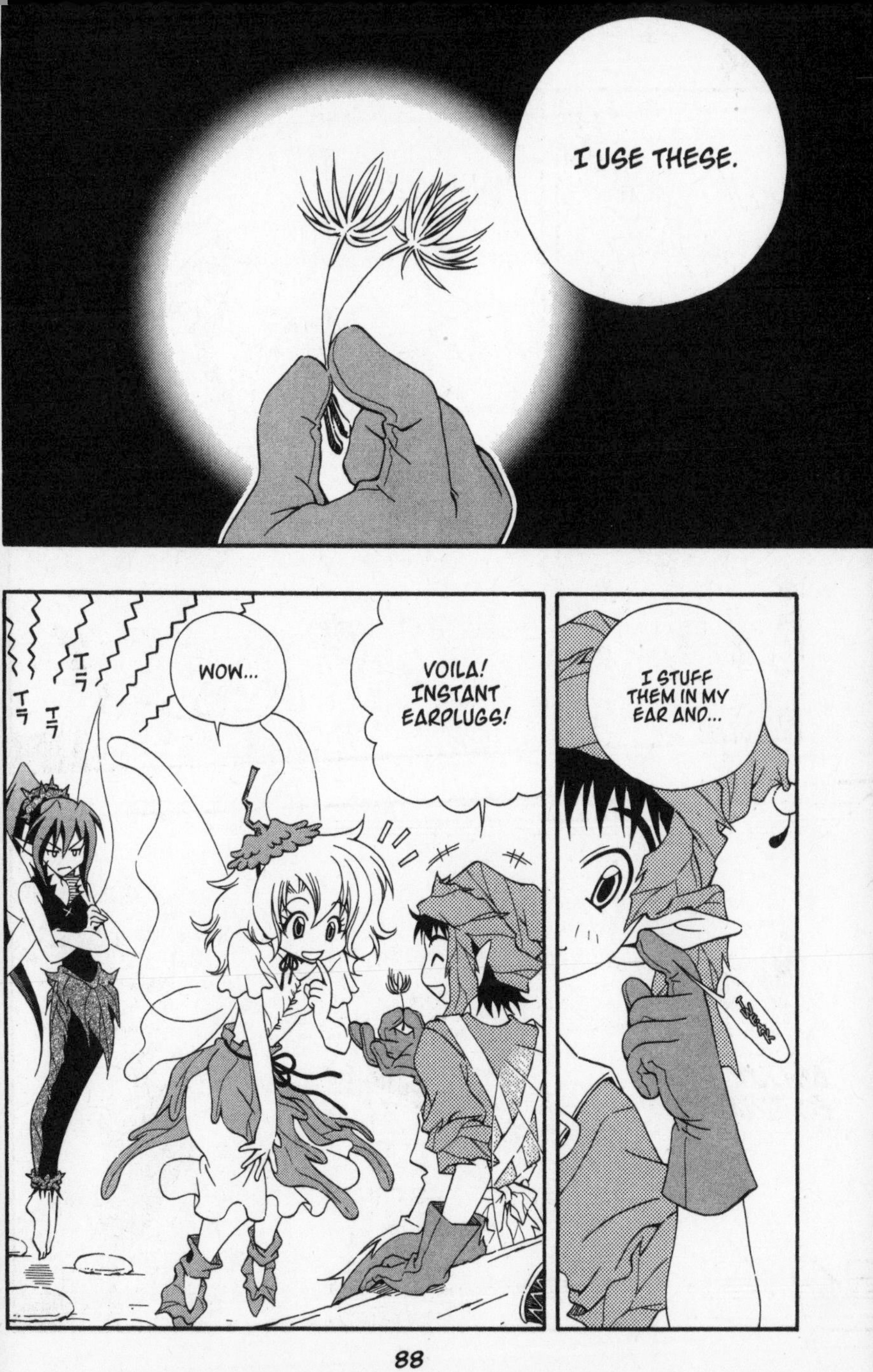
I USE THESE.
I STUFF THEM IN MY EAR AND...
VOILA! INSTANT EARPLUGS!
WOW...
イラ
イラ
イラ

READ THIS WAY

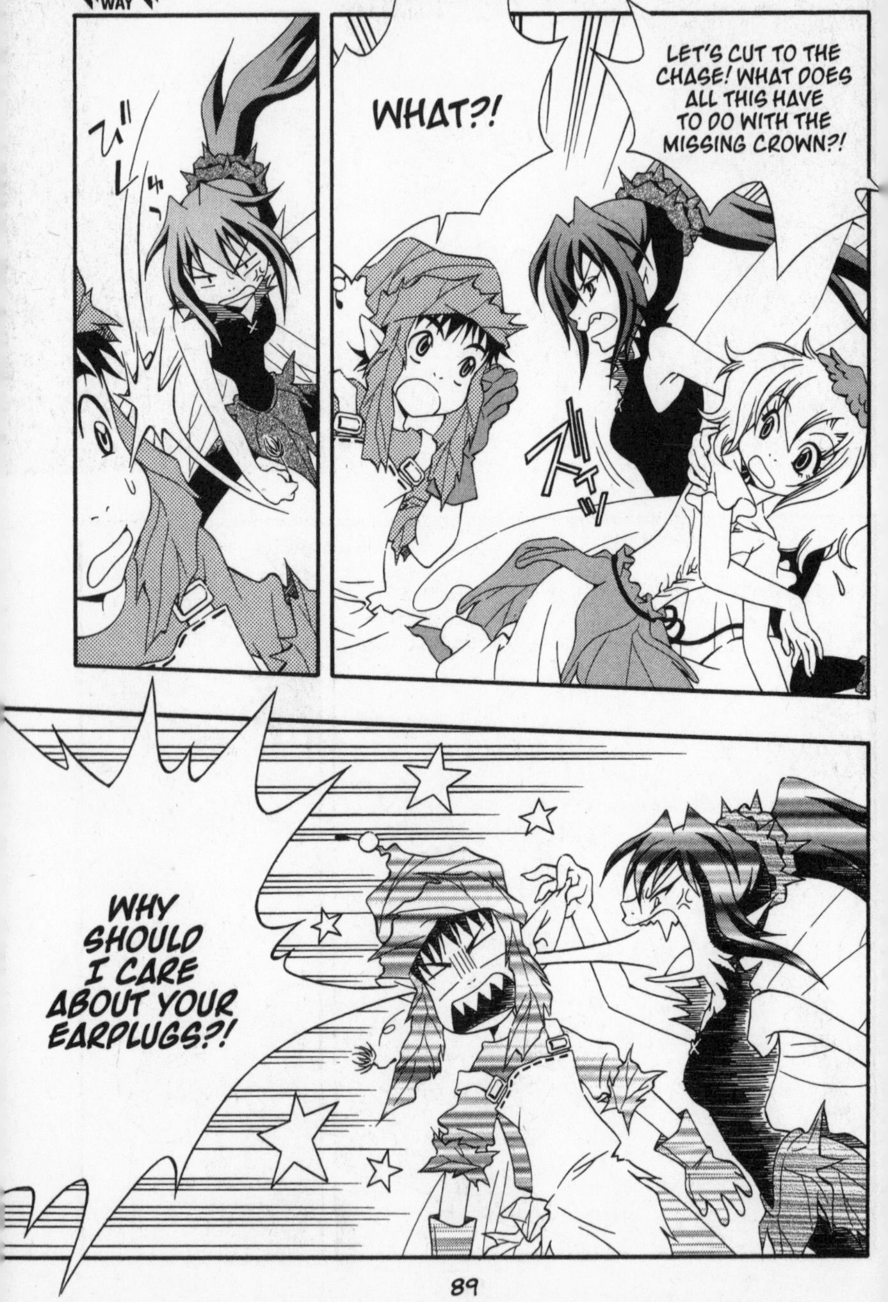
LET'S CUT TO THE CHASE! WHAT DOES ALL THIS HAVE TO DO WITH THE MISSING CROWN?!
WHAT?!
WHY SHOULD I CARE ABOUT YOUR EARPLUGS?!

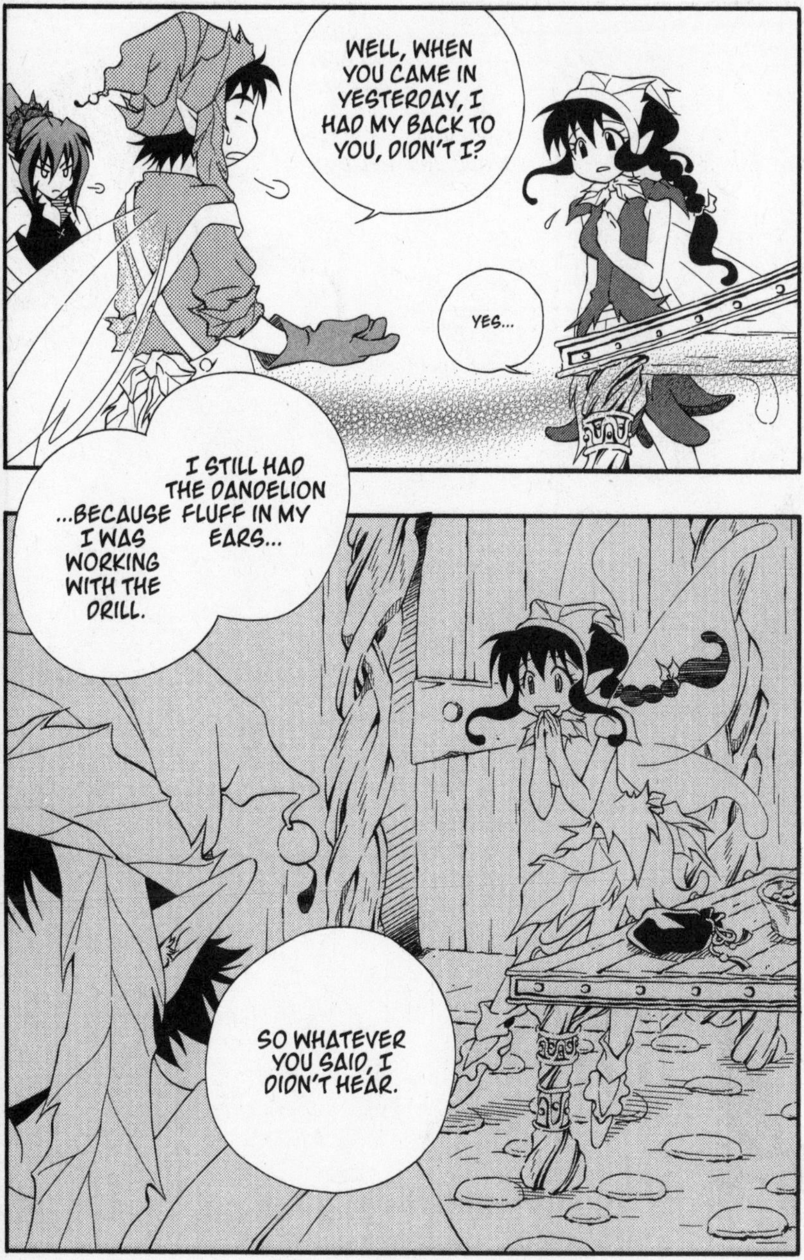
WELL, WHEN YOU CAME IN YESTERDAY, I HAD MY BACK TO YOU, DIDN'T I?
YES...
I STILL HAD THE DANDELION FLUFF IN MY EARS...
...BECAUSE I WAS WORKING WITH THE DRILL.
SO WHATEVER YOU SAID, I DIDN'T HEAR.

READ THIS WAY

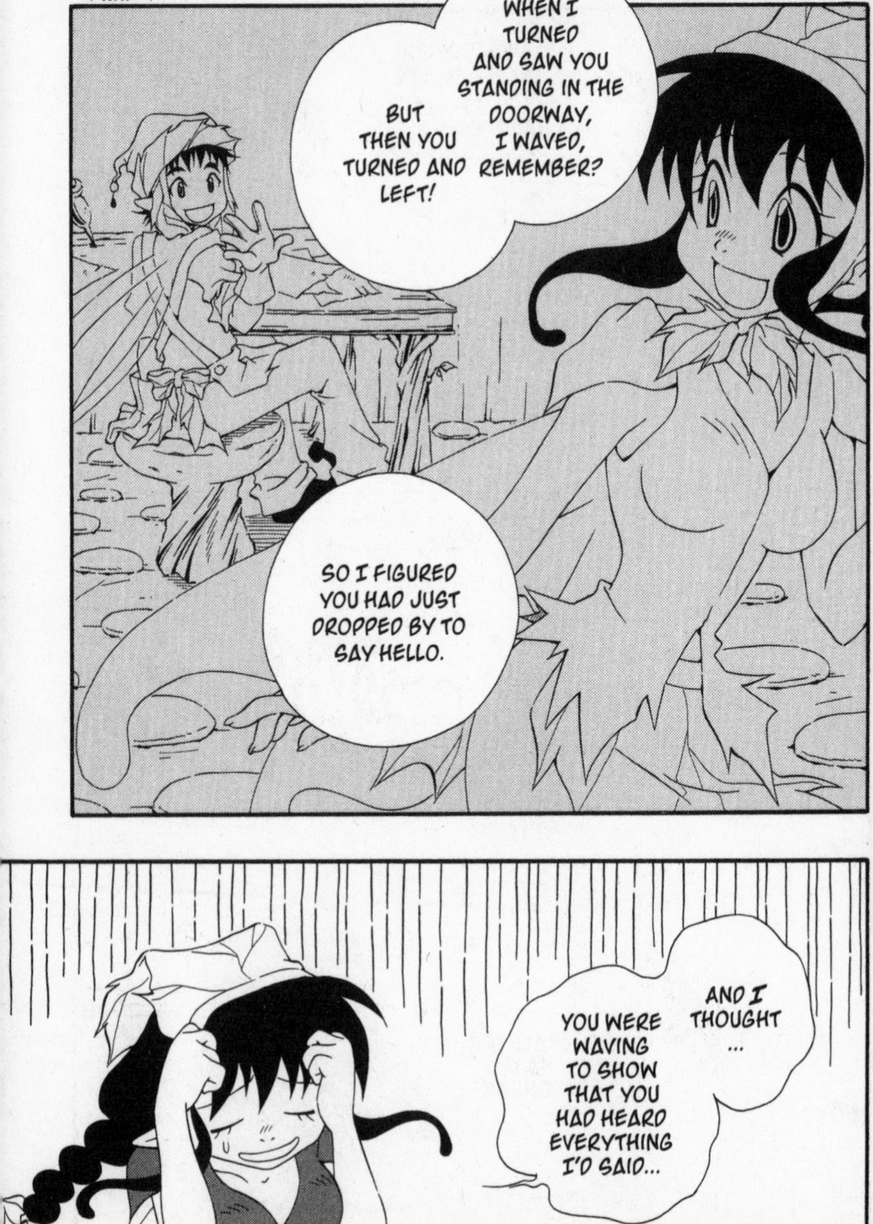
WHEN I TURNED AND SAW YOU STANDING IN THE DOORWAY, I WAVED, REMEMBER?
BUT THEN YOU TURNED AND LEFT!
SO I FIGURED YOU HAD JUST DROPPED BY TO SAY HELLO.
AND I THOUGHT ...
YOU WERE WAVING TO SHOW THAT YOU HAD HEARD EVERYTHING I'D SAID...

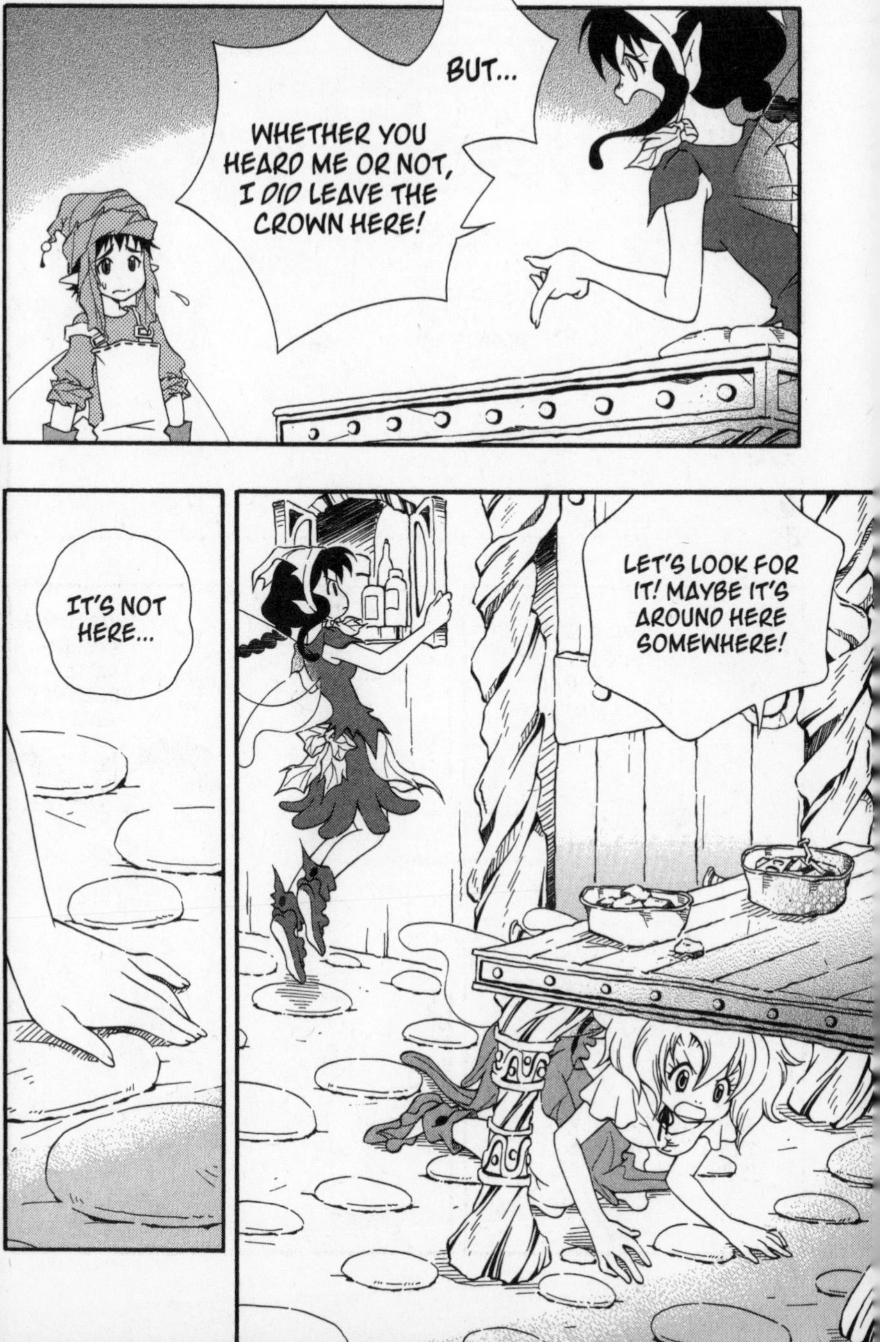
BUT...
WHETHER YOU HEARD ME OR NOT, I *DID* LEAVE THE CROWN HERE!
LET'S LOOK FOR IT! MAYBE IT'S AROUND HERE SOMEWHERE!
IT'S NOT HERE...

READ THIS WAY

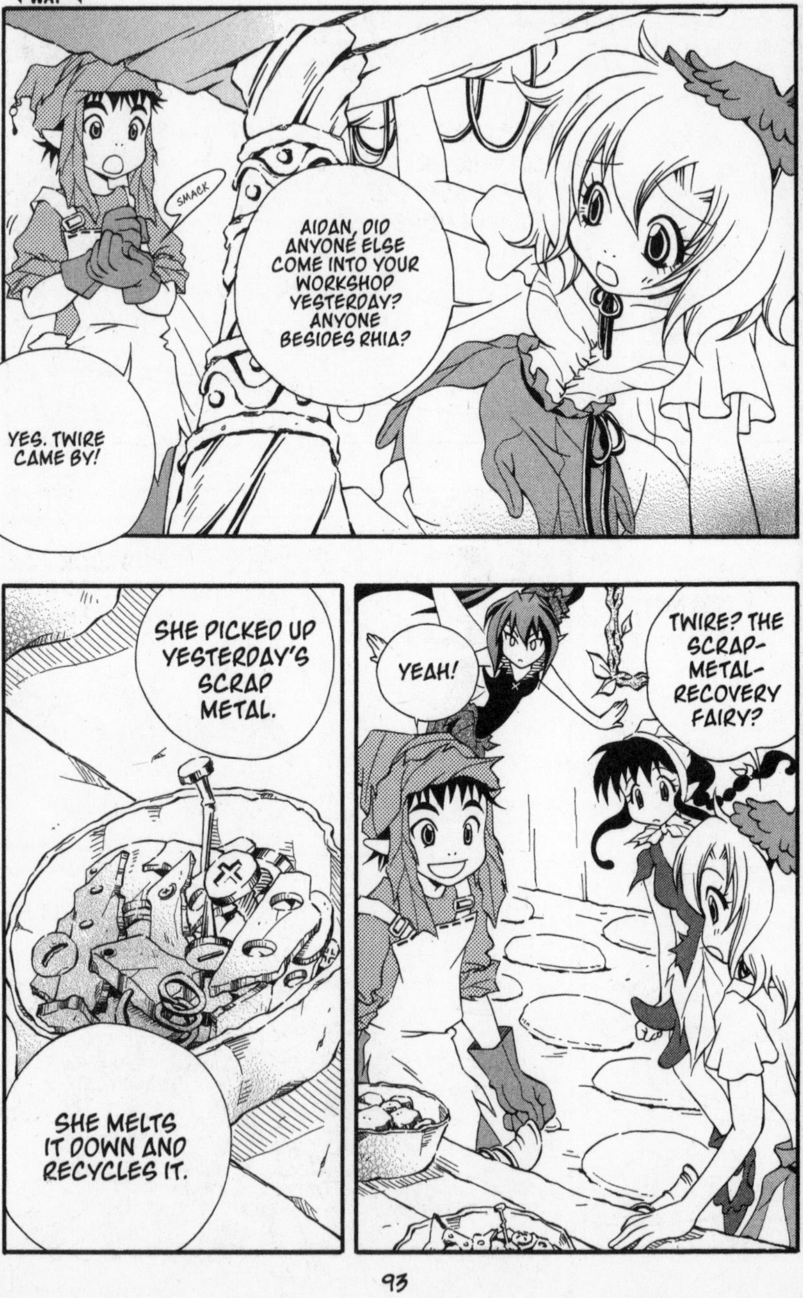

AIDAN, DID ANYONE ELSE COME INTO YOUR WORKSHOP YESTERDAY? ANYONE BESIDES RHIA?
SMACK
YES. TWIRE CAME BY!
TWIRE? THE SCRAP-METAL-RECOVERY FAIRY?
YEAH!
SHE PICKED UP YESTERDAY'S SCRAP METAL.
SHE MELTS IT DOWN AND RECYCLES IT.

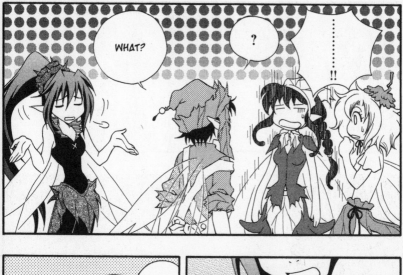

WHAT?

?

·········
!!

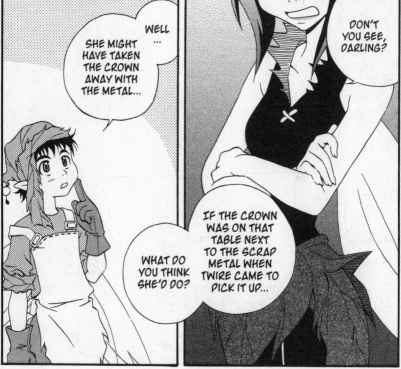

WELL...

SHE MIGHT HAVE TAKEN THE CROWN AWAY WITH THE METAL...

WHAT DO YOU THINK SHE'D DO?

DON'T YOU SEE, DARLING?

IF THE CROWN WAS ON THAT TABLE NEXT TO THE SCRAP METAL WHEN TWIRE CAME TO PICK IT UP...

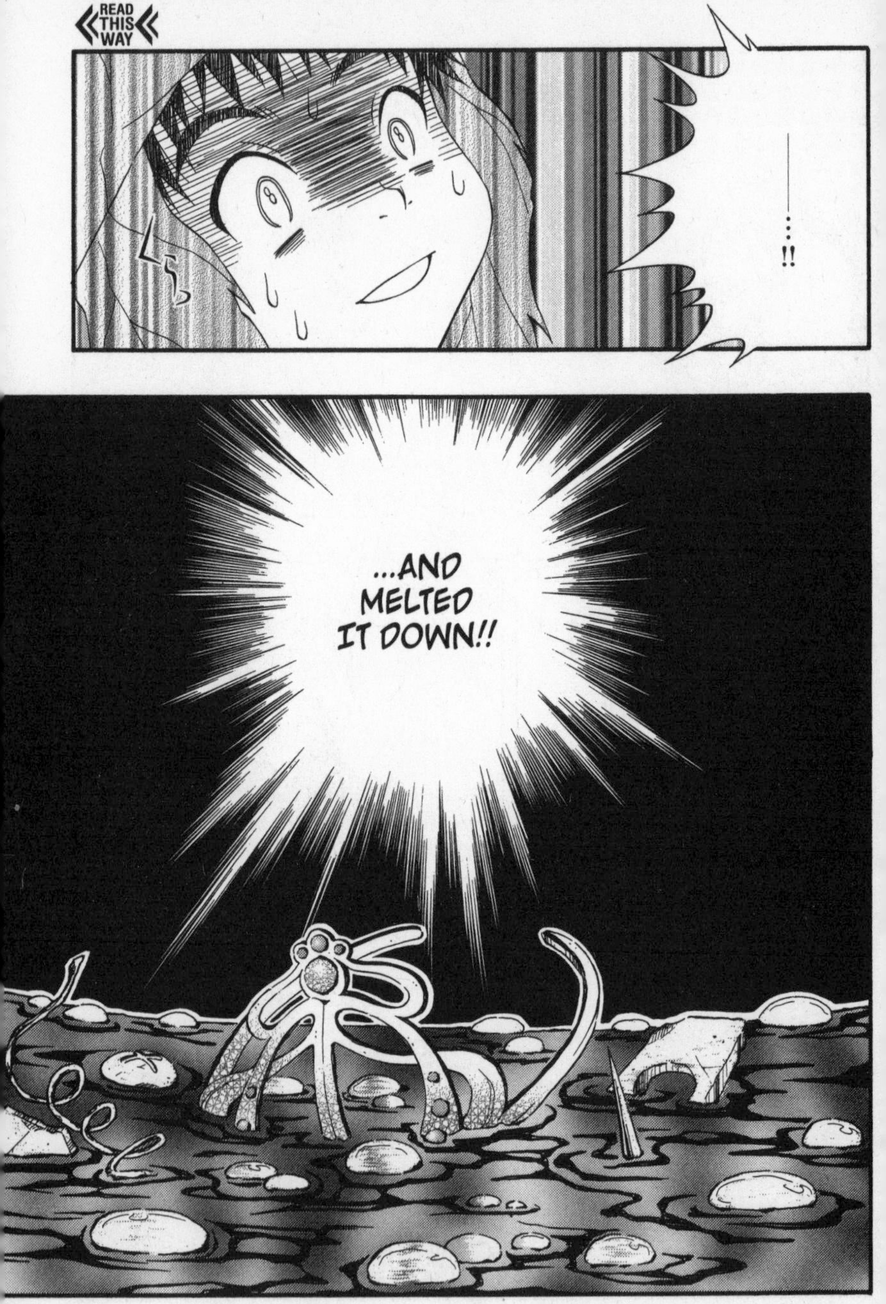
READ THIS WAY
——...!!
...AND MELTED IT DOWN!!

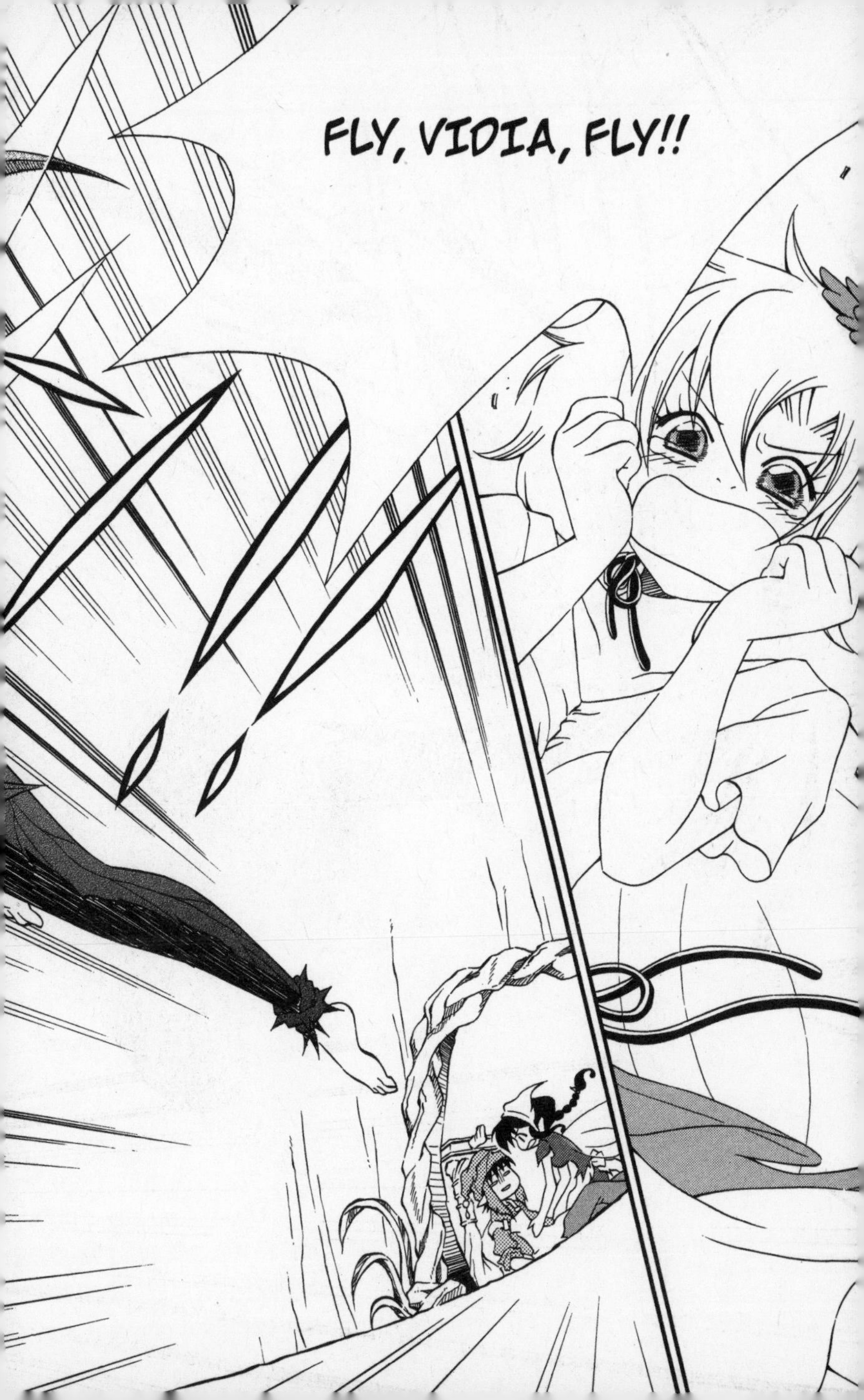
FLY, VIDIA, FLY!!

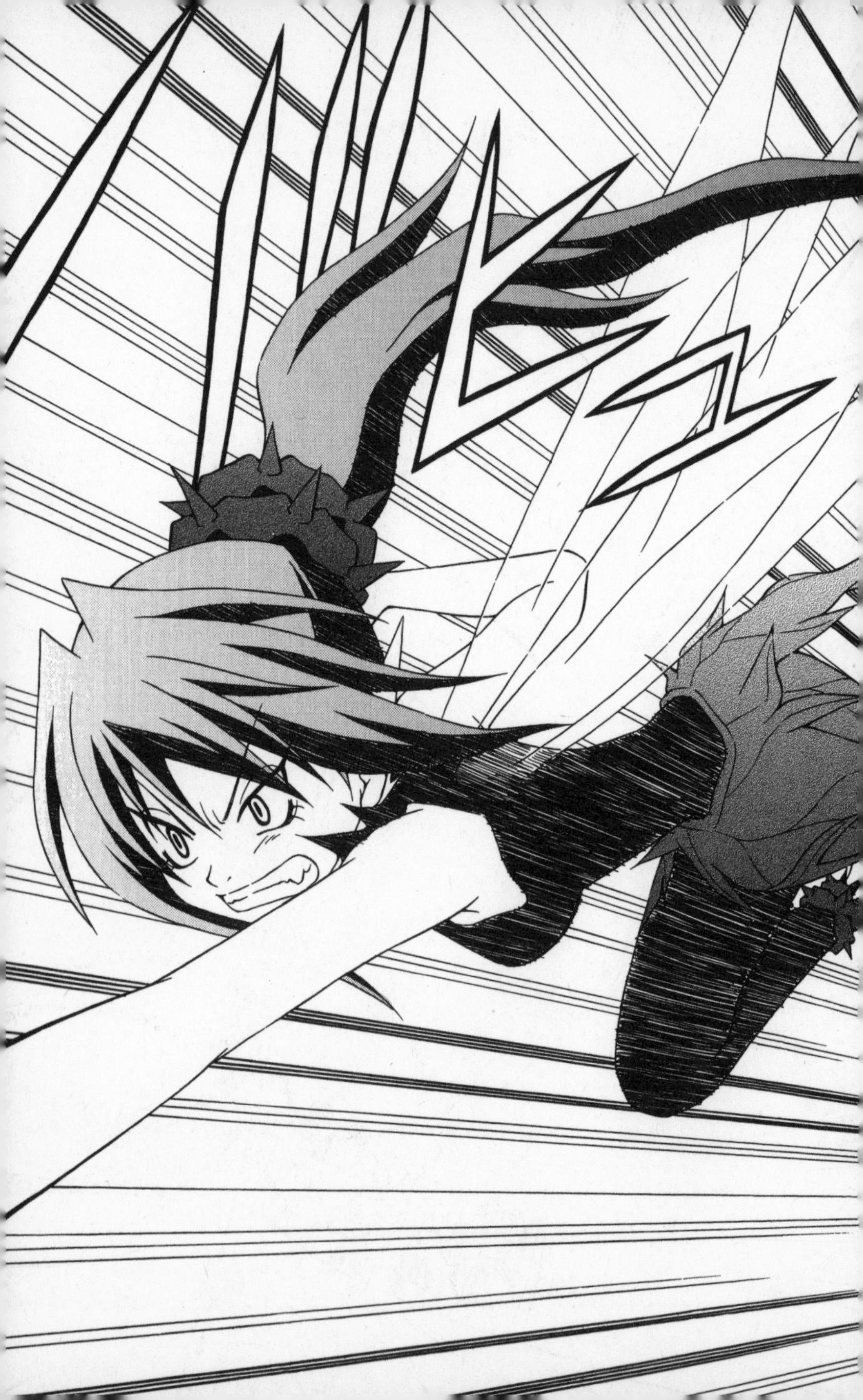

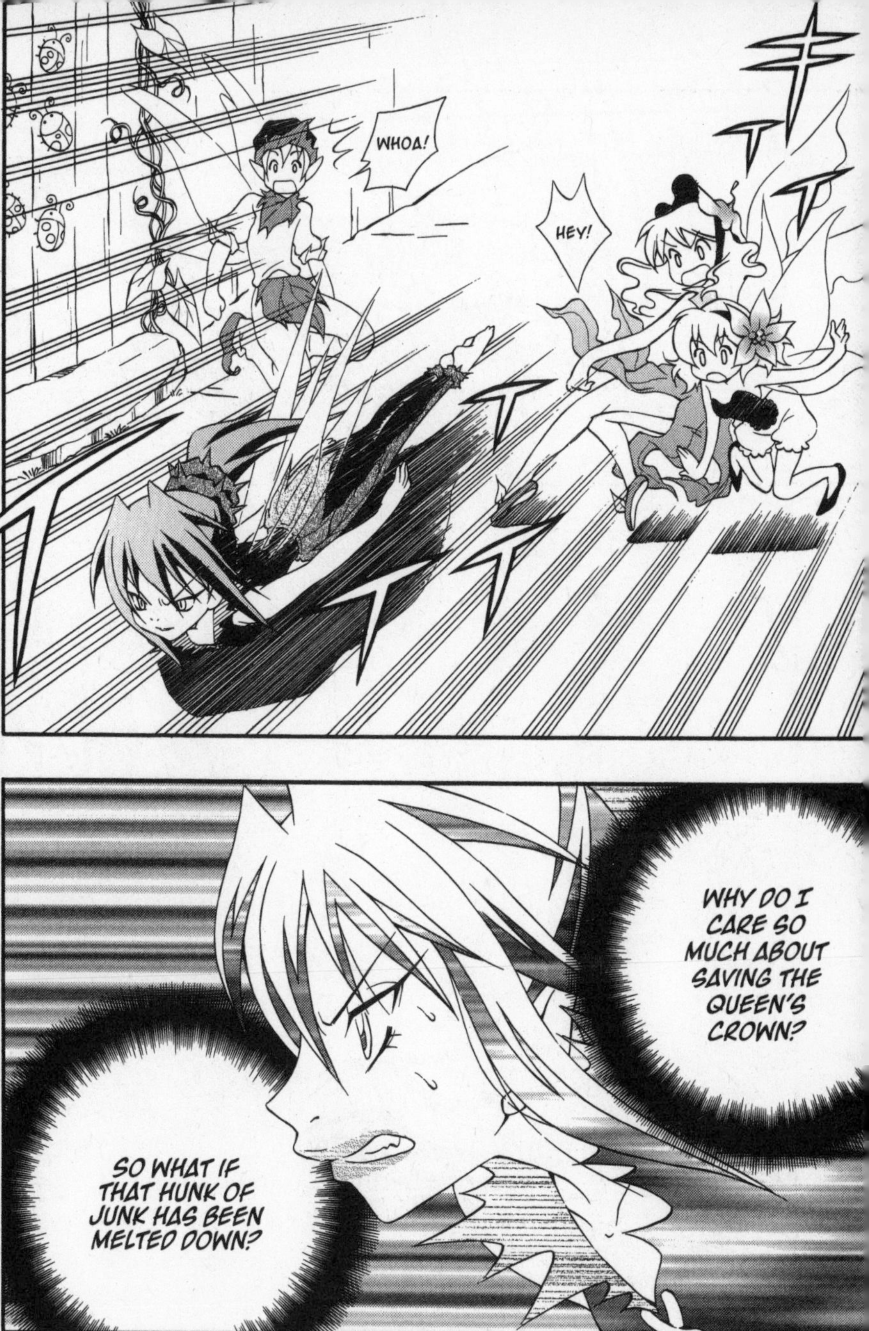
HEY!
WHOA!
WHY DO I CARE SO MUCH ABOUT SAVING THE QUEEN'S CROWN?
SO WHAT IF THAT HUNK OF JUNK HAS BEEN MELTED DOWN?

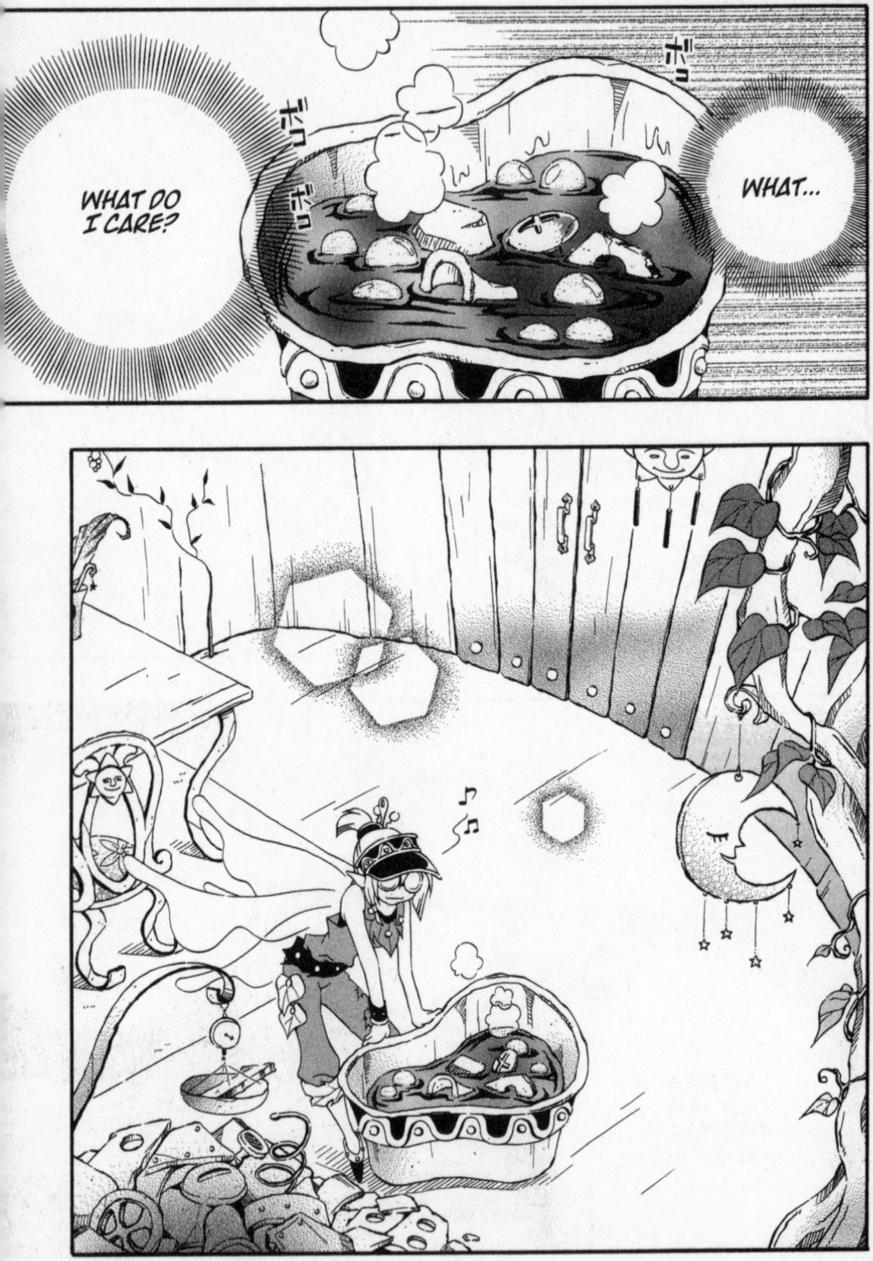
WHAT...
ボコ
ボコ
ボコ
WHAT DO I CARE?

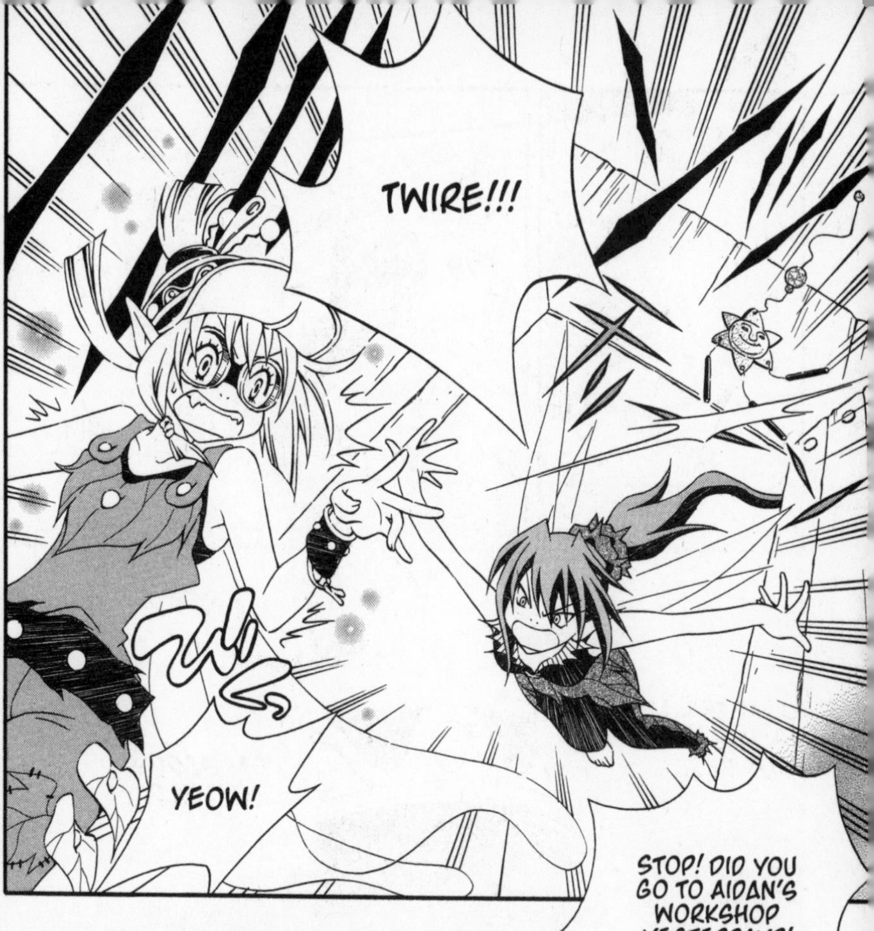
TWIRE!!!
YEOW!
STOP! DID YOU GO TO AIDAN'S WORKSHOP YESTERDAY?!
HUH?
UM... YES...
DID YOU BRING BACK THE CROWN AS WELL?!

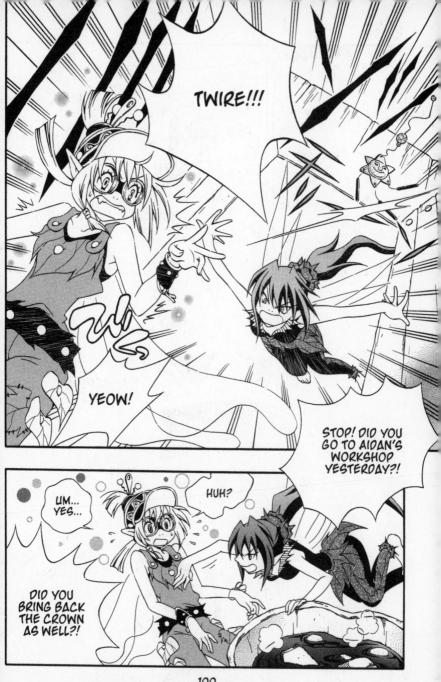

READ THIS WAY

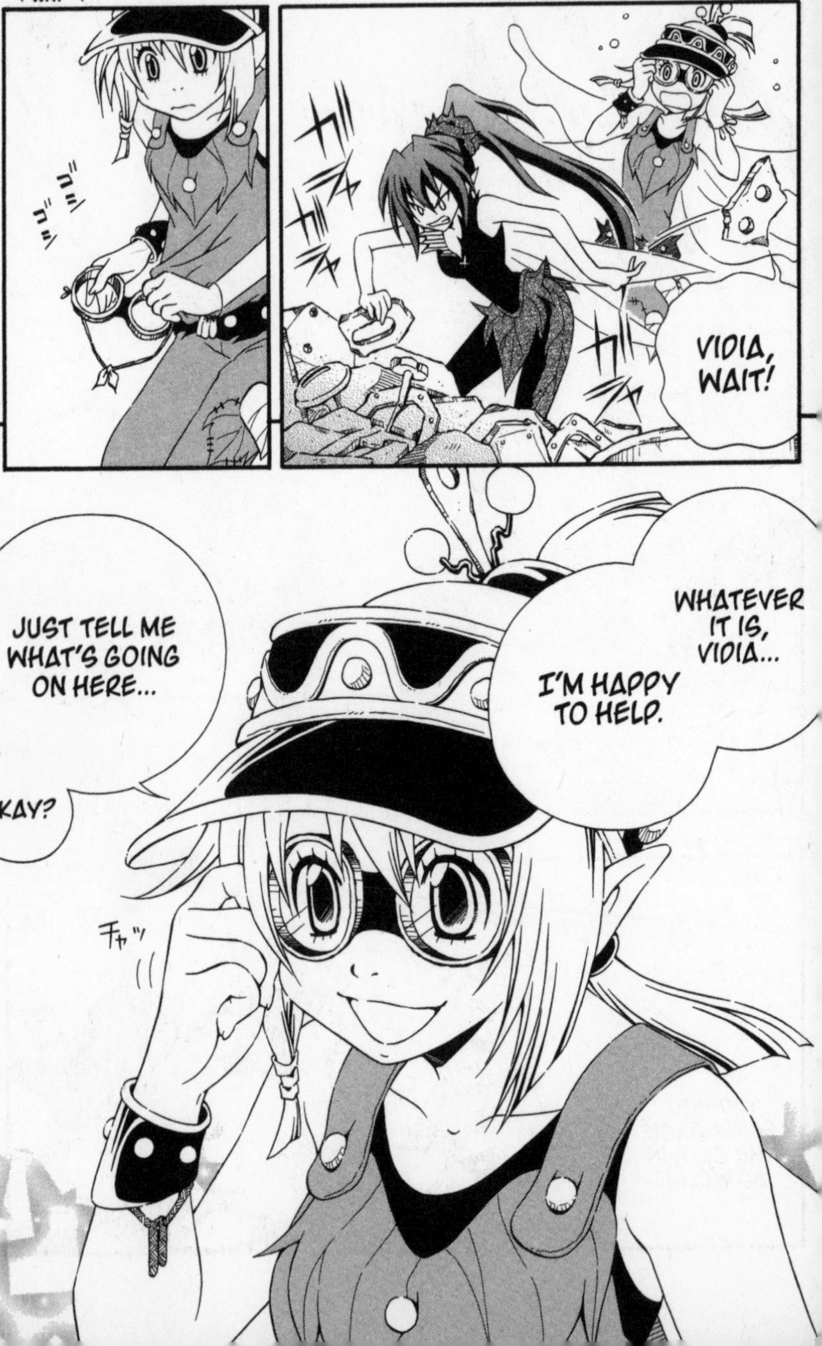
VIDIA, WAIT!
ゴソゴソ
WHATEVER IT IS, VIDIA...
I'M HAPPY TO HELP.
JUST TELL ME WHAT'S GOING ON HERE...
OKAY?
チャッ

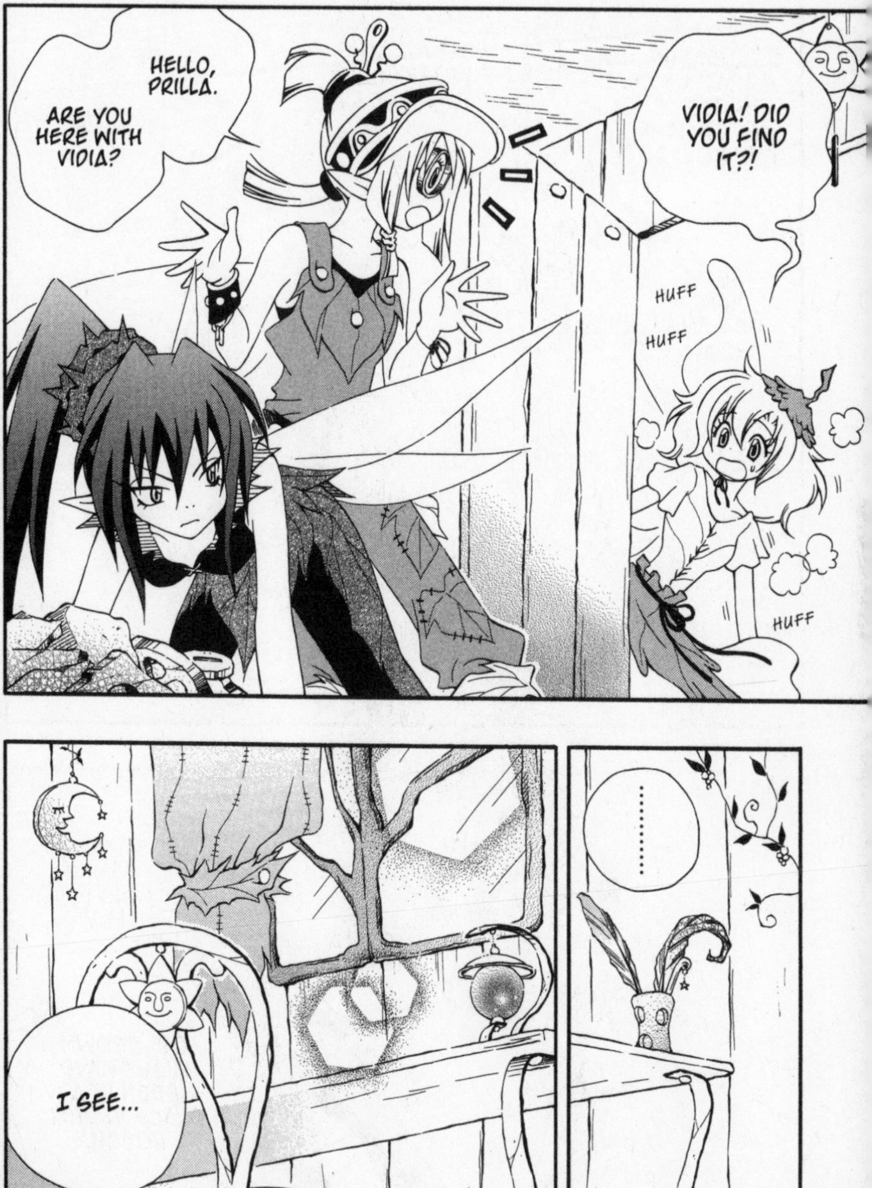
VIDIA! DID YOU FIND IT?!
HUFF
HUFF
HUFF
HELLO, PRILLA.
ARE YOU HERE WITH VIDIA?
......
I SEE...

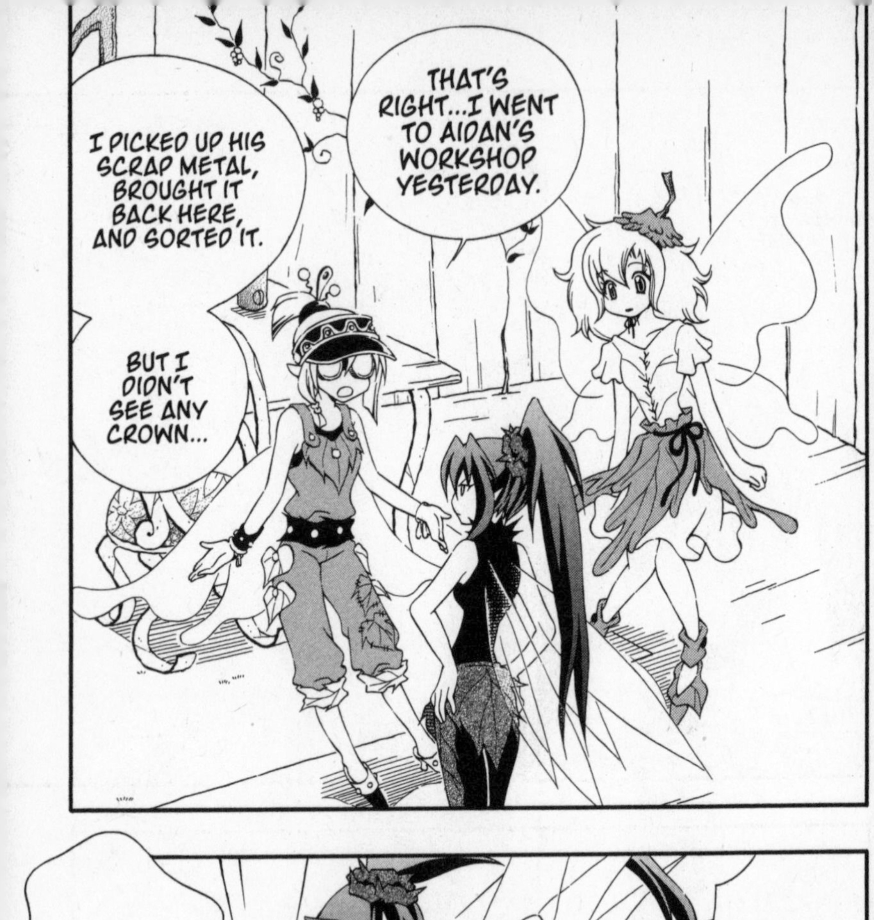
THAT'S RIGHT...I WENT TO AIDAN'S WORKSHOP YESTERDAY.
I PICKED UP HIS SCRAP METAL, BROUGHT IT BACK HERE, AND SORTED IT.
BUT I DIDN'T SEE ANY CROWN...
THINK CAREFULLY, LOVE...
THE CROWN MIGHT HAVE BEEN IN A BLACK VELVET POUCH.
VELVET?!

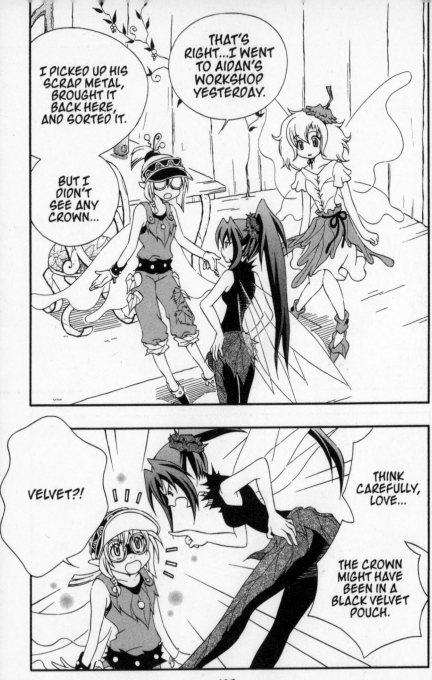

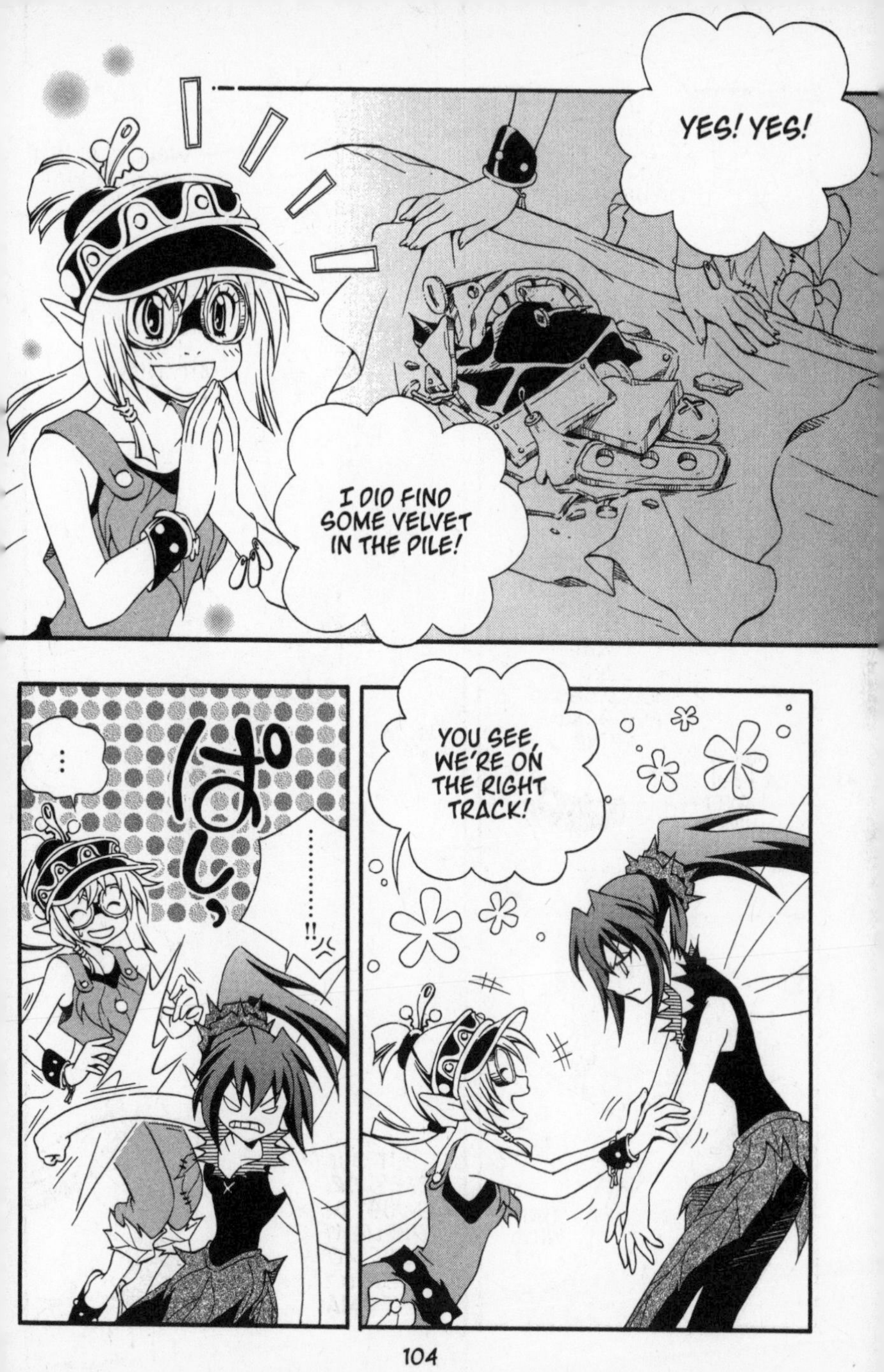
YES! YES!
I DID FIND SOME VELVET IN THE PILE!
YOU SEE, WE'RE ON THE RIGHT TRACK!
ぱし
...
.........!!

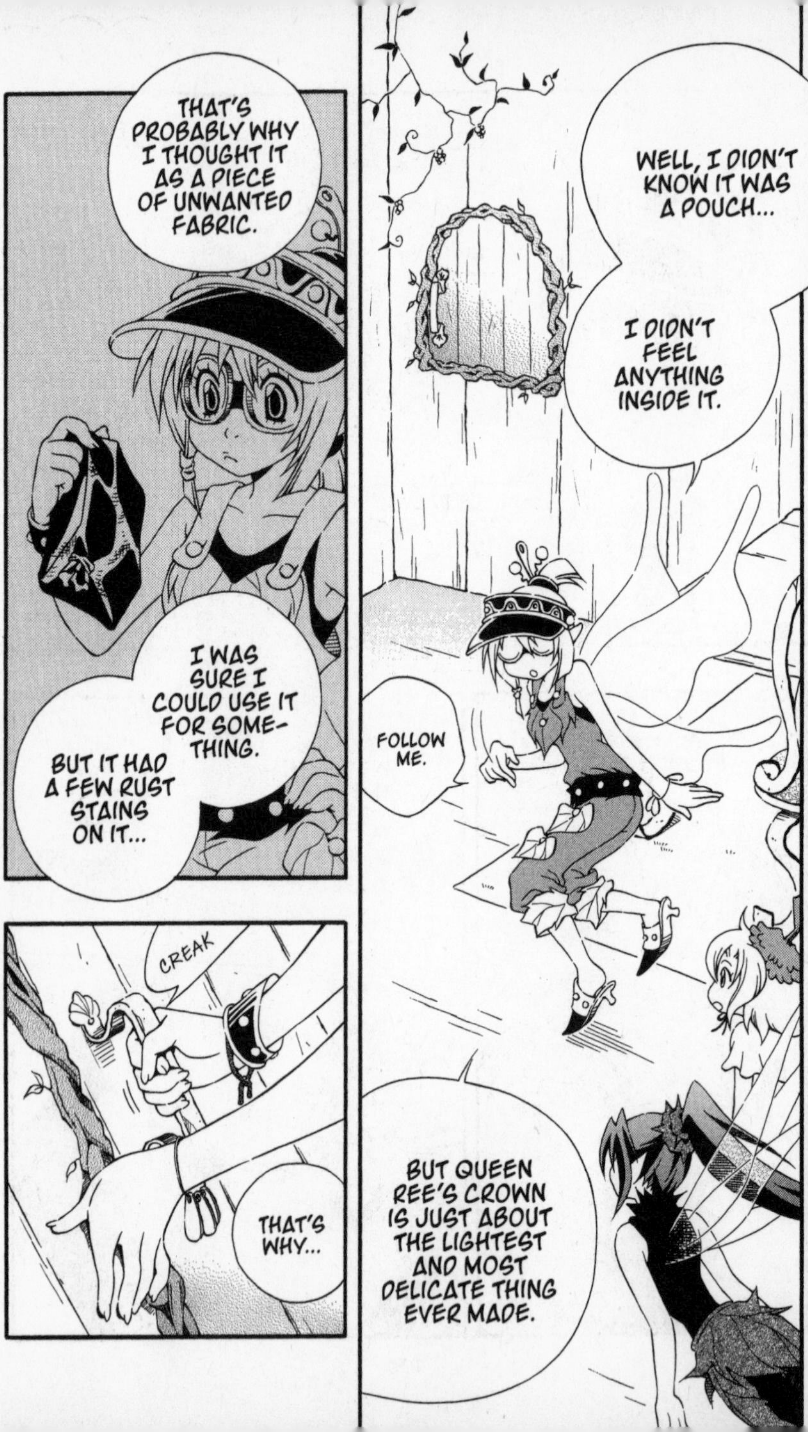
WELL, I DIDN'T KNOW IT WAS A POUCH...
I DIDN'T FEEL ANYTHING INSIDE IT.
FOLLOW ME.
BUT QUEEN REE'S CROWN IS JUST ABOUT THE LIGHTEST AND MOST DELICATE THING EVER MADE.
THAT'S PROBABLY WHY I THOUGHT IT AS A PIECE OF UNWANTED FABRIC.
I WAS SURE I COULD USE IT FOR SOME-THING.
BUT IT HAD A FEW RUST STAINS ON IT...
CREAK
THAT'S WHY...

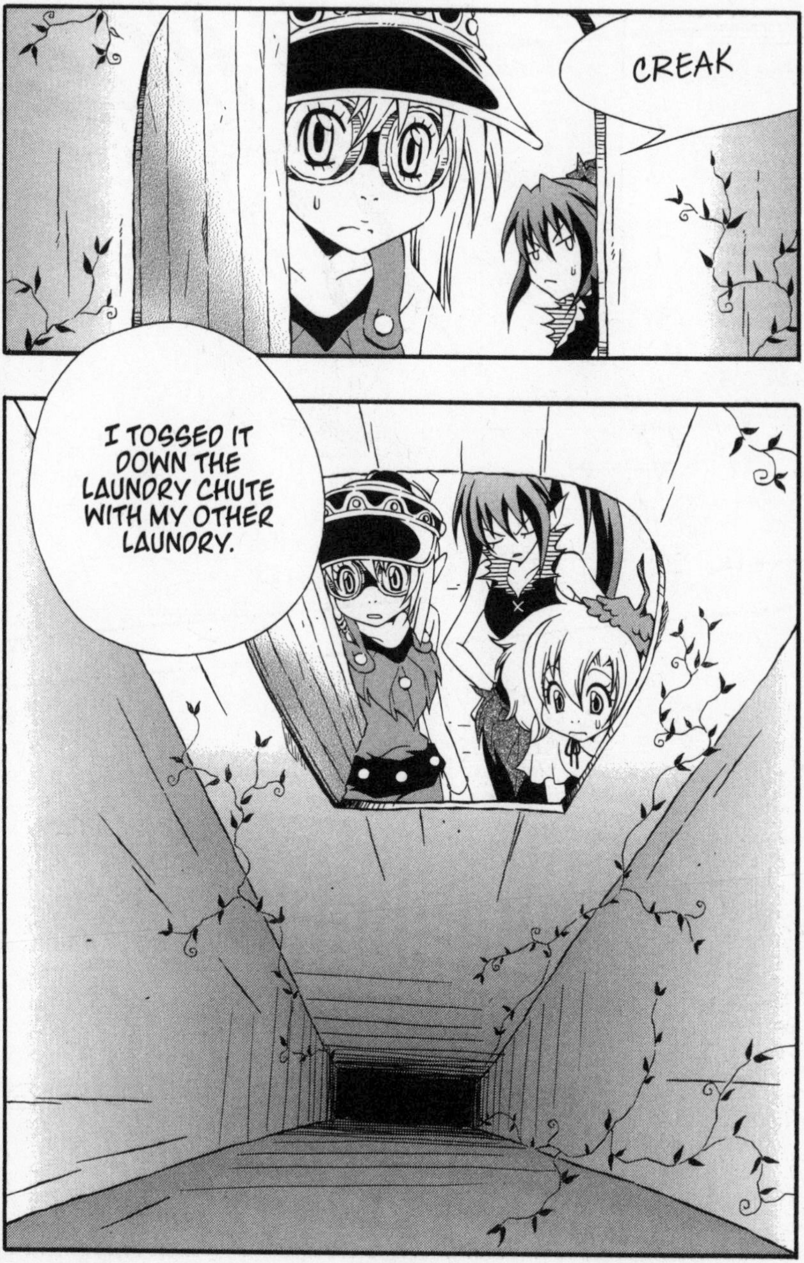
CREAK
I TOSSED IT DOWN THE LAUNDRY CHUTE WITH MY OTHER LAUNDRY.

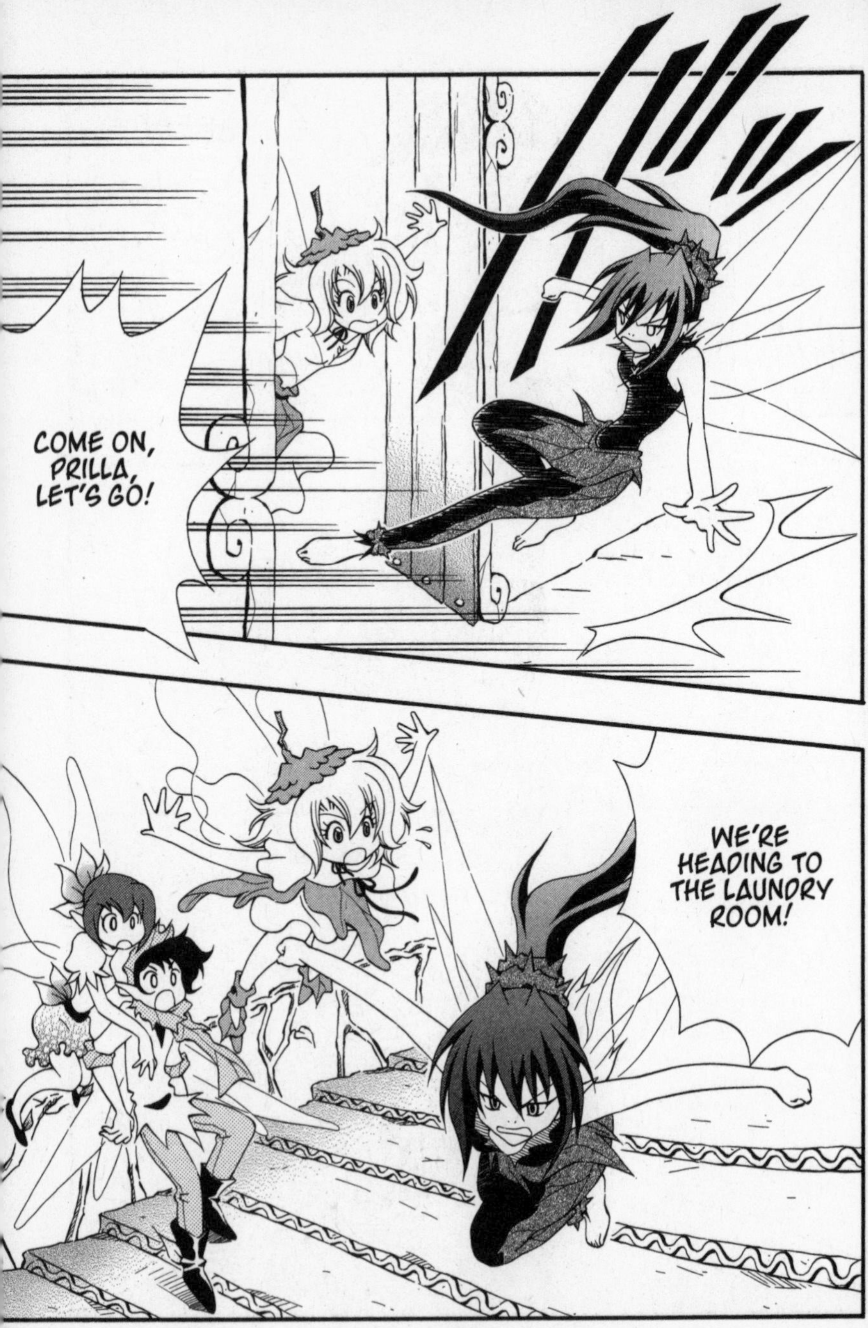
COME ON, PRILLA, LET'S GO!
WE'RE HEADING TO THE LAUNDRY ROOM!

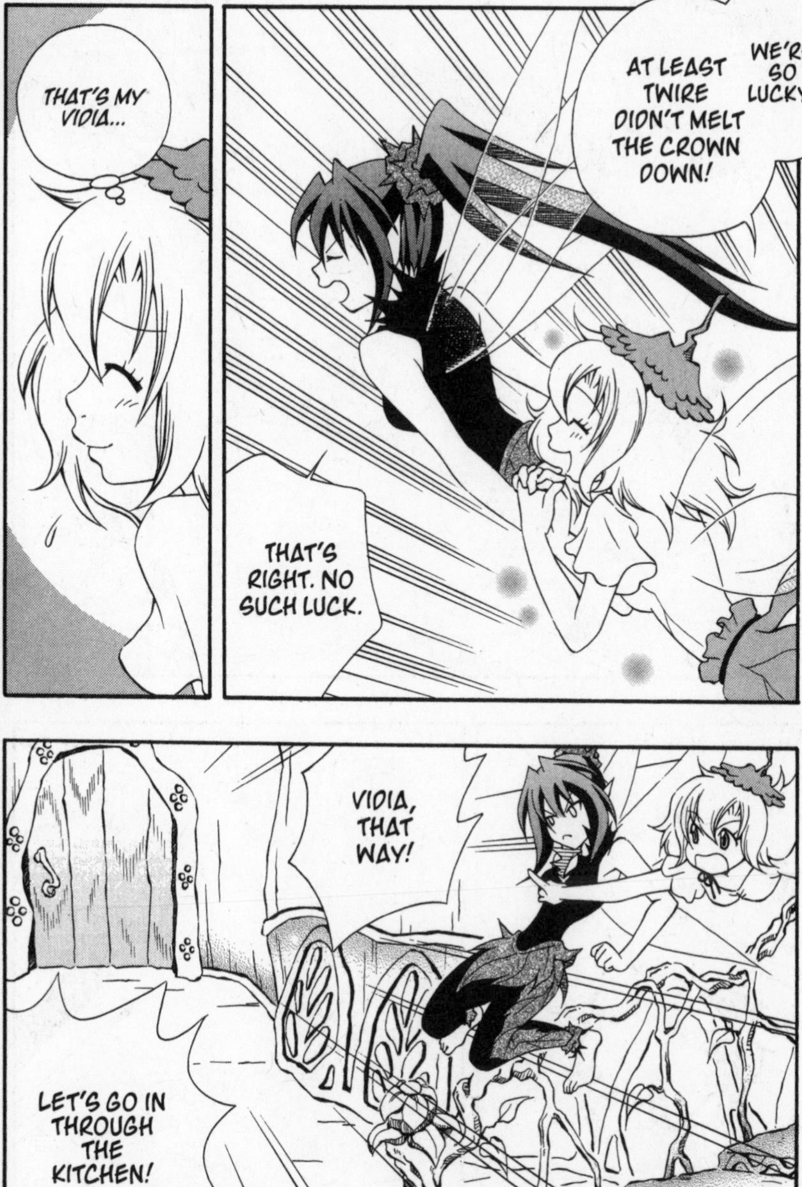
WE'RE SO LUCKY!
AT LEAST TWIRE DIDN'T MELT THE CROWN DOWN!
THAT'S RIGHT. NO SUCH LUCK.
THAT'S MY VIDIA...
VIDIA, THAT WAY!
LET'S GO IN THROUGH THE KITCHEN!

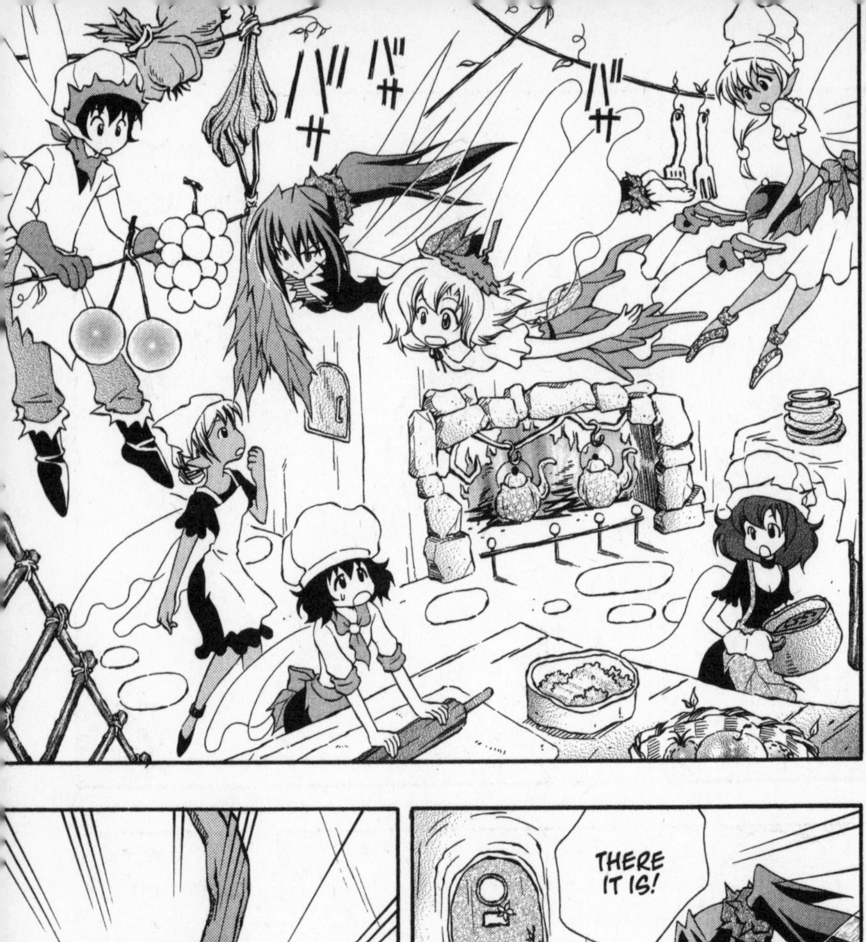
バサ
バサ
バサ

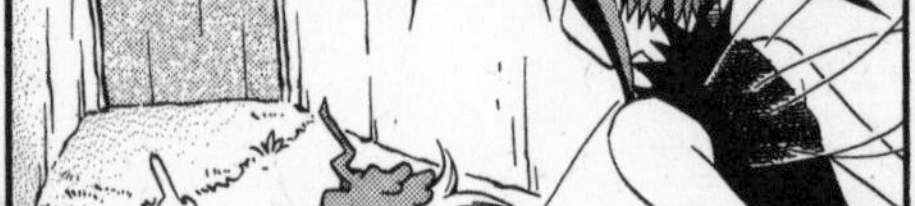
THERE IT IS!

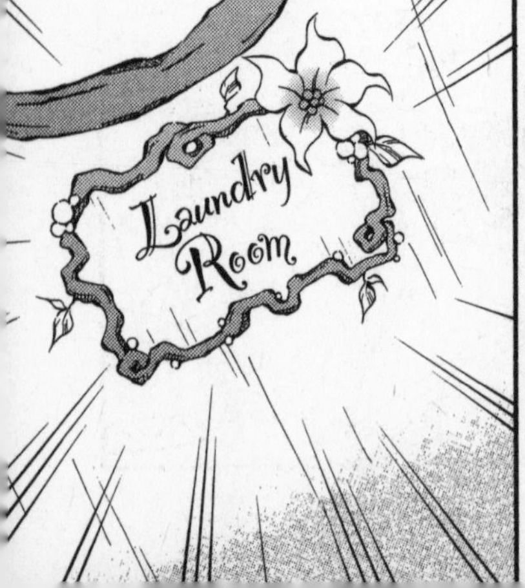
Laundry Room

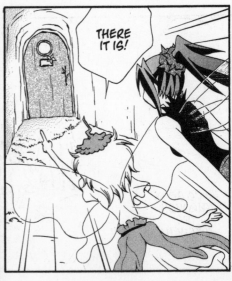

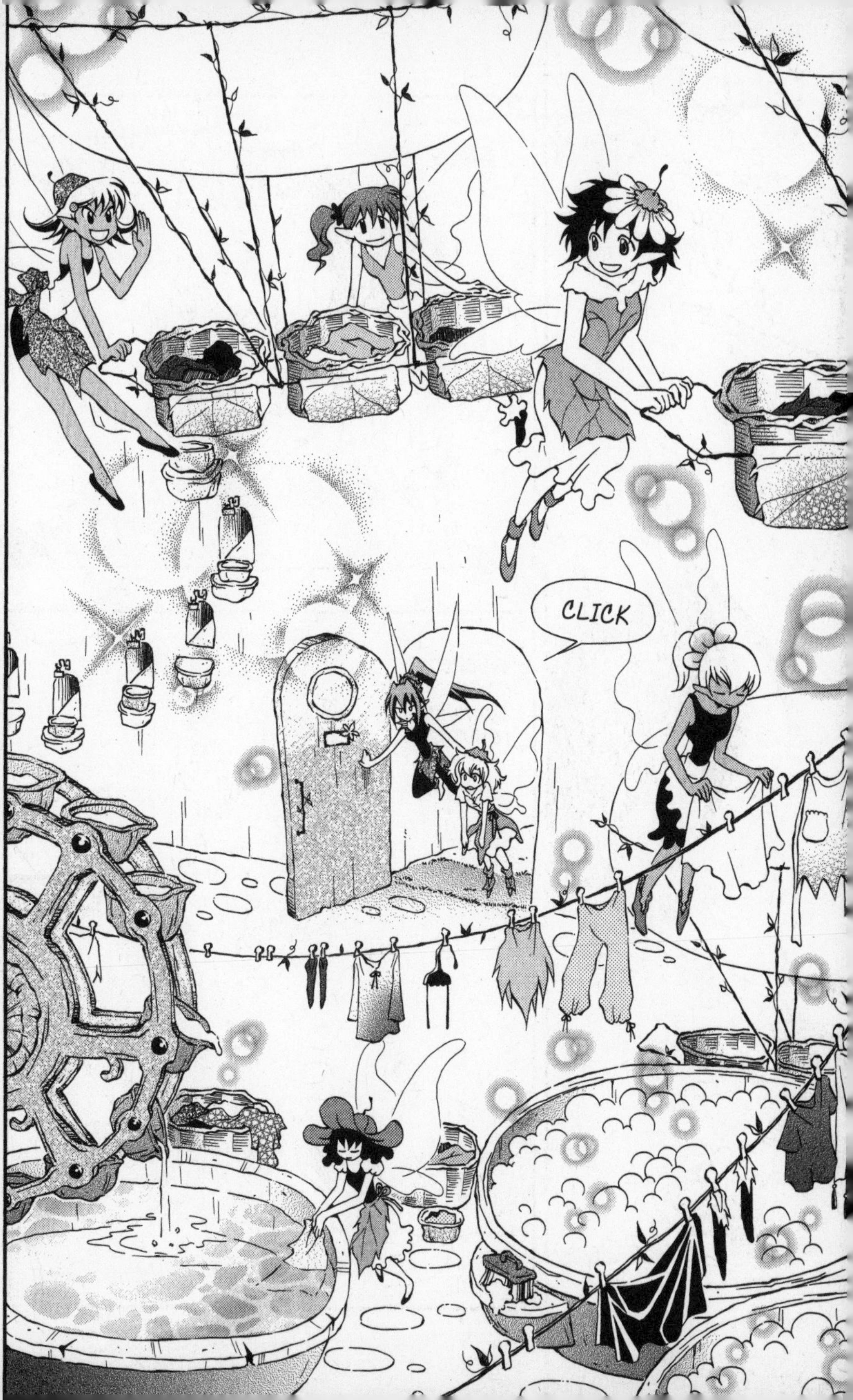
CLICK

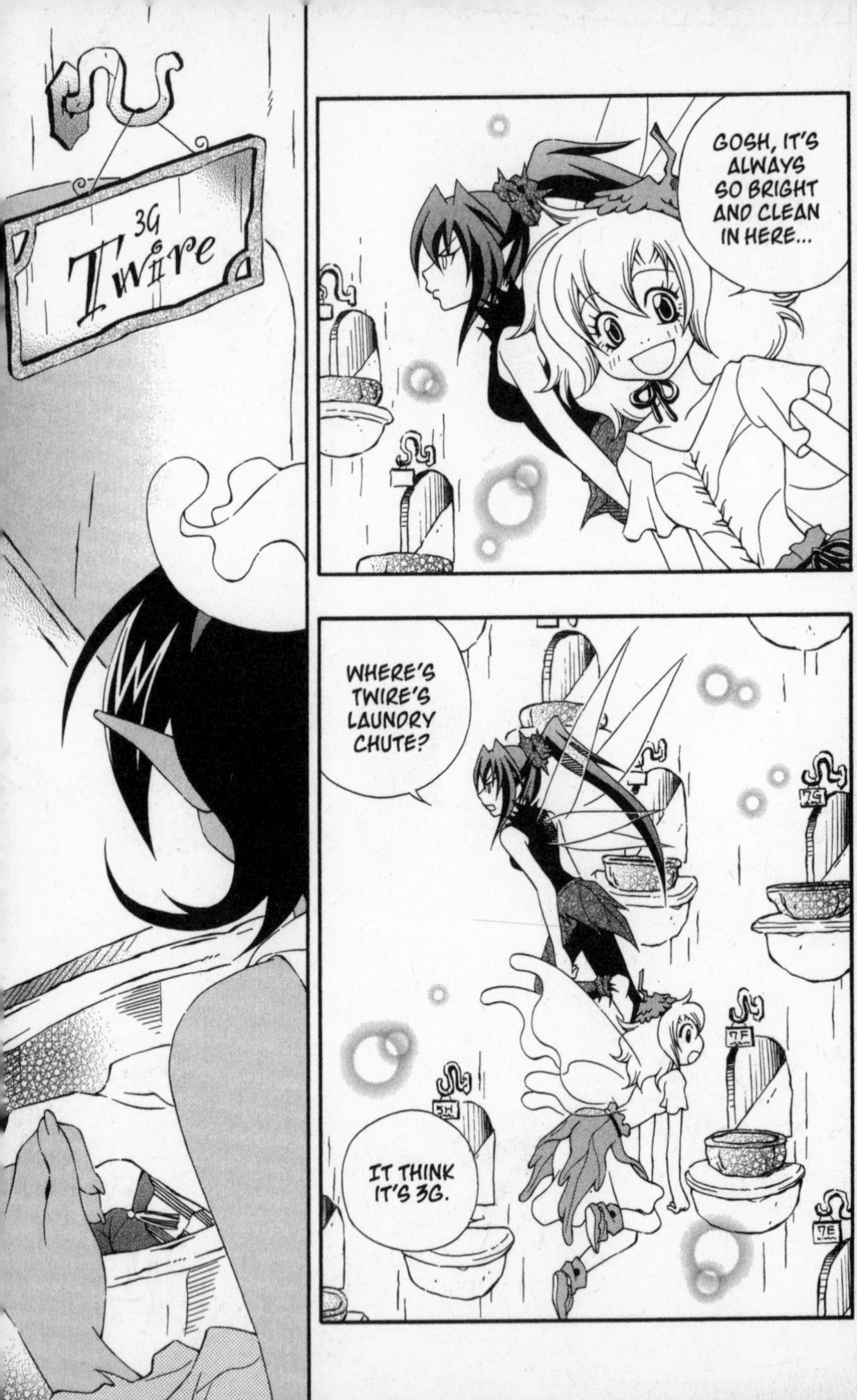
GOSH, IT'S ALWAYS SO BRIGHT AND CLEAN IN HERE...
WHERE'S TWIRE'S LAUNDRY CHUTE?
IT THINK IT'S 3G.
3G
Twire

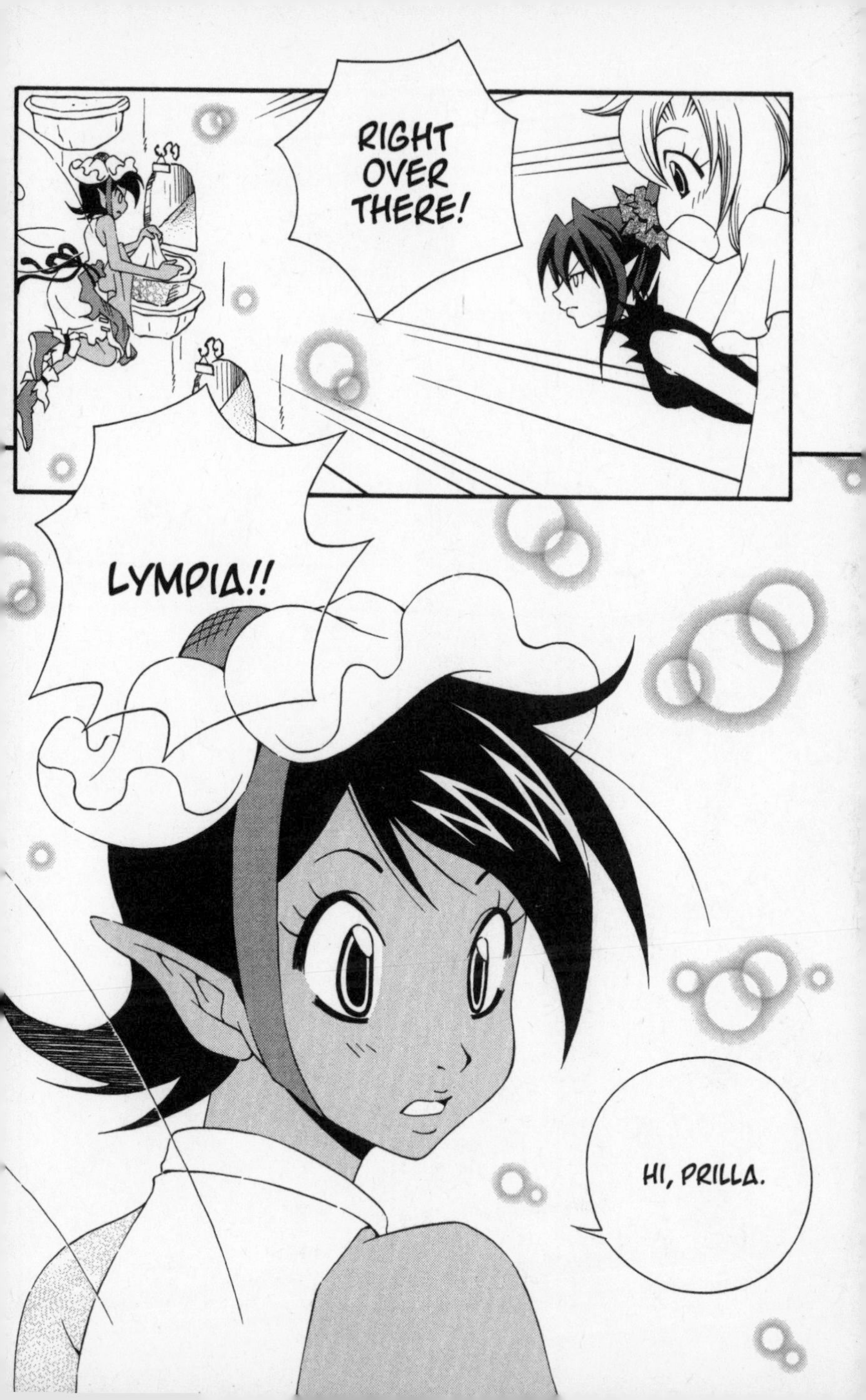
RIGHT OVER THERE!
LYMPIA!!
HI, PRILLA.

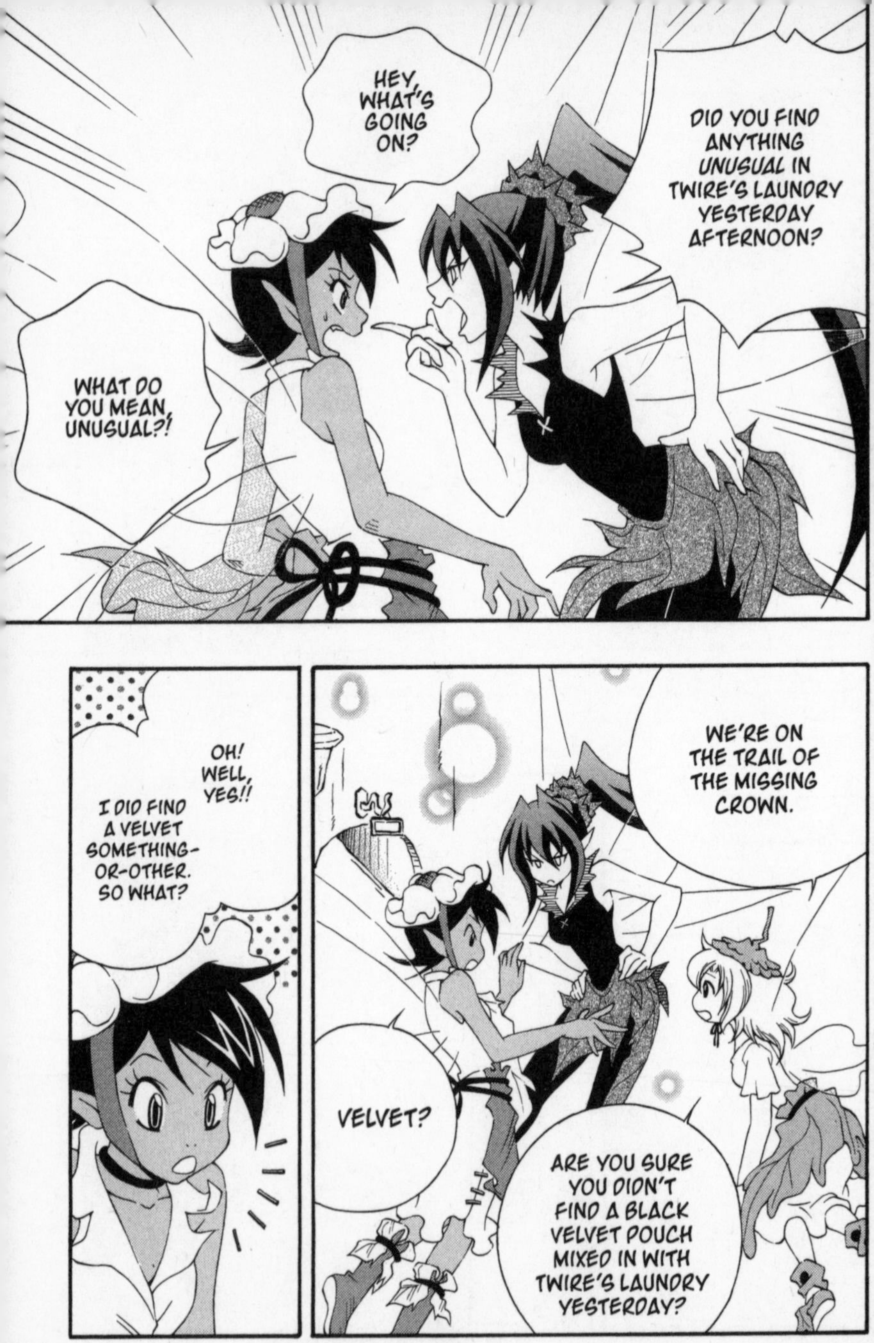
DID YOU FIND ANYTHING UNUSUAL IN TWIRE'S LAUNDRY YESTERDAY AFTERNOON?
HEY, WHAT'S GOING ON?
WHAT DO YOU MEAN, UNUSUAL?!
WE'RE ON THE TRAIL OF THE MISSING CROWN.
ARE YOU SURE YOU DIDN'T FIND A BLACK VELVET POUCH MIXED IN WITH TWIRE'S LAUNDRY YESTERDAY?
VELVET?
OH! WELL, YES!!
I DID FIND A VELVET SOMETHING-OR-OTHER. SO WHAT?

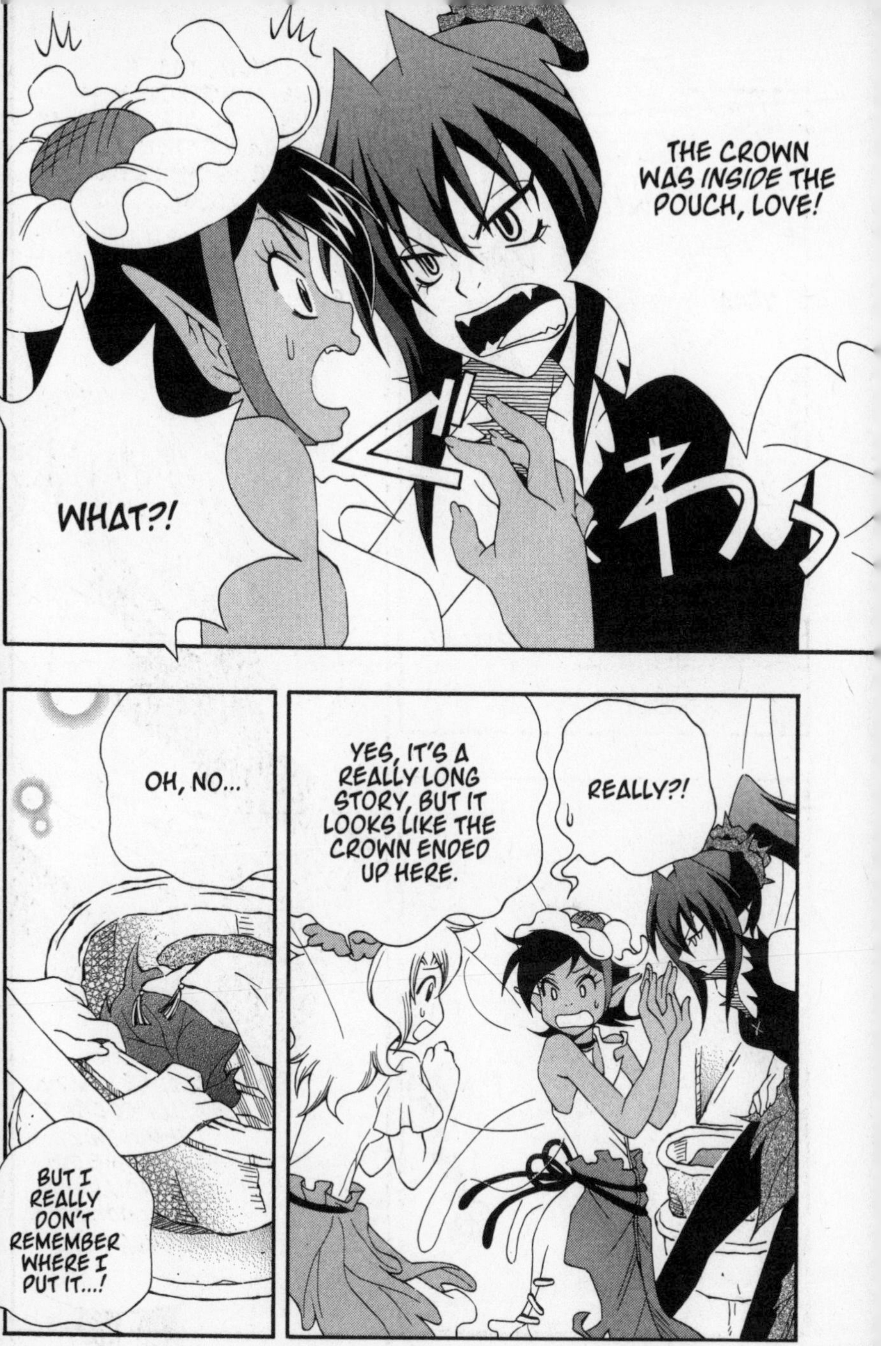
THE CROWN WAS INSIDE THE POUCH, LOVE!
WHAT?!
REALLY?!
YES, IT'S A REALLY LONG STORY, BUT IT LOOKS LIKE THE CROWN ENDED UP HERE.
OH, NO...
BUT I REALLY DON'T REMEMBER WHERE I PUT IT...!

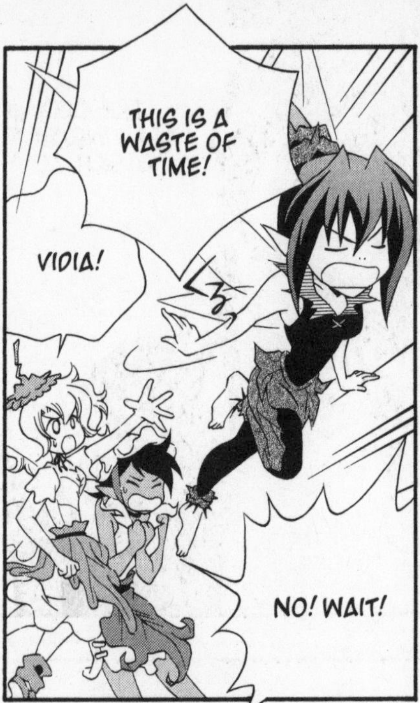
THIS IS A WASTE OF TIME!
VIDIA!
NO! WAIT!
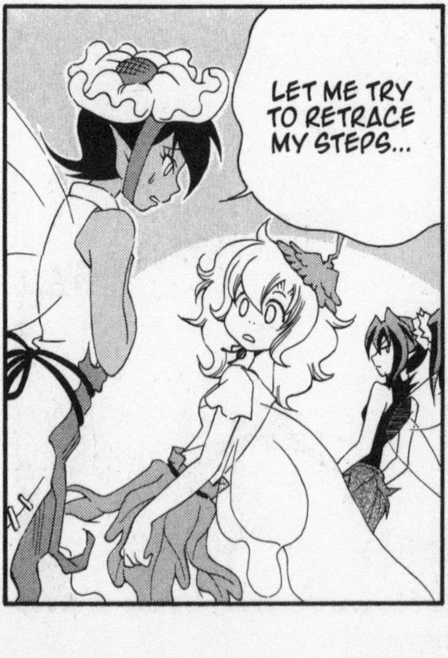
LET ME TRY TO RETRACE MY STEPS...
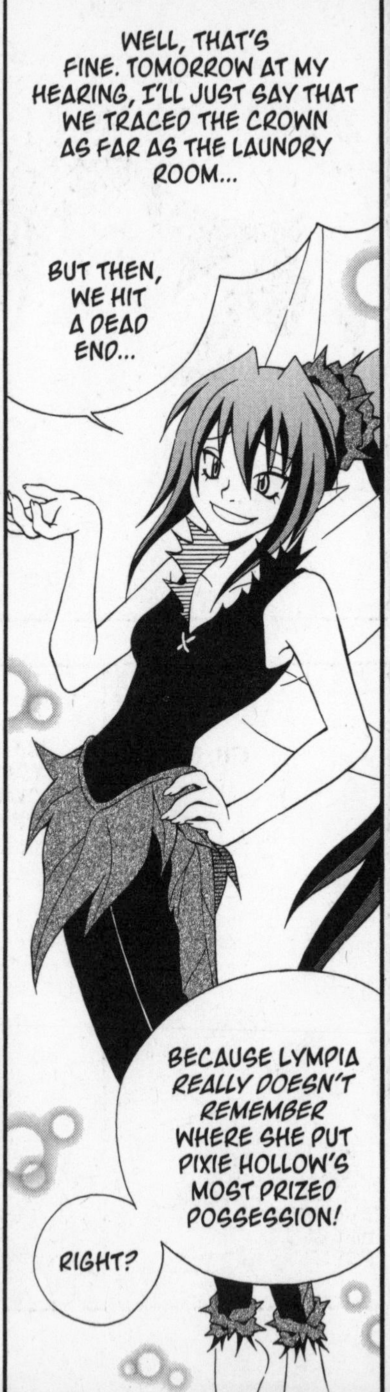
WELL, THAT'S FINE. TOMORROW AT MY HEARING, I'LL JUST SAY THAT WE TRACED THE CROWN AS FAR AS THE LAUNDRY ROOM...
BUT THEN, WE HIT A DEAD END...
BECAUSE LYMPIA REALLY DOESN'T REMEMBER WHERE SHE PUT PIXIE HOLLOW'S MOST PRIZED POSSESSION!
RIGHT?

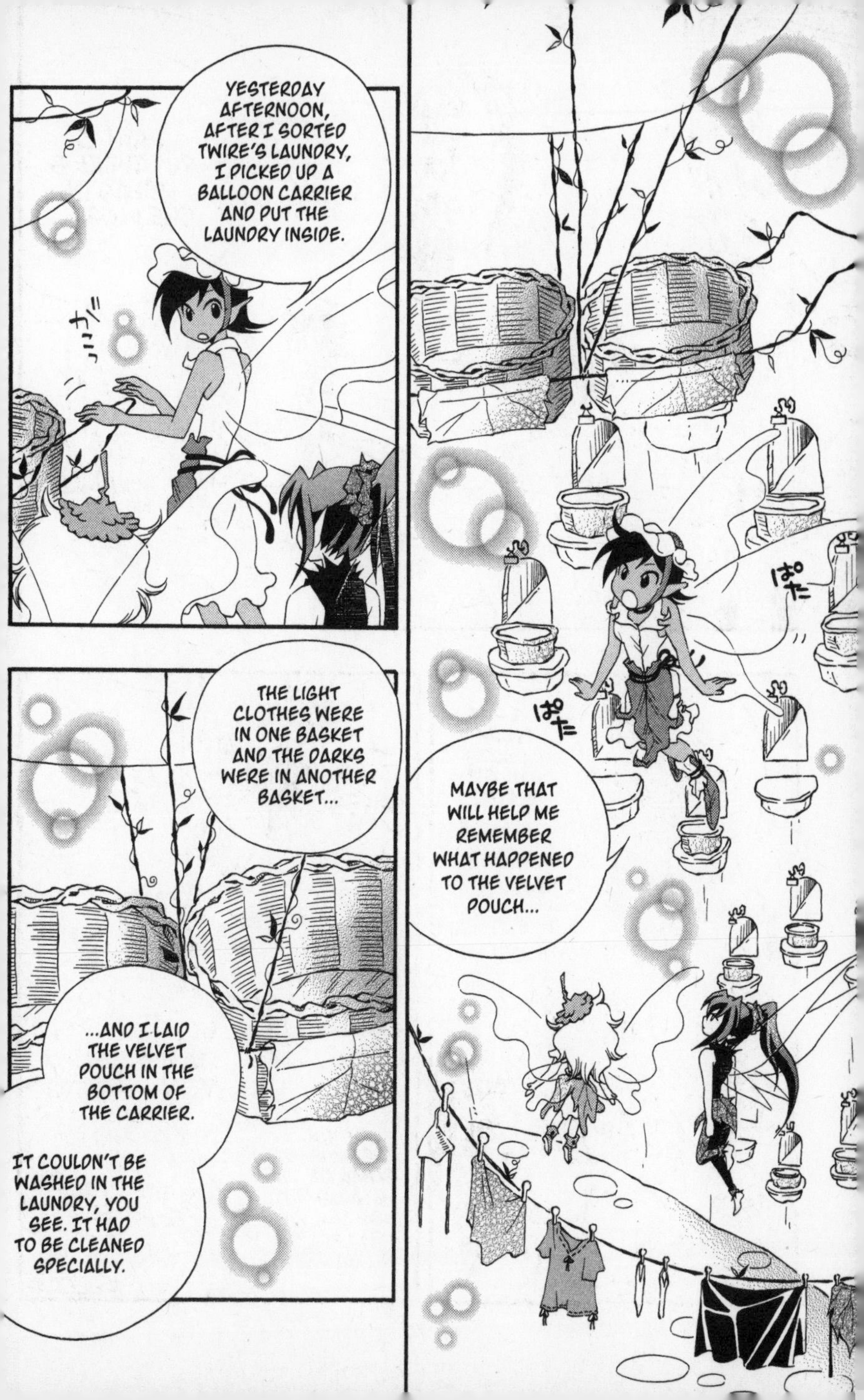

ぱた
ぱた
MAYBE THAT WILL HELP ME REMEMBER WHAT HAPPENED TO THE VELVET POUCH...
YESTERDAY AFTERNOON, AFTER I SORTED TWIRE'S LAUNDRY, I PICKED UP A BALLOON CARRIER AND PUT THE LAUNDRY INSIDE.
THE LIGHT CLOTHES WERE IN ONE BASKET AND THE DARKS WERE IN ANOTHER BASKET...
...AND I LAID THE VELVET POUCH IN THE BOTTOM OF THE CARRIER.
IT COULDN'T BE WASHED IN THE LAUNDRY, YOU SEE. IT HAD TO BE CLEANED SPECIALLY.

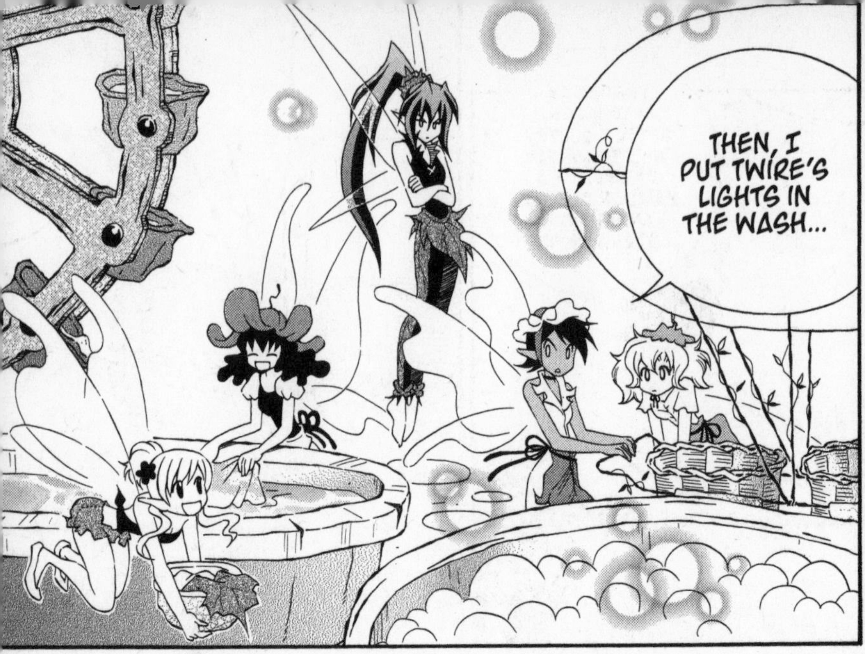
THEN, I PUT TWIRE'S LIGHTS IN THE WASH...

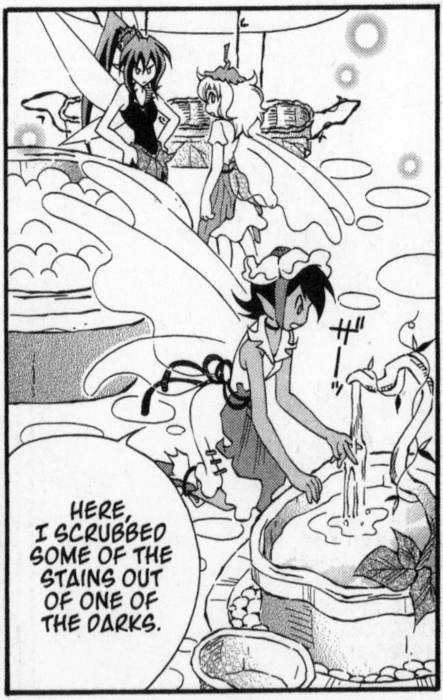
ザーッ
HERE, I SCRUBBED SOME OF THE STAINS OUT OF ONE OF THE DARKS.

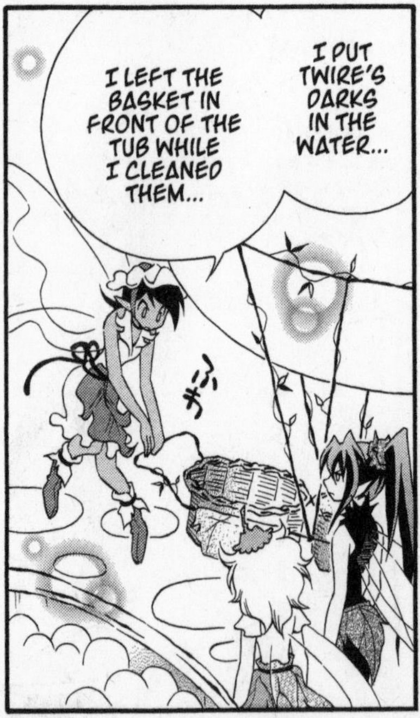
I PUT TWIRE'S DARKS IN THE WATER...
I LEFT THE BASKET IN FRONT OF THE TUB WHILE I CLEANED THEM...

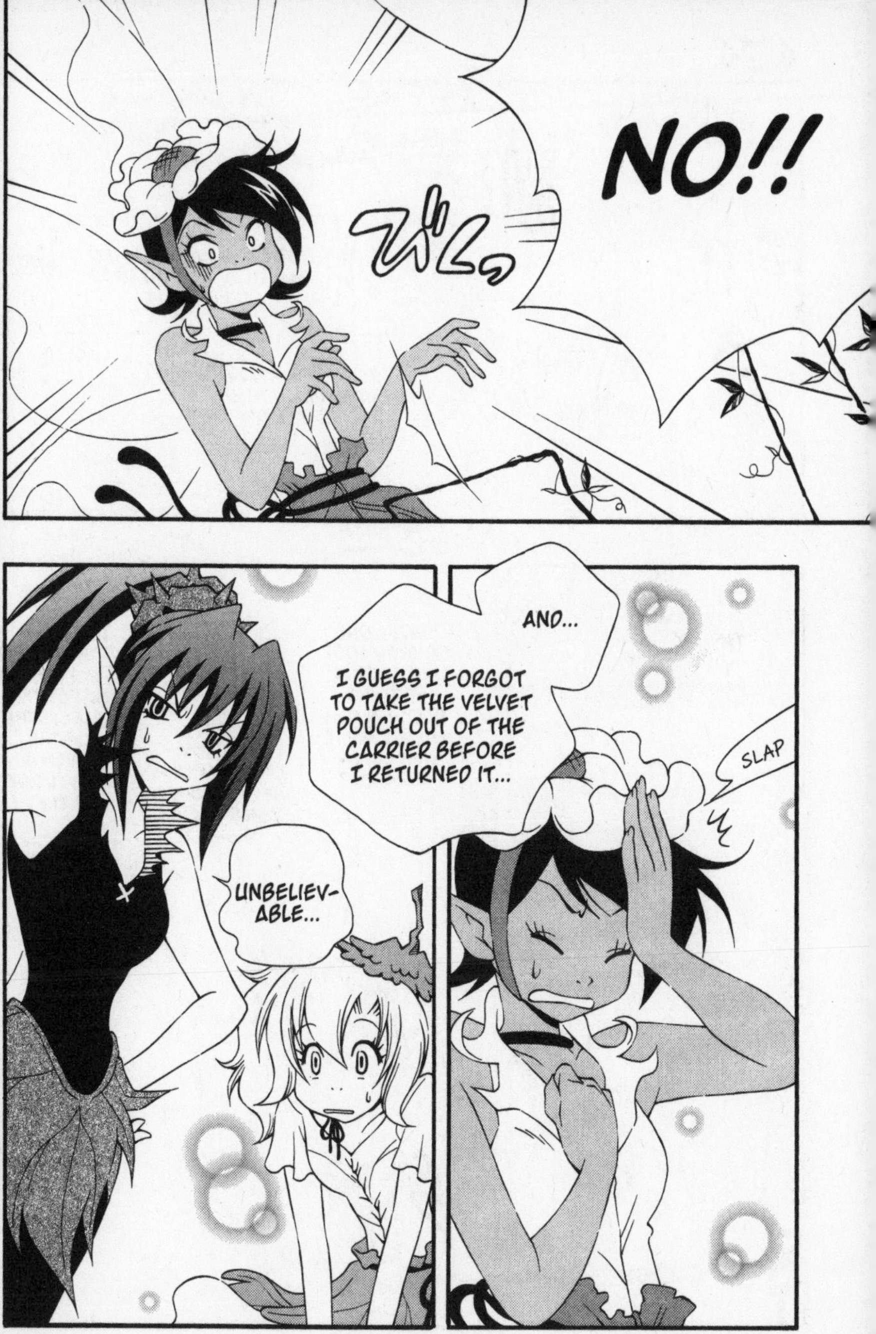
NO!!
びくっ
AND...
I GUESS I FORGOT TO TAKE THE VELVET POUCH OUT OF THE CARRIER BEFORE I RETURNED IT...
SLAP
UNBELIEV-ABLE...

READ THIS WAY

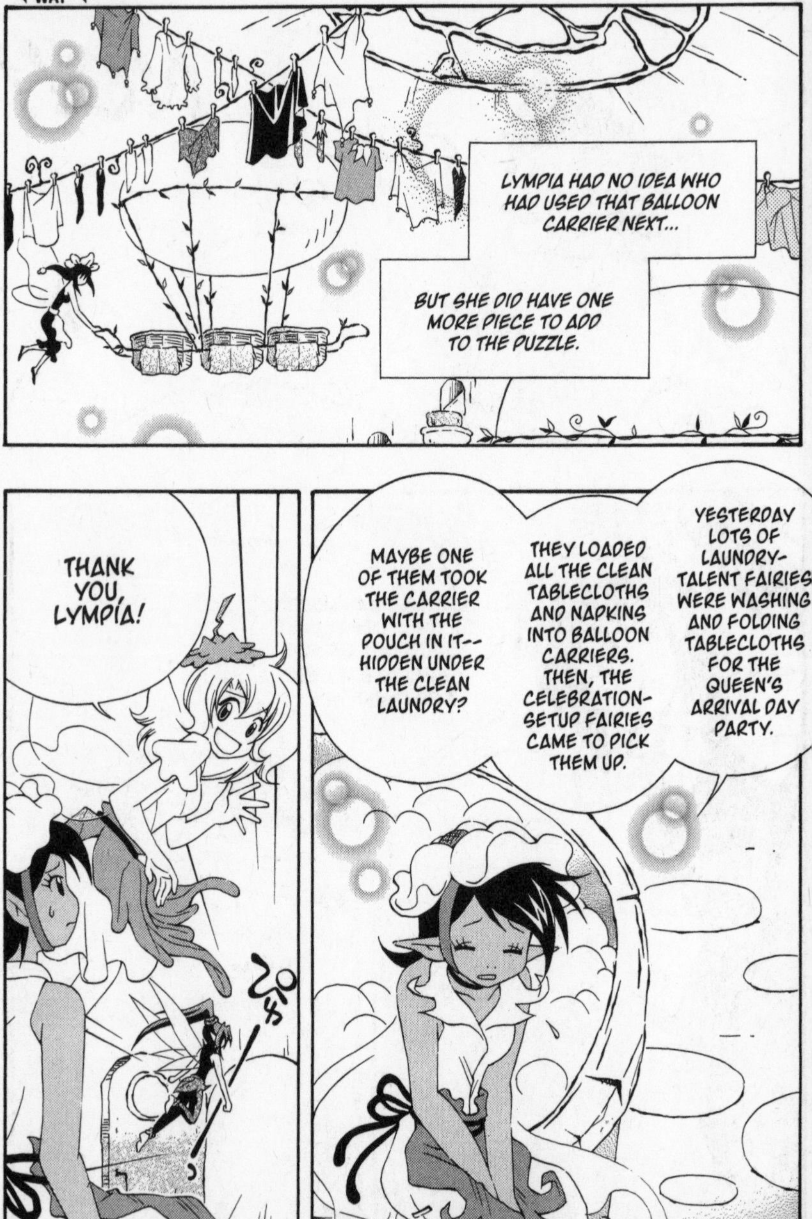
LYMPIA HAD NO IDEA WHO HAD USED THAT BALLOON CARRIER NEXT...
BUT SHE DID HAVE ONE MORE PIECE TO ADD TO THE PUZZLE.
YESTERDAY LOTS OF LAUNDRY-TALENT FAIRIES WERE WASHING AND FOLDING TABLECLOTHS FOR THE QUEEN'S ARRIVAL DAY PARTY.
THEY LOADED ALL THE CLEAN TABLECLOTHS AND NAPKINS INTO BALLOON CARRIERS. THEN, THE CELEBRATION-SETUP FAIRIES CAME TO PICK THEM UP.
MAYBE ONE OF THEM TOOK THE CARRIER WITH THE POUCH IN IT-- HIDDEN UNDER THE CLEAN LAUNDRY?
THANK YOU, LYMPIA!

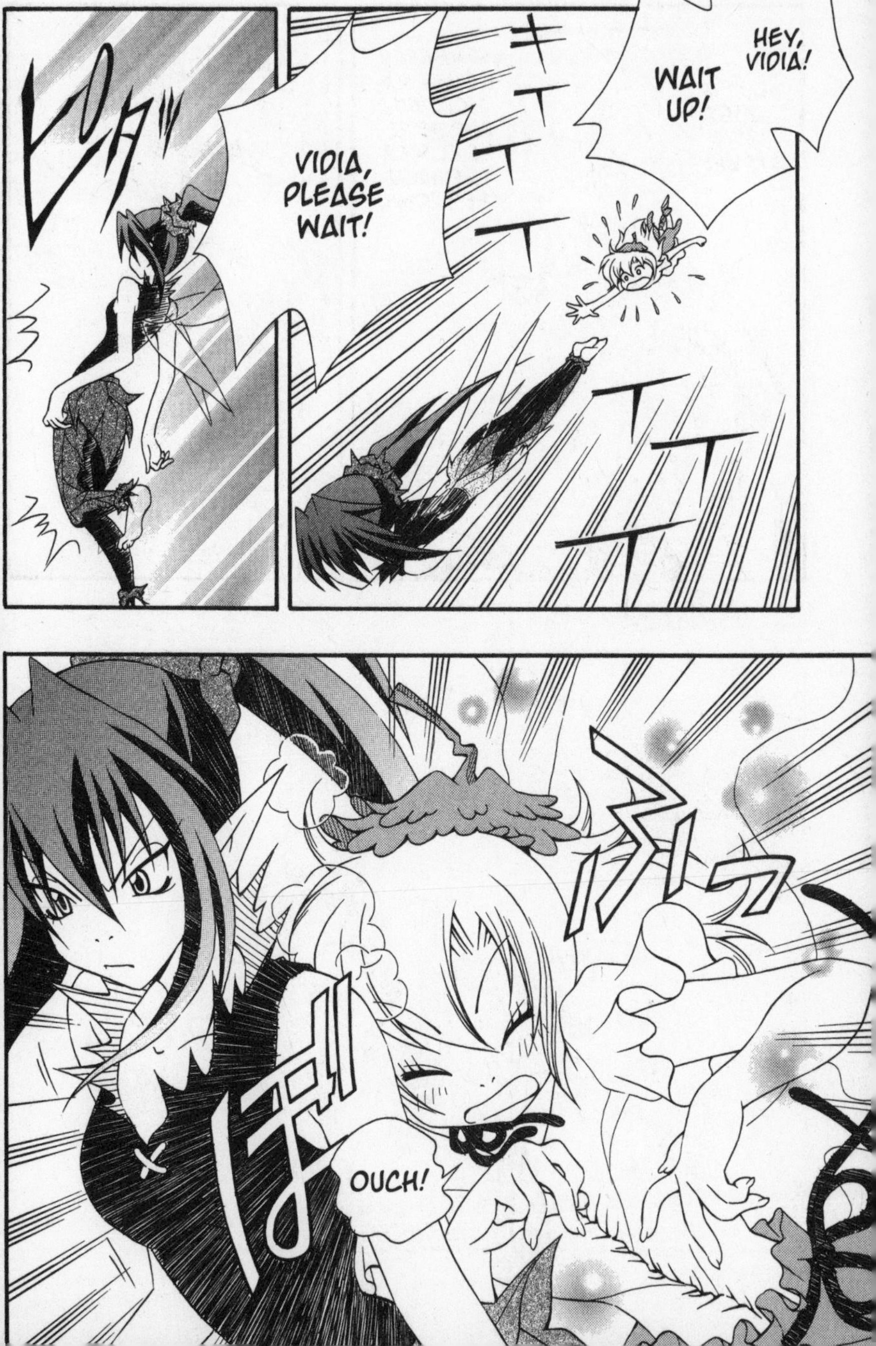
HEY, VIDIA!
WAIT UP!
VIDIA, PLEASE WAIT!
OUCH!

READ THIS WAY

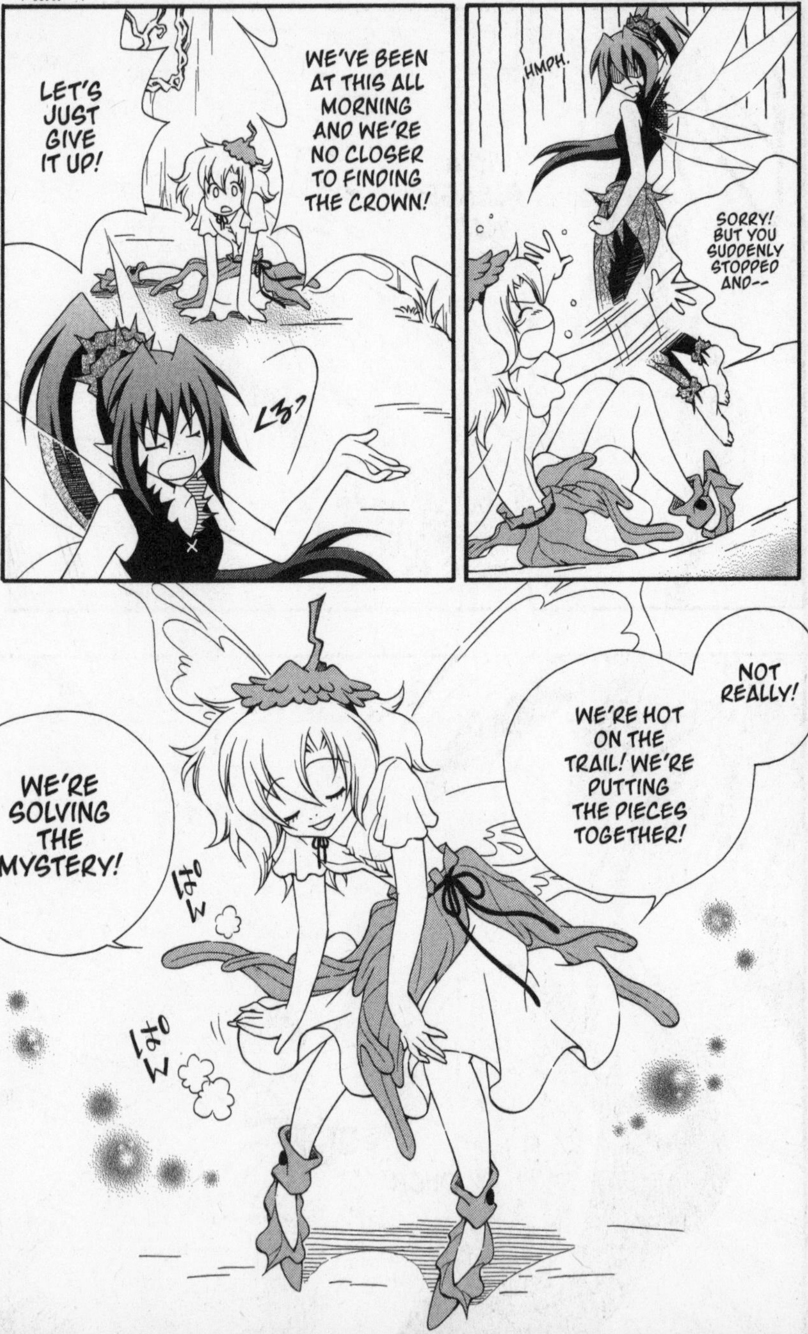
HMPH.
SORRY! BUT YOU SUDDENLY STOPPED AND--
WE'VE BEEN AT THIS ALL MORNING AND WE'RE NO CLOSER TO FINDING THE CROWN!
LET'S JUST GIVE IT UP!
くるっ
NOT REALLY!
WE'RE HOT ON THE TRAIL! WE'RE PUTTING THE PIECES TOGETHER!
WE'RE SOLVING THE MYSTERY!

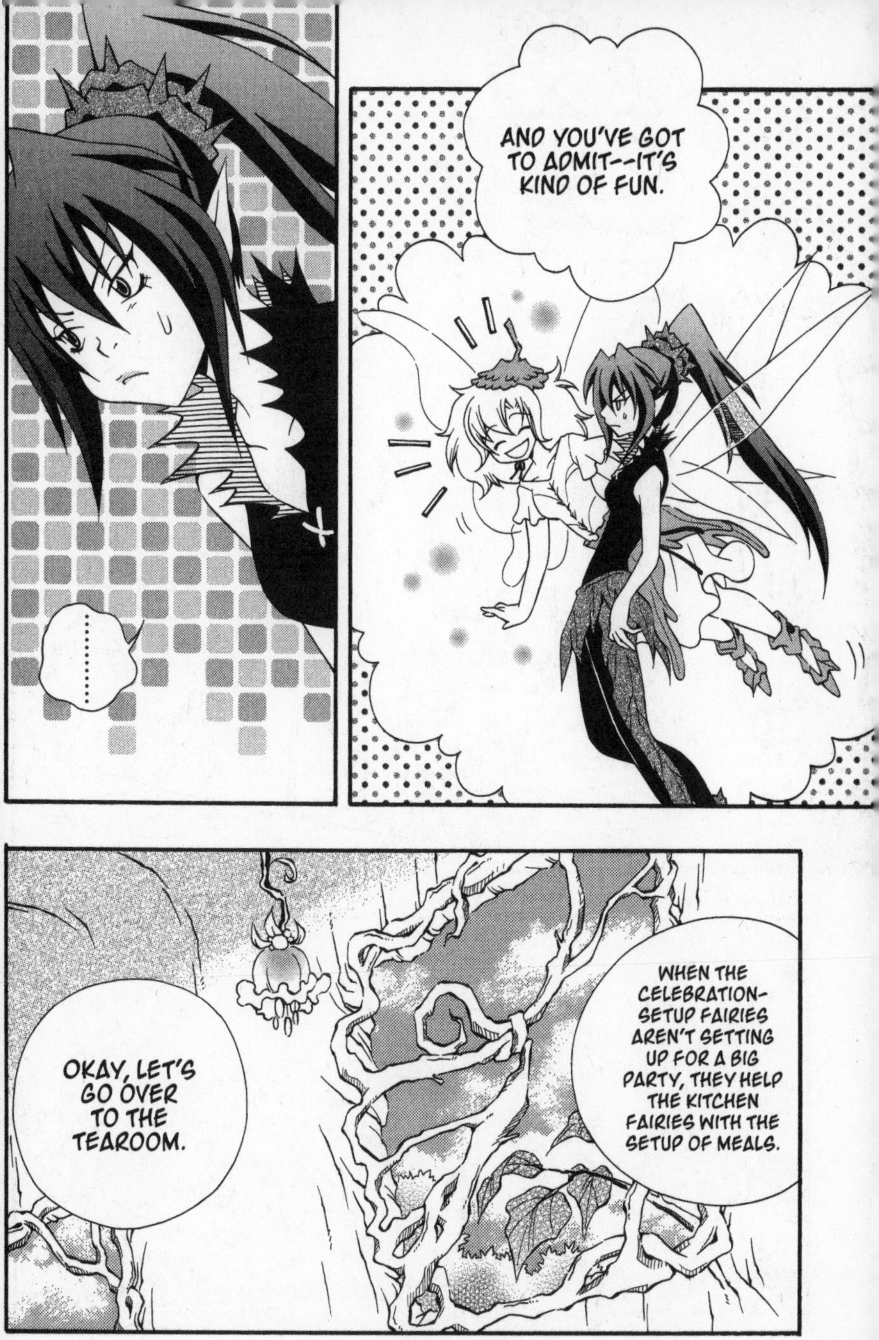
AND YOU'VE GOT TO ADMIT--IT'S KIND OF FUN.
......
WHEN THE CELEBRATION-SETUP FAIRIES AREN'T SETTING UP FOR A BIG PARTY, THEY HELP THE KITCHEN FAIRIES WITH THE SETUP OF MEALS.
OKAY, LET'S GO OVER TO THE TEAROOM.

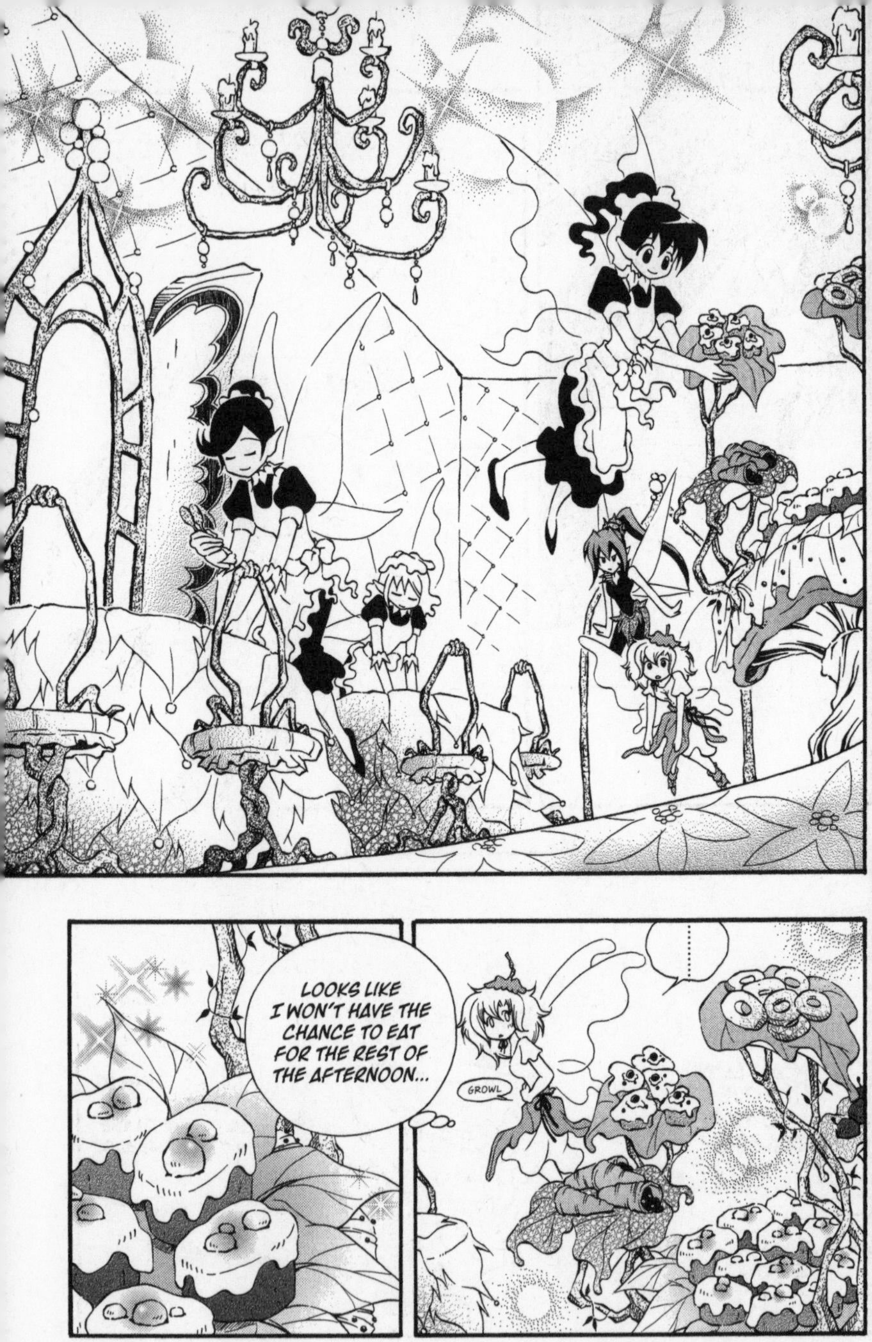
GROWL
LOOKS LIKE I WON'T HAVE THE CHANCE TO EAT FOR THE REST OF THE AFTERNOON...

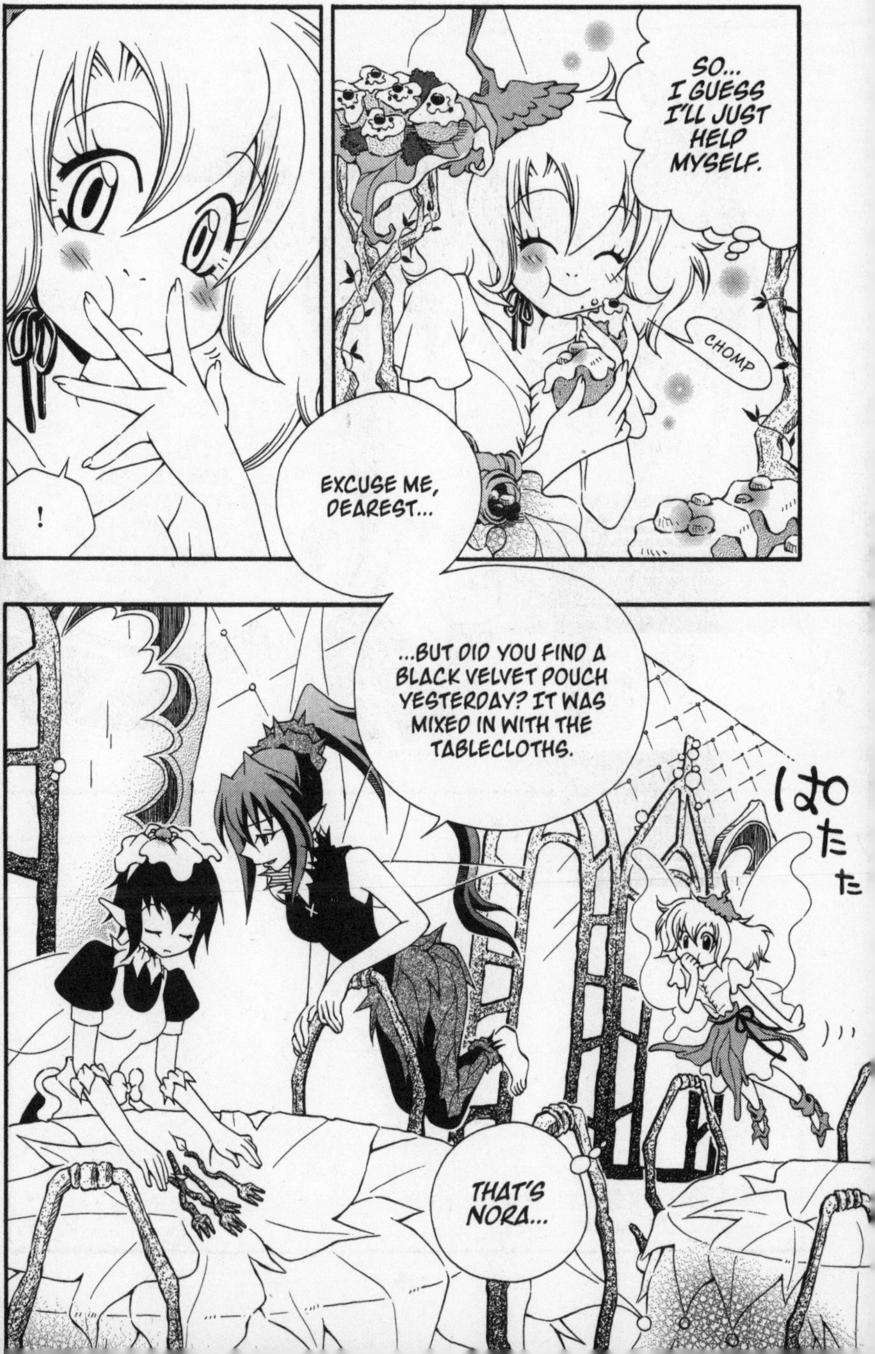
SO... I GUESS I'LL JUST HELP MYSELF.
CHOMP
!
EXCUSE ME, DEAREST...
...BUT DID YOU FIND A BLACK VELVET POUCH YESTERDAY? IT WAS MIXED IN WITH THE TABLECLOTHS.
ぱたた
THAT'S NORA...

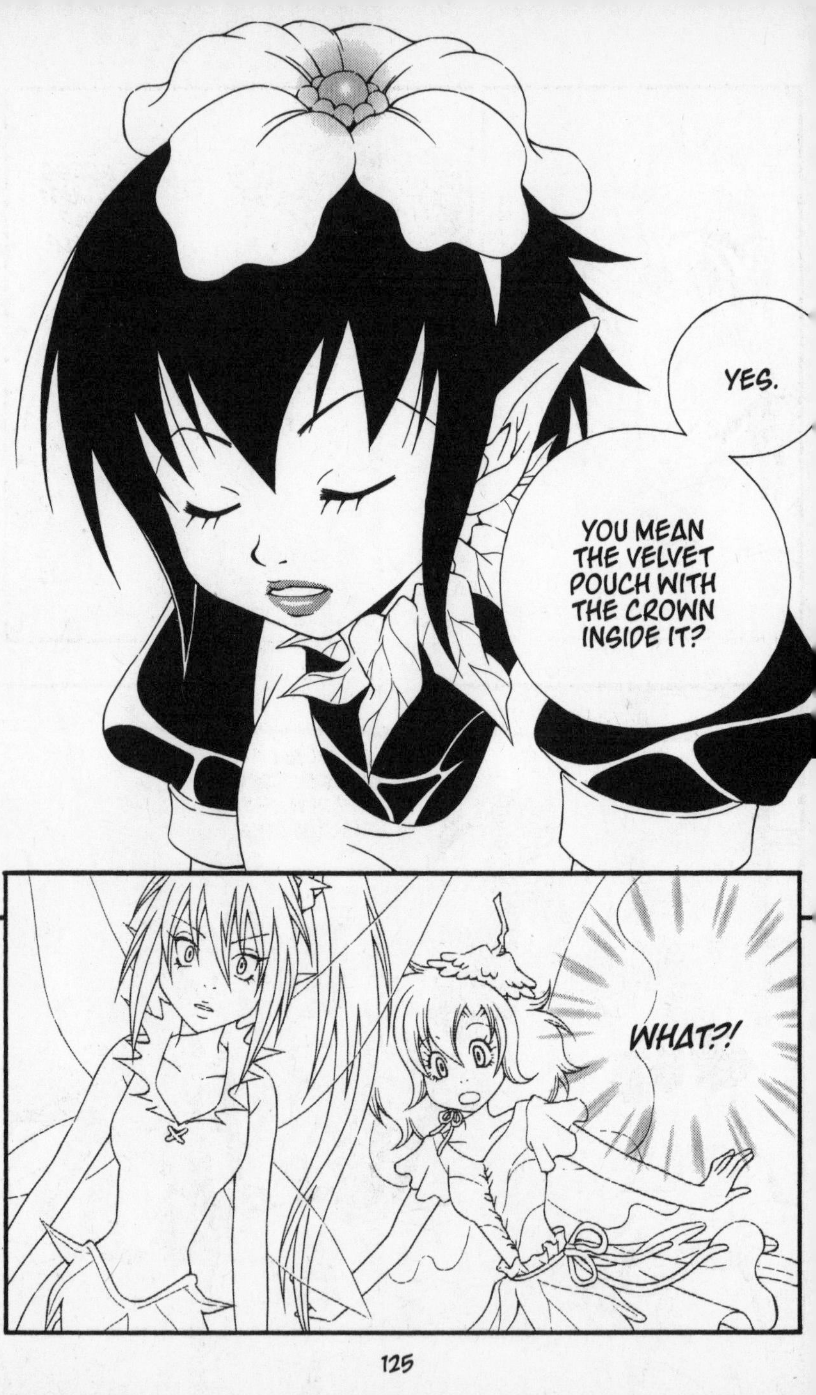
YES.
YOU MEAN THE VELVET POUCH WITH THE CROWN INSIDE IT?
WHAT?!

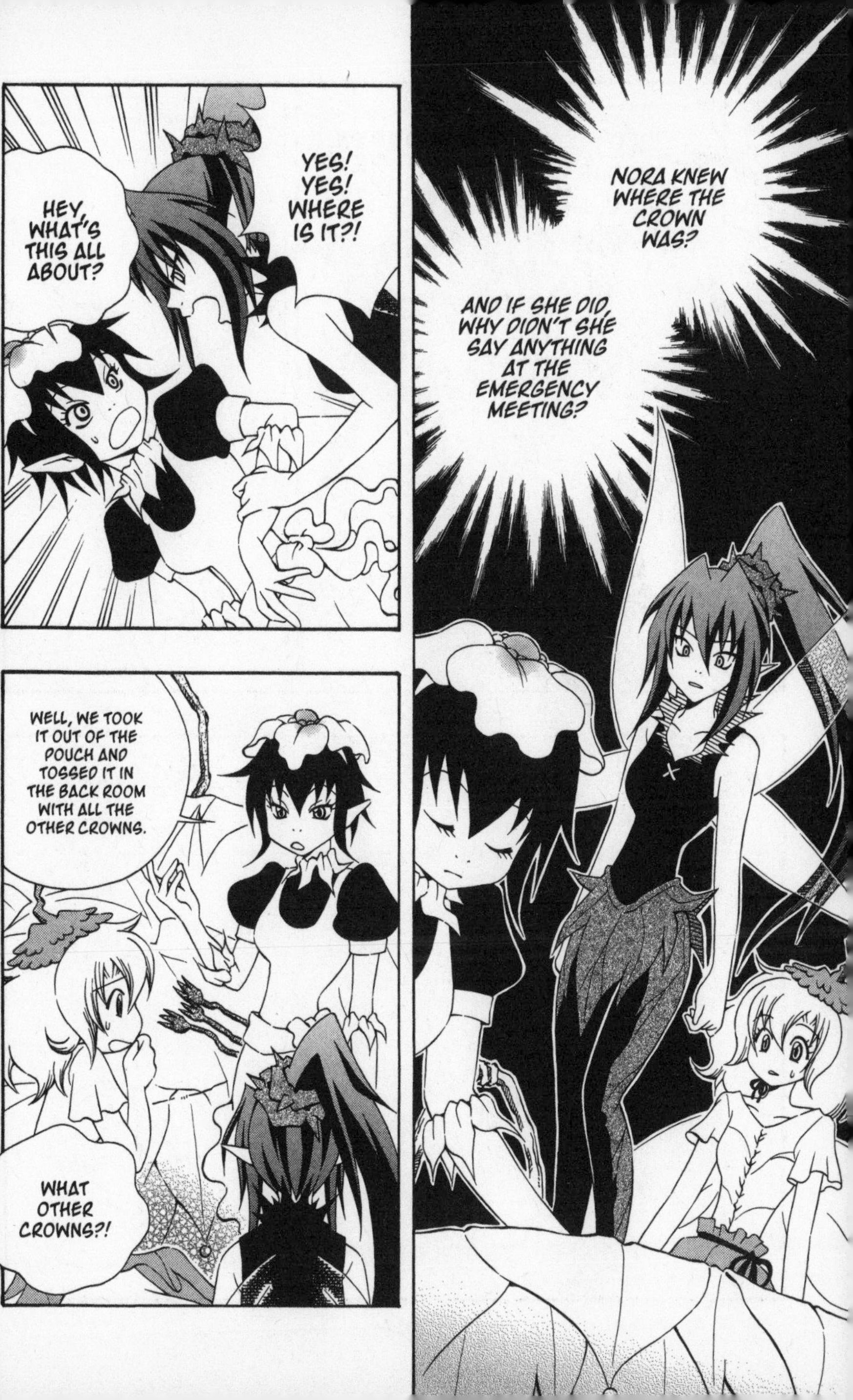
NORA KNEW WHERE THE CROWN WAS?
AND IF SHE DID, WHY DIDN'T SHE SAY ANYTHING AT THE EMERGENCY MEETING?
YES! YES! WHERE IS IT?!
HEY, WHAT'S THIS ALL ABOUT?
WELL, WE TOOK IT OUT OF THE POUCH AND TOSSED IT IN THE BACK ROOM WITH ALL THE OTHER CROWNS.
WHAT OTHER CROWNS?!

READ THIS WAY

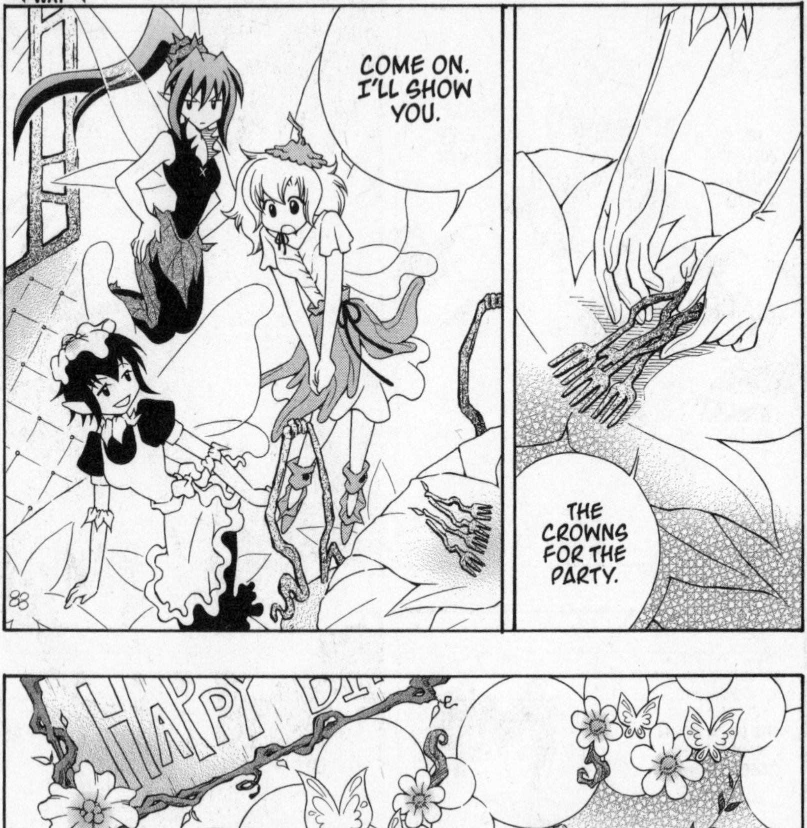
THE CROWNS FOR THE PARTY.
COME ON. I'LL SHOW YOU.
HAPPY

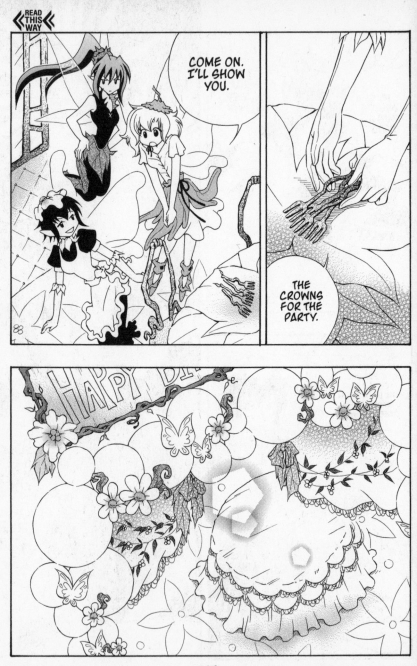

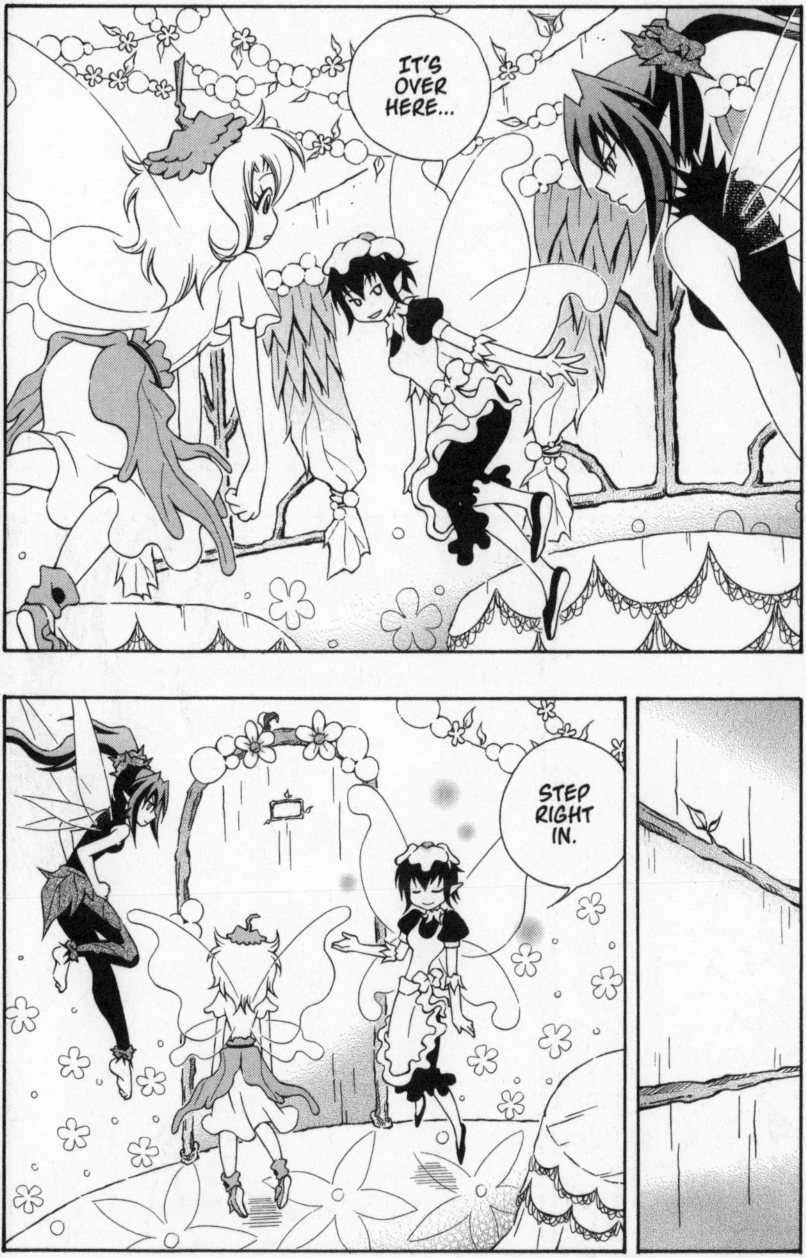
IT'S OVER HERE...
STEP RIGHT IN.

READ THIS WAY

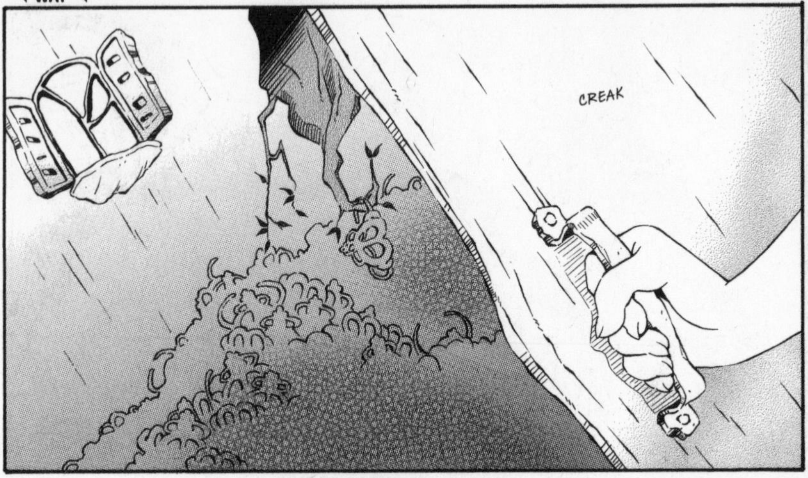
CREAK

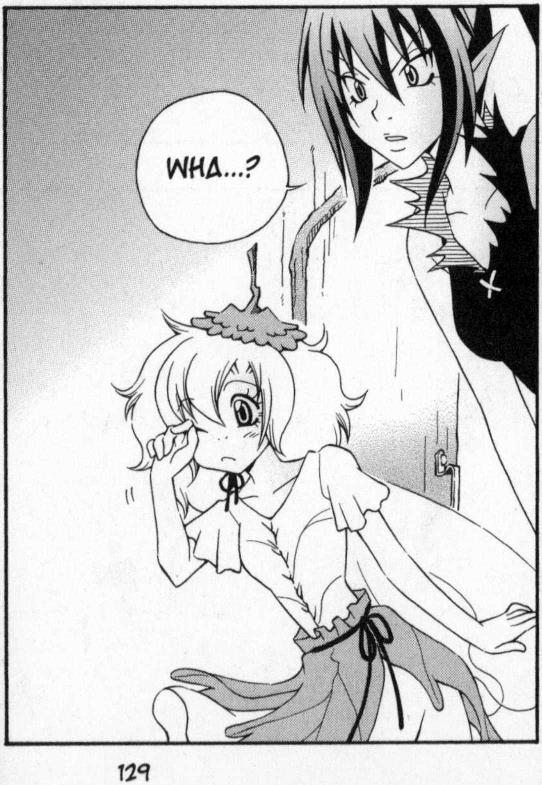
WHA...?

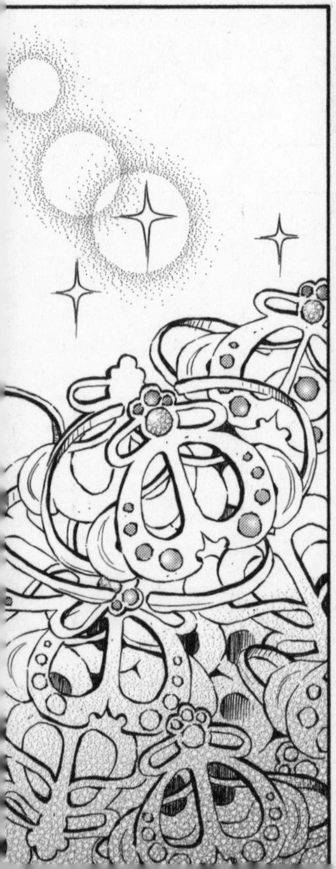

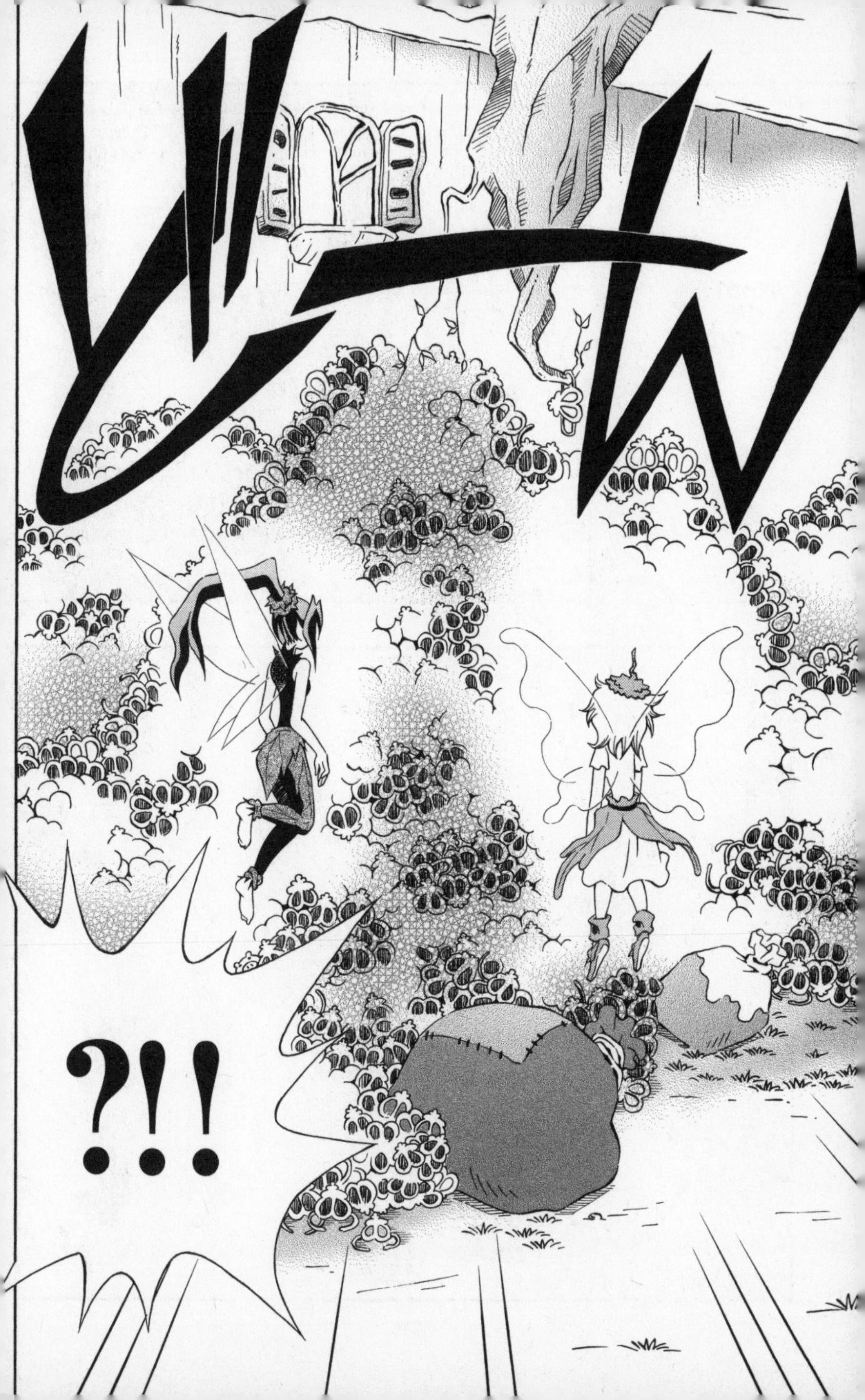
?!!

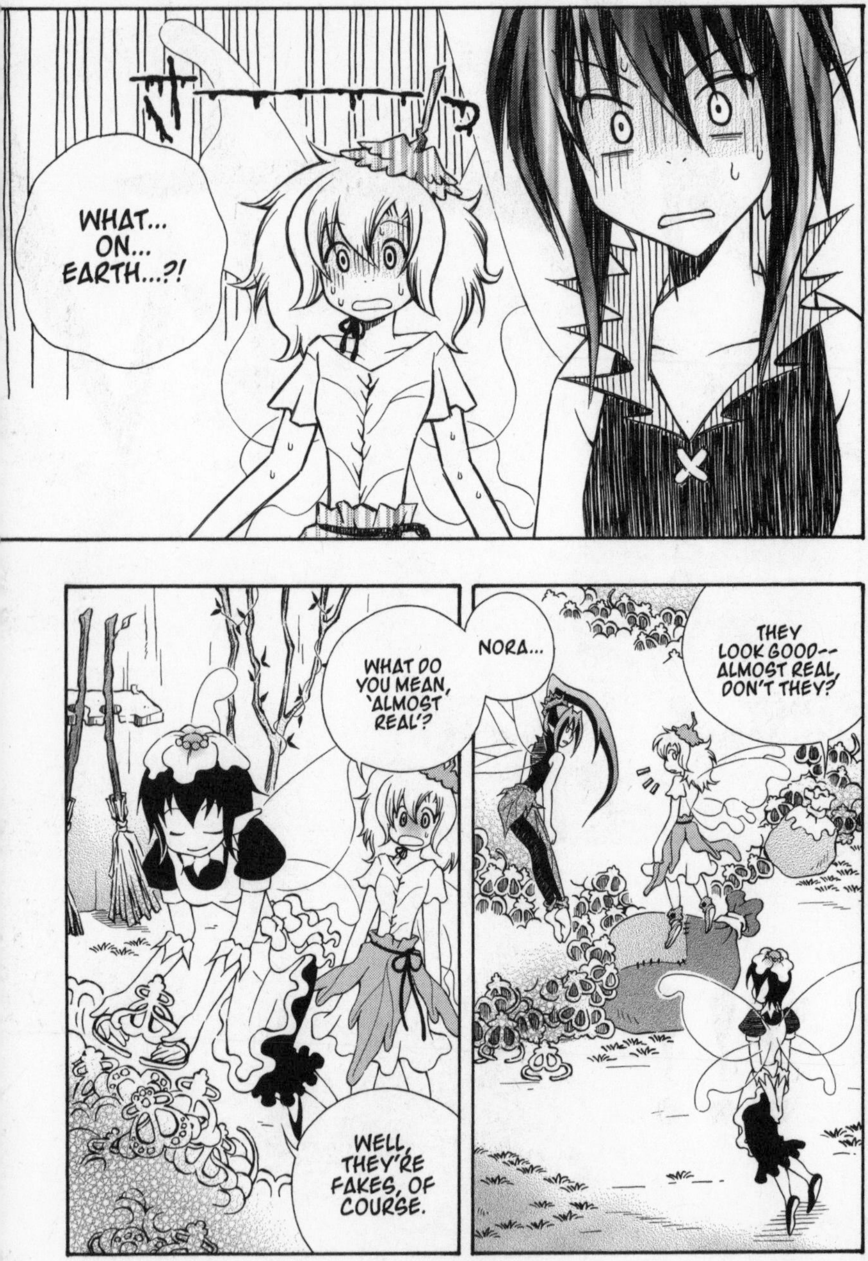
WHAT... ON... EARTH...?!
THEY LOOK GOOD-- ALMOST REAL, DON'T THEY?
NORA...
WHAT DO YOU MEAN, 'ALMOST REAL'?
WELL, THEY'RE FAKES, OF COURSE.

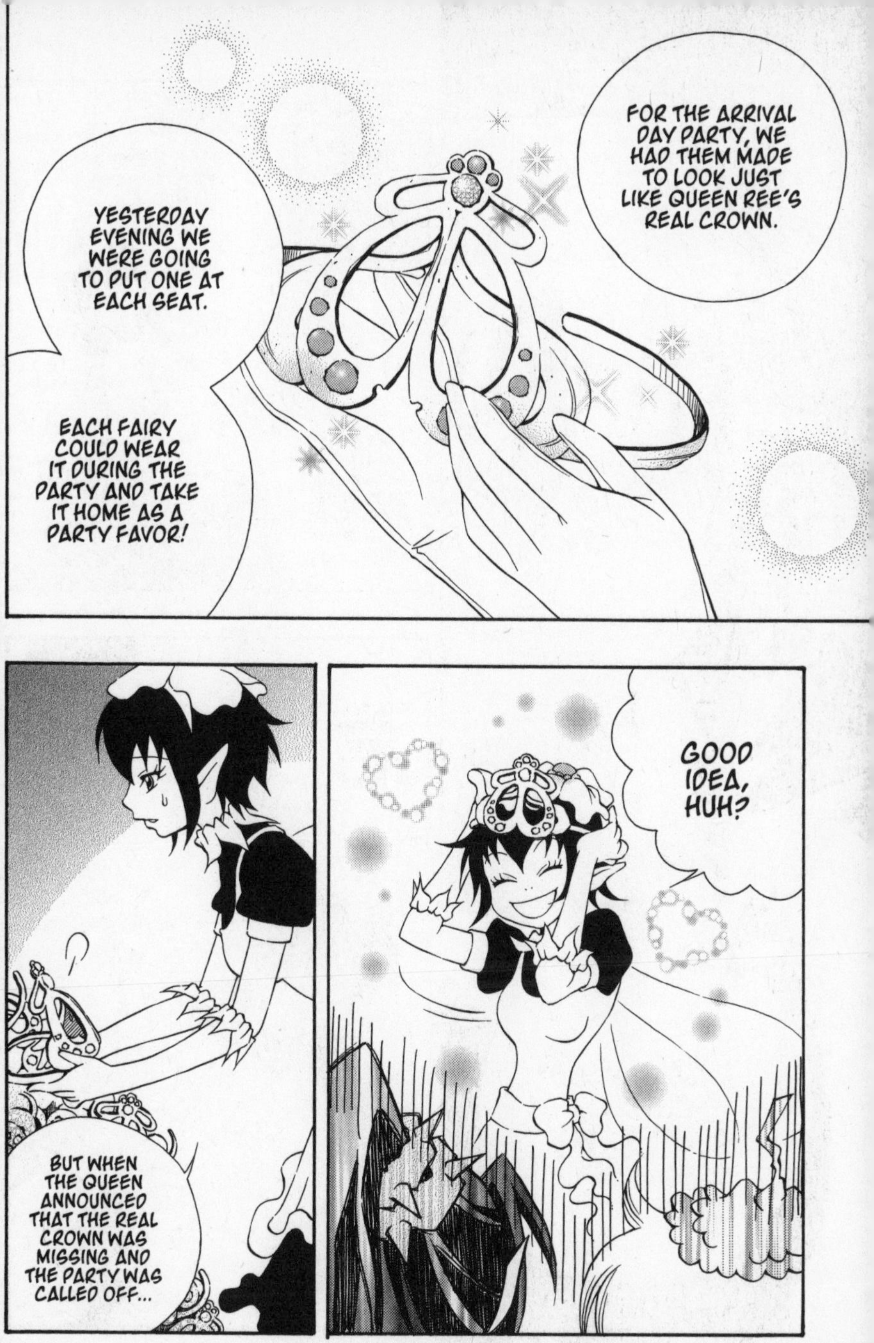
FOR THE ARRIVAL DAY PARTY, WE HAD THEM MADE TO LOOK JUST LIKE QUEEN REE'S REAL CROWN.
YESTERDAY EVENING WE WERE GOING TO PUT ONE AT EACH SEAT.
EACH FAIRY COULD WEAR IT DURING THE PARTY AND TAKE IT HOME AS A PARTY FAVOR!
GOOD IDEA, HUH?
BUT WHEN THE QUEEN ANNOUNCED THAT THE REAL CROWN WAS MISSING AND THE PARTY WAS CALLED OFF...

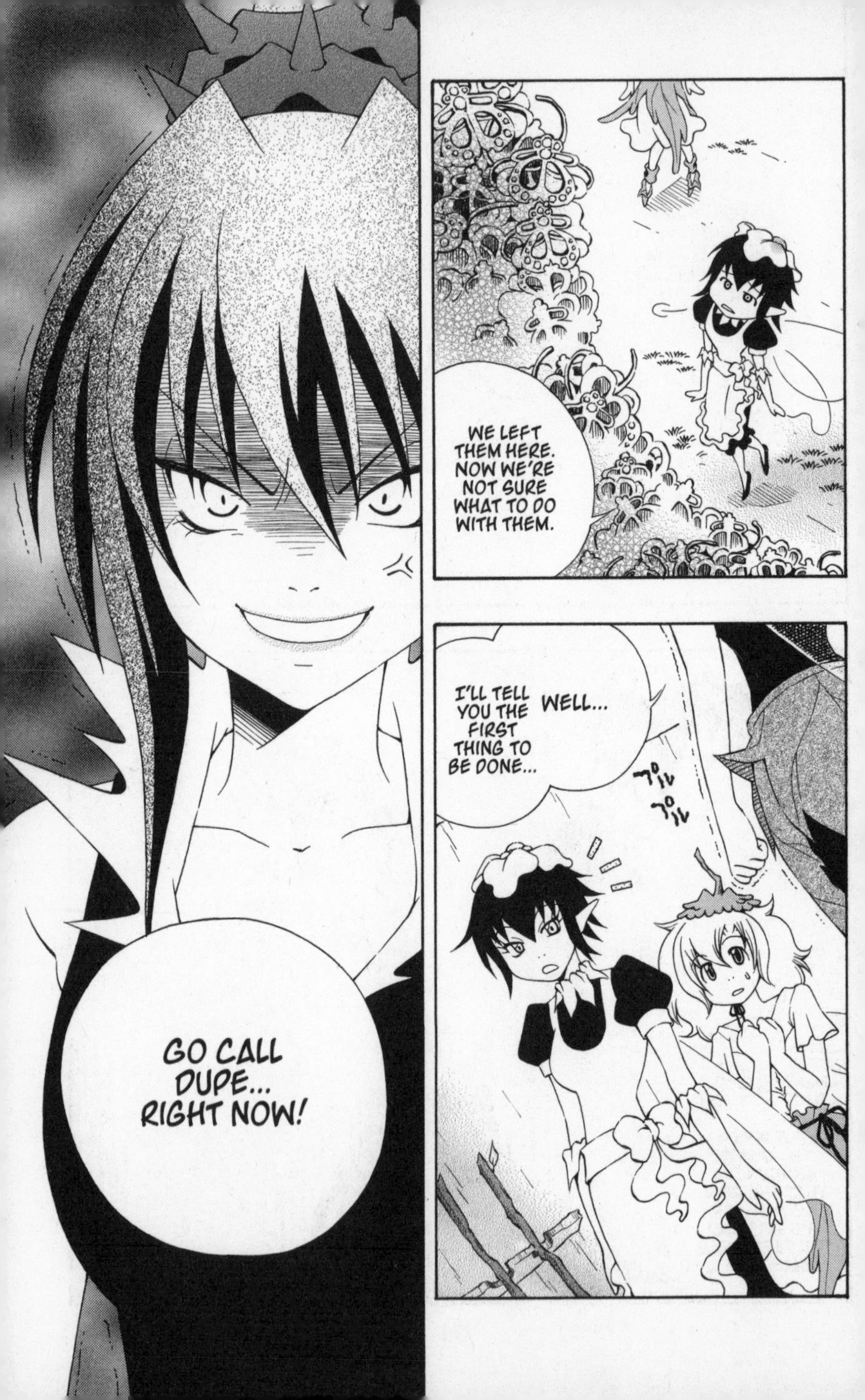
WE LEFT THEM HERE. NOW WE'RE NOT SURE WHAT TO DO WITH THEM.
WELL...
I'LL TELL YOU THE FIRST THING TO BE DONE...
プル
プル
GO CALL DUPE... RIGHT NOW!

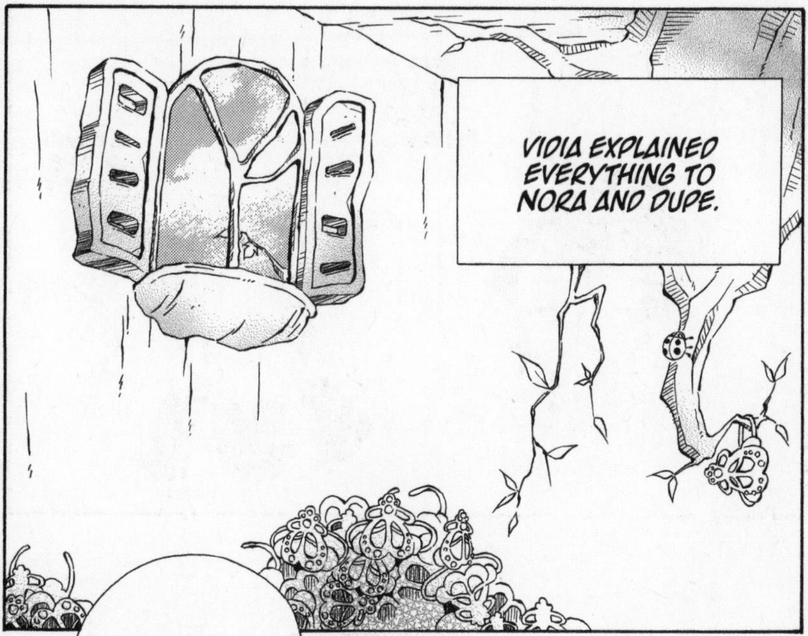
VIDIA EXPLAINED EVERYTHING TO NORA AND DUPE.

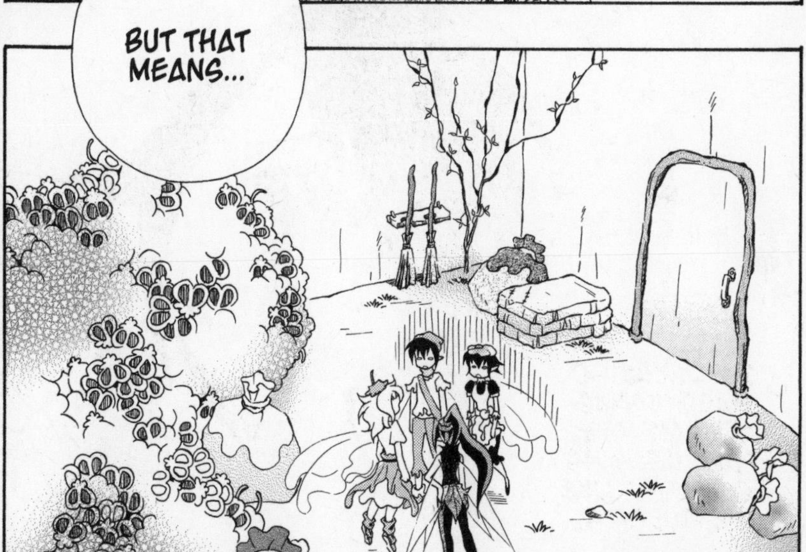
BUT THAT MEANS...

READ THIS WAY

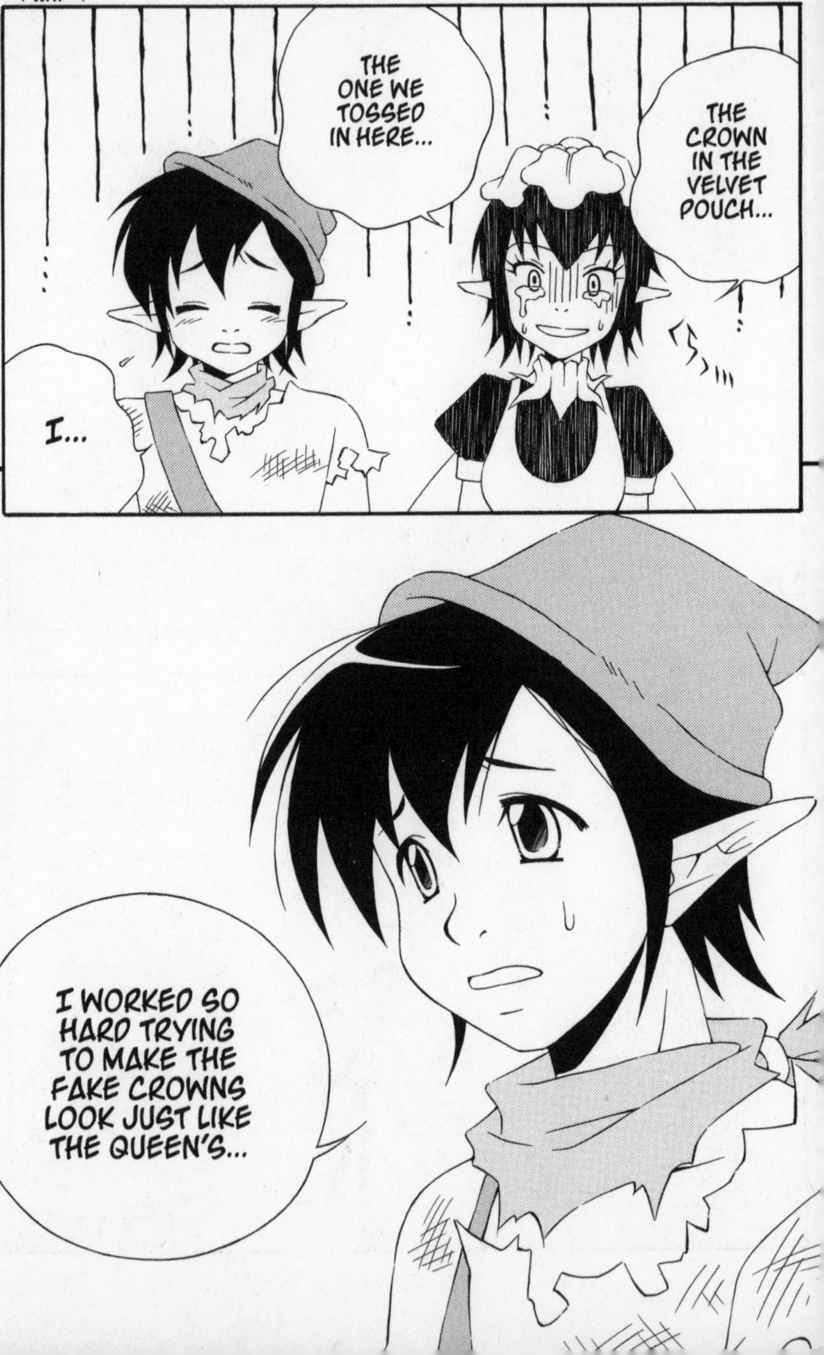
THE CROWN IN THE VELVET POUCH...
THE ONE WE TOSSED IN HERE...
I...
I WORKED SO HARD TRYING TO MAKE THE FAKE CROWNS LOOK JUST LIKE THE QUEEN'S...

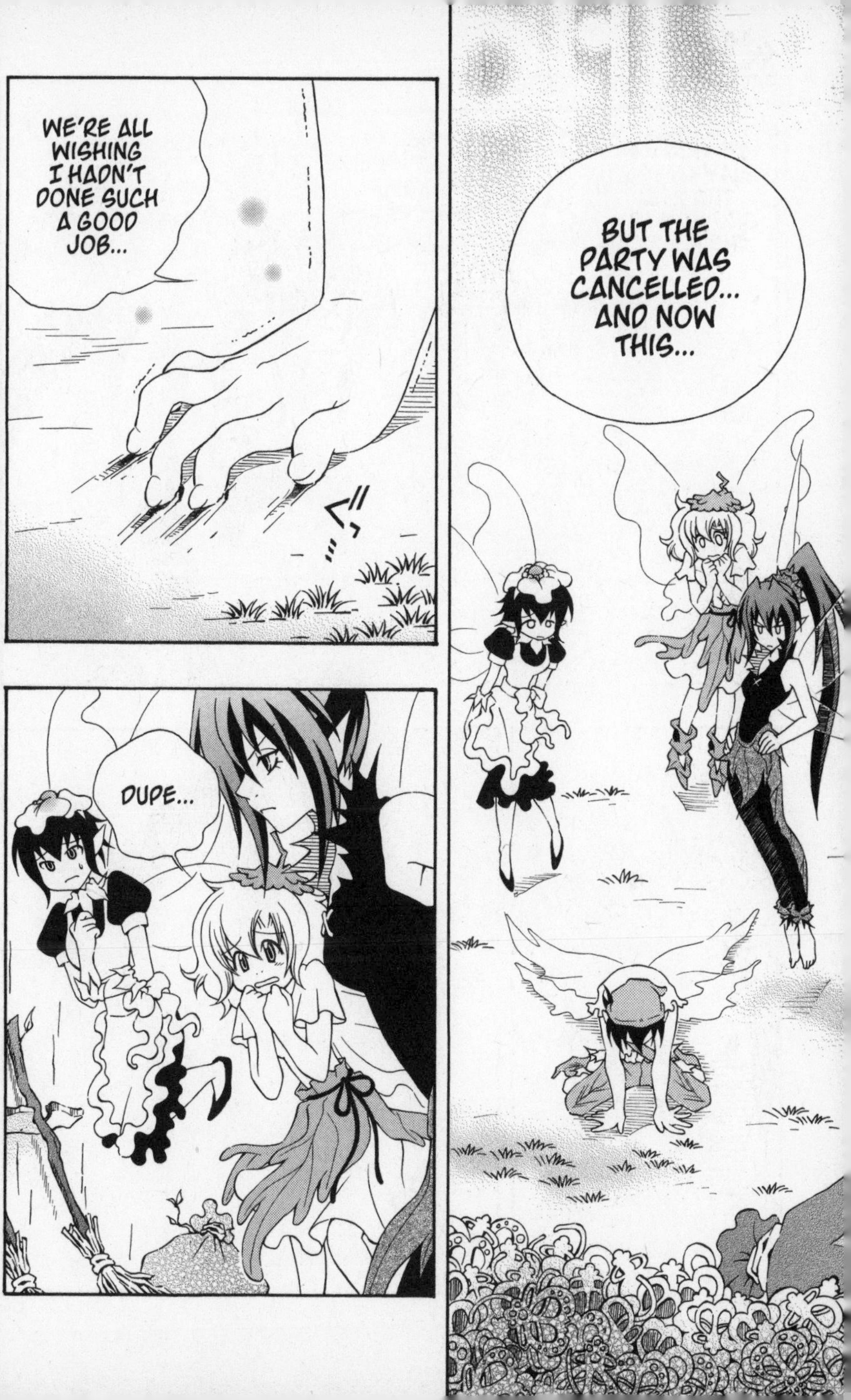
BUT THE PARTY WAS CANCELLED... AND NOW THIS...
WE'RE ALL WISHING I HADN'T DONE SUCH A GOOD JOB...
DUPE...

READ THIS WAY

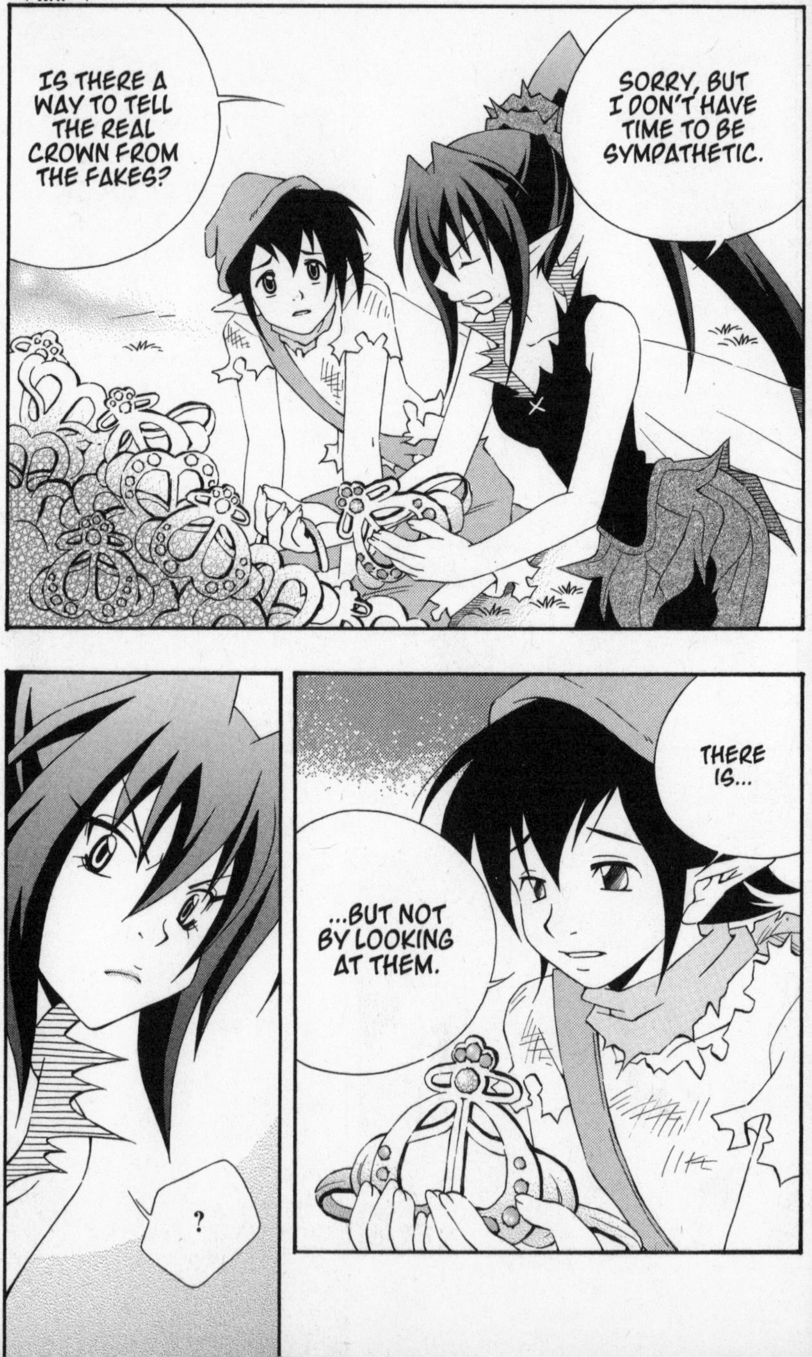
SORRY, BUT I DON'T HAVE TIME TO BE SYMPATHETIC.
IS THERE A WAY TO TELL THE REAL CROWN FROM THE FAKES?
THERE IS...
...BUT NOT BY LOOKING AT THEM.
?

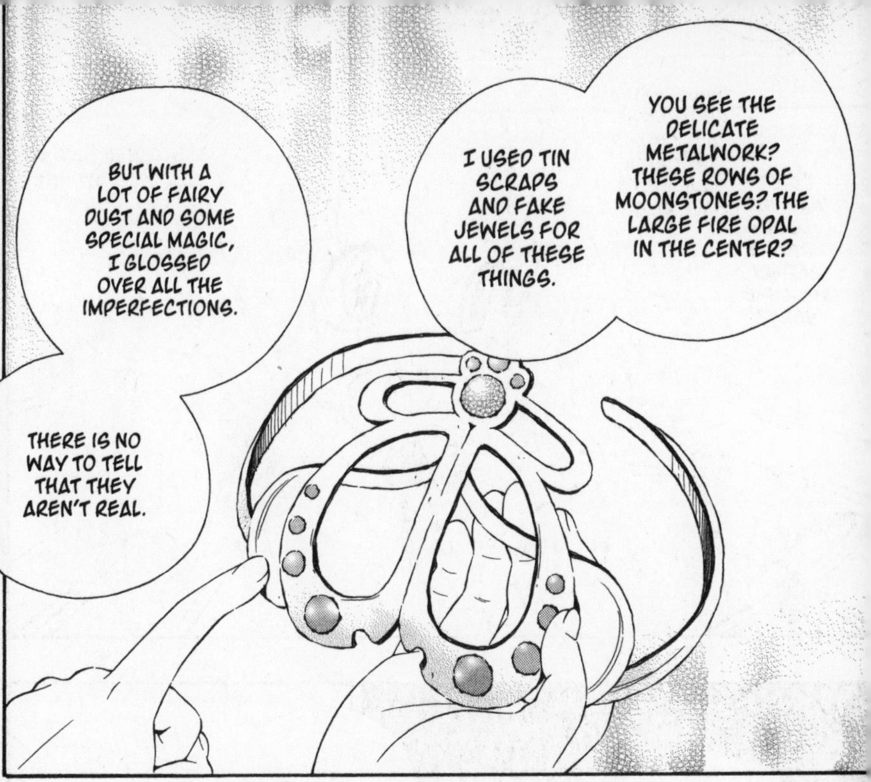
YOU SEE THE DELICATE METALWORK? THESE ROWS OF MOONSTONES? THE LARGE FIRE OPAL IN THE CENTER?
I USED TIN SCRAPS AND FAKE JEWELS FOR ALL OF THESE THINGS.
BUT WITH A LOT OF FAIRY DUST AND SOME SPECIAL MAGIC, I GLOSSED OVER ALL THE IMPERFECTIONS.
THERE IS NO WAY TO TELL THAT THEY AREN'T REAL.

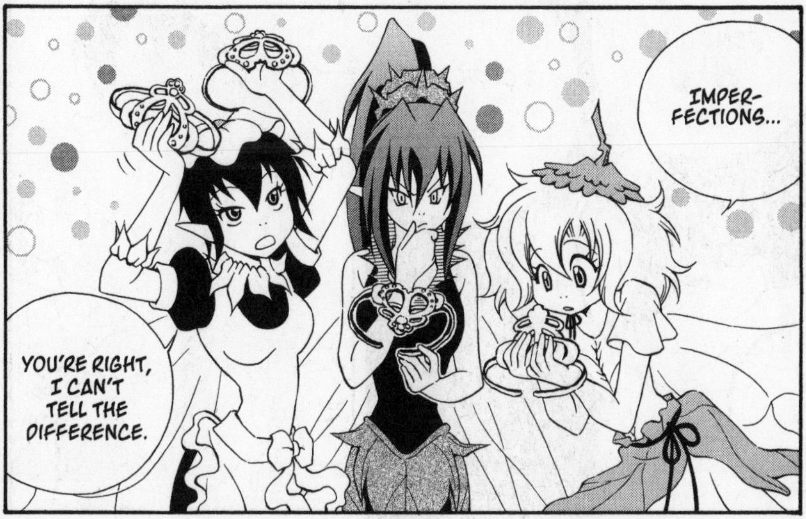
IMPER-FECTIONS...
YOU'RE RIGHT, I CAN'T TELL THE DIFFERENCE.

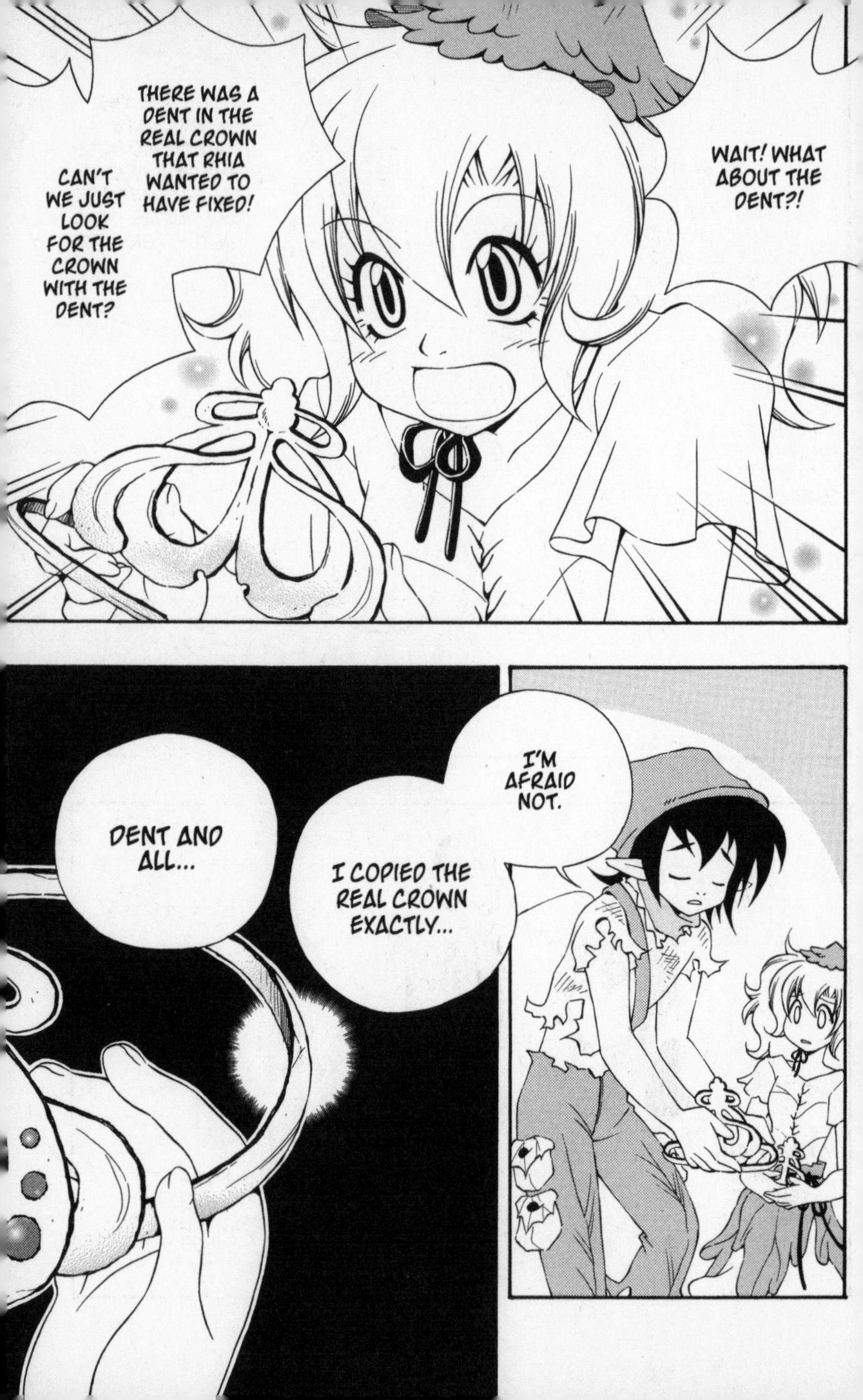
WAIT! WHAT ABOUT THE DENT?!
THERE WAS A DENT IN THE REAL CROWN THAT RHIA WANTED TO HAVE FIXED!
CAN'T WE JUST LOOK FOR THE CROWN WITH THE DENT?
I'M AFRAID NOT.
I COPIED THE REAL CROWN EXACTLY...
DENT AND ALL...

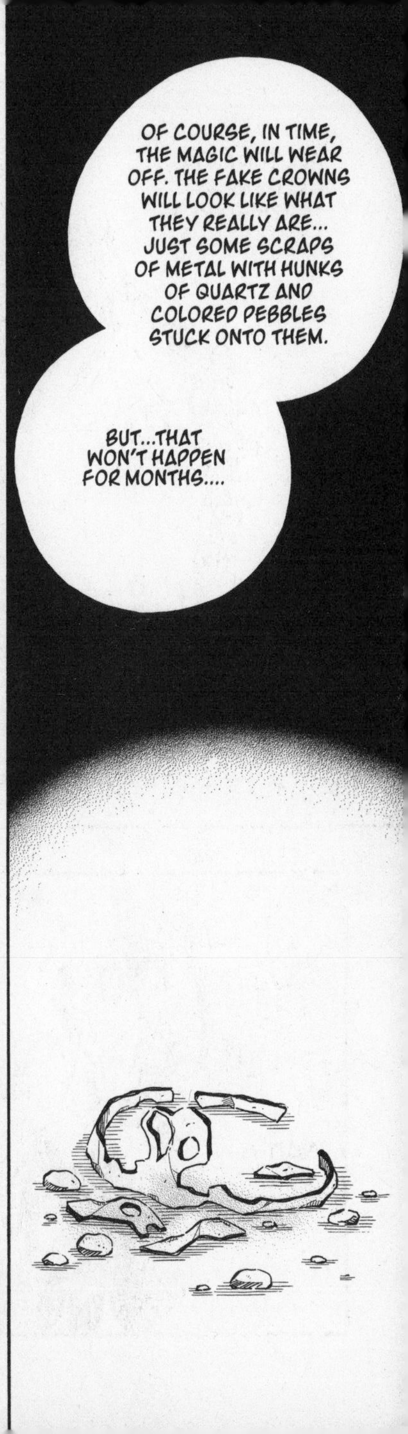
OF COURSE, IN TIME, THE MAGIC WILL WEAR OFF. THE FAKE CROWNS WILL LOOK LIKE WHAT THEY REALLY ARE... JUST SOME SCRAPS OF METAL WITH HUNKS OF QUARTZ AND COLORED PEBBLES STUCK ONTO THEM.
BUT...THAT WON'T HAPPEN FOR MONTHS....

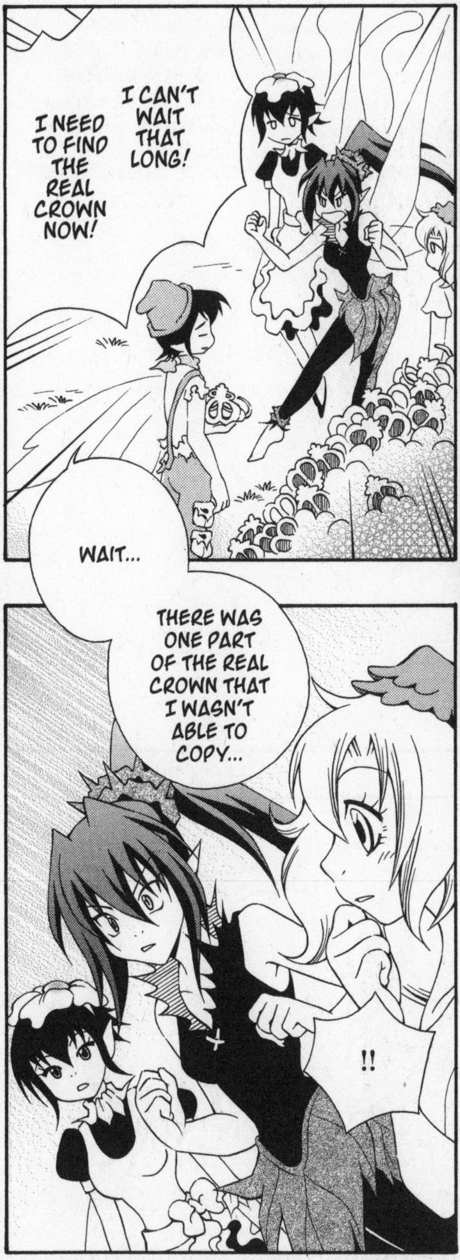
I CAN'T WAIT THAT LONG!
I NEED TO FIND THE REAL CROWN NOW!
WAIT...
THERE WAS ONE PART OF THE REAL CROWN THAT I WASN'T ABLE TO COPY...
!!

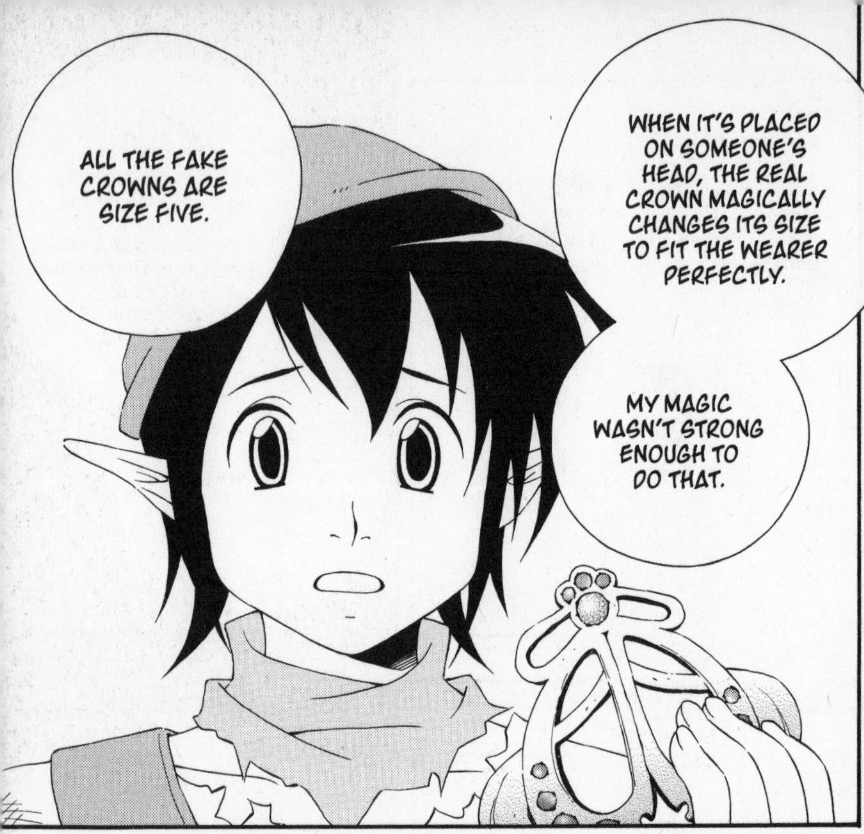
WHEN IT'S PLACED ON SOMEONE'S HEAD, THE REAL CROWN MAGICALLY CHANGES ITS SIZE TO FIT THE WEARER PERFECTLY.
MY MAGIC WASN'T STRONG ENOUGH TO DO THAT.
ALL THE FAKE CROWNS ARE SIZE FIVE.

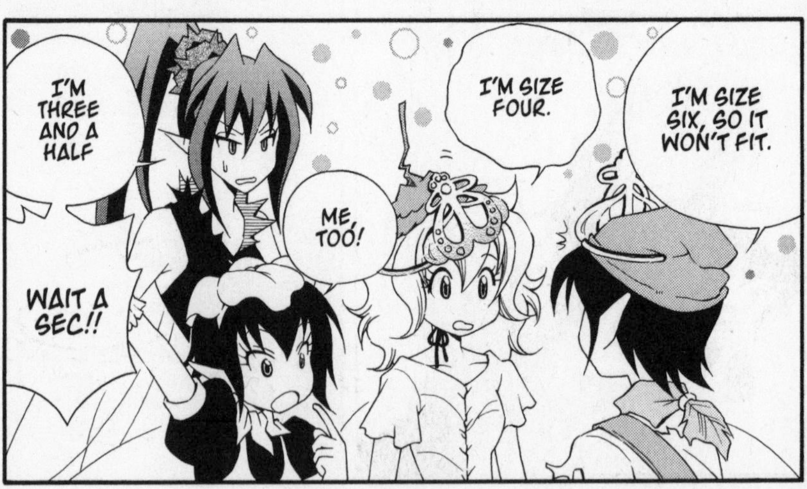
I'M SIZE SIX, SO IT WON'T FIT.
I'M SIZE FOUR.
ME, TOO!
I'M THREE AND A HALF
WAIT A SEC!!

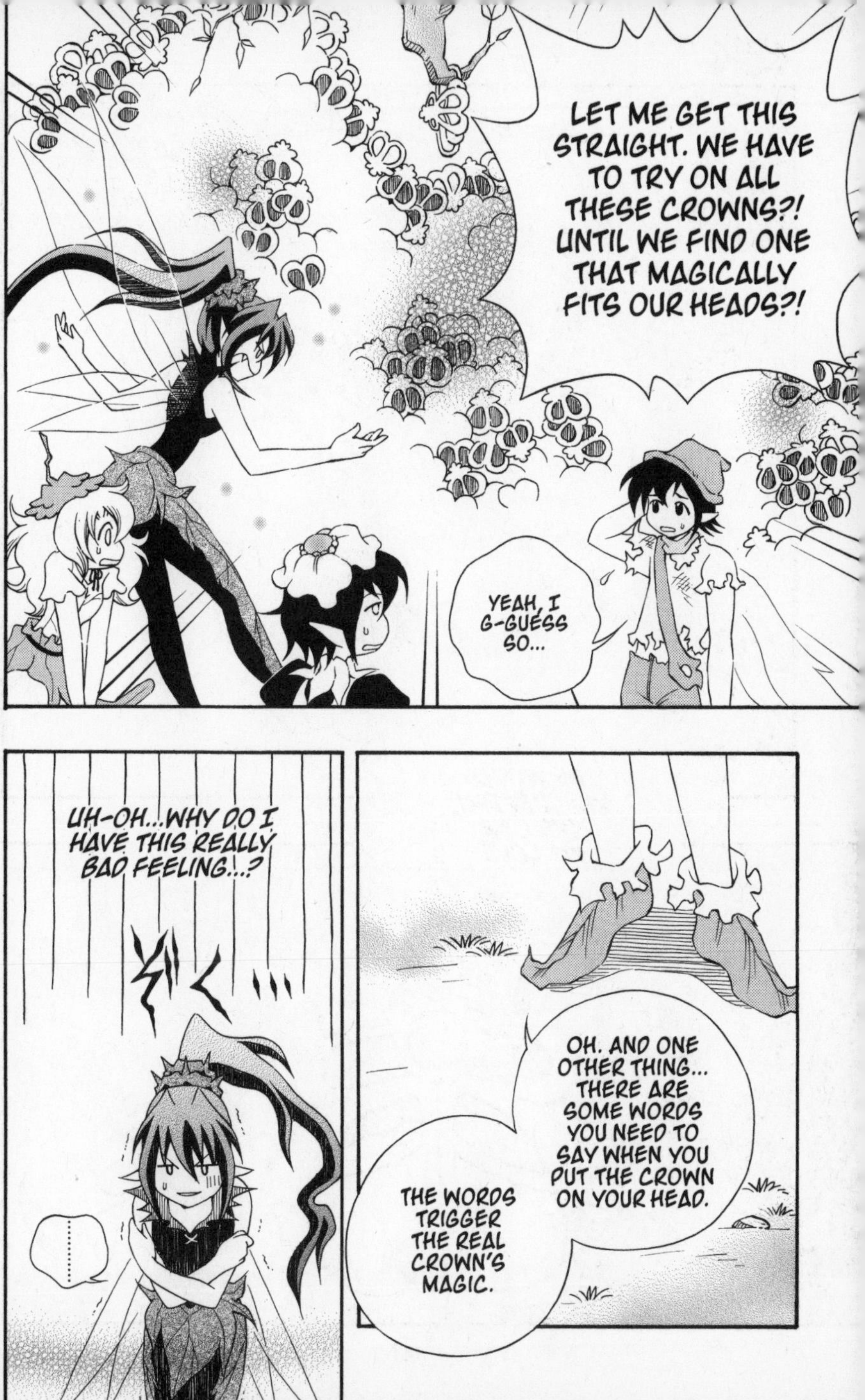
LET ME GET THIS STRAIGHT. WE HAVE TO TRY ON ALL THESE CROWNS?! UNTIL WE FIND ONE THAT MAGICALLY FITS OUR HEADS?!
YEAH, I G-GUESS SO...
OH. AND ONE OTHER THING... THERE ARE SOME WORDS YOU NEED TO SAY WHEN YOU PUT THE CROWN ON YOUR HEAD.
THE WORDS TRIGGER THE REAL CROWN'S MAGIC.
UH-OH...WHY DO I HAVE THIS REALLY BAD FEELING...?
......

READ THIS WAY

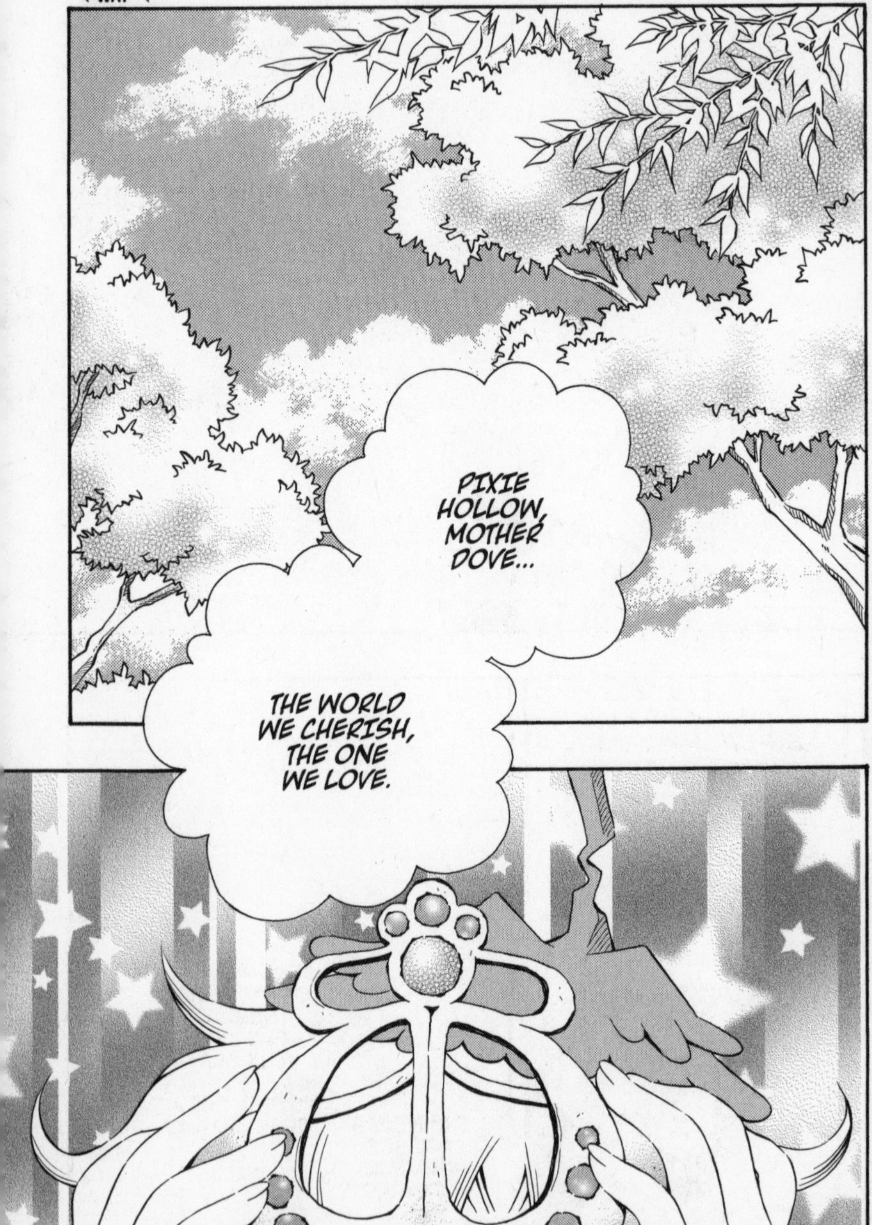
PIXIE HOLLOW, MOTHER DOVE...
THE WORLD WE CHERISH, THE ONE WE LOVE.

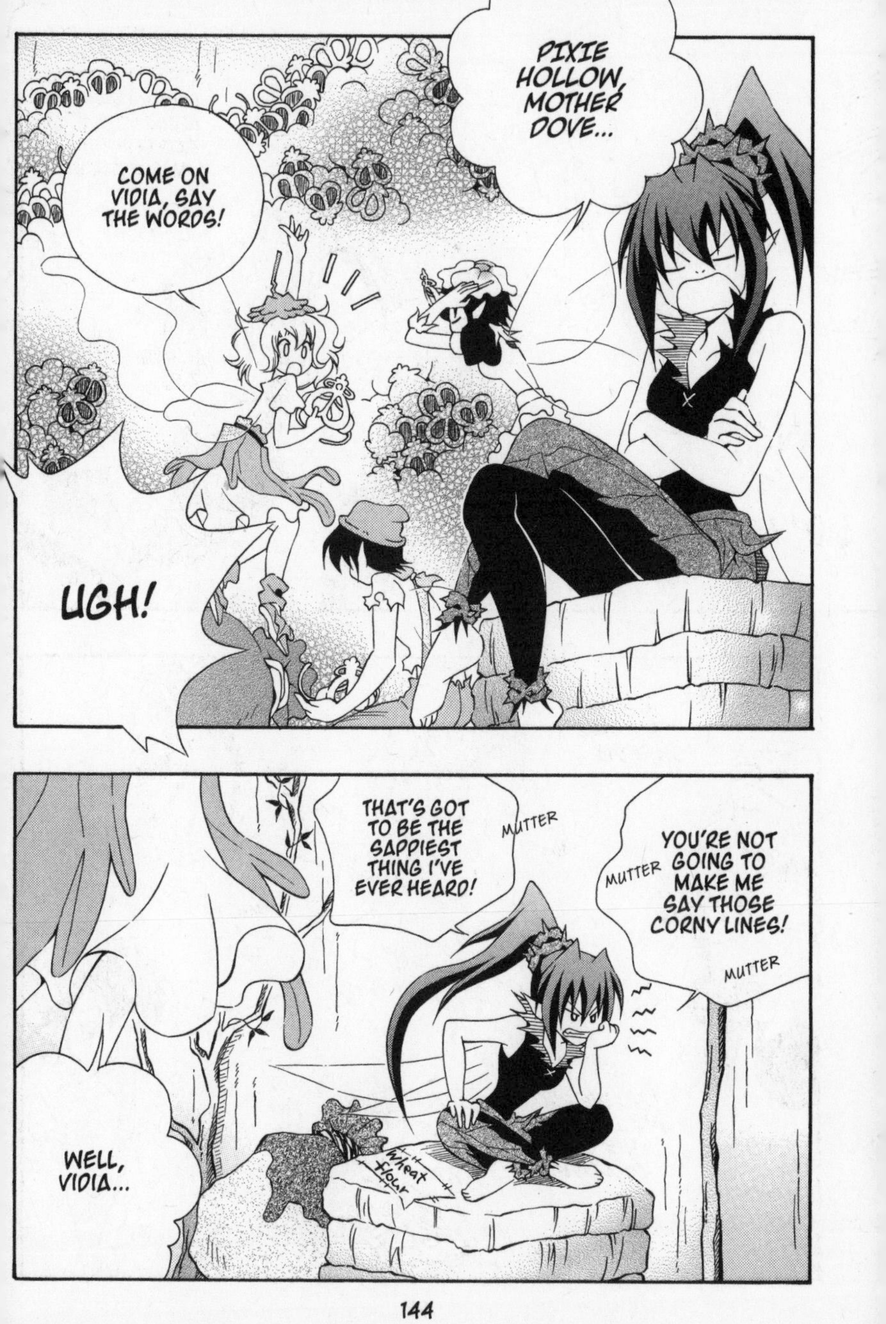
PIXIE HOLLOW, MOTHER DOVE...
COME ON VIDIA, SAY THE WORDS!
UGH!
MUTTER
YOU'RE NOT GOING TO MAKE ME SAY THOSE CORNY LINES!
MUTTER
MUTTER
THAT'S GOT TO BE THE SAPPIEST THING I'VE EVER HEARD!
Wheat flour
WELL, VIDIA...

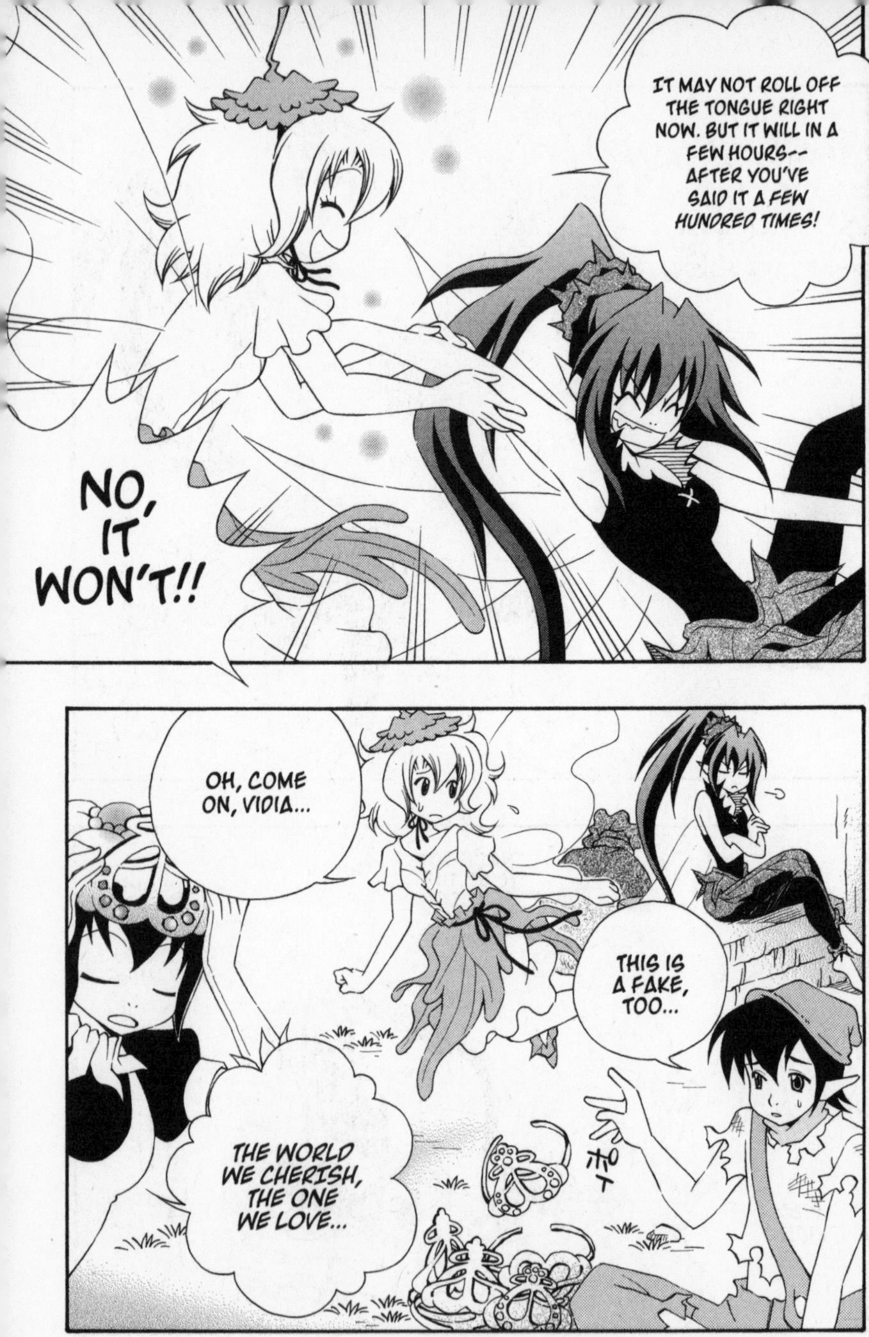
IT MAY NOT ROLL OFF THE TONGUE RIGHT NOW. BUT IT WILL IN A FEW HOURS-- AFTER YOU'VE SAID IT A FEW HUNDRED TIMES!
NO, IT WON'T!!
OH, COME ON, VIDIA...
THIS IS A FAKE, TOO...
ポト
THE WORLD WE CHERISH, THE ONE WE LOVE...

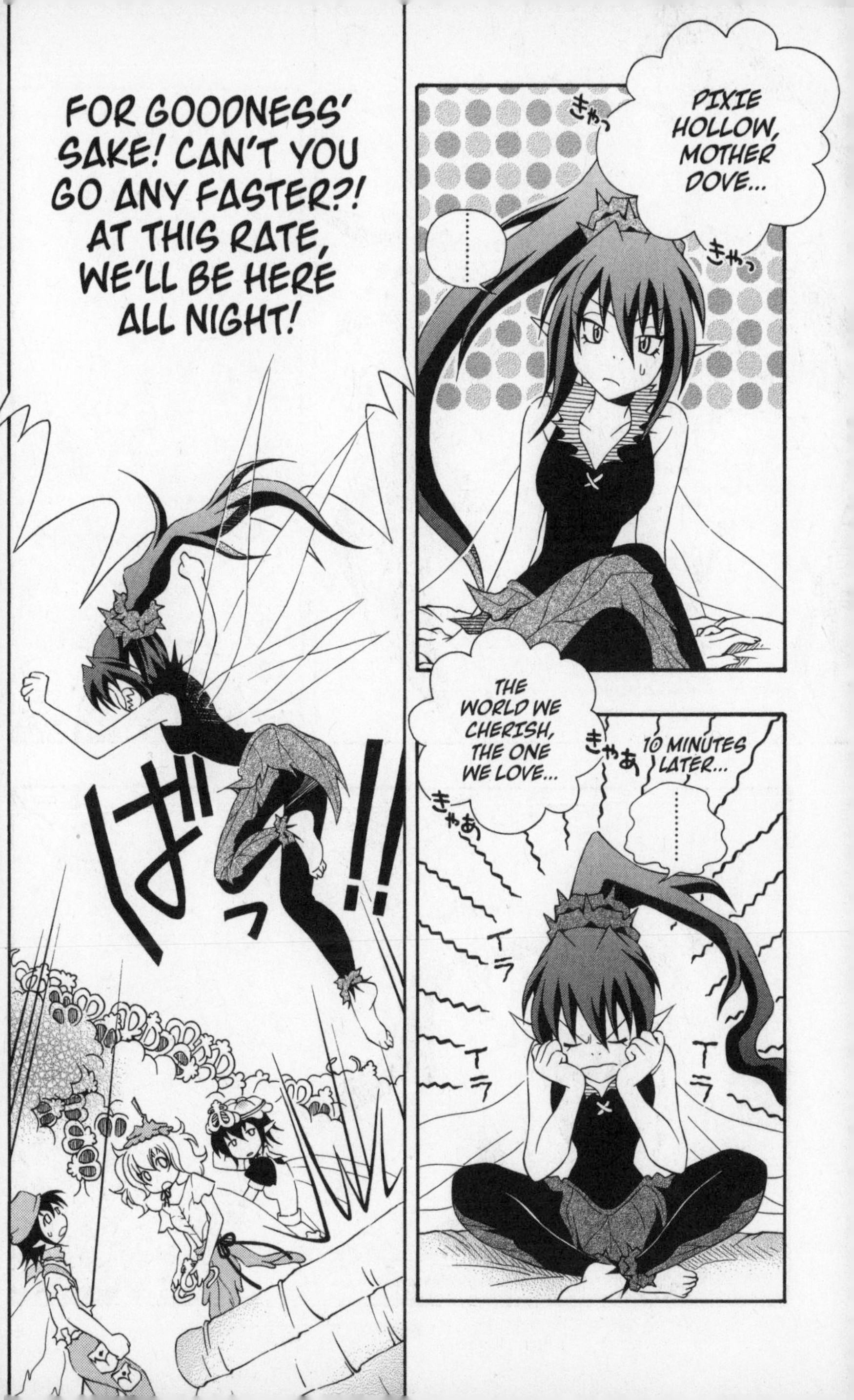

きゃっ
PIXIE HOLLOW, MOTHER DOVE...
......
きゃっ
THE WORLD WE CHERISH, THE ONE WE LOVE...
きゃあ
10 MINUTES LATER...
......
きゃあ
イラ
イラ
FOR GOODNESS' SAKE! CAN'T YOU GO ANY FASTER?! AT THIS RATE, WE'LL BE HERE ALL NIGHT!
ばっ!!

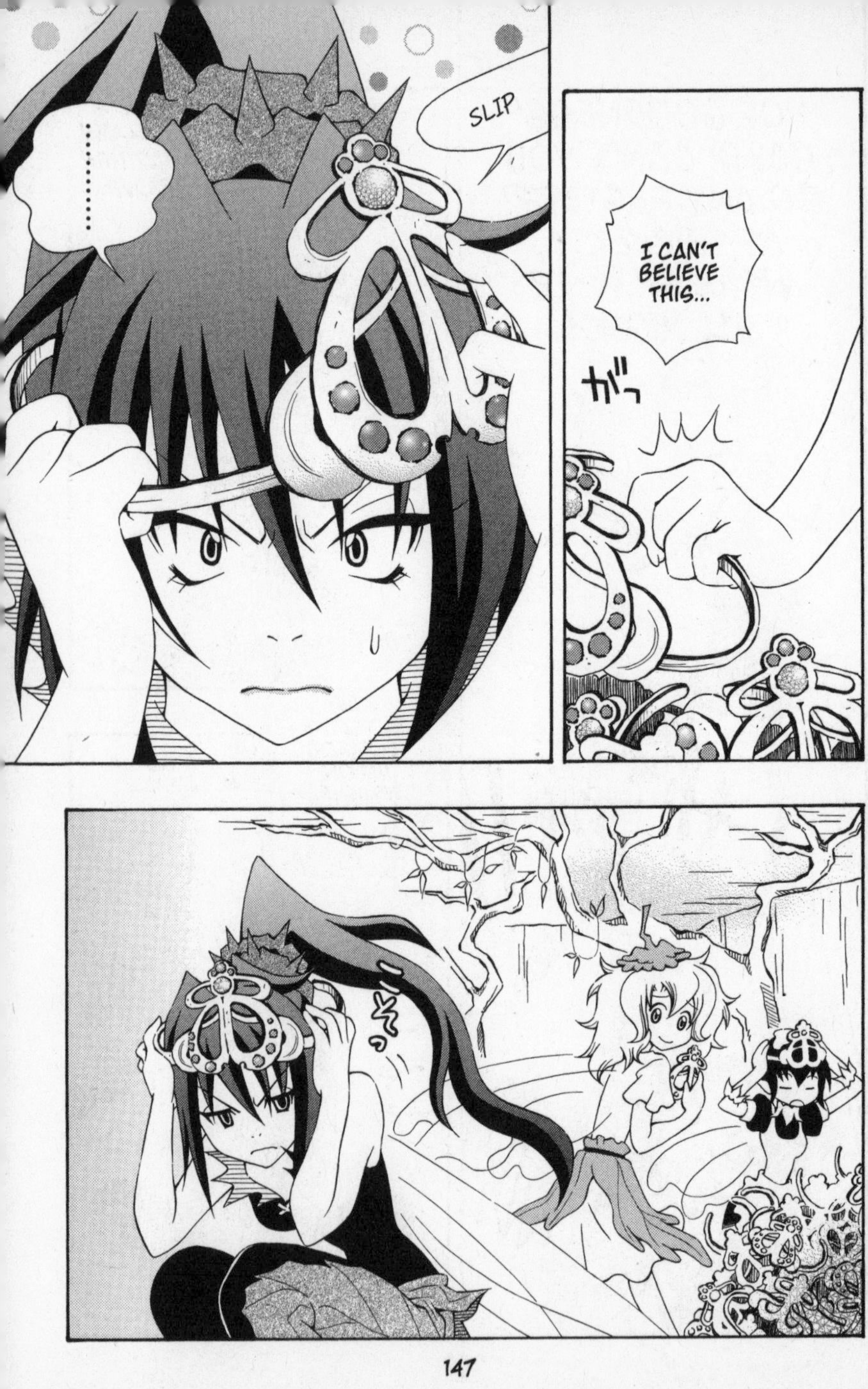
I CAN'T BELIEVE THIS...
ガッ
SLIP
......
こそっ

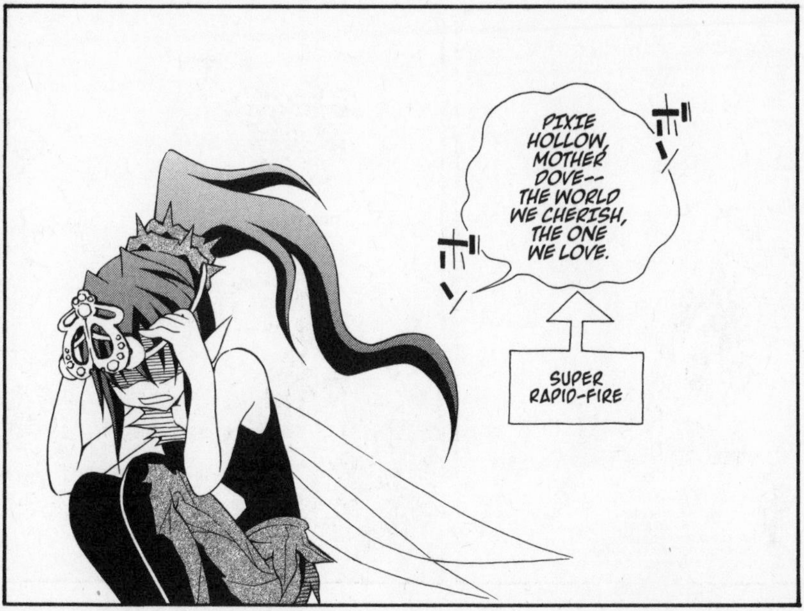
PIXIE HOLLOW, MOTHER DOVE-- THE WORLD WE CHERISH, THE ONE WE LOVE.
SUPER RAPID-FIRE

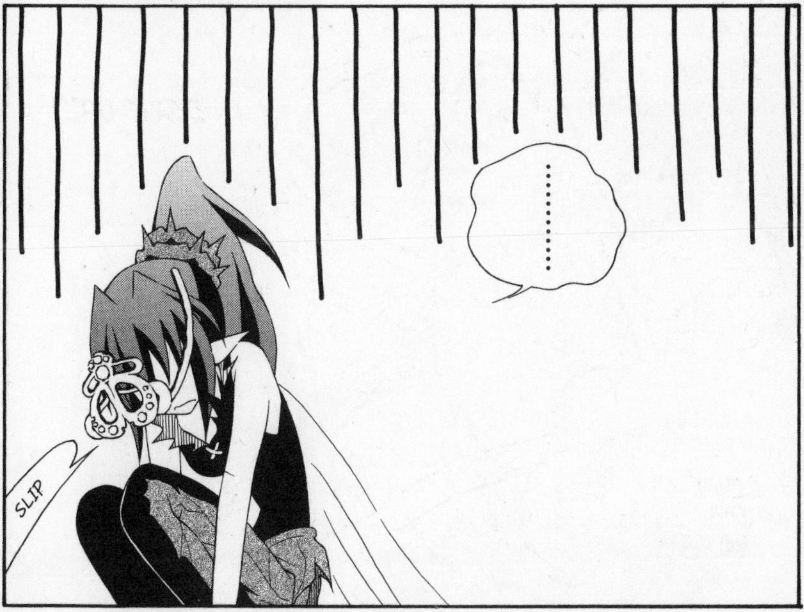
......
SLIP

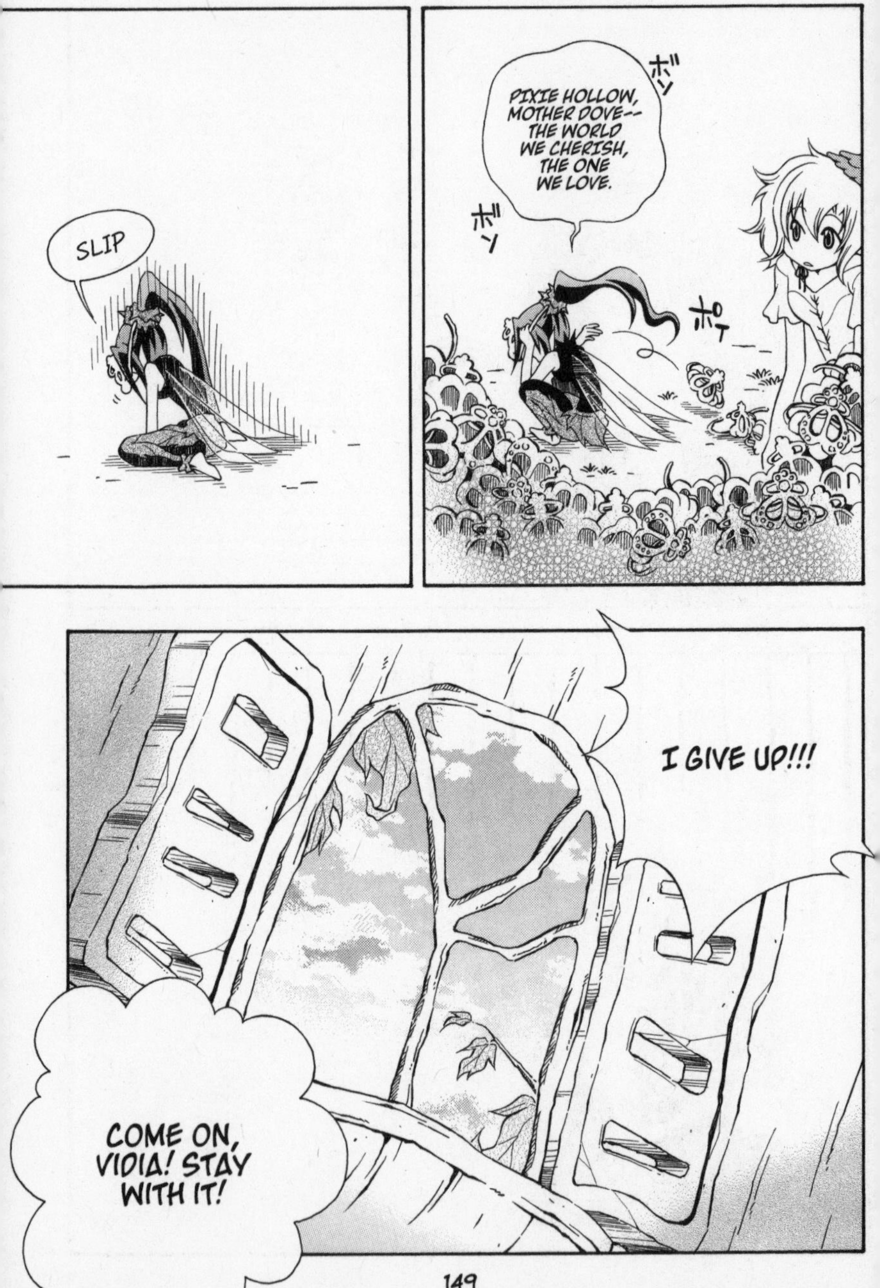
ボン
PIXIE HOLLOW, MOTHER DOVE-- THE WORLD WE CHERISH, THE ONE WE LOVE.
ボン
ポテ
SLIP
I GIVE UP!!!
COME ON, VIDIA! STAY WITH IT!

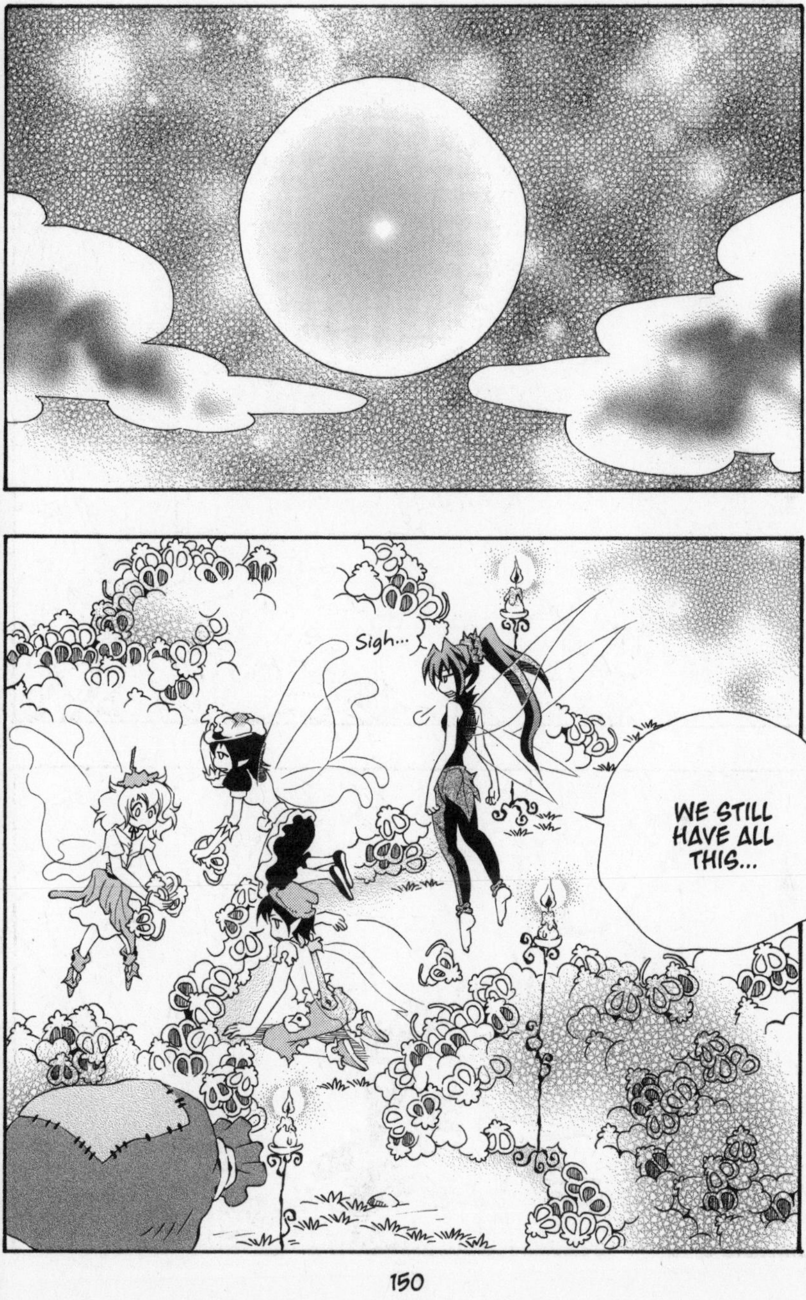
Sigh...
WE STILL HAVE ALL THIS...

READ THIS WAY

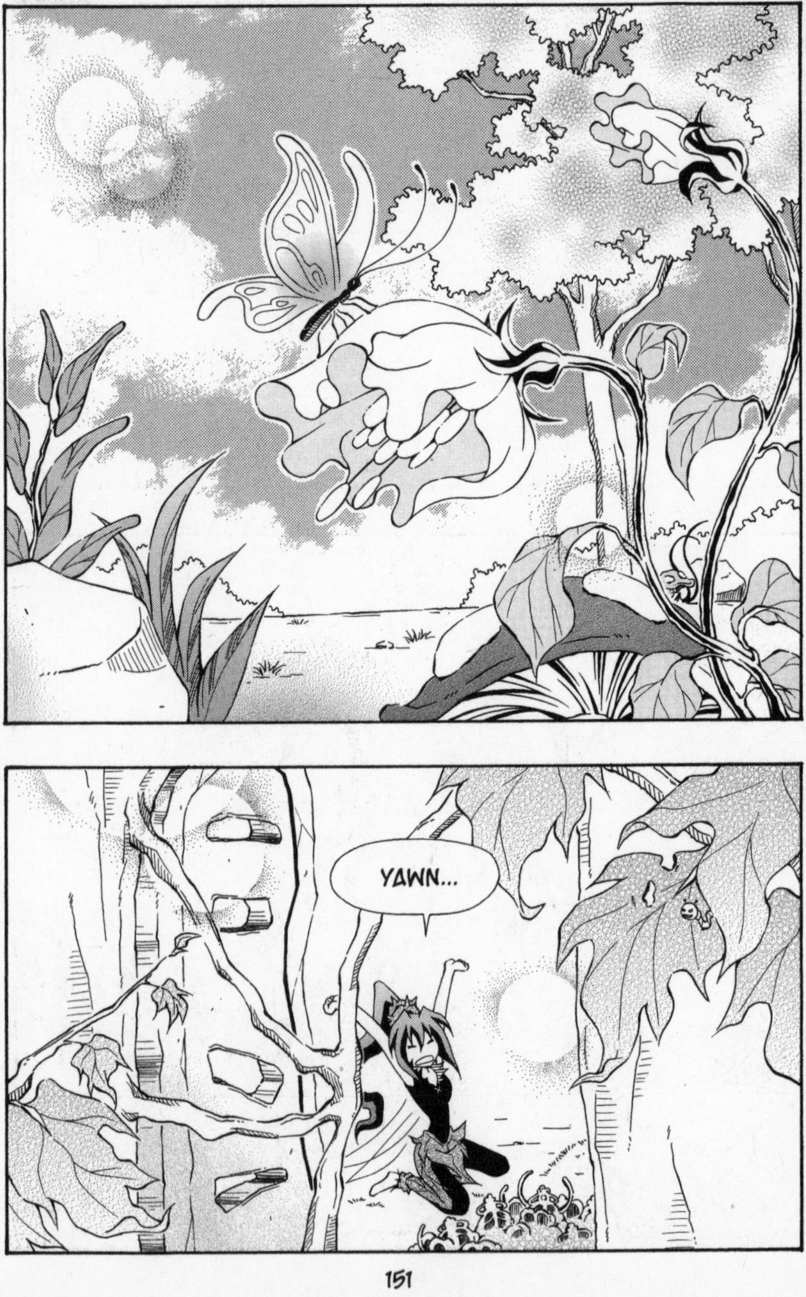
YAWN...

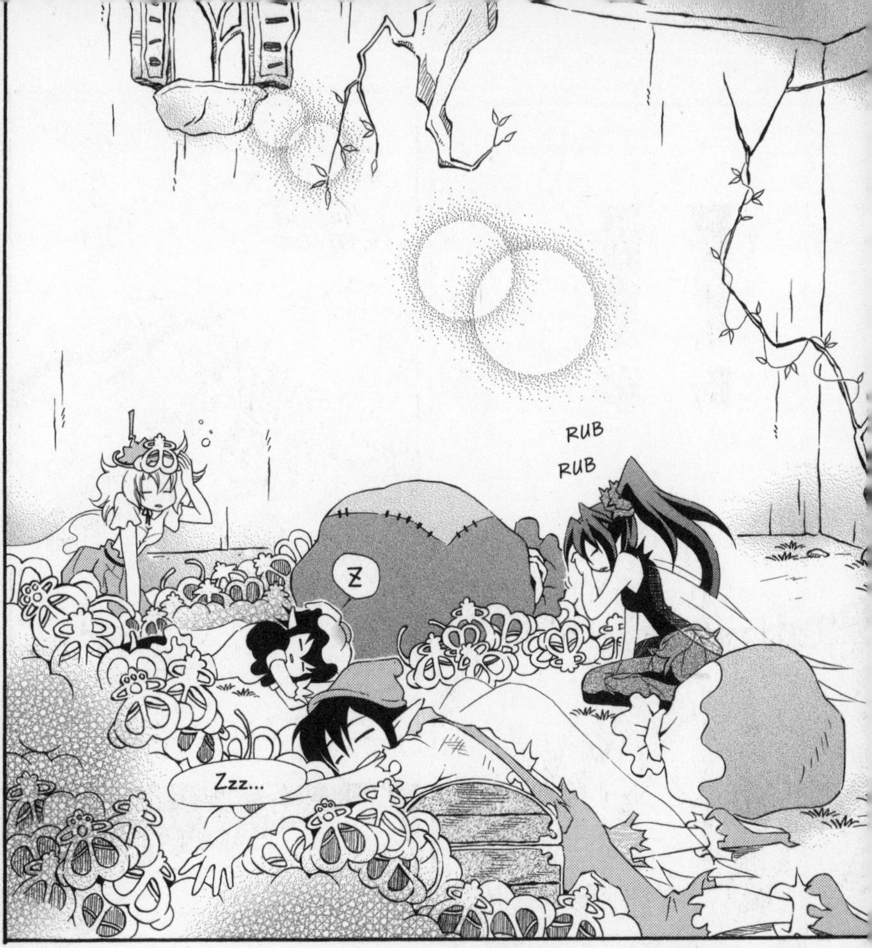
RUB
RUB
Z
Zzz...

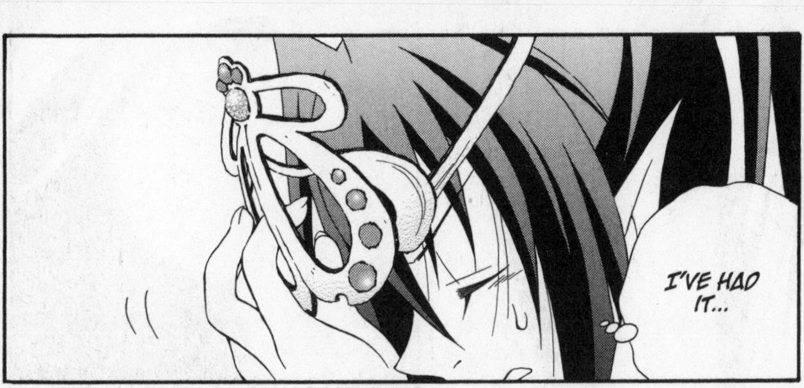
I'VE HAD IT...

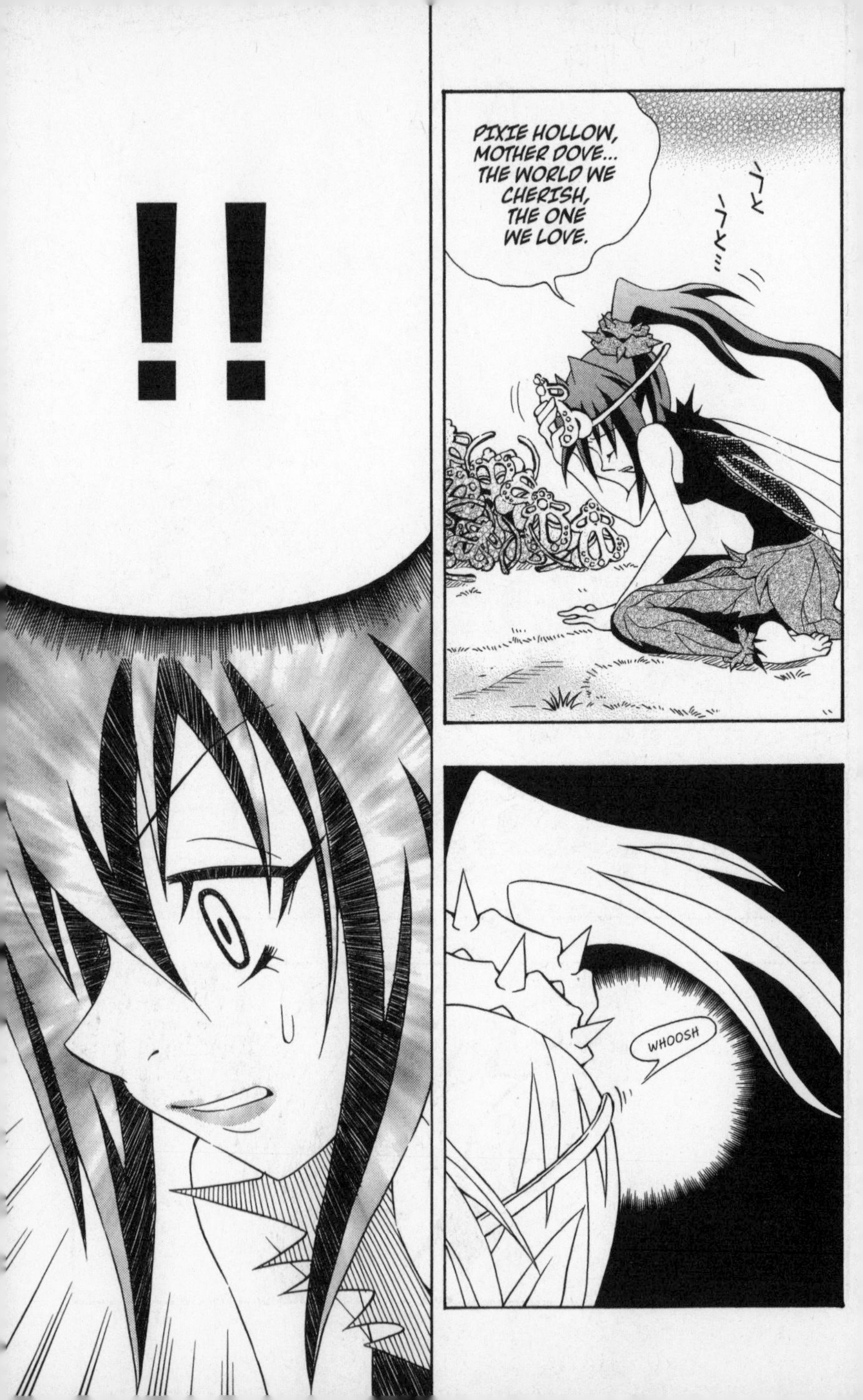
PIXIE HOLLOW, MOTHER DOVE... THE WORLD WE CHERISH, THE ONE WE LOVE.
WHOOSH
!!

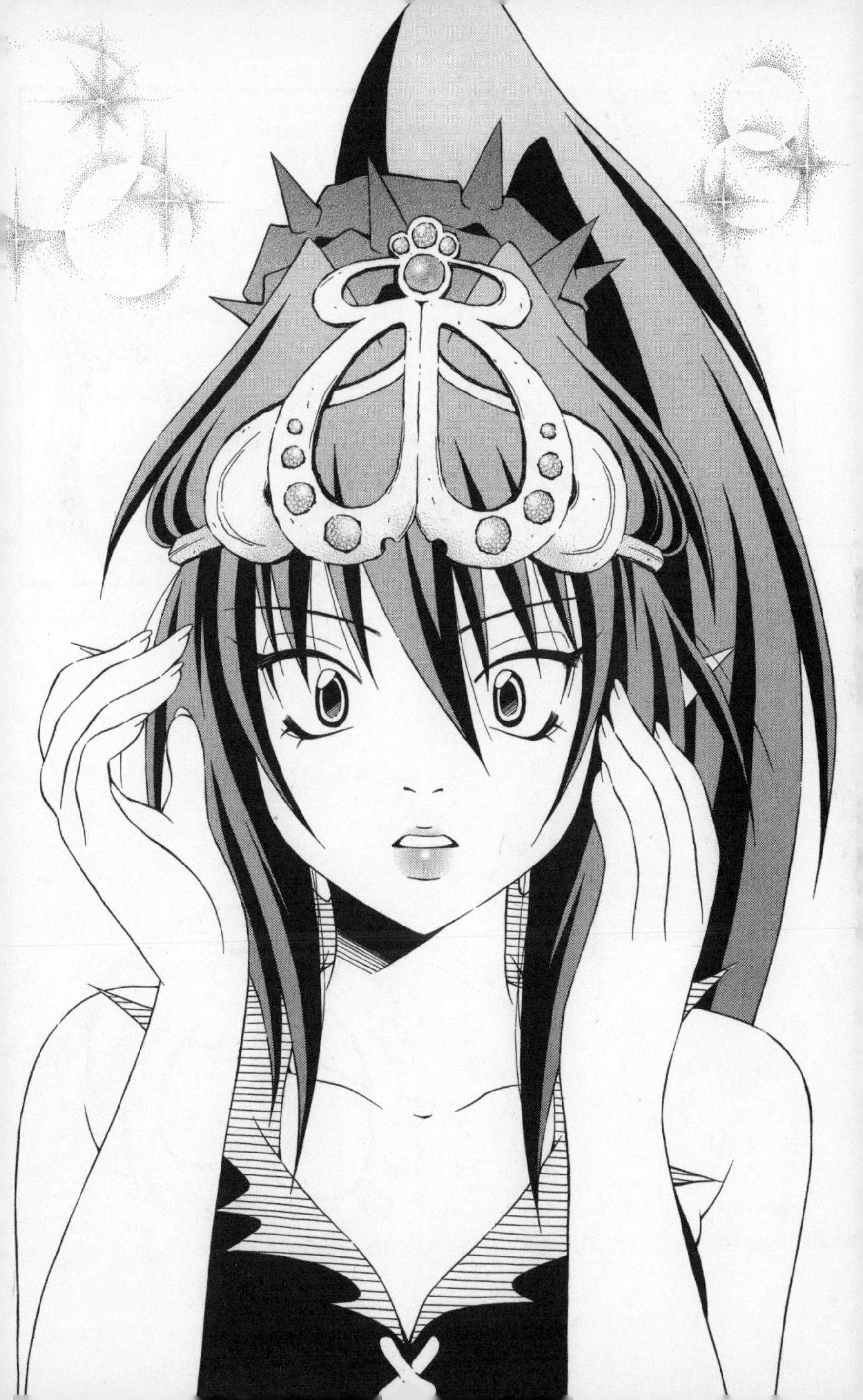

READ THIS WAY

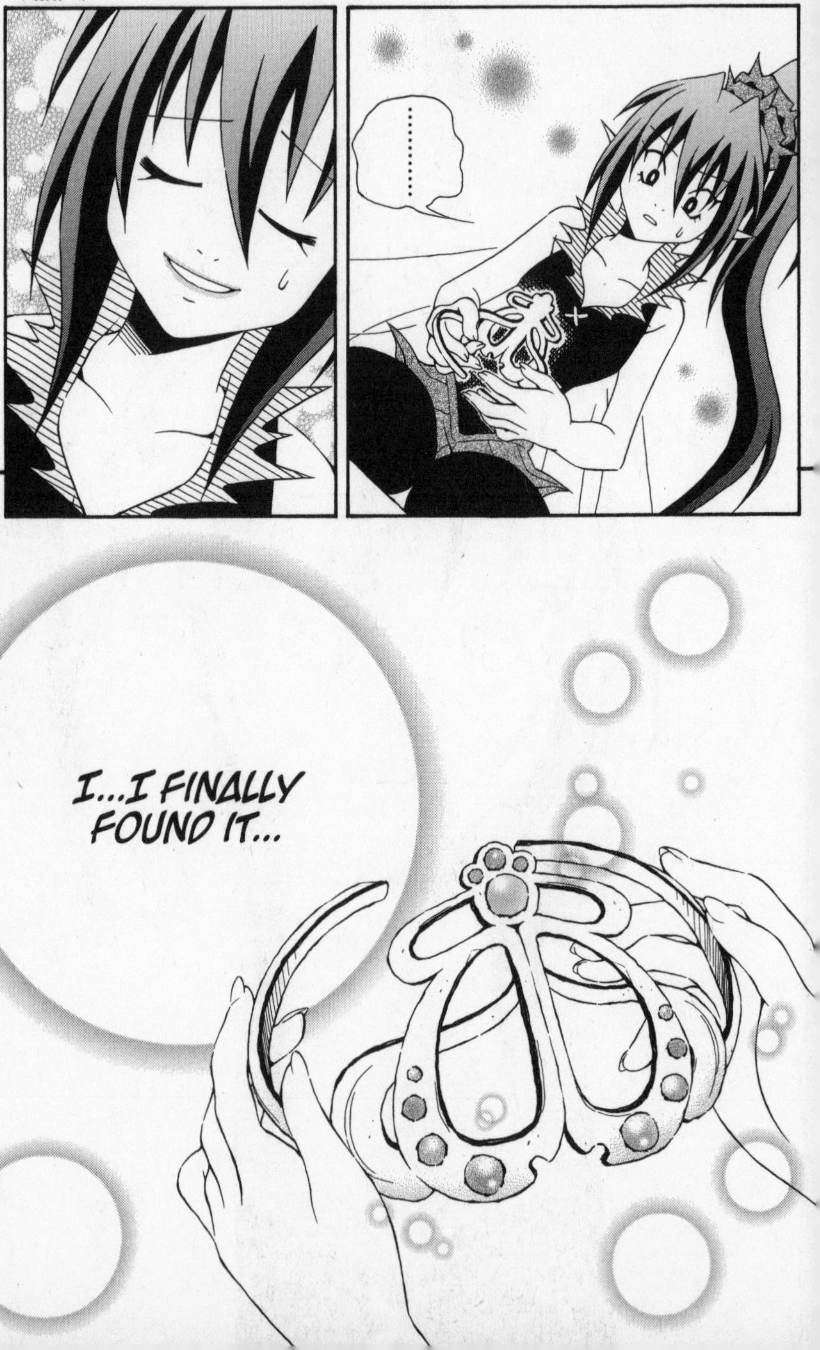
......
I...I FINALLY FOUND IT...

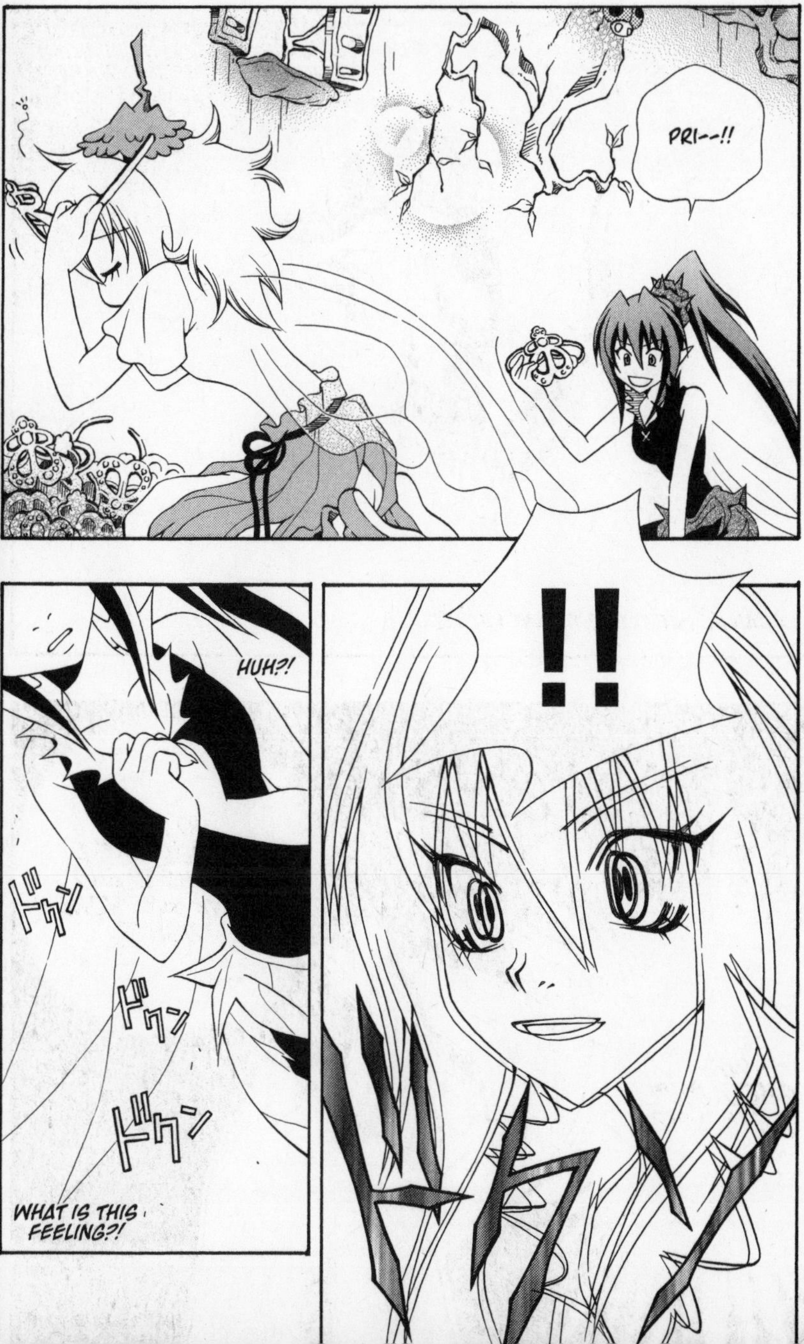
PRI--!!
!!
HUH?!
ドクン
ドクン
ドクン
WHAT IS THIS FEELING?!

READ THIS WAY

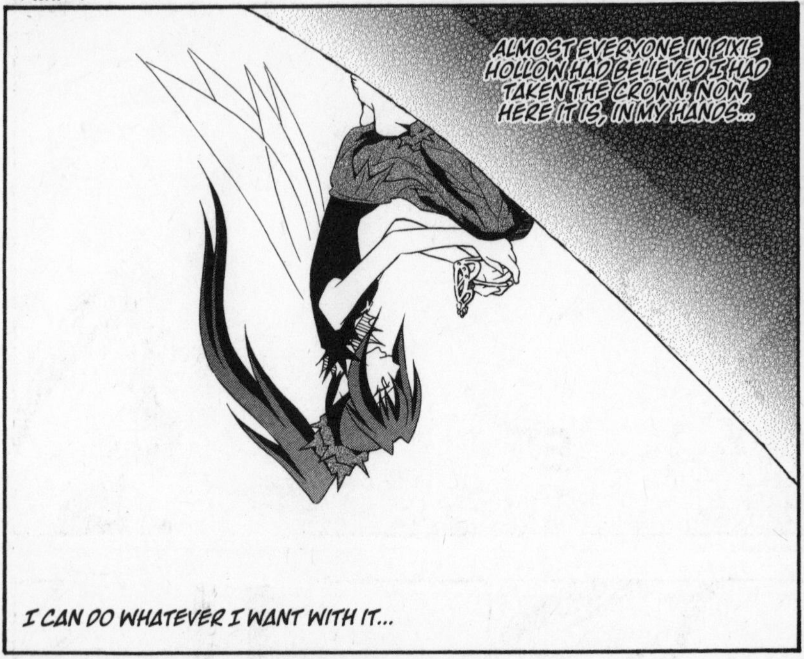
ALMOST EVERYONE IN PIXIE HOLLOW HAD BELIEVED I HAD TAKEN THE CROWN. NOW, HERE IT IS, IN MY HANDS...
I CAN DO WHATEVER I WANT WITH IT...

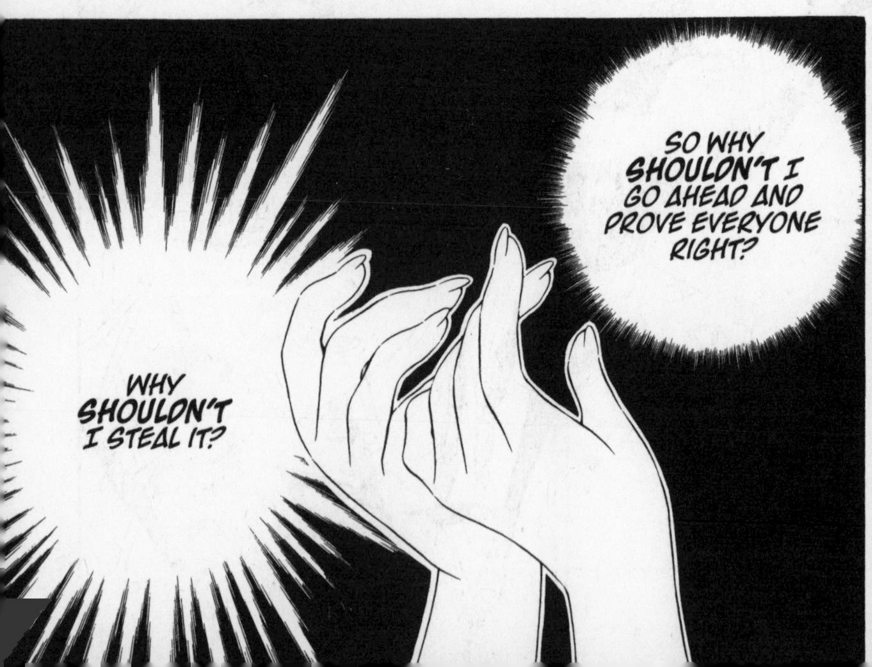
SO WHY **SHOULDN'T** I GO AHEAD AND PROVE EVERYONE RIGHT?
WHY **SHOULDN'T** I STEAL IT?

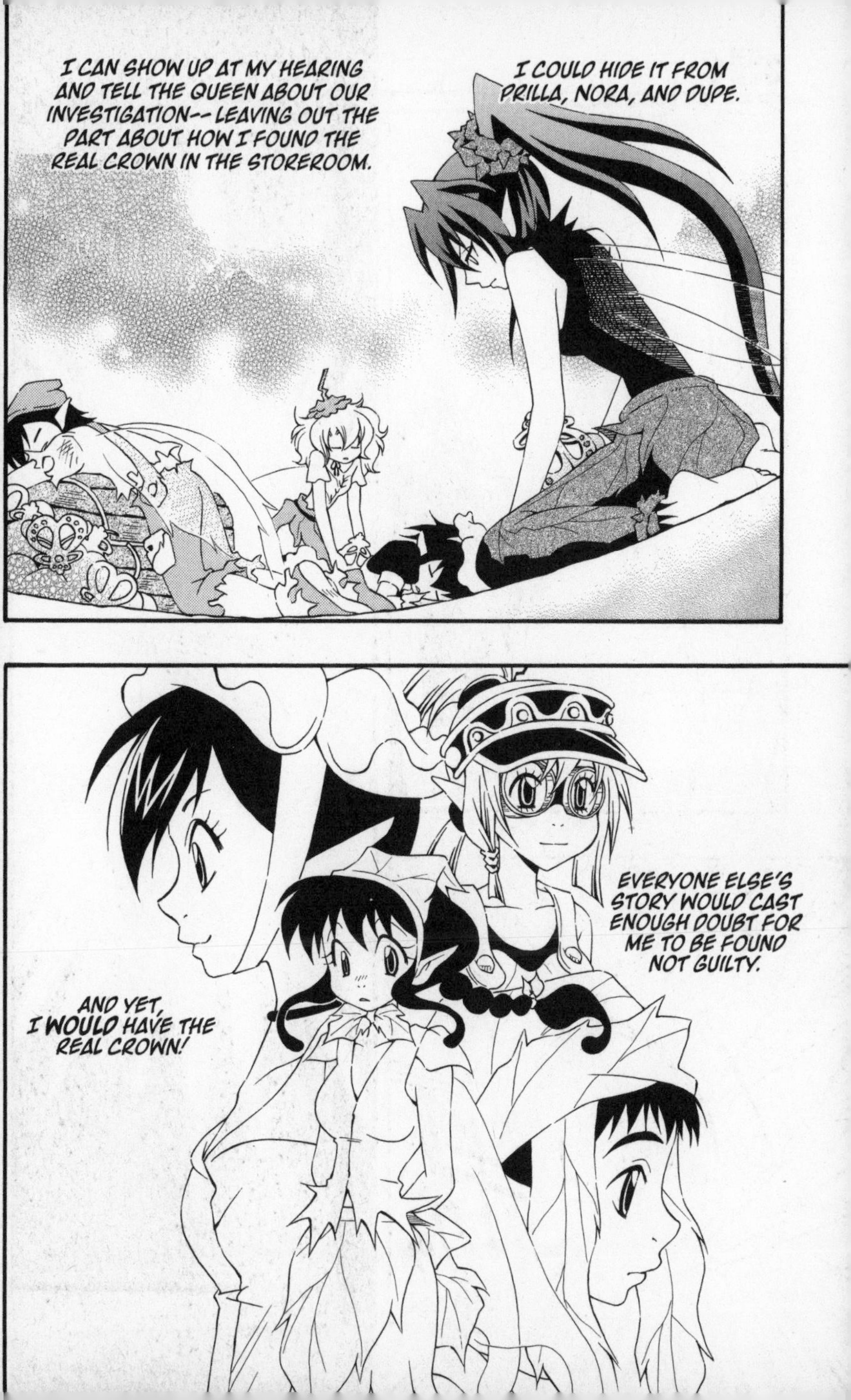
I COULD HIDE IT FROM PRILLA, NORA, AND DUPE.
I CAN SHOW UP AT MY HEARING AND TELL THE QUEEN ABOUT OUR INVESTIGATION-- LEAVING OUT THE PART ABOUT HOW I FOUND THE REAL CROWN IN THE STOREROOM.
EVERYONE ELSE'S STORY WOULD CAST ENOUGH DOUBT FOR ME TO BE FOUND NOT GUILTY.
AND YET, I WOULD HAVE THE REAL CROWN!

READ THIS WAY

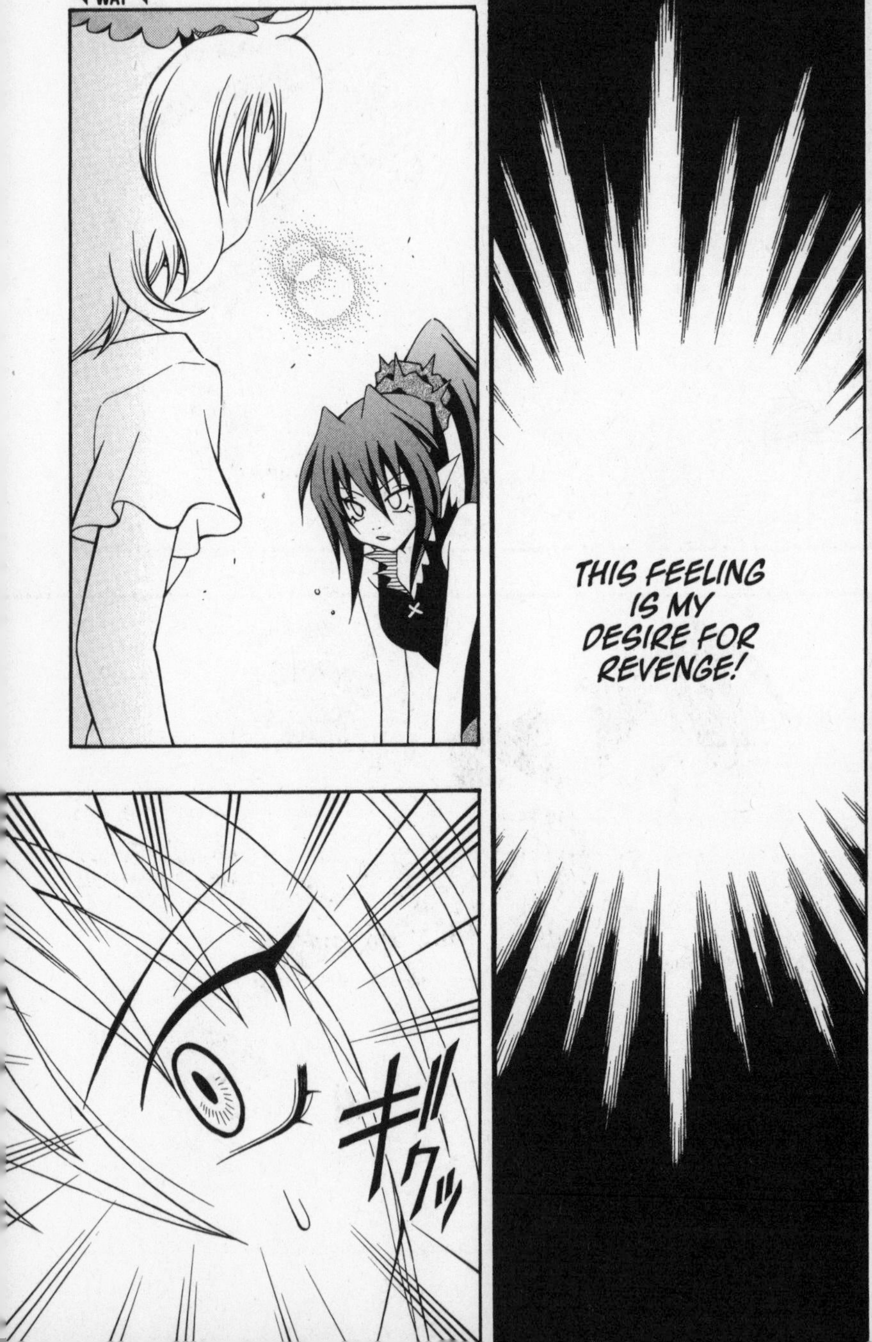
THIS FEELING IS MY DESIRE FOR REVENGE!
ギクッ

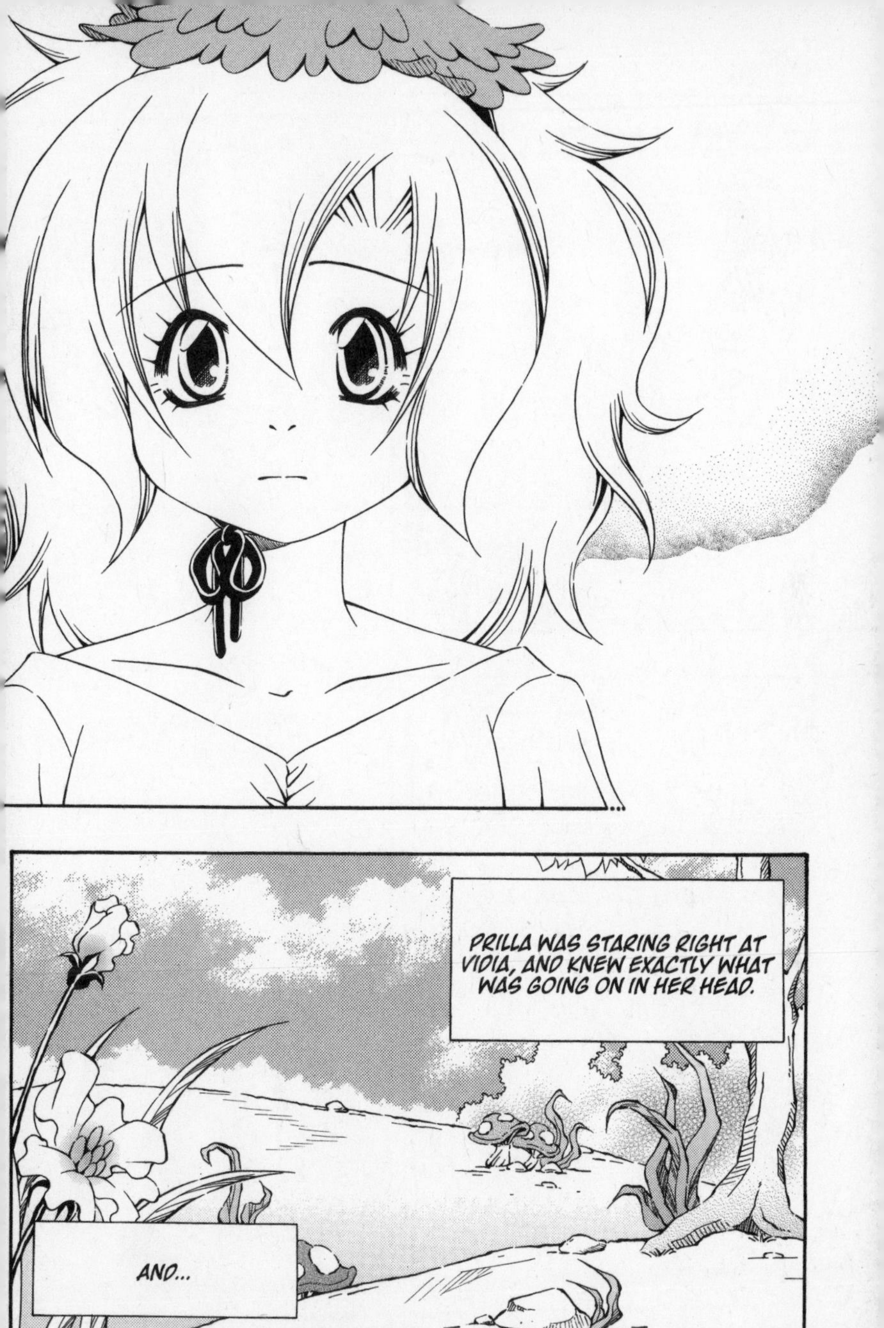
PRILLA WAS STARING RIGHT AT VIDIA, AND KNEW EXACTLY WHAT WAS GOING ON IN HER HEAD.
AND...

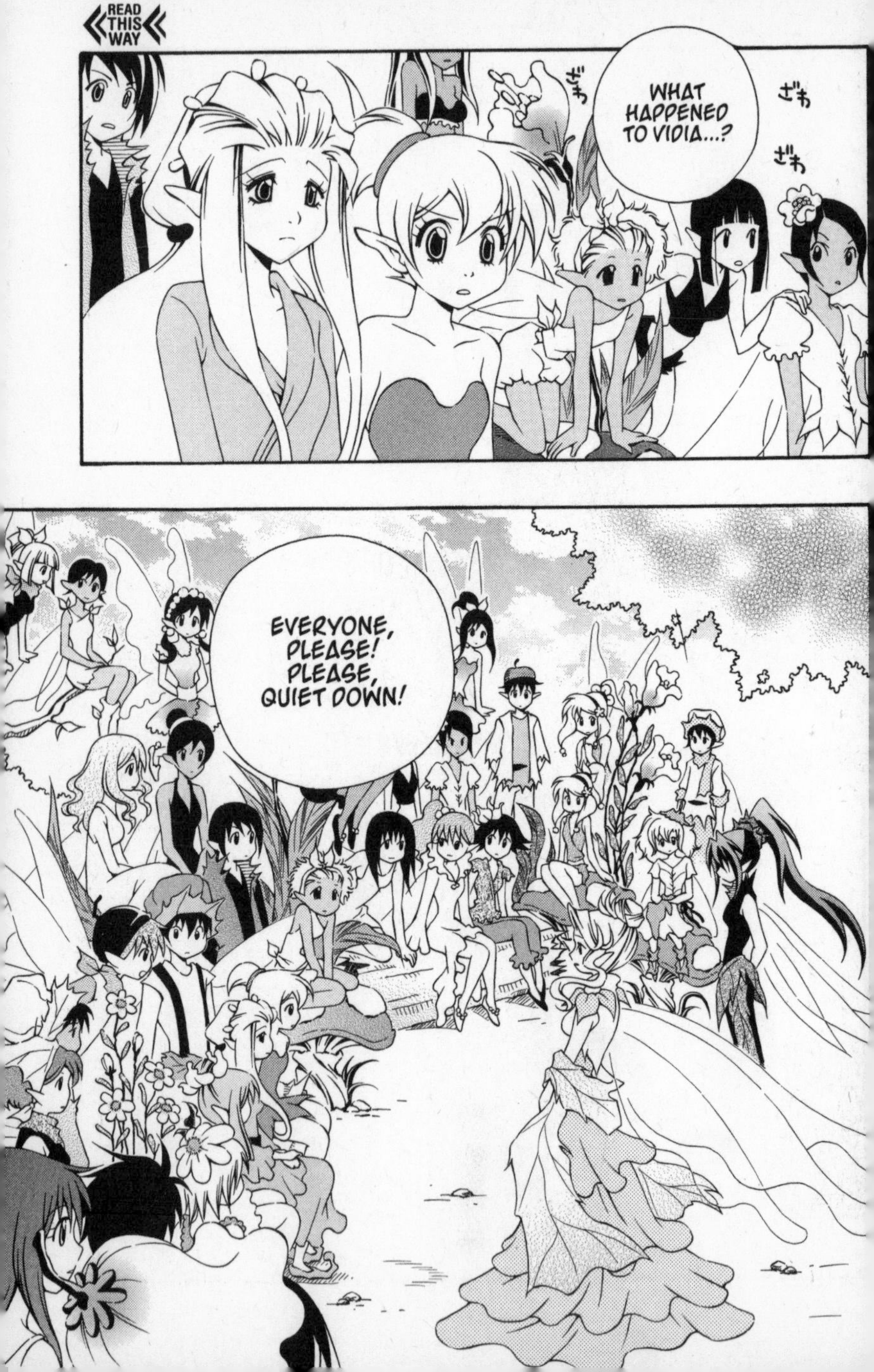
READ THIS WAY
ざわ
WHAT HAPPENED TO VIDIA...?
ざわ
ざわ
EVERYONE, PLEASE! PLEASE, QUIET DOWN!

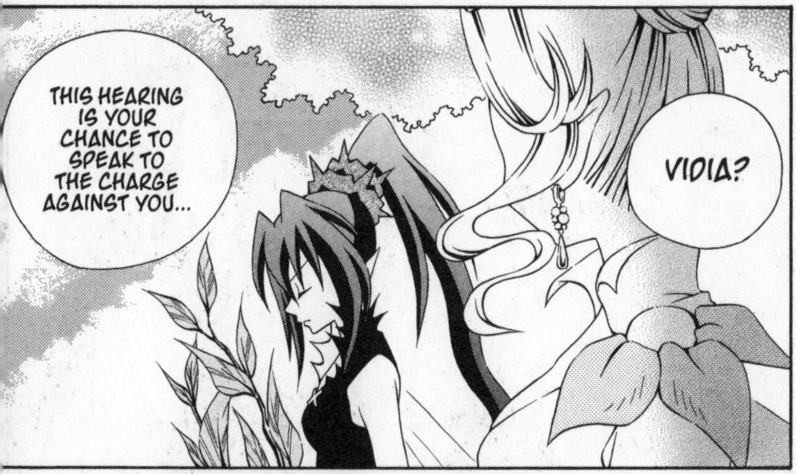
VIDIA?
THIS HEARING IS YOUR CHANCE TO SPEAK TO THE CHARGE AGAINST YOU...
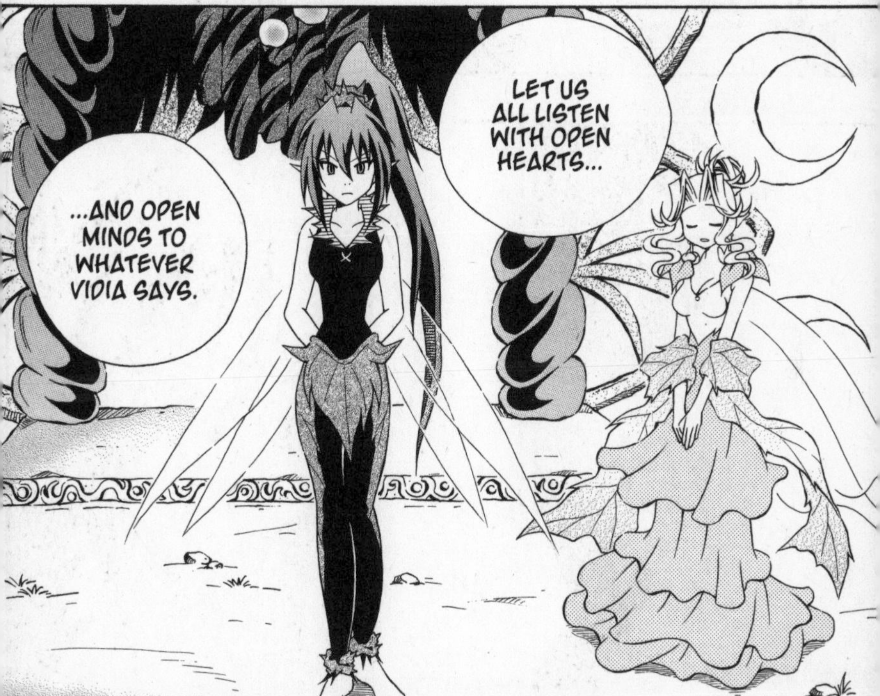
LET US ALL LISTEN WITH OPEN HEARTS...
...AND OPEN MINDS TO WHATEVER VIDIA SAYS.

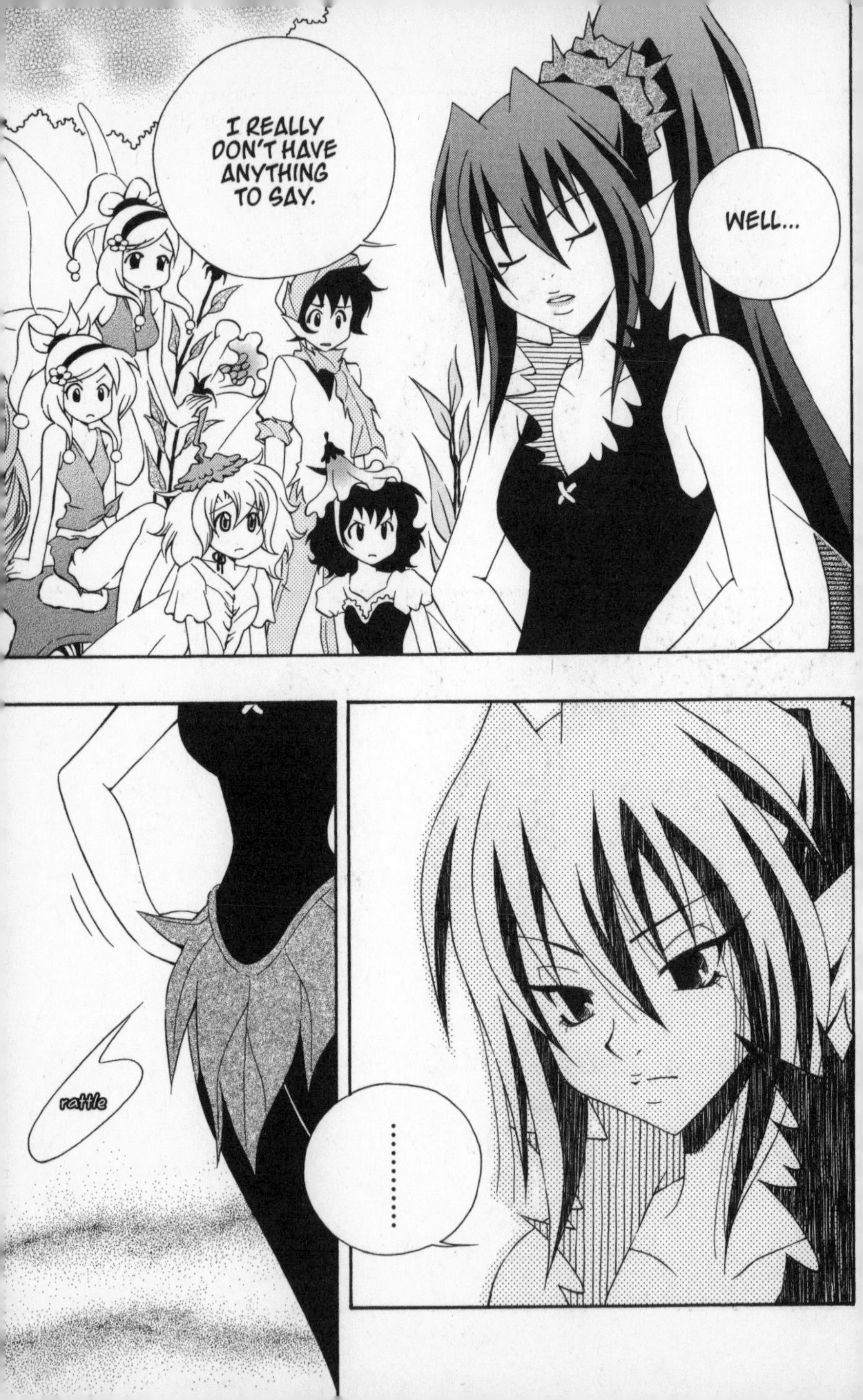
WELL...
I REALLY DON'T HAVE ANYTHING TO SAY.
....
rattle

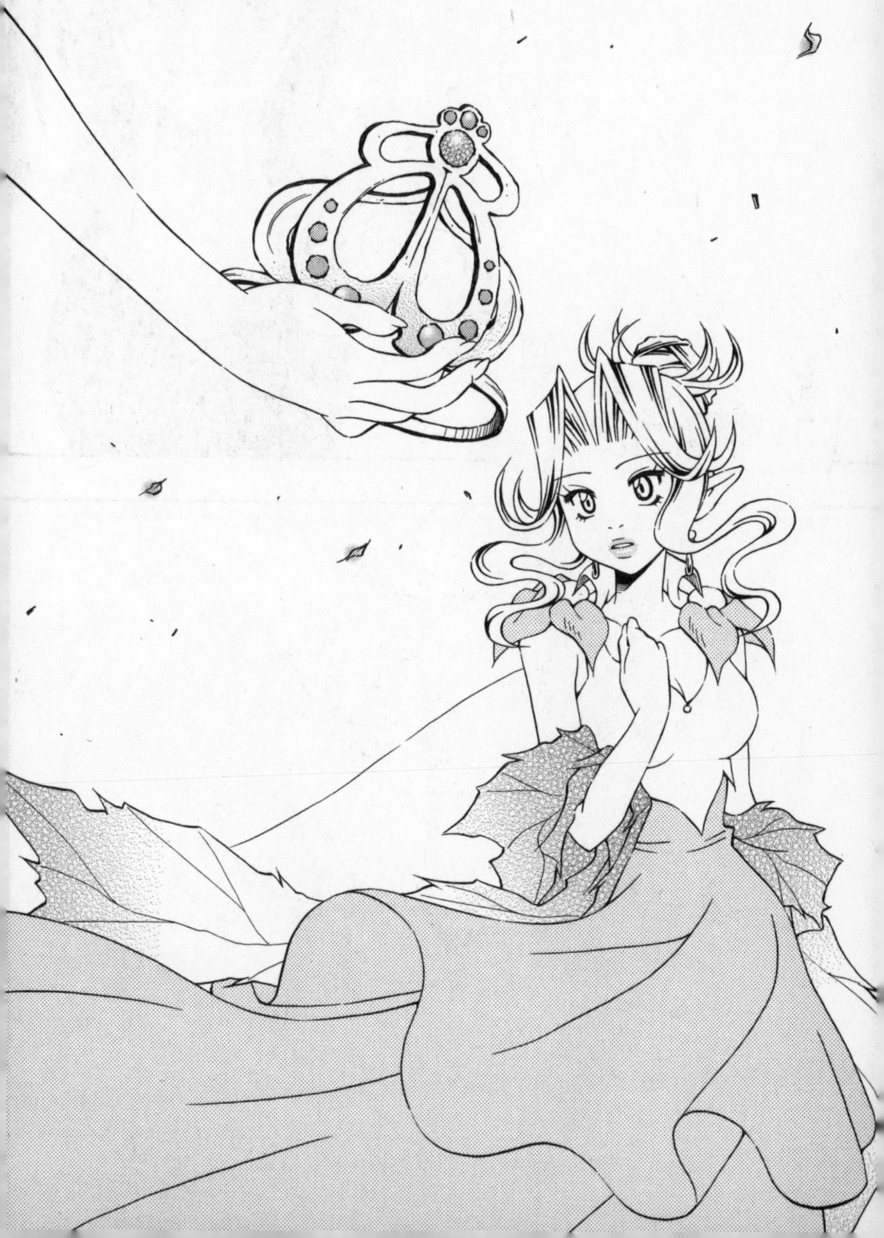

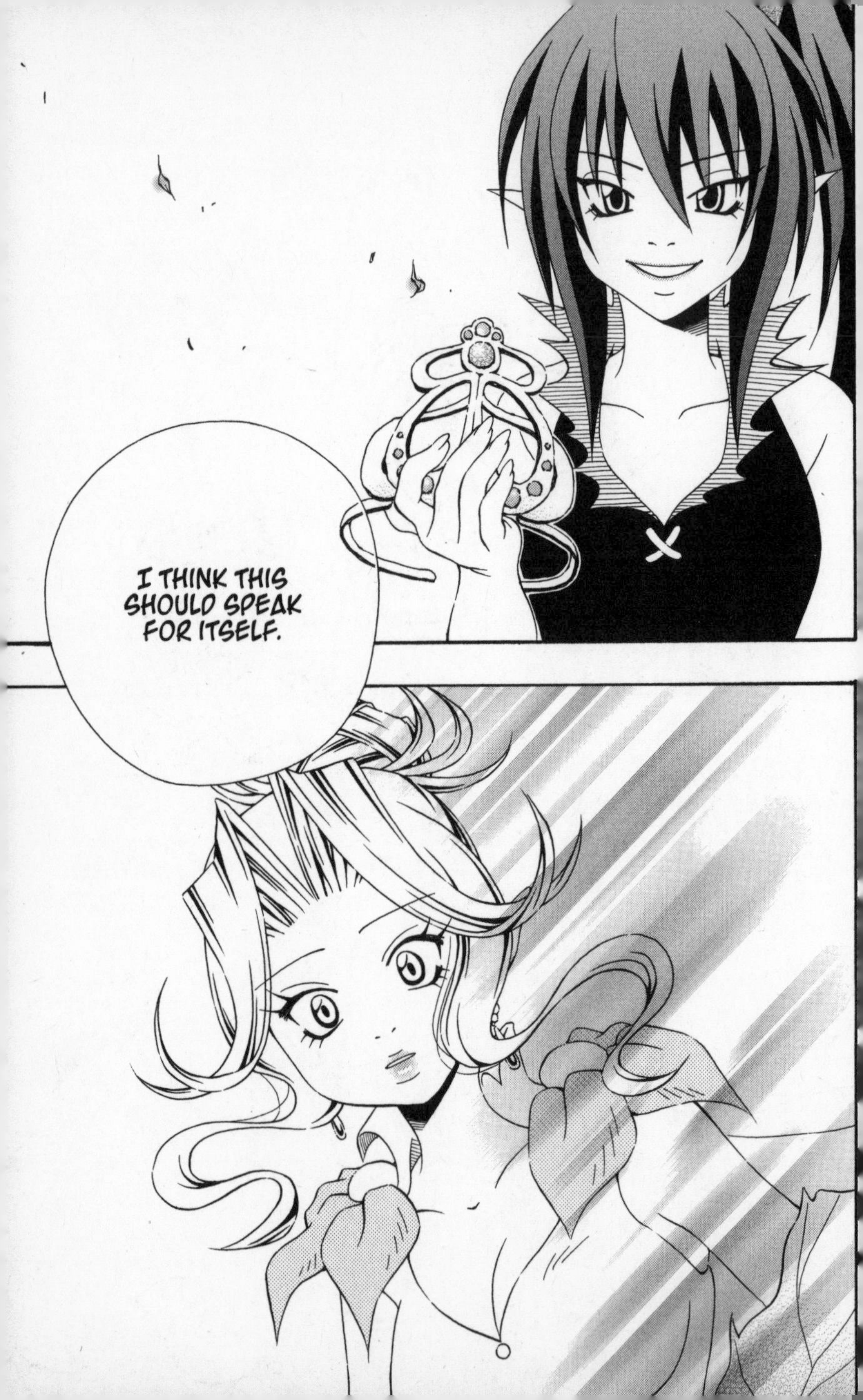
I THINK THIS SHOULD SPEAK FOR ITSELF.

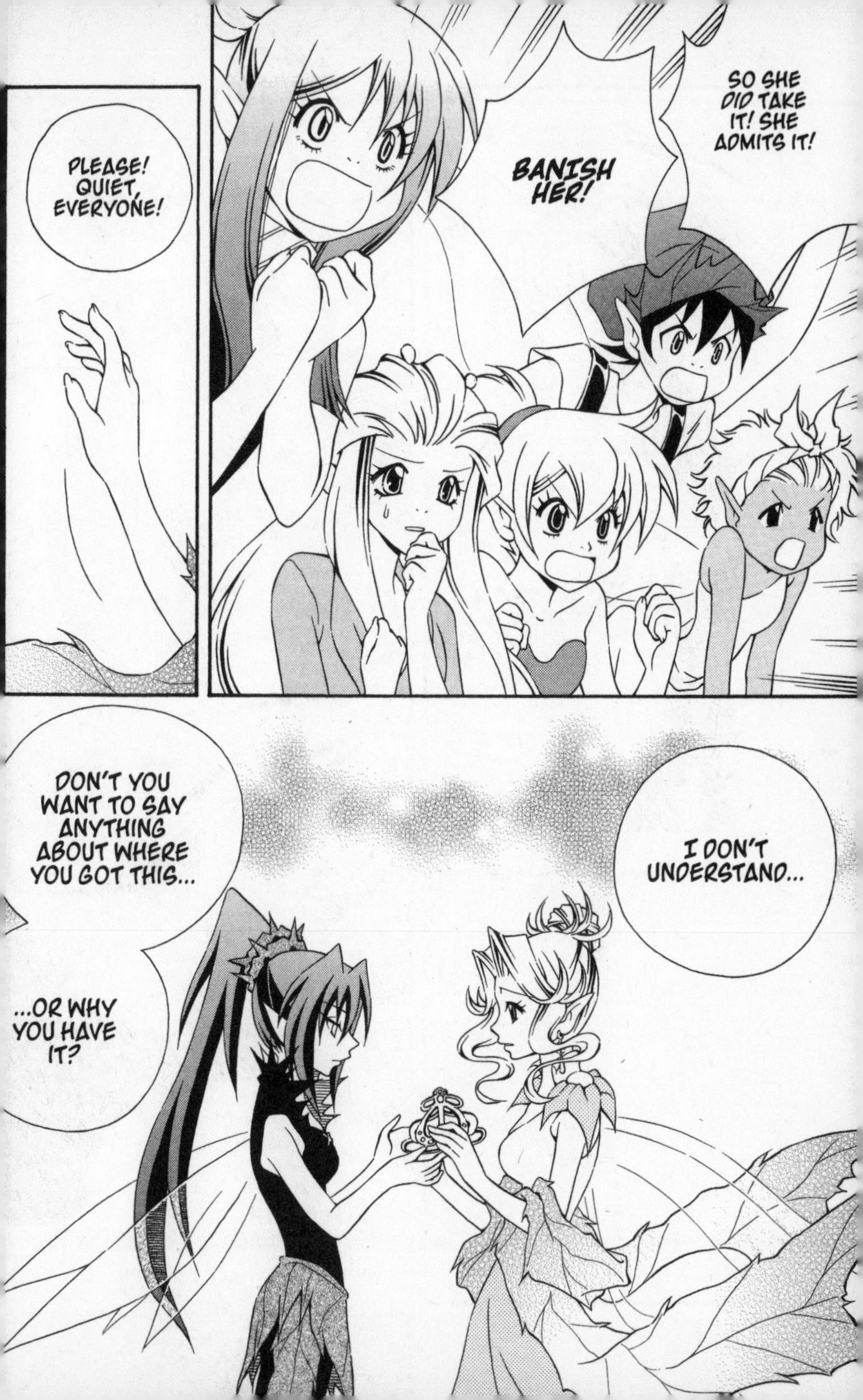
SO SHE DID TAKE IT! SHE ADMITS IT!
BANISH HER!
PLEASE! QUIET, EVERYONE!
DON'T YOU WANT TO SAY ANYTHING ABOUT WHERE YOU GOT THIS...
...OR WHY YOU HAVE IT?
I DON'T UNDERSTAND...

READ THIS WAY

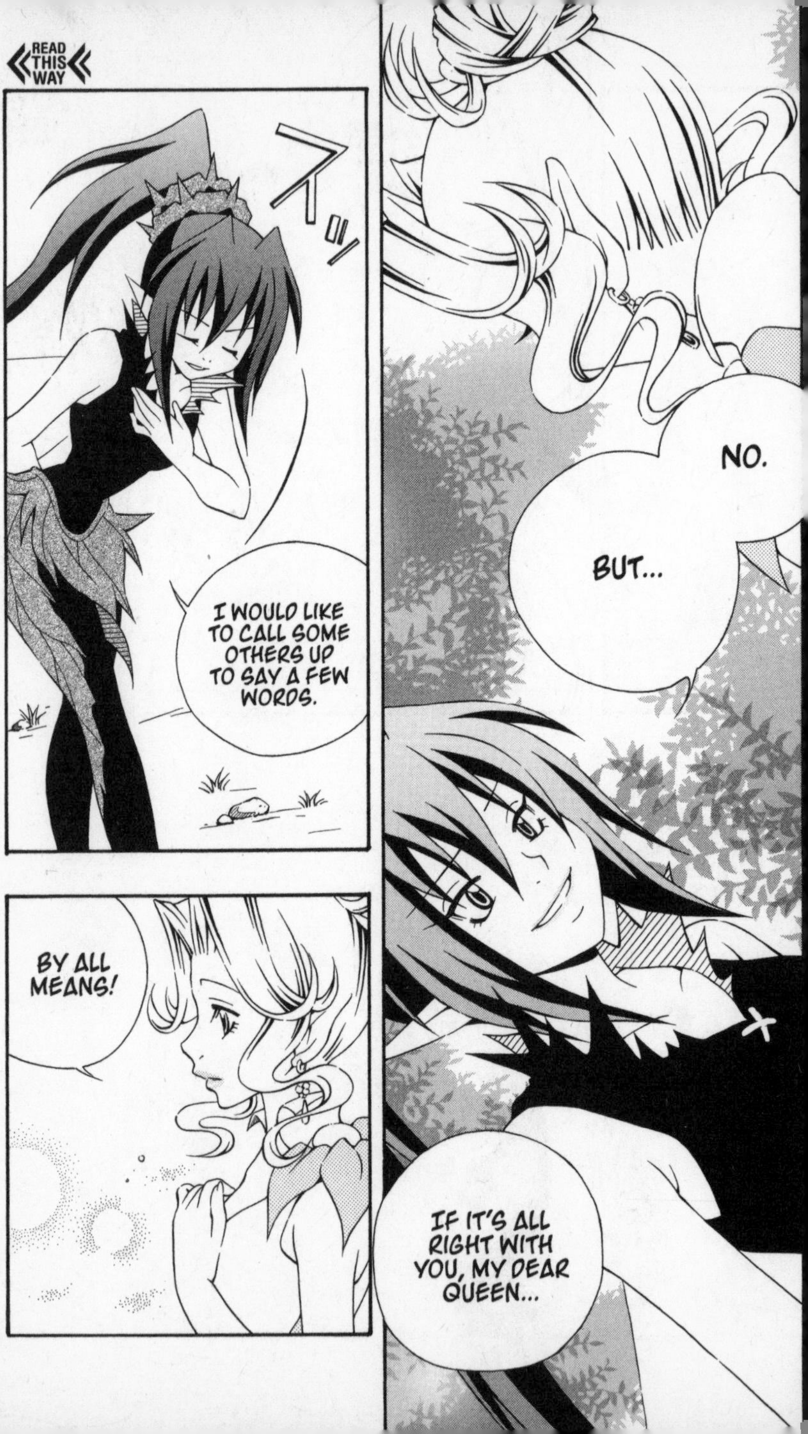

NO.
BUT...
IF IT'S ALL RIGHT WITH YOU, MY DEAR QUEEN...
スイッ
I WOULD LIKE TO CALL SOME OTHERS UP TO SAY A FEW WORDS.
BY ALL MEANS!

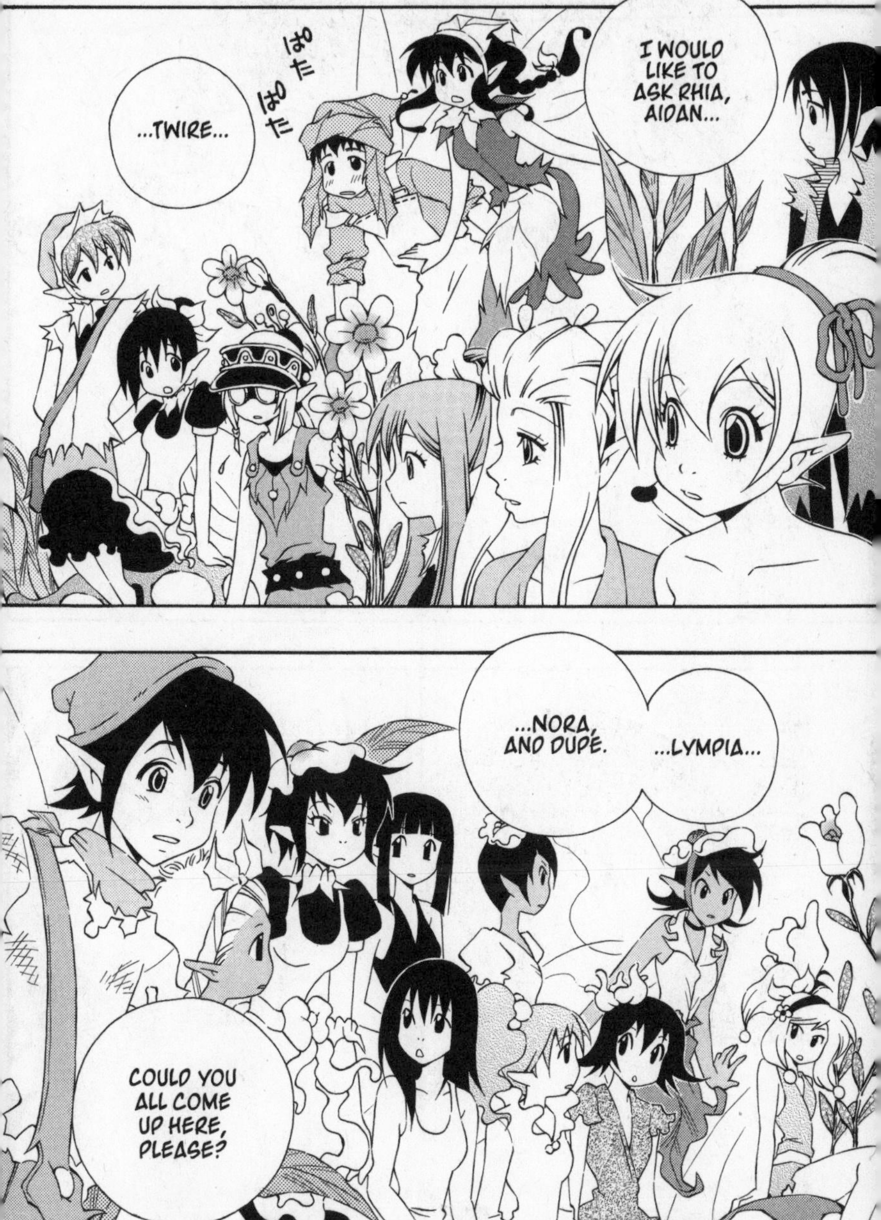
I WOULD LIKE TO ASK RHIA, AIDAN...
ぱた ぱた
...TWIRE...
...LYMPIA...
...NORA, AND DUPE.
COULD YOU ALL COME UP HERE, PLEASE?

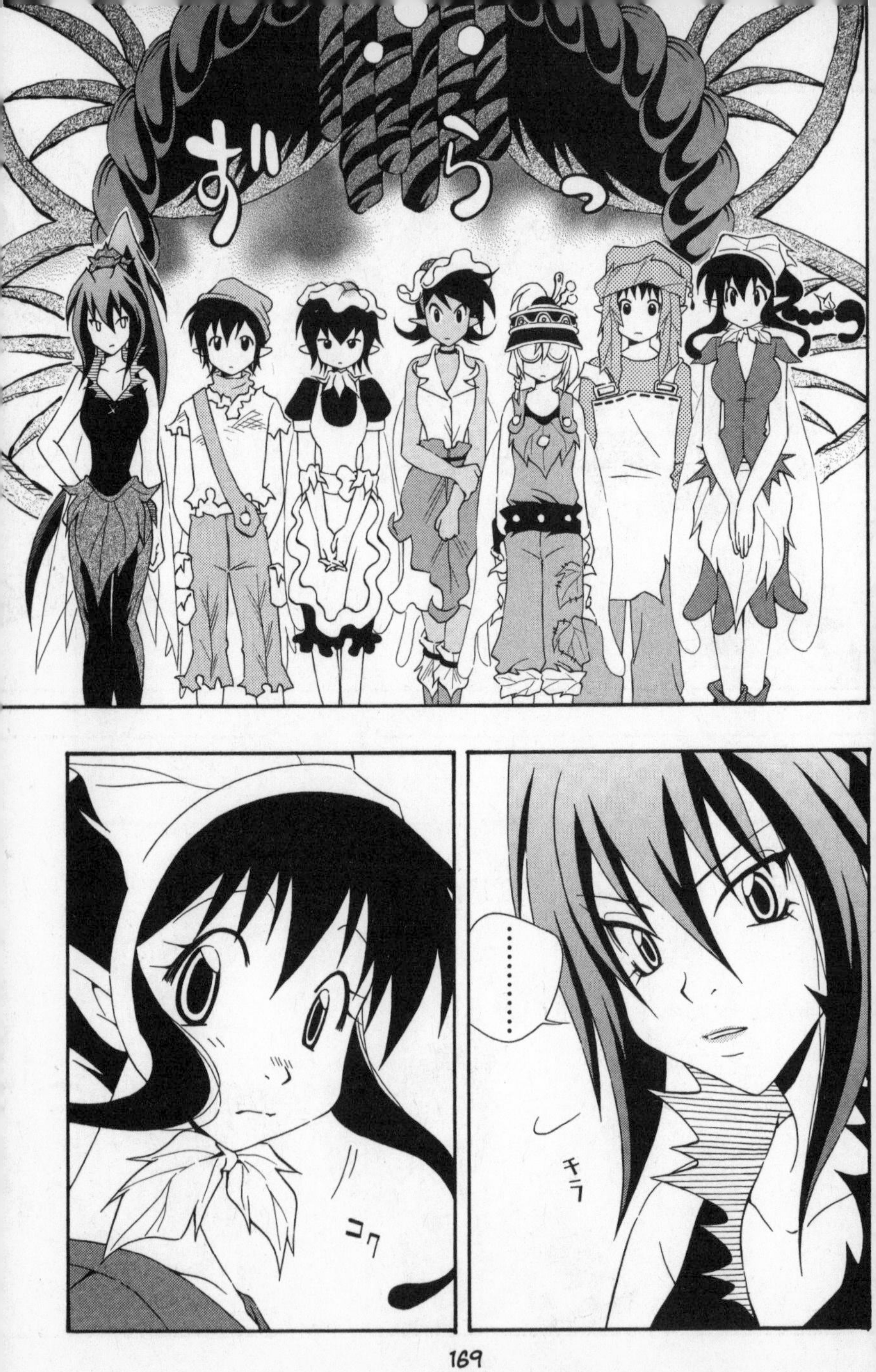
ずらっ
……
キラ
コク

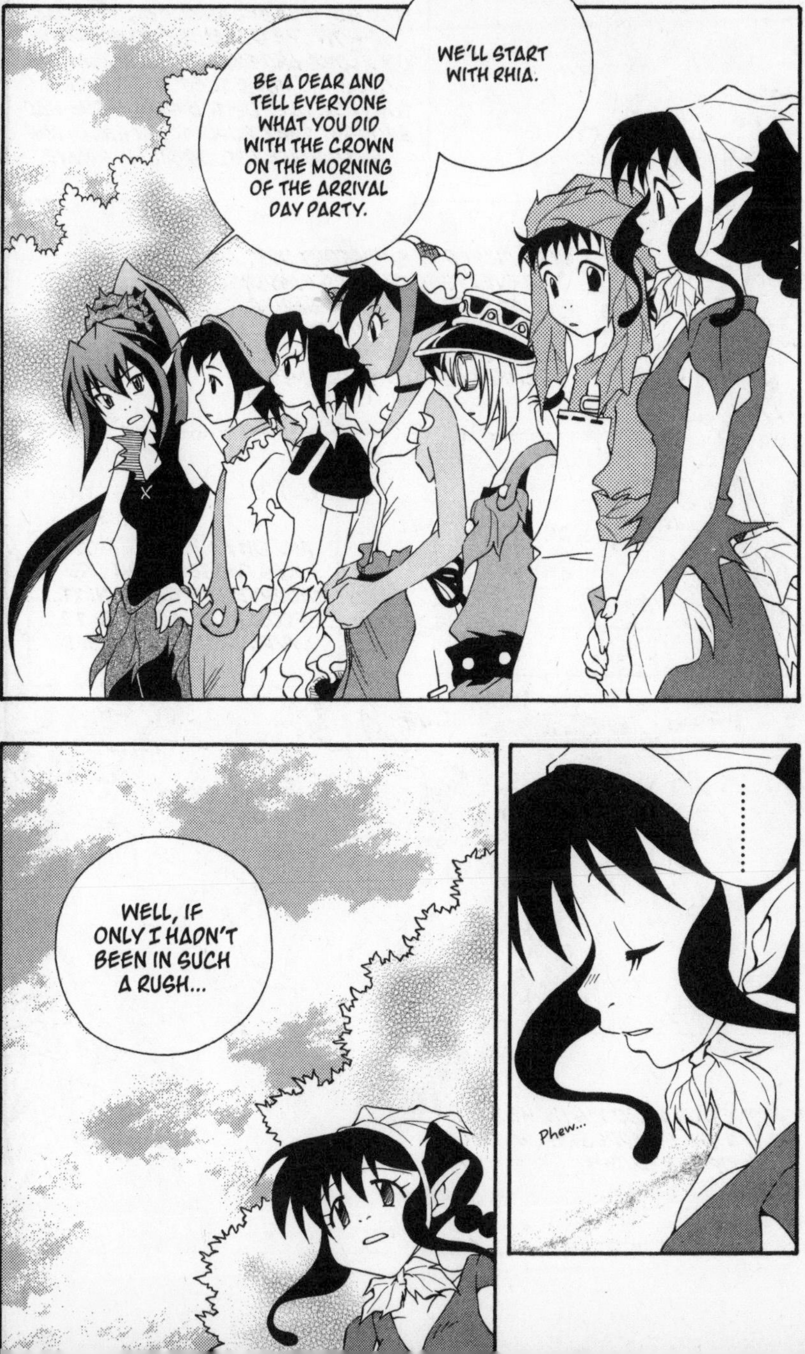
WE'LL START WITH RHIA.
BE A DEAR AND TELL EVERYONE WHAT YOU DID WITH THE CROWN ON THE MORNING OF THE ARRIVAL DAY PARTY.
....
Phew...
WELL, IF ONLY I HADN'T BEEN IN SUCH A RUSH...

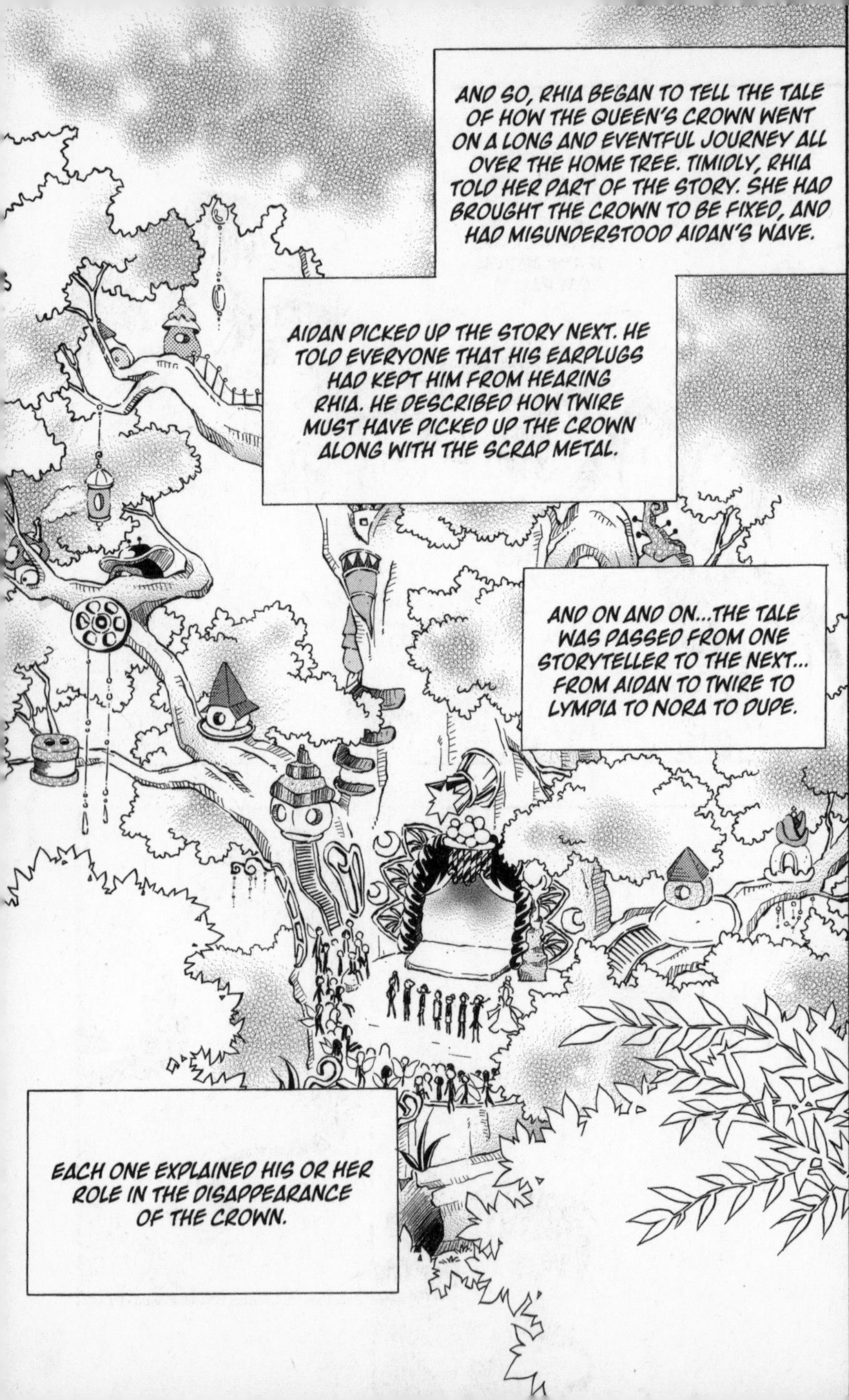
AND SO, RHIA BEGAN TO TELL THE TALE OF HOW THE QUEEN'S CROWN WENT ON A LONG AND EVENTFUL JOURNEY ALL OVER THE HOME TREE. TIMIDLY, RHIA TOLD HER PART OF THE STORY. SHE HAD BROUGHT THE CROWN TO BE FIXED, AND HAD MISUNDERSTOOD AIDAN'S WAVE.
AIDAN PICKED UP THE STORY NEXT. HE TOLD EVERYONE THAT HIS EARPLUGS HAD KEPT HIM FROM HEARING RHIA. HE DESCRIBED HOW TWIRE MUST HAVE PICKED UP THE CROWN ALONG WITH THE SCRAP METAL.
AND ON AND ON...THE TALE WAS PASSED FROM ONE STORYTELLER TO THE NEXT... FROM AIDAN TO TWIRE TO LYMPIA TO NORA TO DUPE.
EACH ONE EXPLAINED HIS OR HER ROLE IN THE DISAPPEARANCE OF THE CROWN.

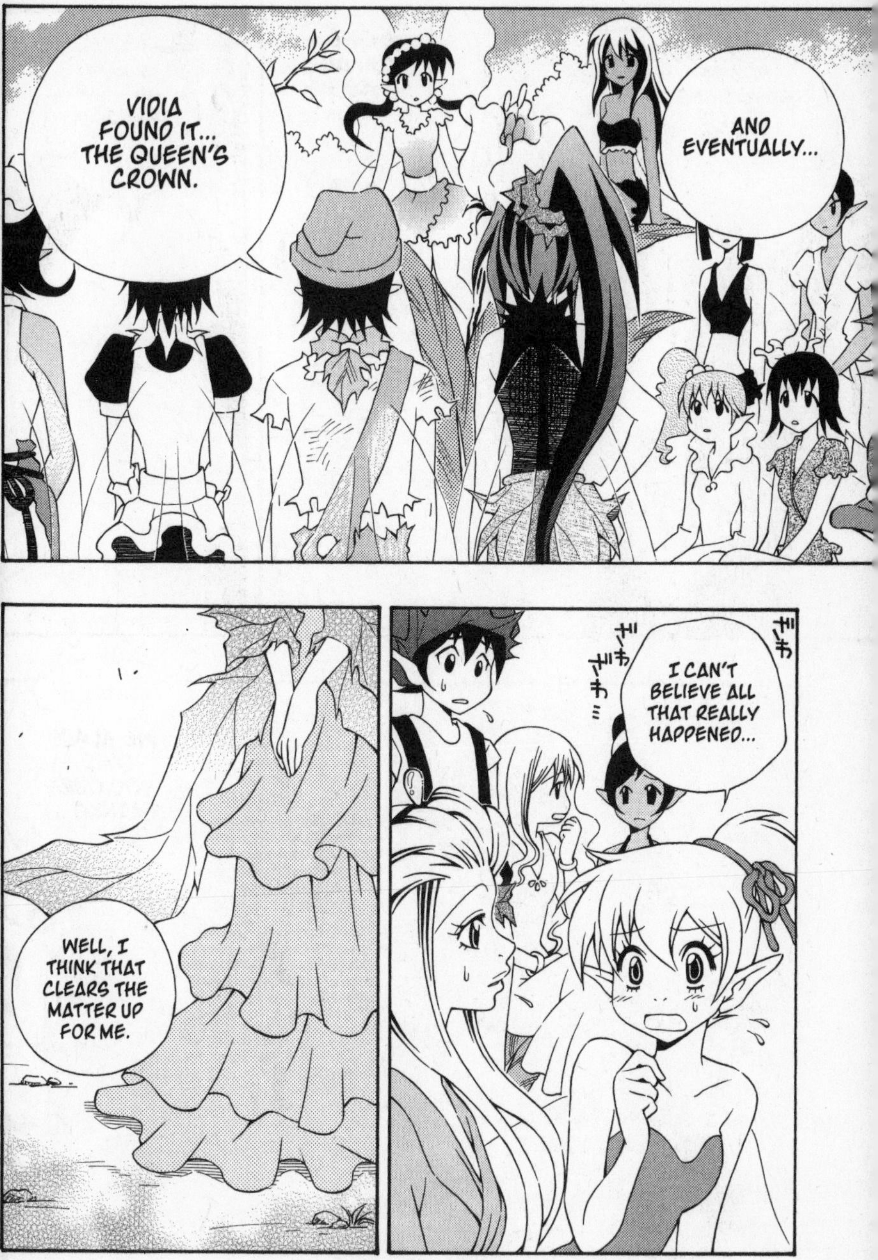
AND EVENTUALLY...
VIDIA FOUND IT... THE QUEEN'S CROWN.
ざわ ざわ ざわ
I CAN'T BELIEVE ALL THAT REALLY HAPPENED...
WELL, I THINK THAT CLEARS THE MATTER UP FOR ME.

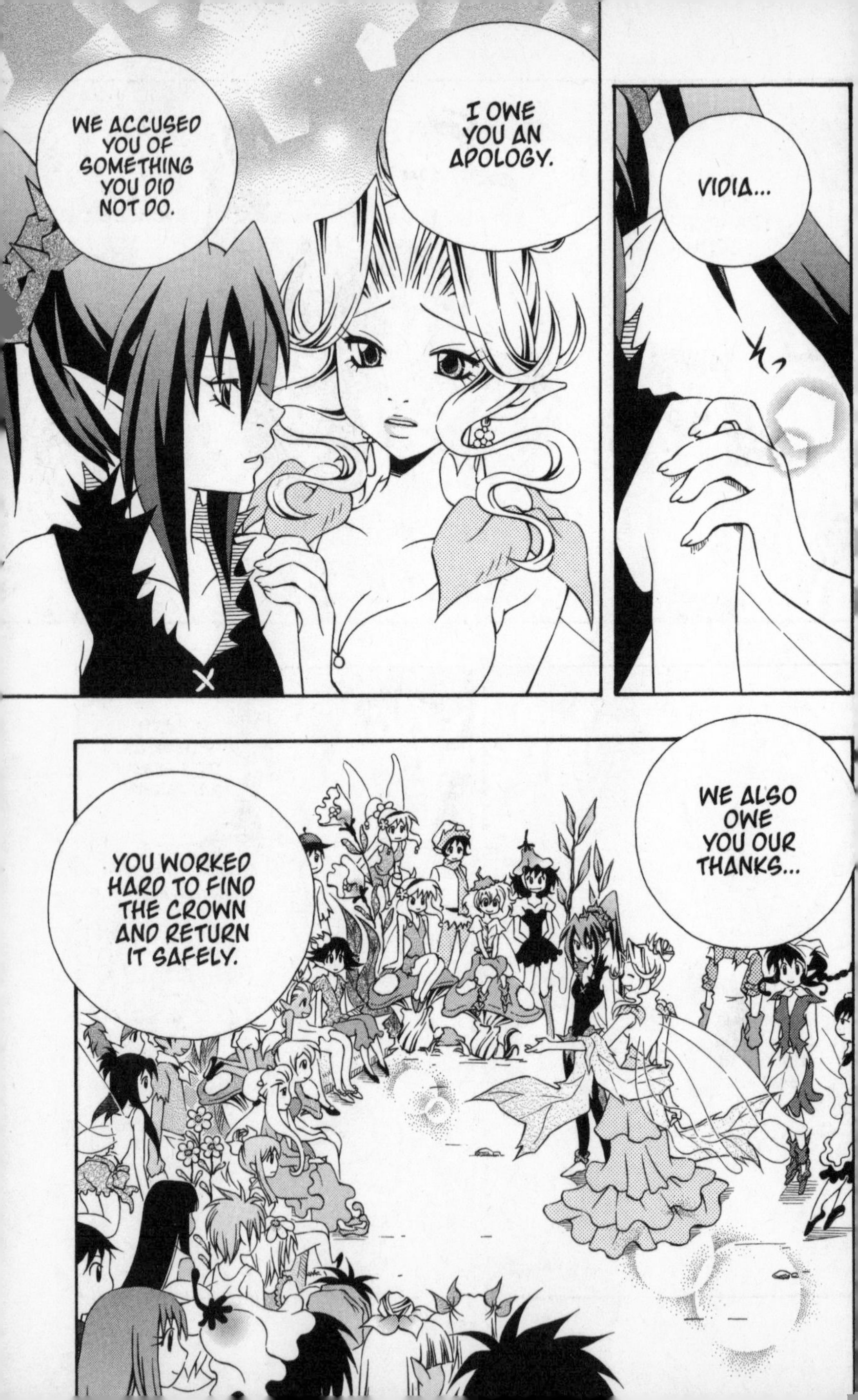
VIDIA...
I OWE YOU AN APOLOGY.
WE ACCUSED YOU OF SOMETHING YOU DID NOT DO.
WE ALSO OWE YOU OUR THANKS...
YOU WORKED HARD TO FIND THE CROWN AND RETURN IT SAFELY.

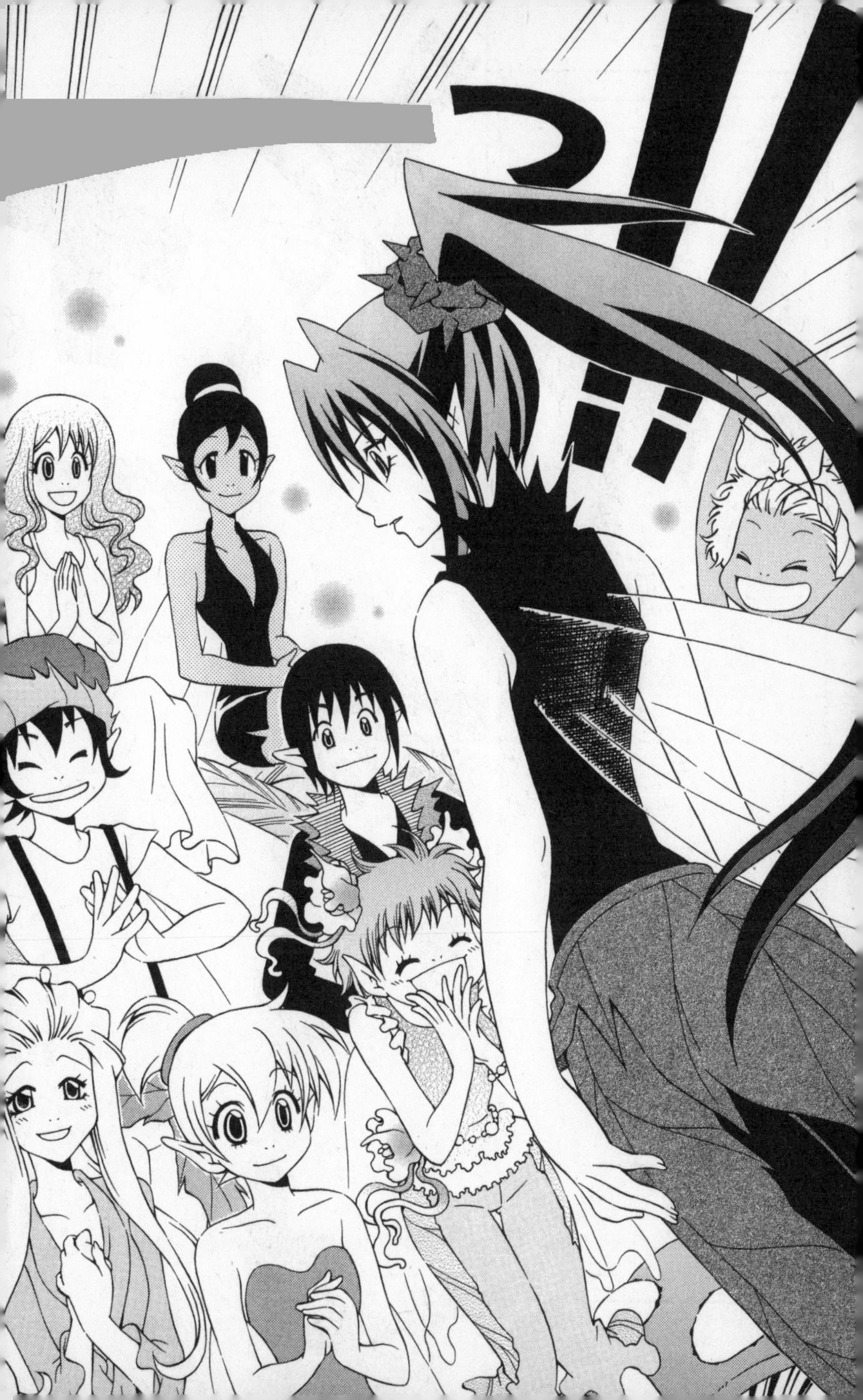

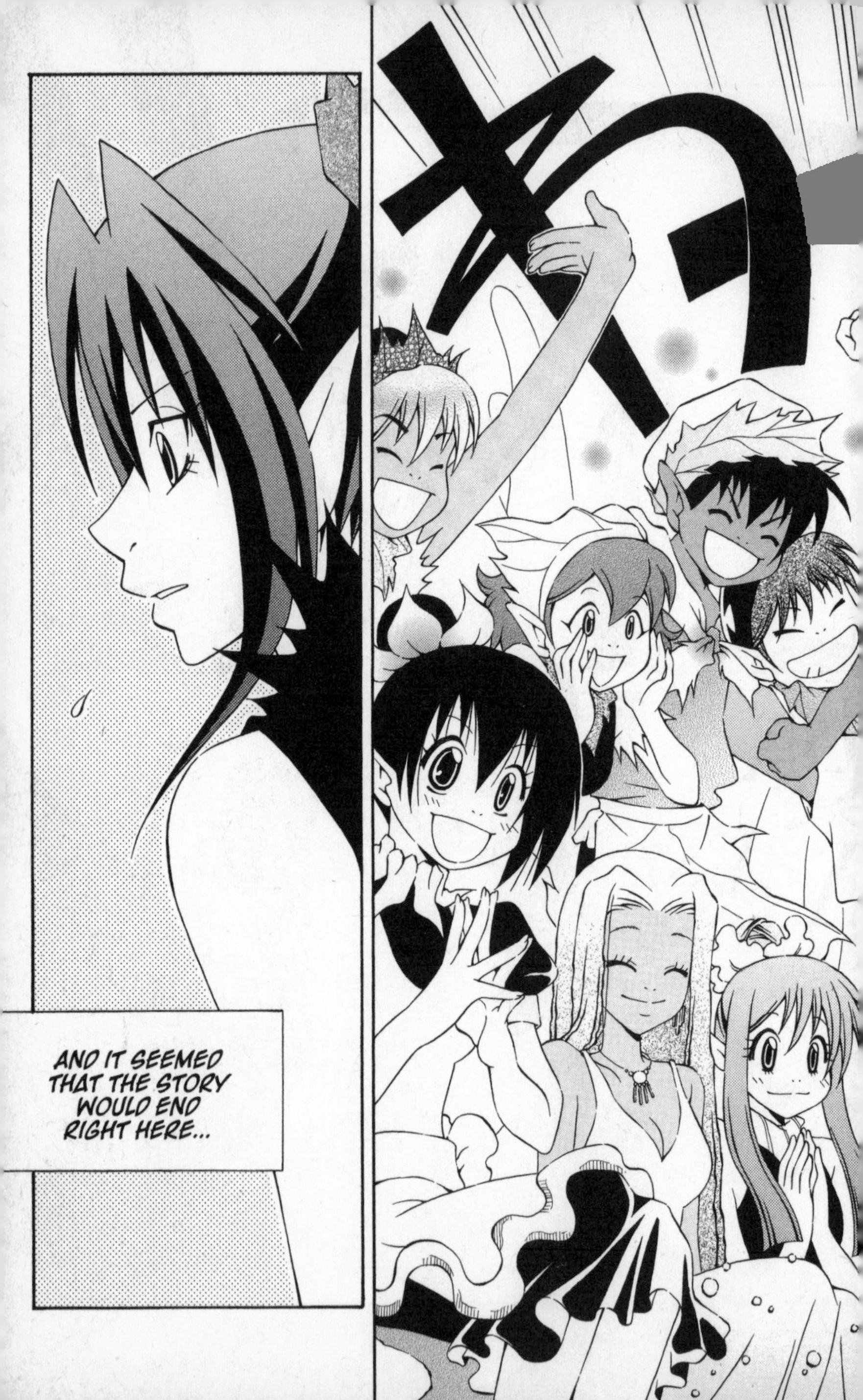
AND IT SEEMED THAT THE STORY WOULD END RIGHT HERE...

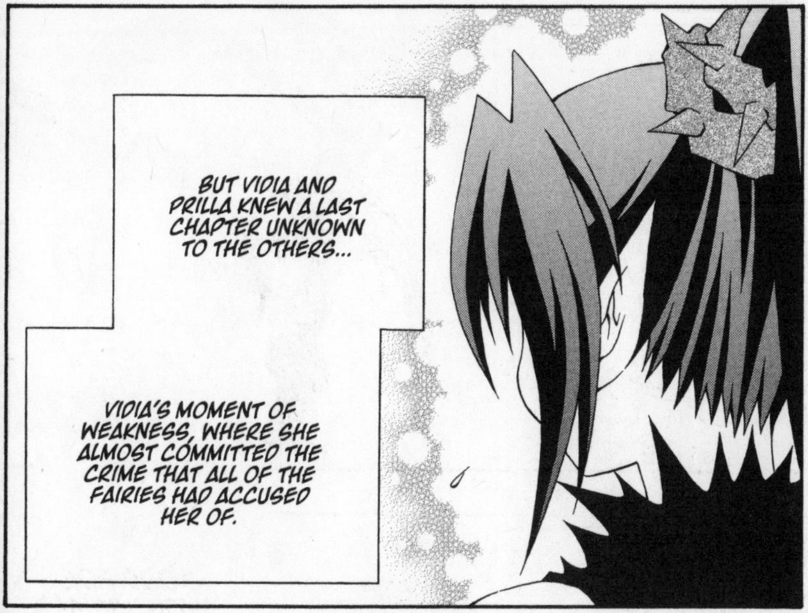
BUT VIDIA AND PRILLA KNEW A LAST CHAPTER UNKNOWN TO THE OTHERS...
VIDIA'S MOMENT OF WEAKNESS, WHERE SHE ALMOST COMMITTED THE CRIME THAT ALL OF THE FAIRIES HAD ACCUSED HER OF.
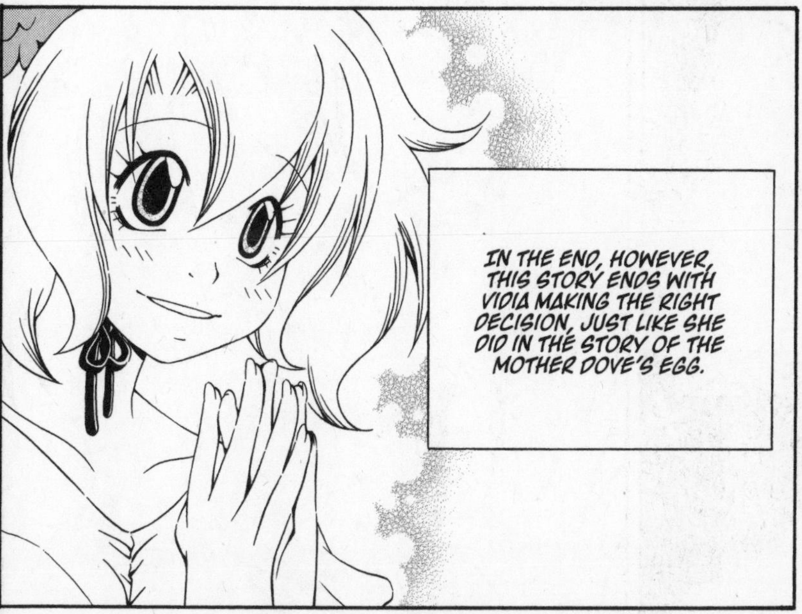
IN THE END, HOWEVER, THIS STORY ENDS WITH VIDIA MAKING THE RIGHT DECISION, JUST LIKE SHE DID IN THE STORY OF THE MOTHER DOVE'S EGG.

READ THIS WAY

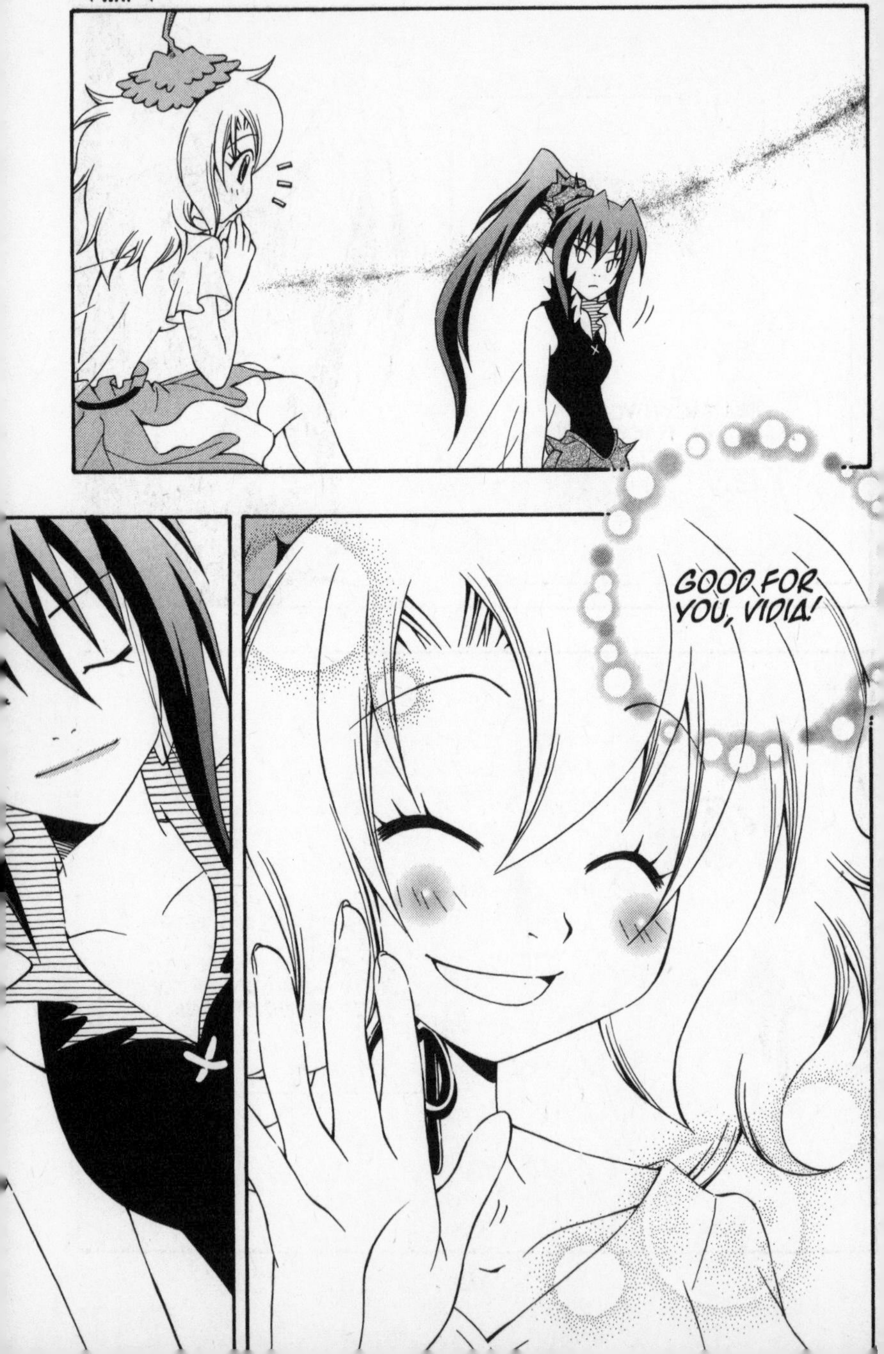
GOOD FOR YOU, VIDIA!

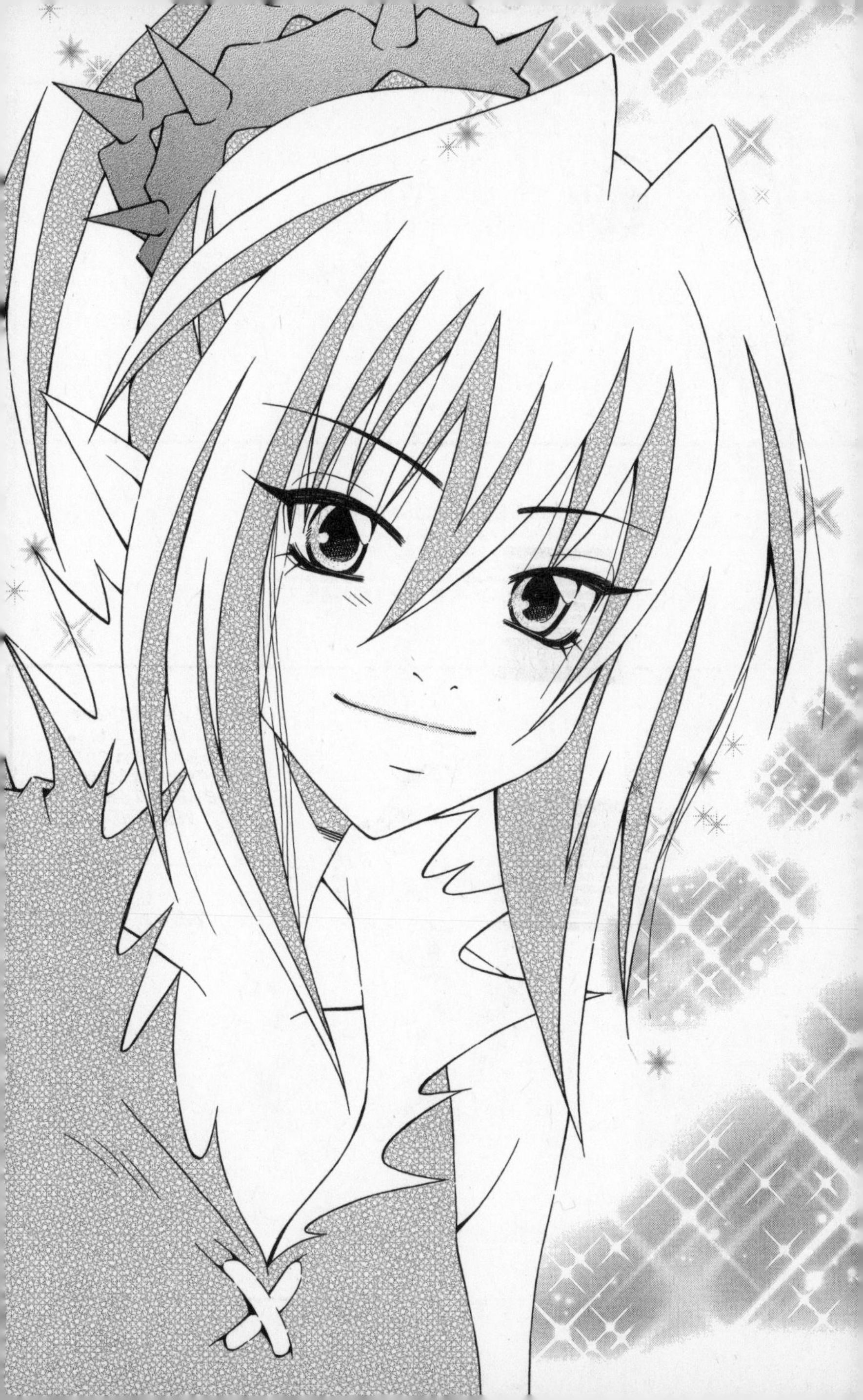

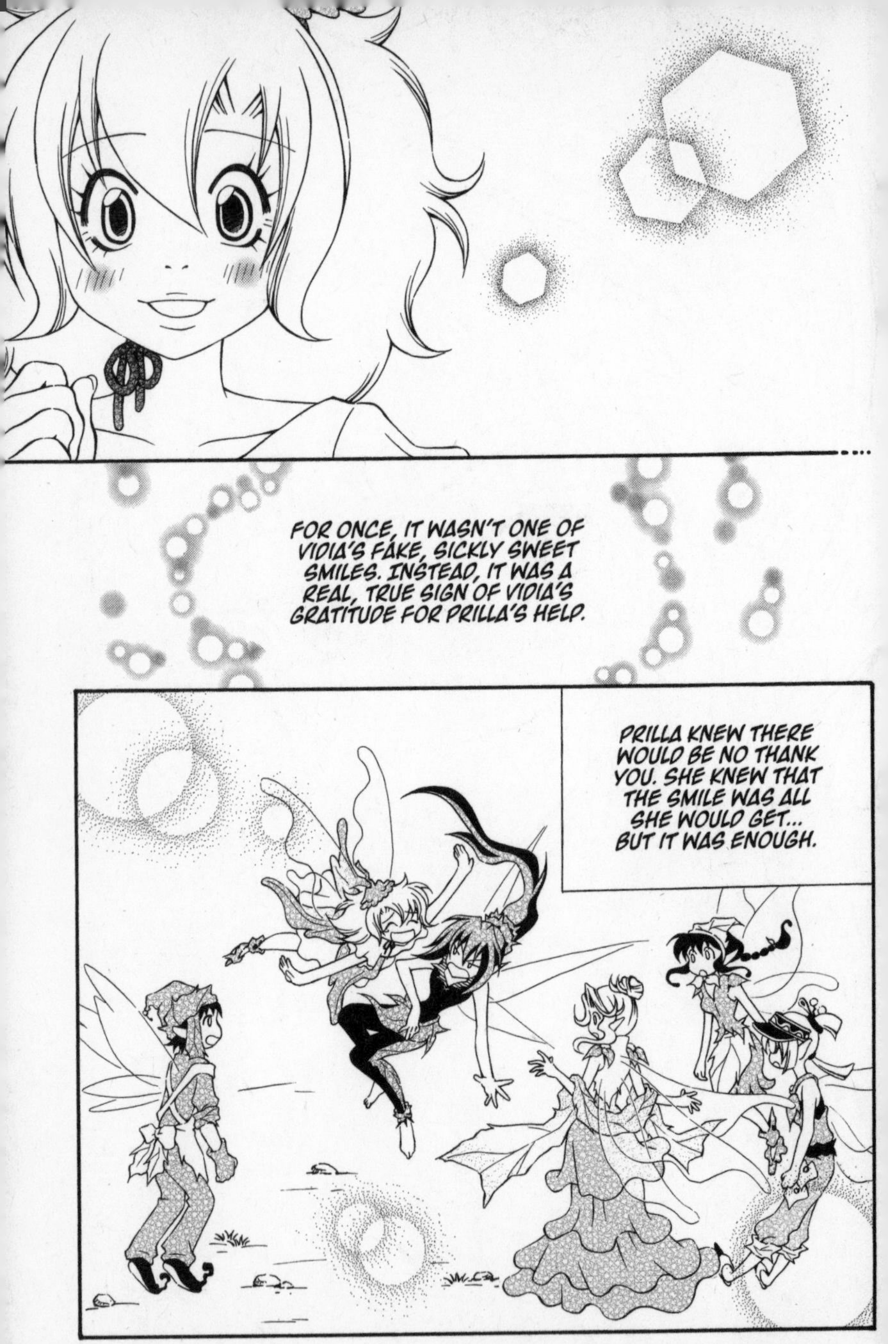
FOR ONCE, IT WASN'T ONE OF VIDIA'S FAKE, SICKLY SWEET SMILES. INSTEAD, IT WAS A REAL, TRUE SIGN OF VIDIA'S GRATITUDE FOR PRILLA'S HELP.
PRILLA KNEW THERE WOULD BE NO THANK YOU. SHE KNEW THAT THE SMILE WAS ALL SHE WOULD GET... BUT IT WAS ENOUGH.

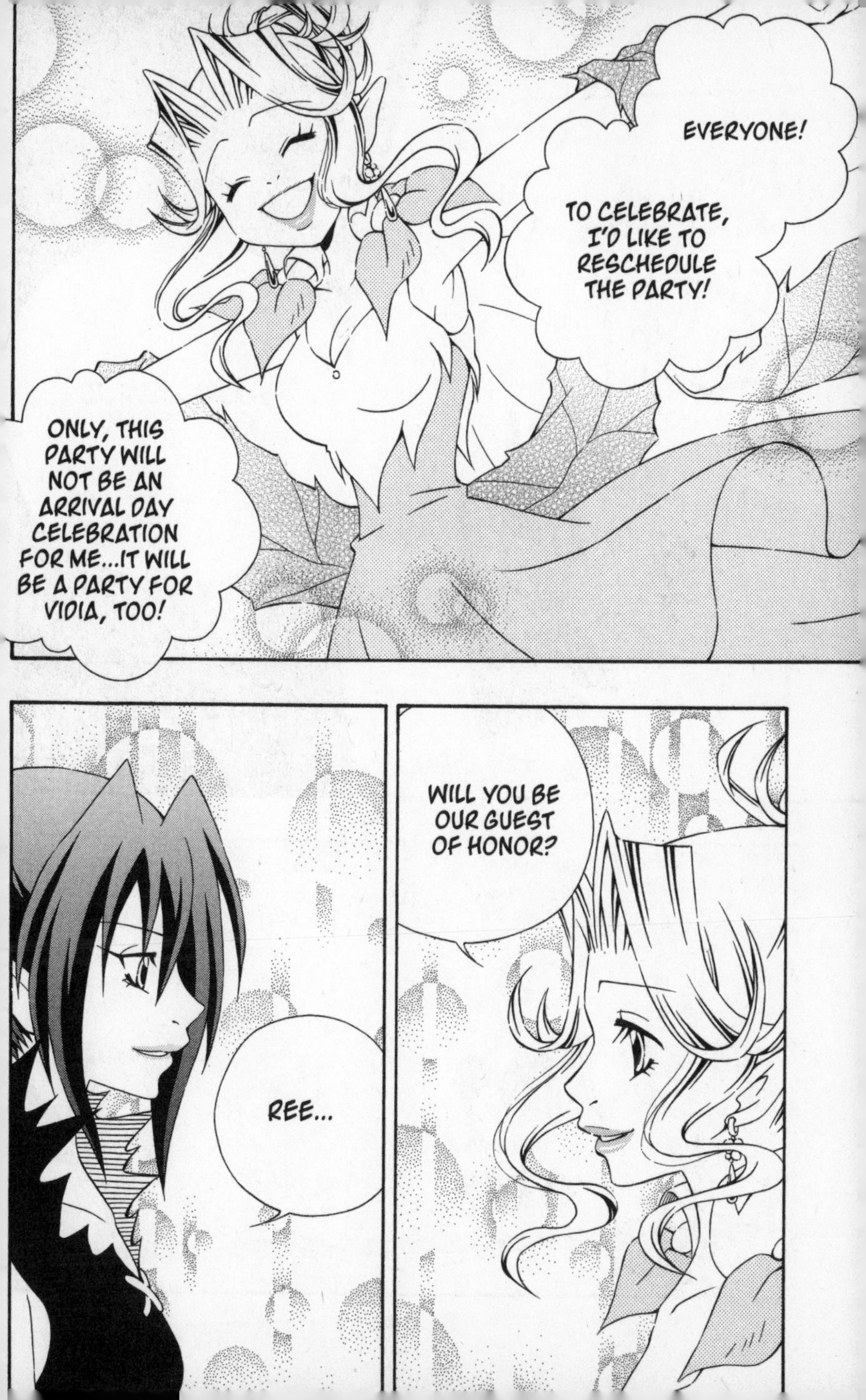
EVERYONE!
TO CELEBRATE, I'D LIKE TO RESCHEDULE THE PARTY!
ONLY, THIS PARTY WILL NOT BE AN ARRIVAL DAY CELEBRATION FOR ME...IT WILL BE A PARTY FOR VIDIA, TOO!
WILL YOU BE OUR GUEST OF HONOR?
REE...

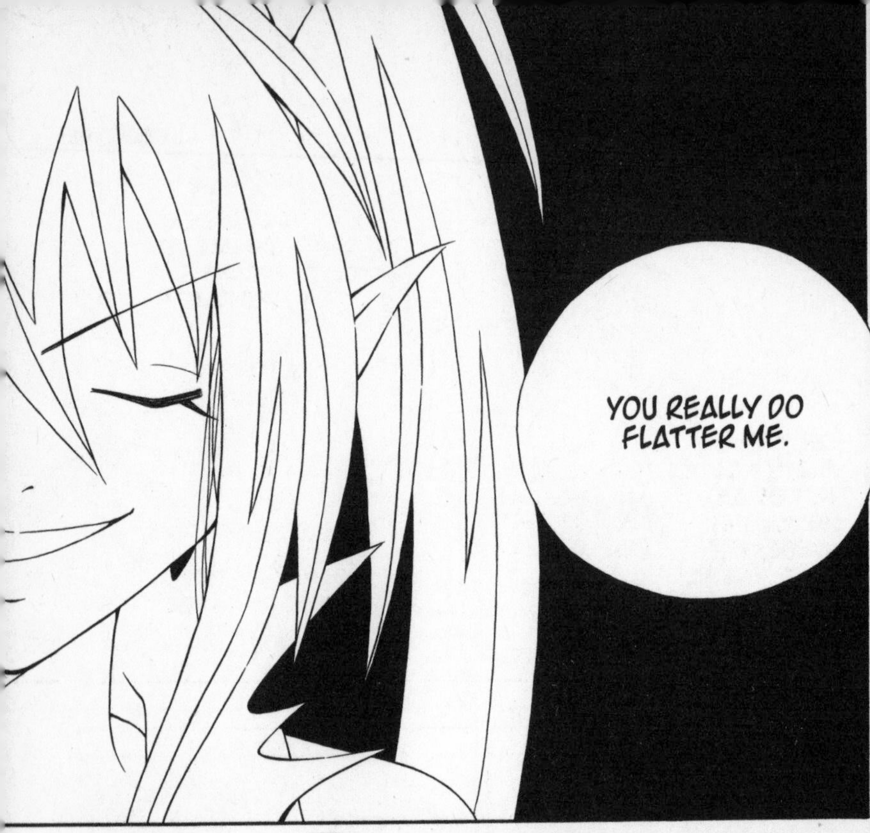
YOU REALLY DO FLATTER ME.

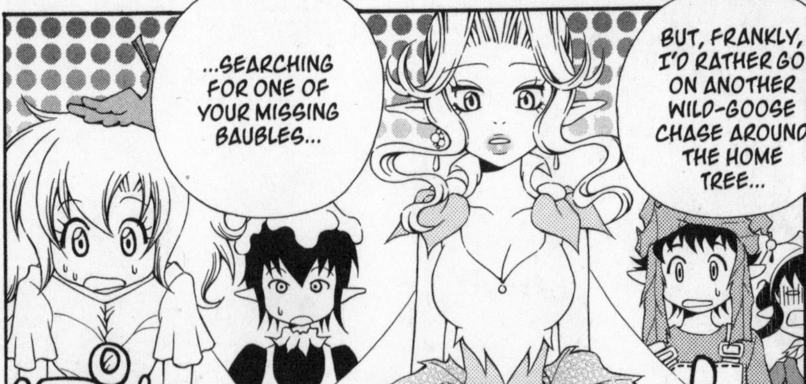
BUT, FRANKLY, I'D RATHER GO ON ANOTHER WILD-GOOSE CHASE AROUND THE HOME TREE...
...SEARCHING FOR ONE OF YOUR MISSING BAUBLES...
ぽわ〜ん

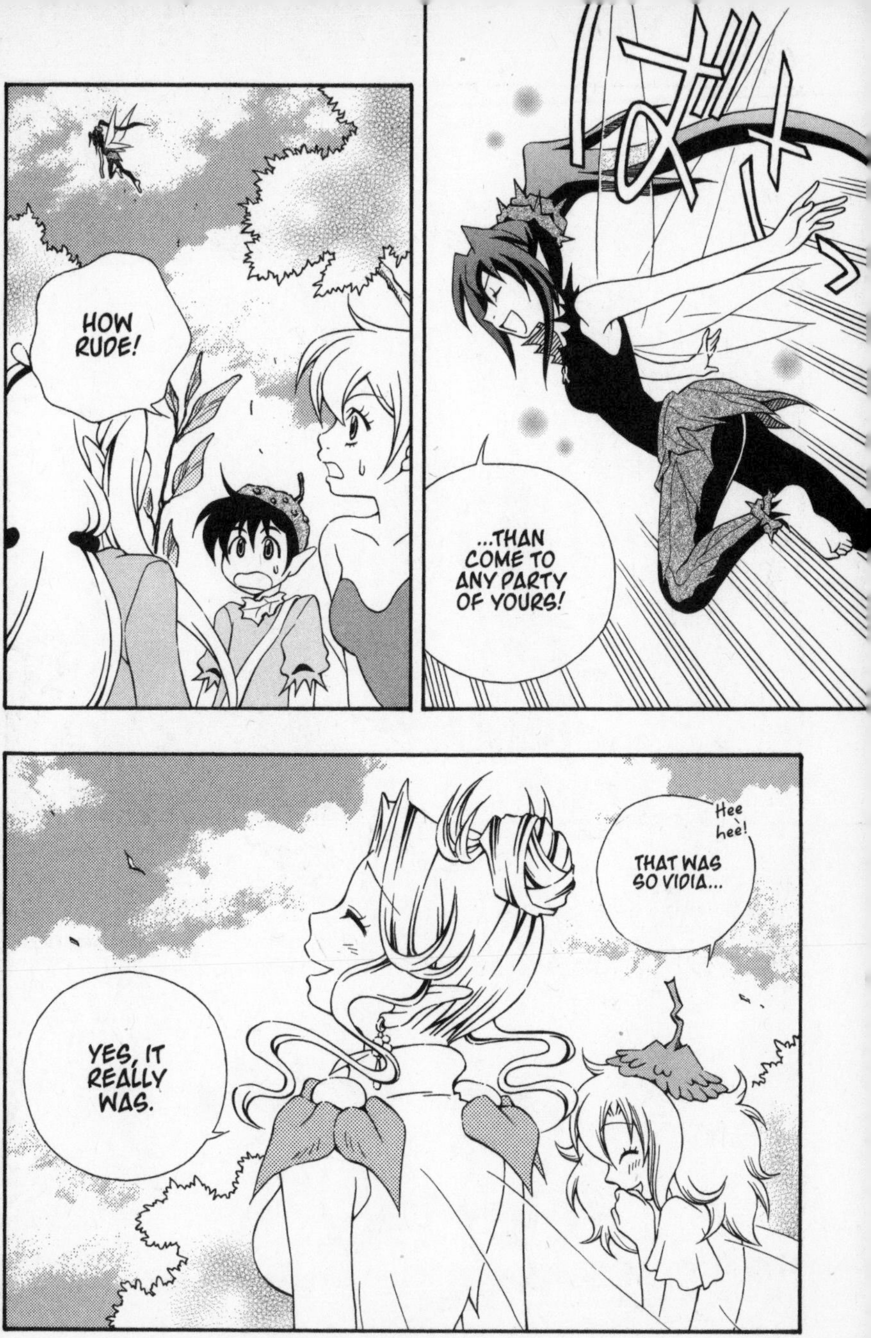
...THAN COME TO ANY PARTY OF YOURS!
HOW RUDE!
Hee hee!
THAT WAS SO VIDIA...
YES, IT REALLY WAS.

READ THIS WAY

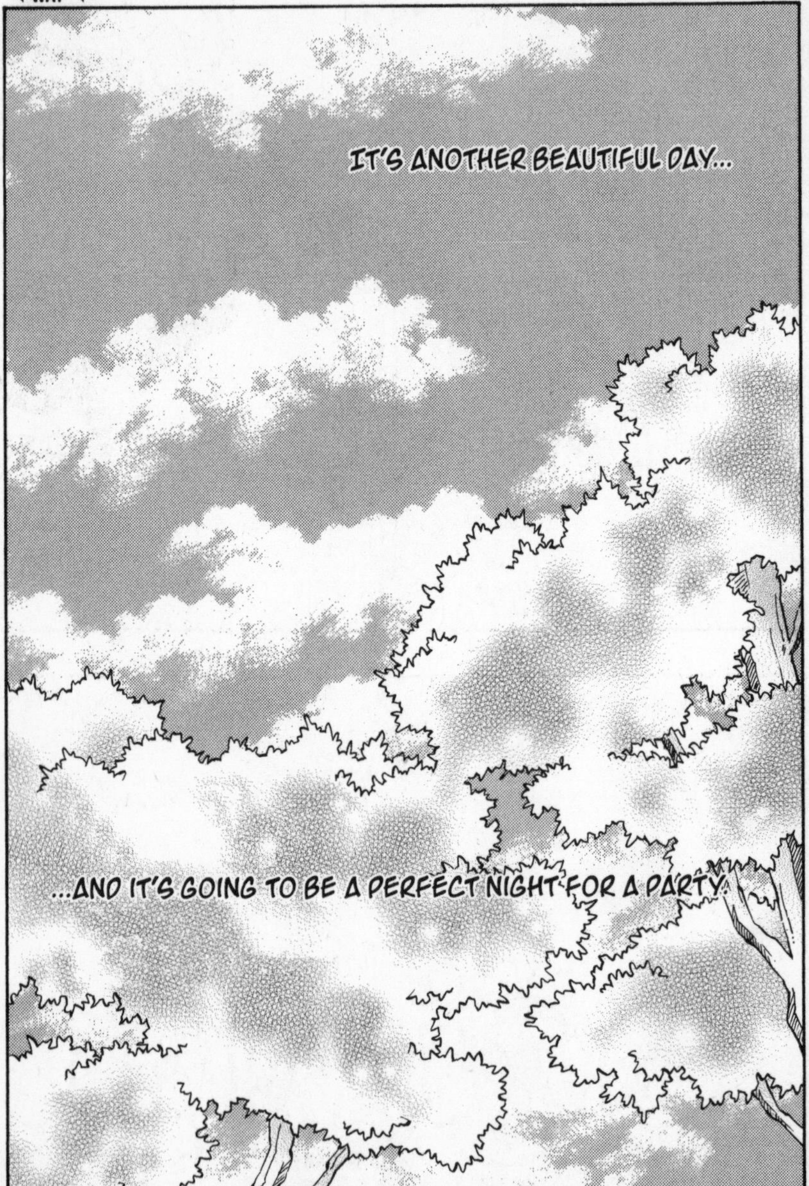
IT'S ANOTHER BEAUTIFUL DAY...
...AND IT'S GOING TO BE A PERFECT NIGHT FOR A PARTY.

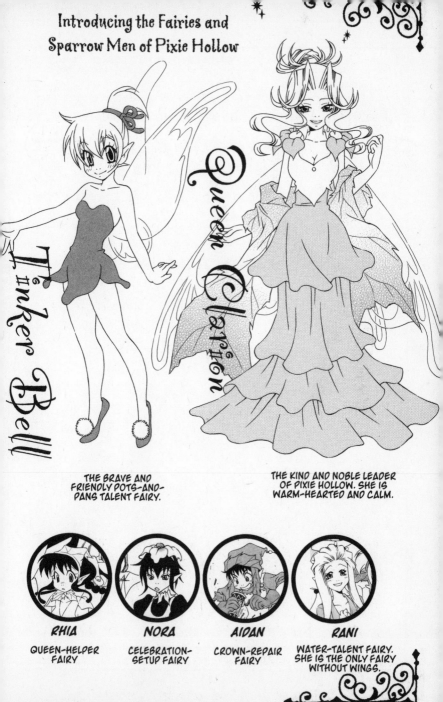

Introducing the Fairies and Sparrow Men of Pixie Hollow

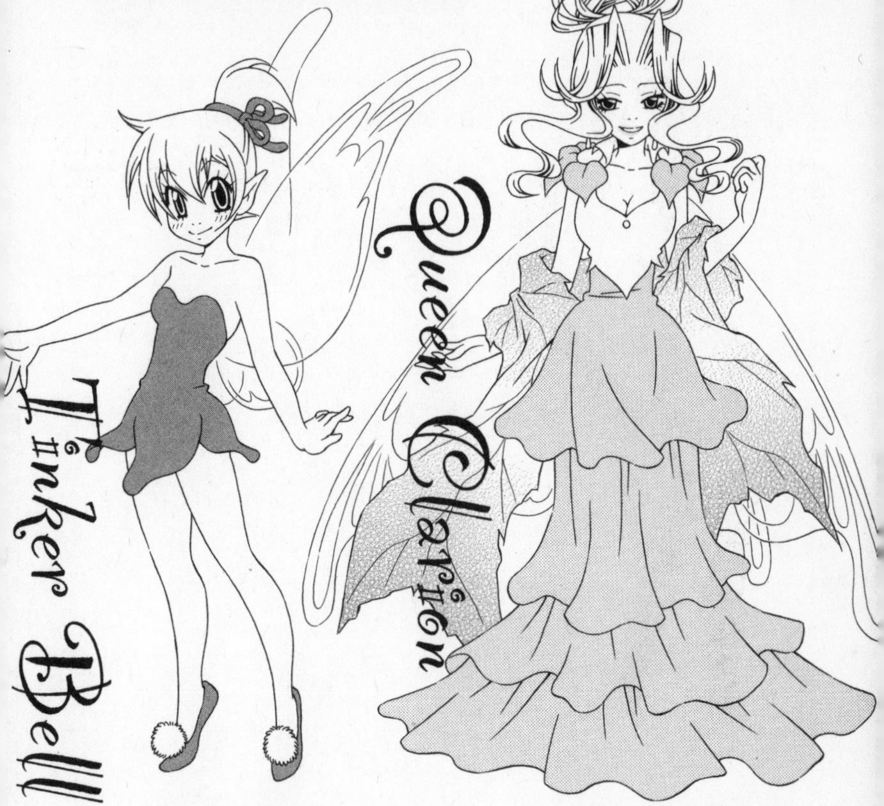
Tinker Bell
Queen Clarion

Tinker Bell: THE BRAVE AND FRIENDLY POTS-AND-PANS TALENT FAIRY.

Queen Clarion: THE KIND AND NOBLE LEADER OF PIXIE HOLLOW. SHE IS WARM-HEARTED AND CALM.

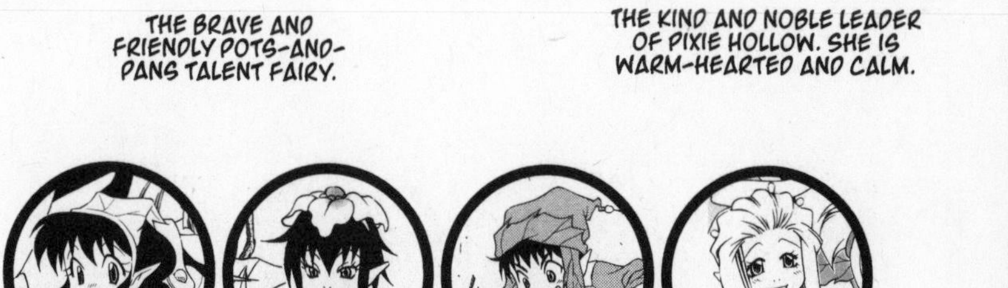

RHIA
QUEEN-HELPER FAIRY

NORA
CELEBRATION-SETUP FAIRY

AIDAN
CROWN-REPAIR FAIRY

RANI
WATER-TALENT FAIRY. SHE IS THE ONLY FAIRY WITHOUT WINGS.

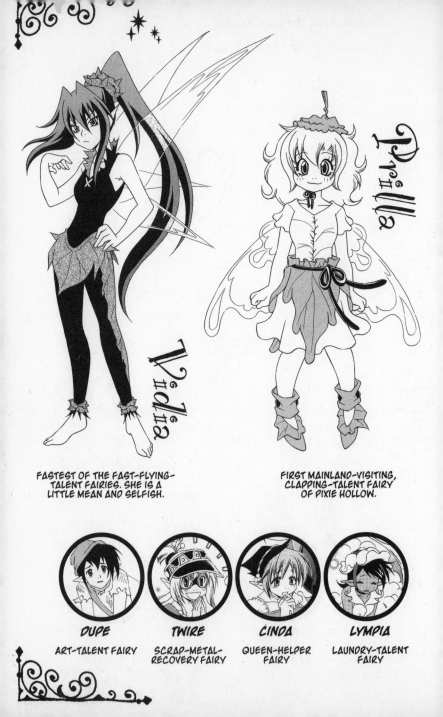

Vidia

FASTEST OF THE FAST-FLYING-TALENT FAIRIES. SHE IS A LITTLE MEAN AND SELFISH.

Prilla

FIRST MAINLAND-VISITING, CLAPPING-TALENT FAIRY OF PIXIE HOLLOW.

DUPE

ART-TALENT FAIRY

TWIRE

SCRAP-METAL-RECOVERY FAIRY

CINDA

QUEEN-HELPER FAIRY

LYMPIA

LAUNDRY-TALENT FAIRY

chicchakute kawaii

Diary Of Cute Little Fairies

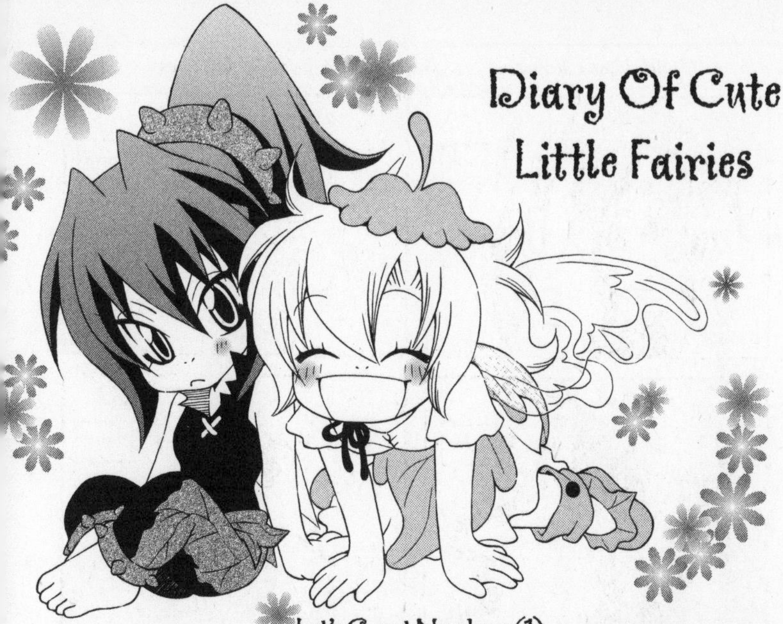

Let's Count Numbers (1)

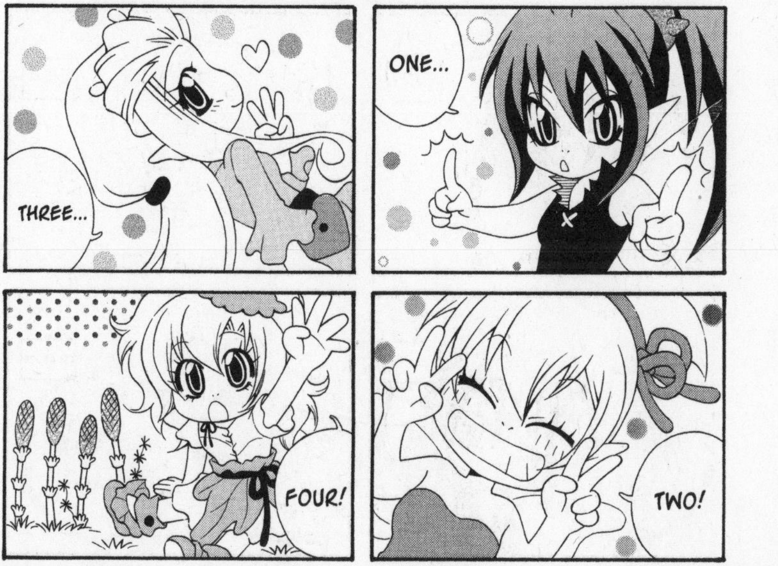
ONE...
TWO!
THREE...
FOUR!

精日記ちっちゃくてかわいい 妖精日記 chicchakute kawaii 妖精日記 チッチャクテカワイイ 妖
ちっちゃくてかわいい 妖精日記 chicchakute kawaii 妖精日記 チッチャ

Tink's Mood Swings

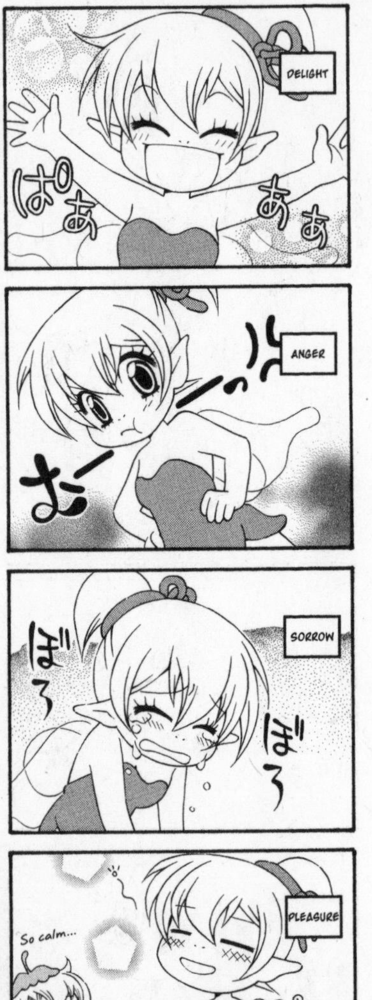
DELIGHT
ぱぁ
ああ
ANGER
っ
むー
SORROW
ぽろ
ぽろ
PLEASURE
So calm...
Ahhh...
TOTALLY RELAXED... ♡

Vidia's Mood Swings

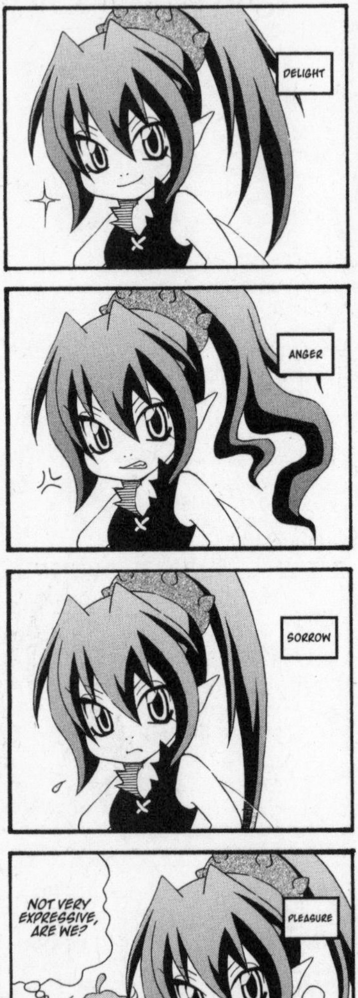
DELIGHT
ANGER
SORROW
PLEASURE
NOT VERY EXPRESSIVE, ARE WE?
Sheesh!

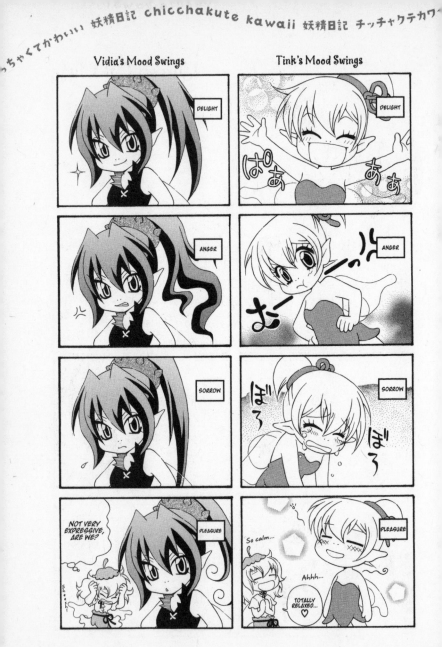

A Cup Of Tea

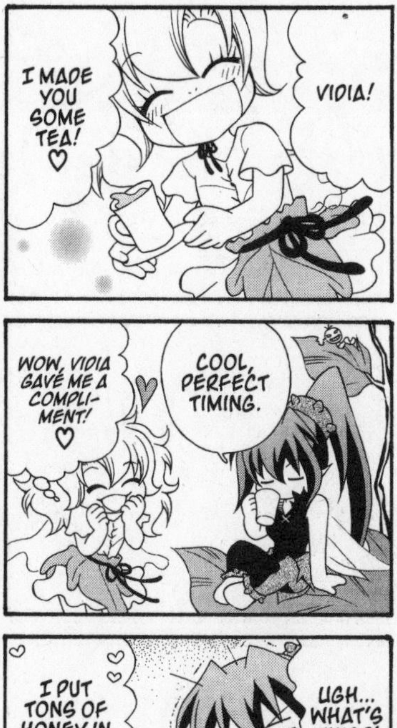
VIDIA!
I MADE YOU SOME TEA! ♡
COOL, PERFECT TIMING.
WOW, VIDIA GAVE ME A COMPLIMENT! ♡
UGH... WHAT'S THIS?!
I PUT TONS OF HONEY IN IT! ♡
FORGET ABOUT MY "COOL" REMARK!
ガビーン
YOU'RE SO MEAN!

Another Cup Of Tea

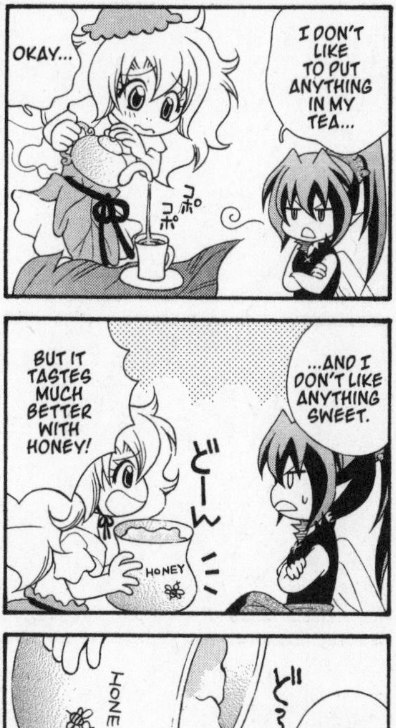
I DON'T LIKE TO PUT ANYTHING IN MY TEA...
コポコポ
OKAY...
...AND I DON'T LIKE ANYTHING SWEET.
どーん
BUT IT TASTES MUCH BETTER WITH HONEY!
HONEY
どろ〜〜っ
THE MORE YOU PUT, THE BETTER IT TASTES...
HONEY
GLORP
HERE YOU GO! ♡
ぱあっ
WERE YOU LISTENING?!

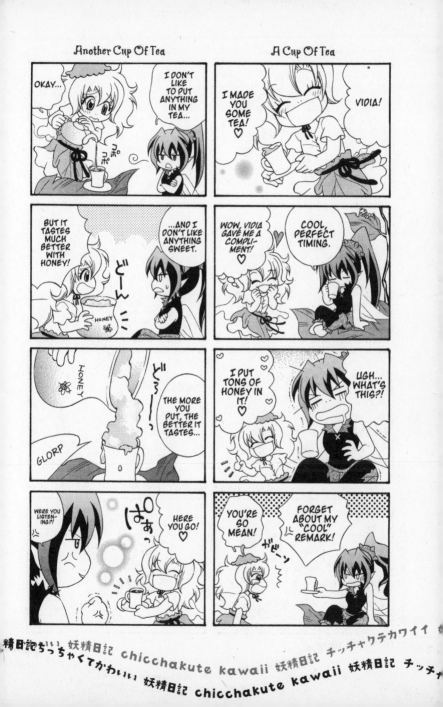

Let's Count Numbers (2)

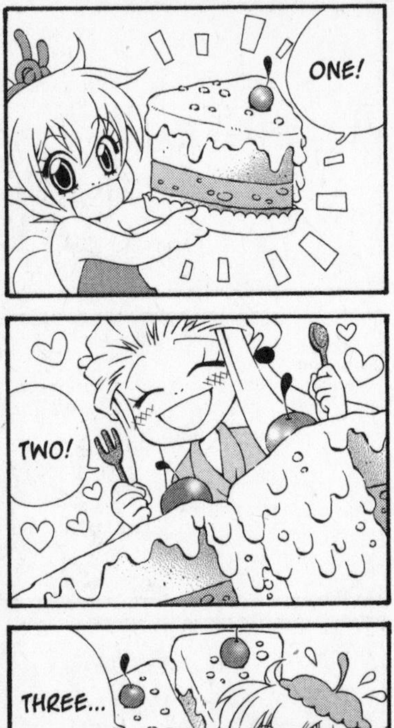
ONE!
TWO!
THREE...
FOUR.

Let's Nap Together

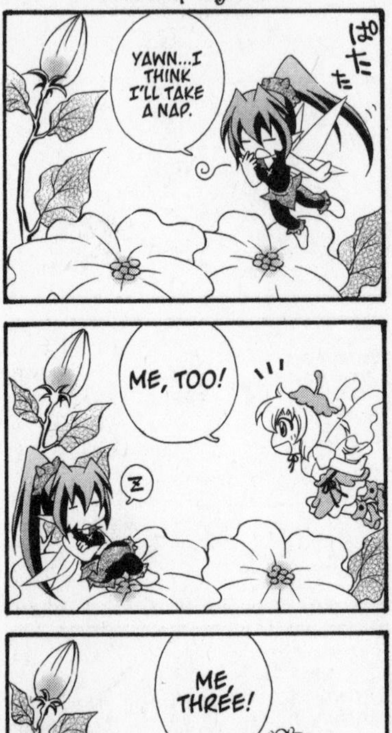
ぱたた
YAWN...I THINK I'LL TAKE A NAP.
ME, TOO!
z
ME, THREE!
Ahhh...
Yawn!
SEE YOU...
...IN VOLUME 2! ♡

To Be Continued In Volume 2 (Probably)

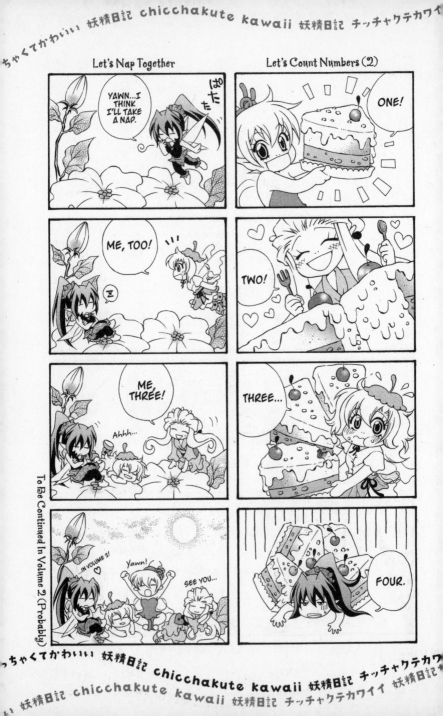

Check out the next Disney Fairies Manga!

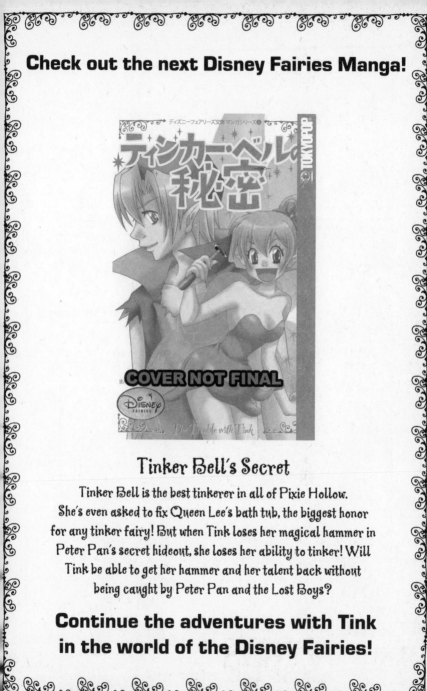

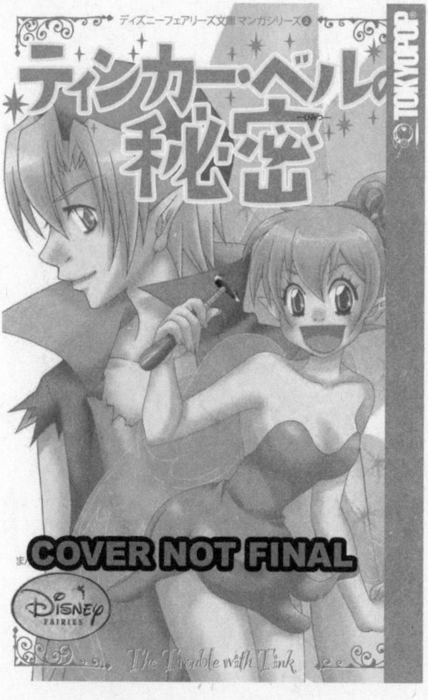
ディズニーフェアリーズ文庫マンガシリーズ②
ティンカー・ベルの秘密
TOKYOPOP
COVER NOT FINAL
DISNEY FAIRIES
The Trouble with Tink

Tinker Bell's Secret

Tinker Bell is the best tinkerer in all of Pixie Hollow. She's even asked to fix Queen Lee's bath tub, the biggest honor for any tinker fairy! But when Tink loses her magical hammer in Peter Pan's secret hideout, she loses her ability to tinker! Will Tink be able to get her hammer and her talent back without being caught by Peter Pan and the Lost Boys?

Continue the adventures with Tink in the world of the Disney Fairies!

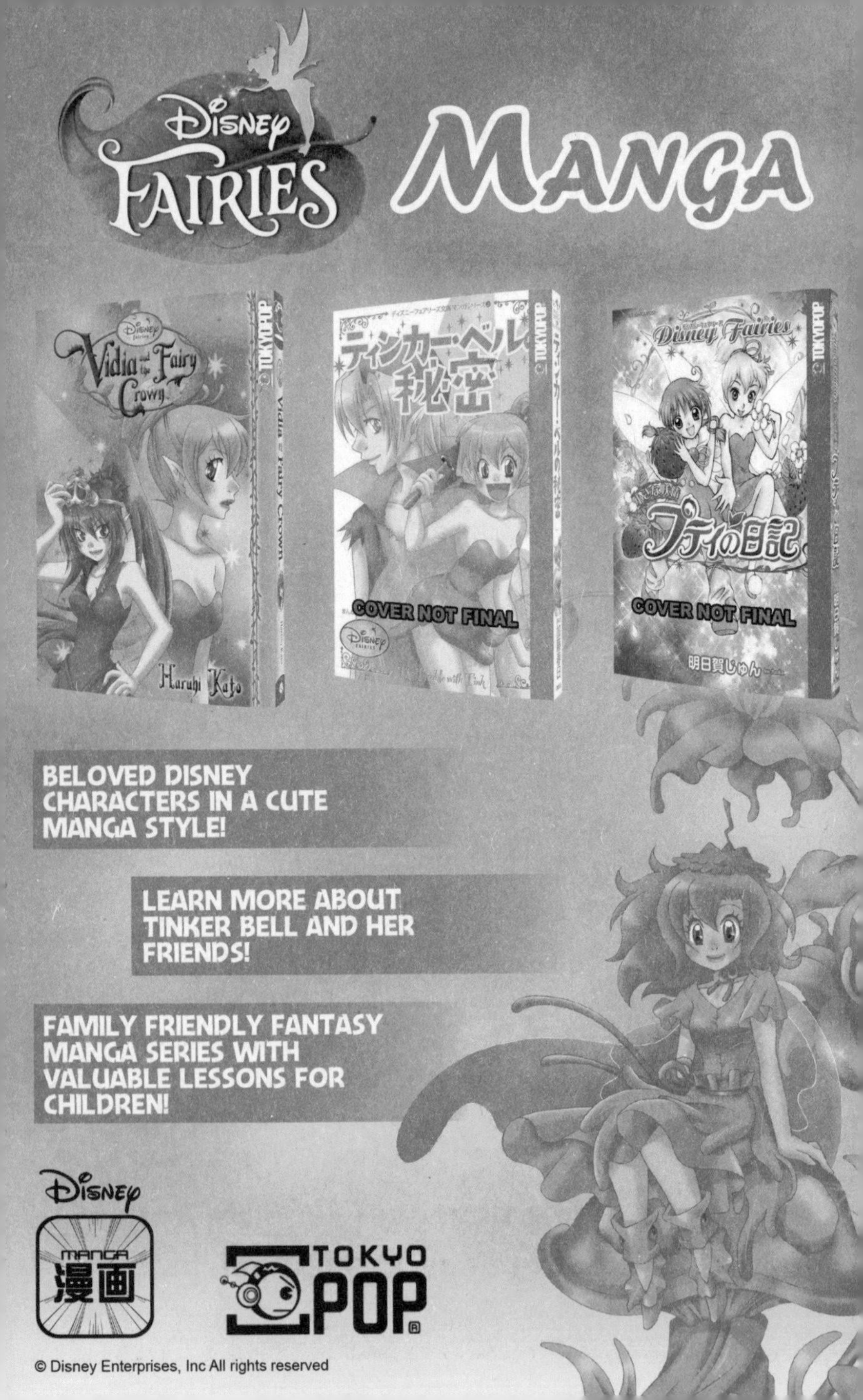
Disney Fairies
Manga
Vidia and the Fairy Crown
Haruhi Kato
ティンカー・ベルの秘密
COVER NOT FINAL
Disney Fairies
プティの日記
COVER NOT FINAL
明日賀じゅん
BELOVED DISNEY CHARACTERS IN A CUTE MANGA STYLE!
LEARN MORE ABOUT TINKER BELL AND HER FRIENDS!
FAMILY FRIENDLY FANTASY MANGA SERIES WITH VALUABLE LESSONS FOR CHILDREN!
Disney
MANGA 漫画
TOKYO POP
© Disney Enterprises, Inc All rights reserved

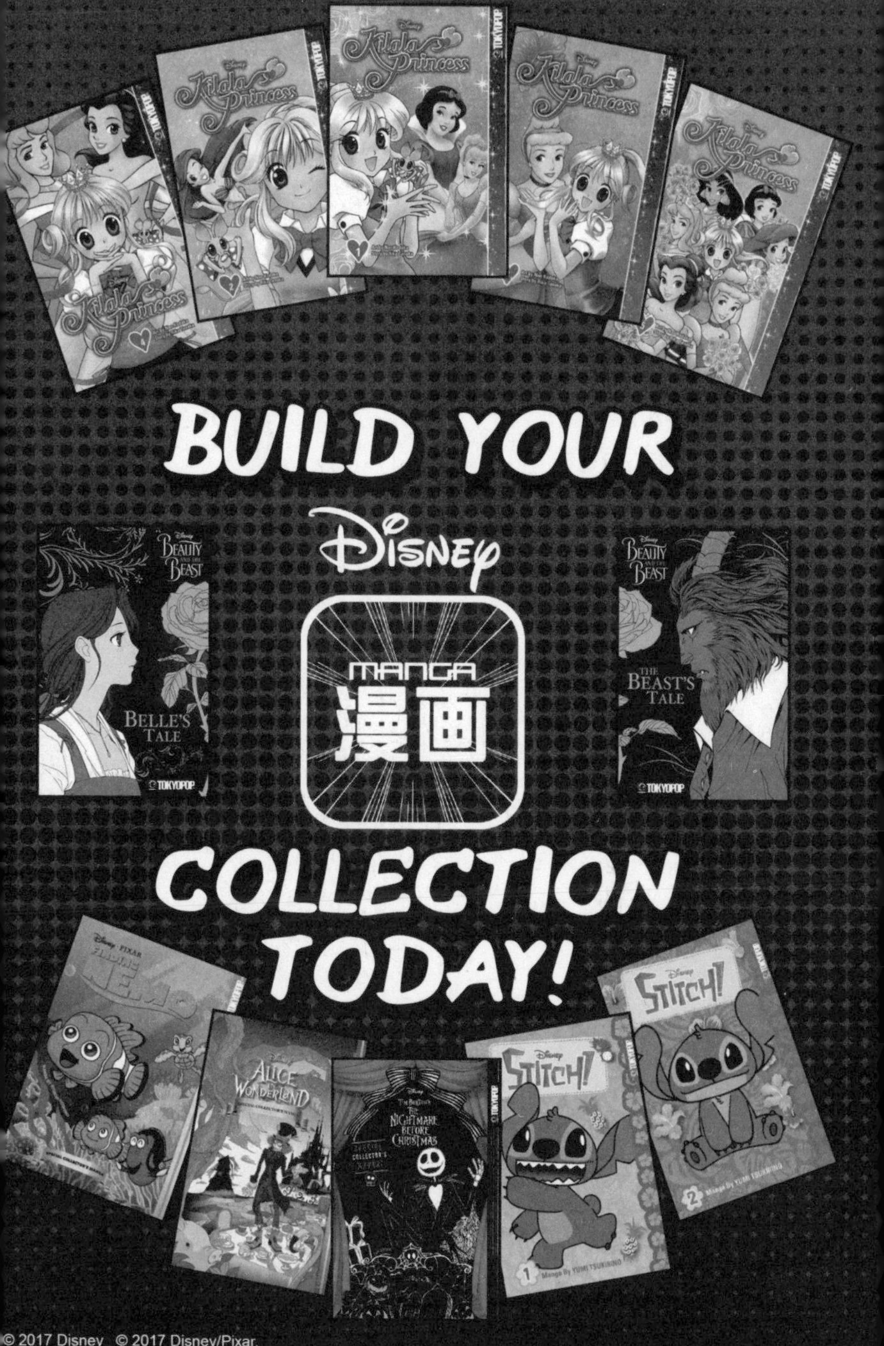
BUILD YOUR
DISNEY
MANGA
漫画
COLLECTION TODAY!

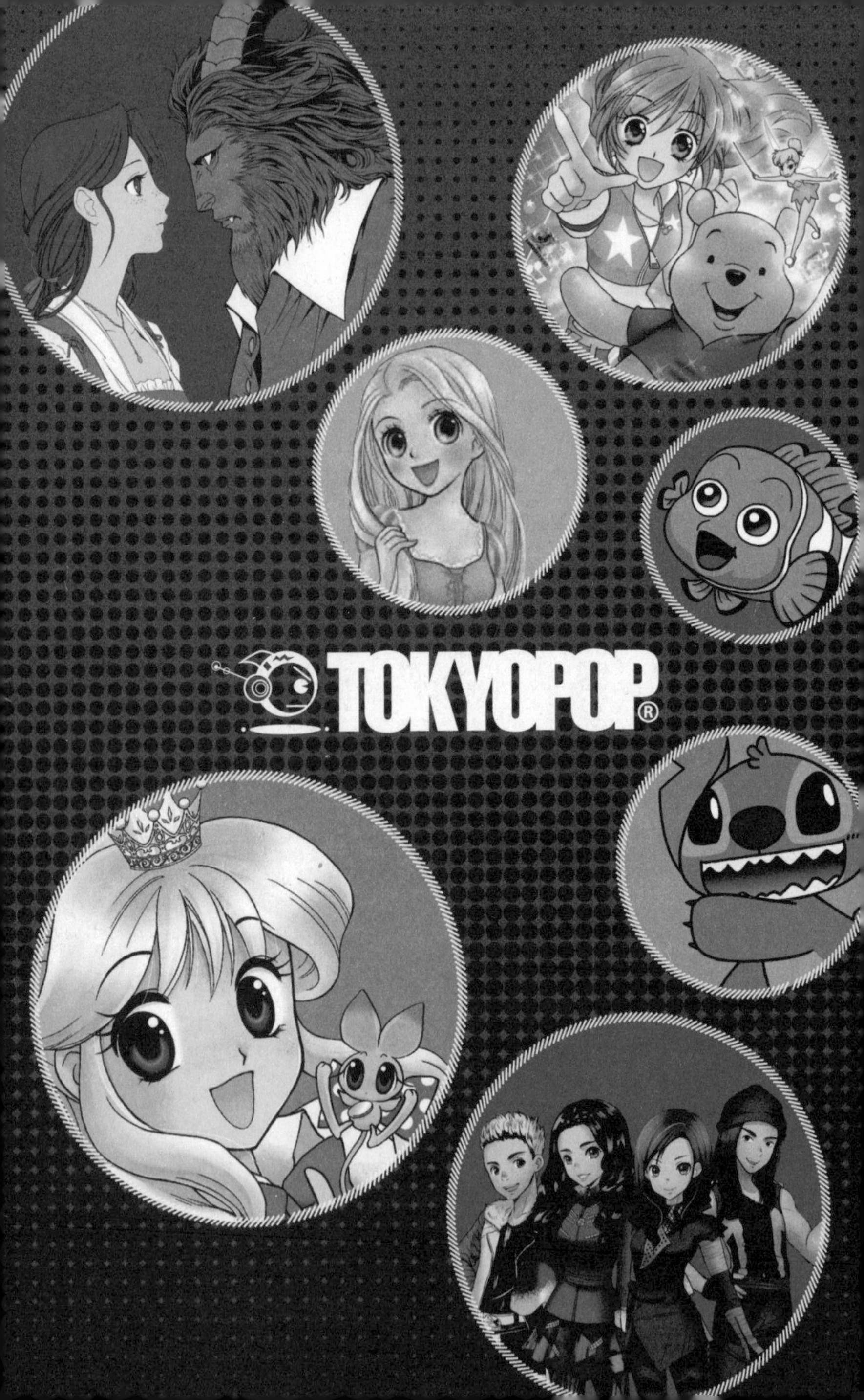
TOKYOPOP®

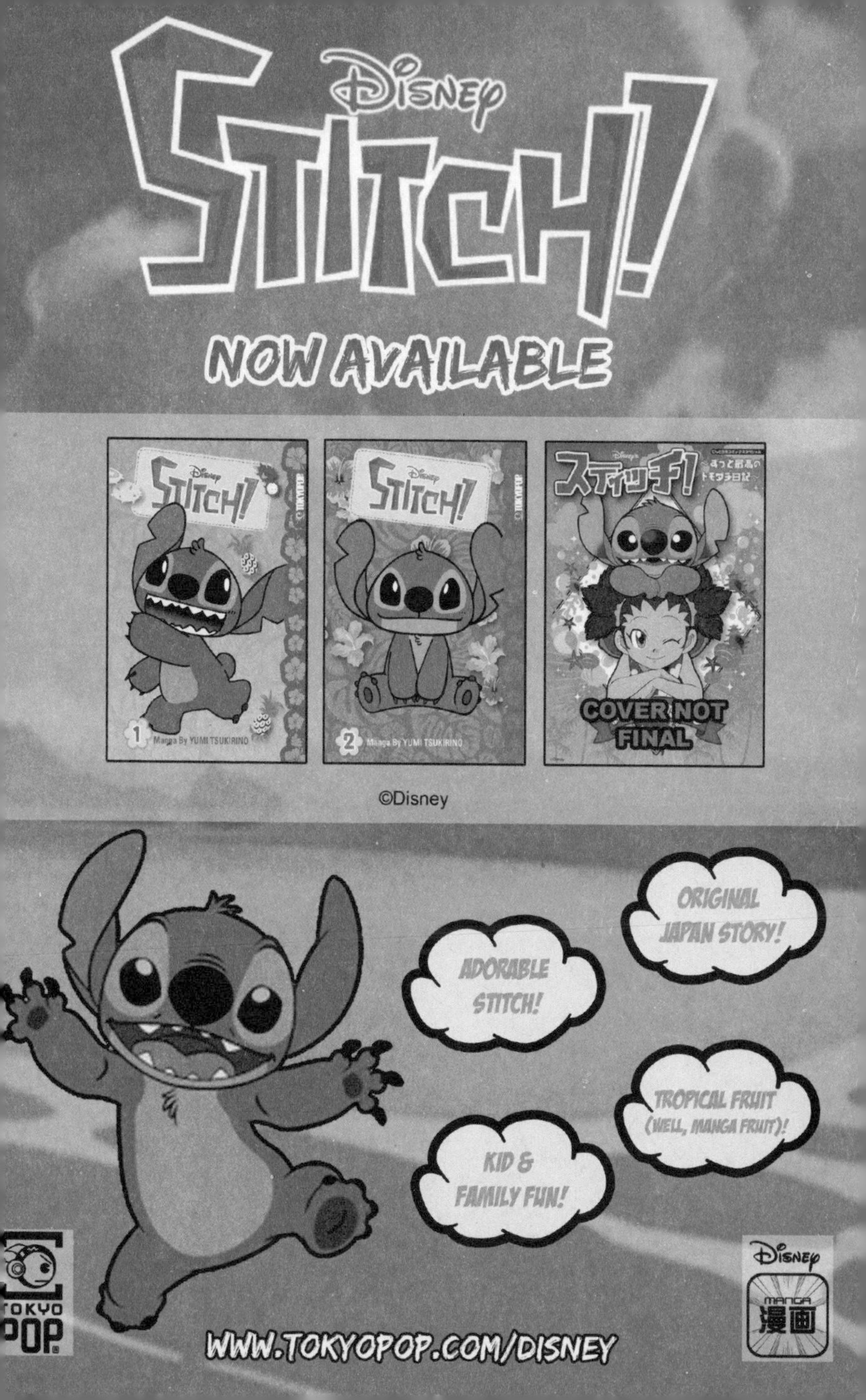
Disney
STITCH!
NOW AVAILABLE
Disney STITCH!
TOKYOPOP
1 Manga By YUMI TSUKIRINO
Disney STITCH!
TOKYOPOP
2 Manga By YUMI TSUKIRINO
スティッチ!
COVER NOT FINAL
©Disney
ORIGINAL JAPAN STORY!
ADORABLE STITCH!
TROPICAL FRUIT (WELL, MANGA FRUIT)!
KID & FAMILY FUN!
TOKYO POP
Disney
MANGA 漫画
WWW.TOKYOPOP.COM/DISNEY

MAGICAL ★DANCE

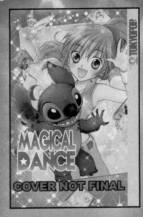

MAGICAL ★DANCE

COVER NOT FINAL

Rin joins a troupe with her fellow students and soon realizes that she has two left feet. She practices day and night but is discouraged by the lack of results and almost gives up on her dreams. Impressed by her passion and dedication, Tinker Bell appears to give her a little encouragement in the form of Disney magic!

FROM THE CREATOR OF DISNEY KILALA PRINCESS!

Disney

MANGA
漫画

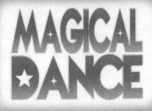

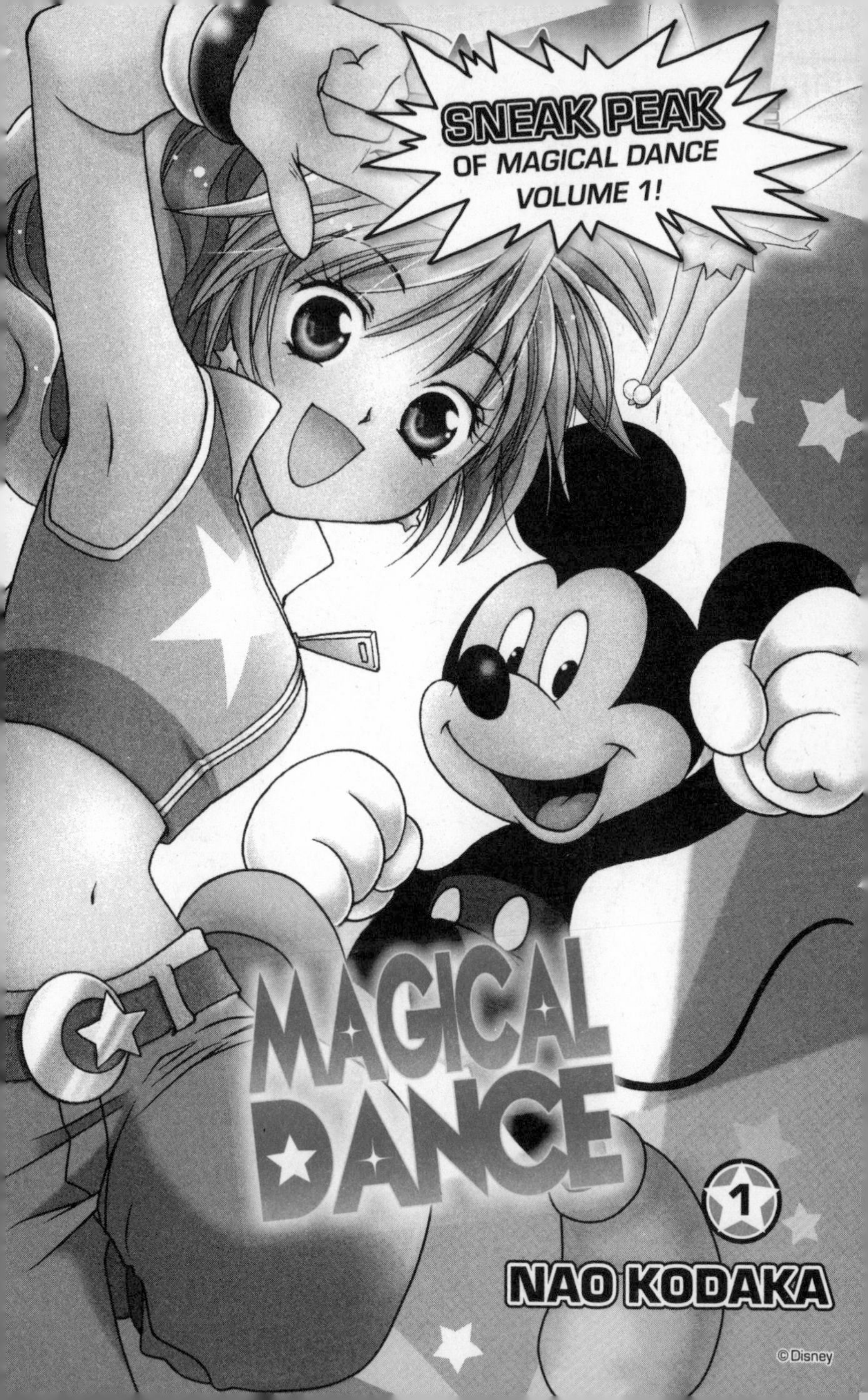
SNEAK PEAK
OF MAGICAL DANCE
VOLUME 1!
MAGICAL DANCE
1
NAO KODAKA
©Disney

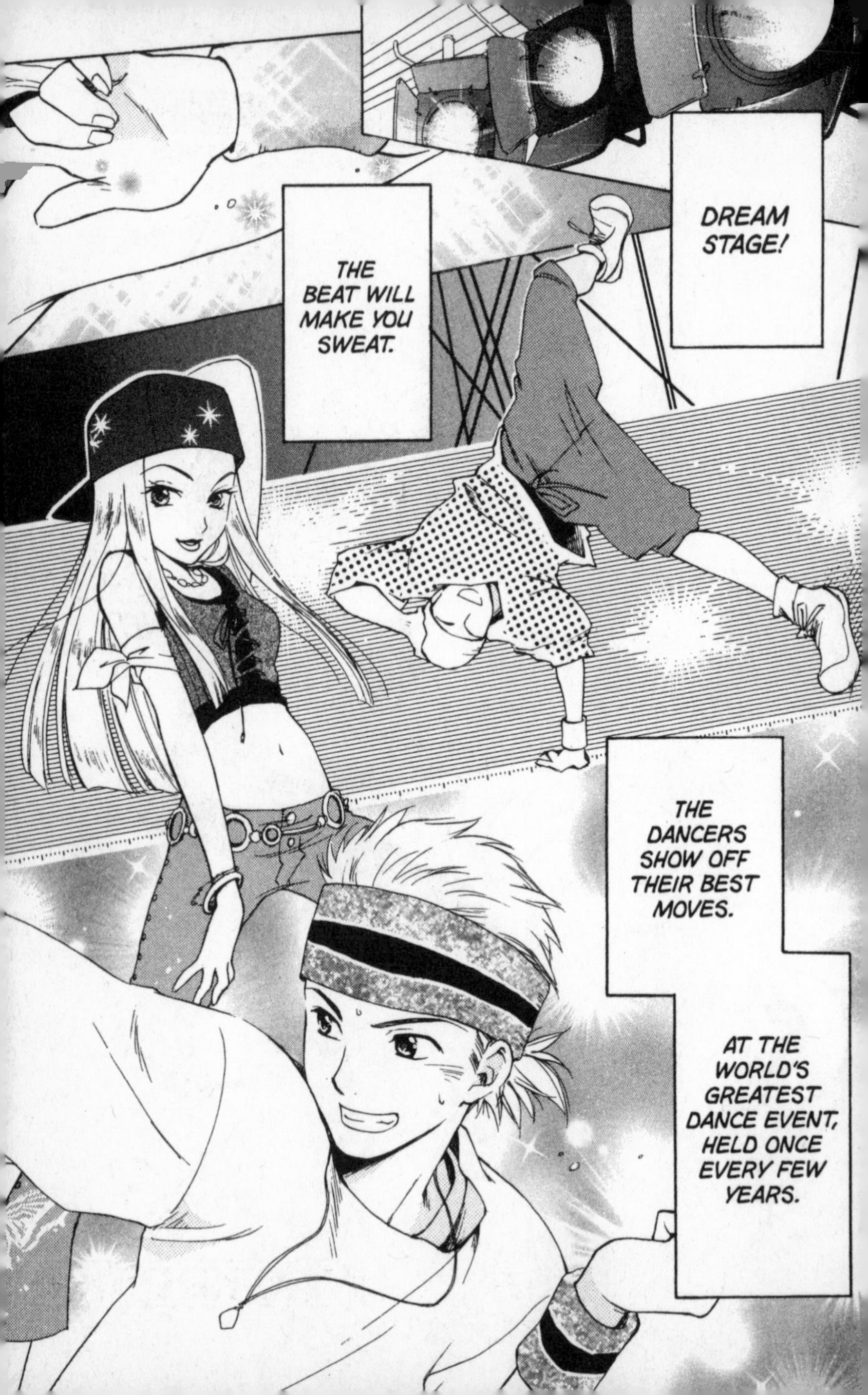
DREAM STAGE!
THE BEAT WILL MAKE YOU SWEAT.
THE DANCERS SHOW OFF THEIR BEST MOVES.
AT THE WORLD'S GREATEST DANCE EVENT, HELD ONCE EVERY FEW YEARS.

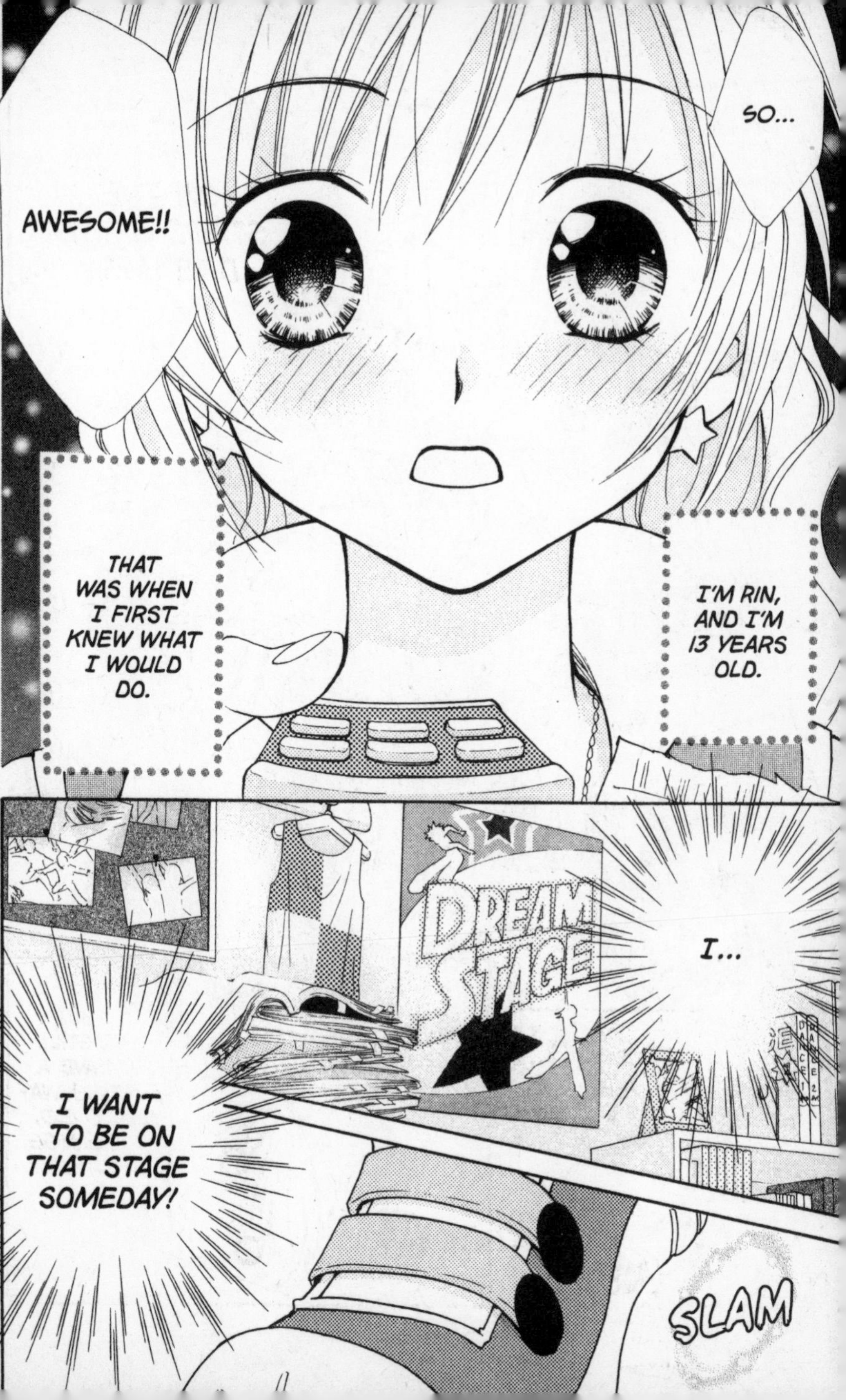
SO...
AWESOME!!
I'M RIN, AND I'M 13 YEARS OLD.
THAT WAS WHEN I FIRST KNEW WHAT I WOULD DO.
I...
DREAM STAGE
I WANT TO BE ON THAT STAGE SOMEDAY!
SLAM

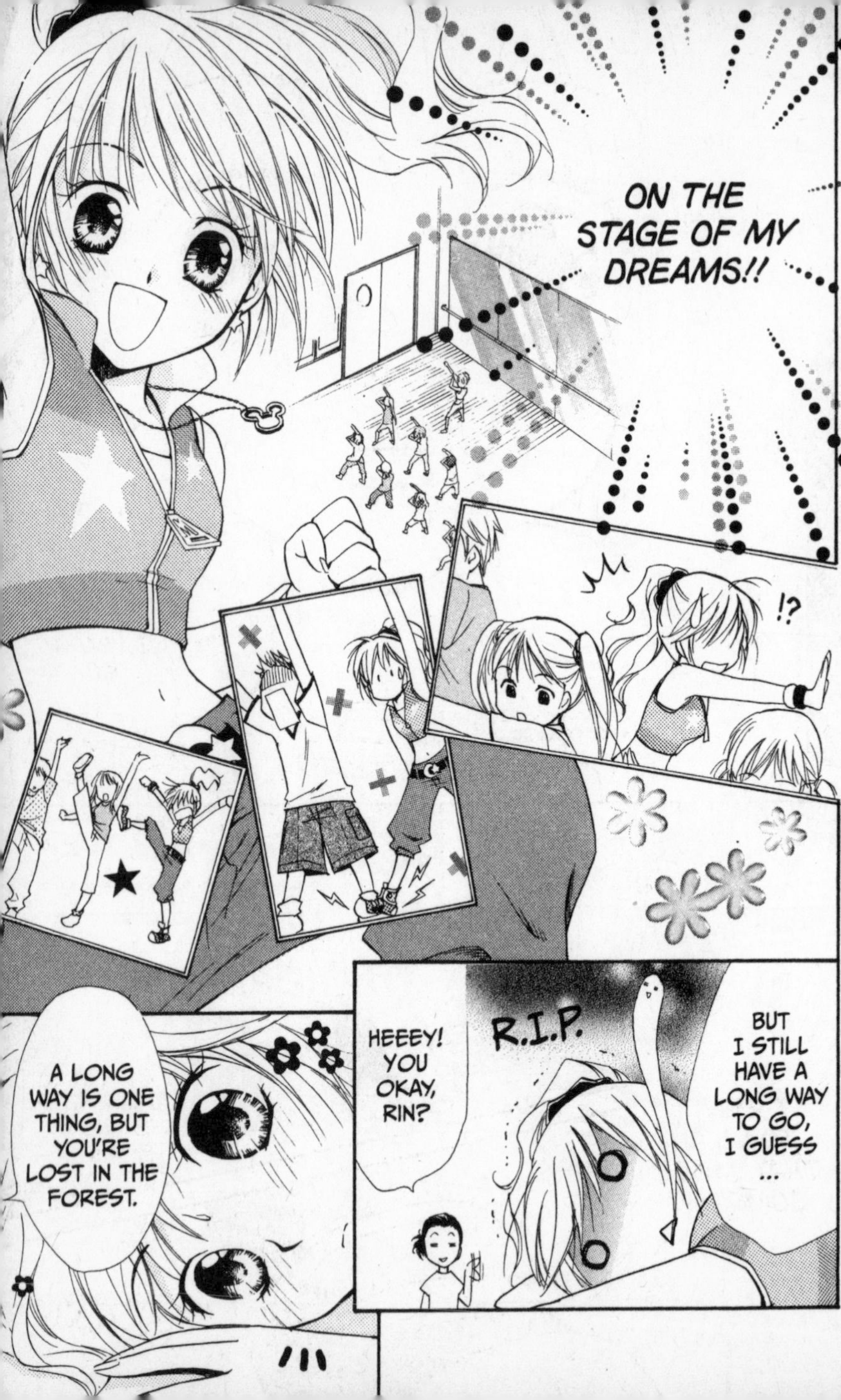
ON THE STAGE OF MY DREAMS!!
!?
BUT I STILL HAVE A LONG WAY TO GO, I GUESS ...
R.I.P.
HEEEY! YOU OKAY, RIN?
A LONG WAY IS ONE THING, BUT YOU'RE LOST IN THE FOREST.

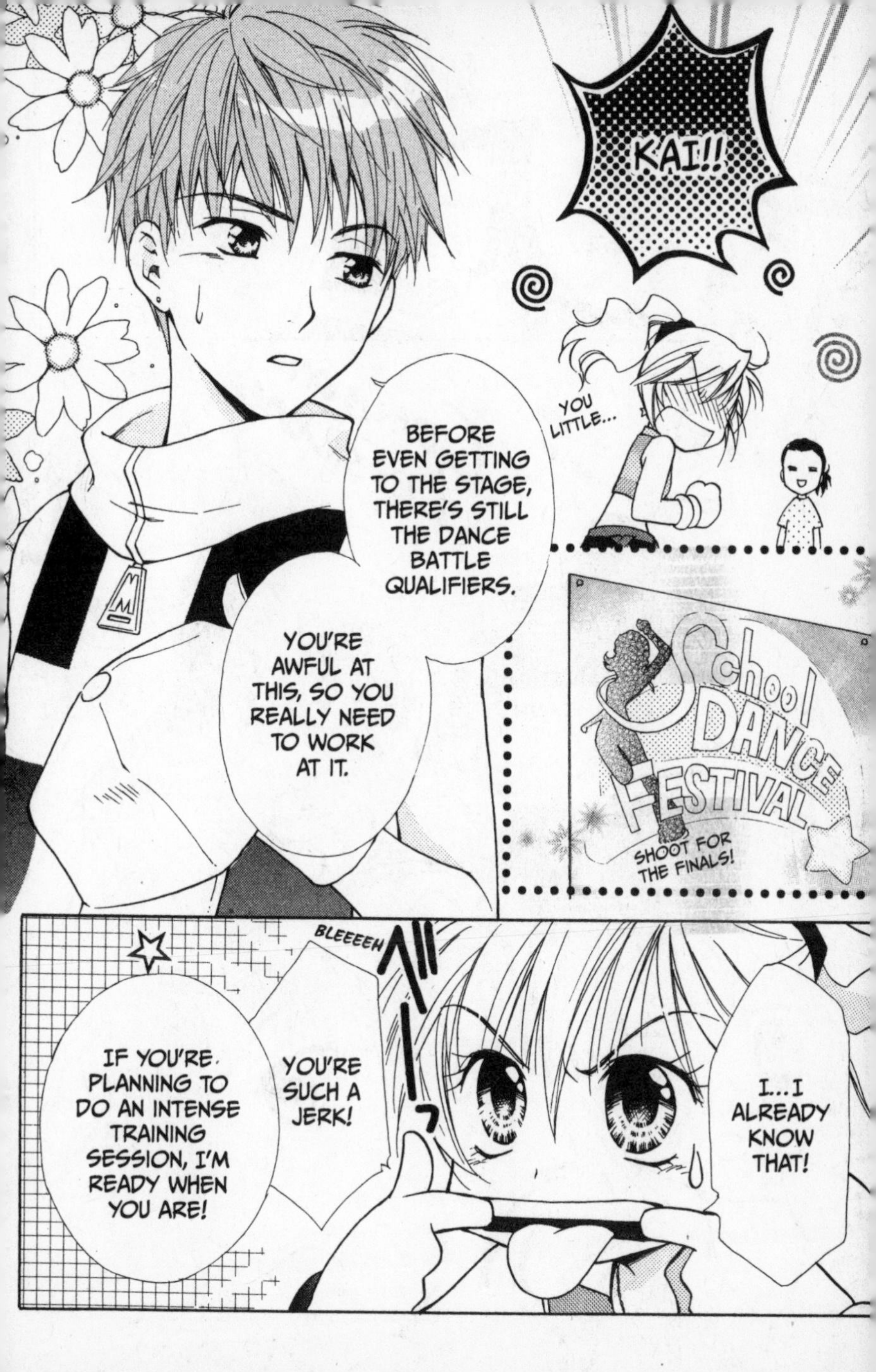
KAI!!
YOU LITTLE...
School DANCE FESTIVAL
SHOOT FOR THE FINALS!
BEFORE EVEN GETTING TO THE STAGE, THERE'S STILL THE DANCE BATTLE QUALIFIERS.
YOU'RE AWFUL AT THIS, SO YOU REALLY NEED TO WORK AT IT.
I...I ALREADY KNOW THAT!
BLEEEEH
YOU'RE SUCH A JERK!
IF YOU'RE PLANNING TO DO AN INTENSE TRAINING SESSION, I'M READY WHEN YOU ARE!

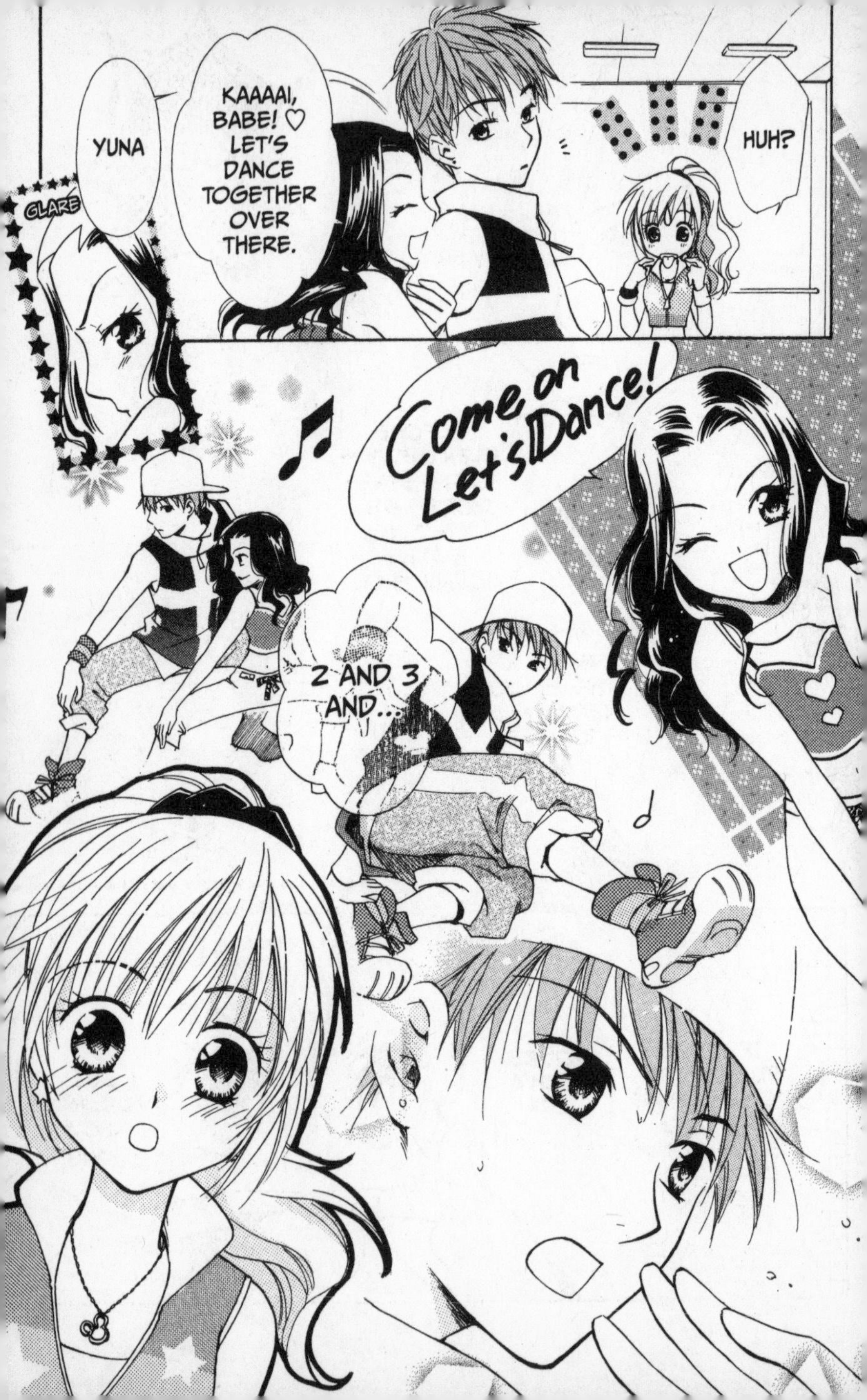
HUH?
KAAAAI, BABE! ♡ LET'S DANCE TOGETHER OVER THERE.
YUNA
GLARE
Come on Let's Dance!
2 AND 3 AND...

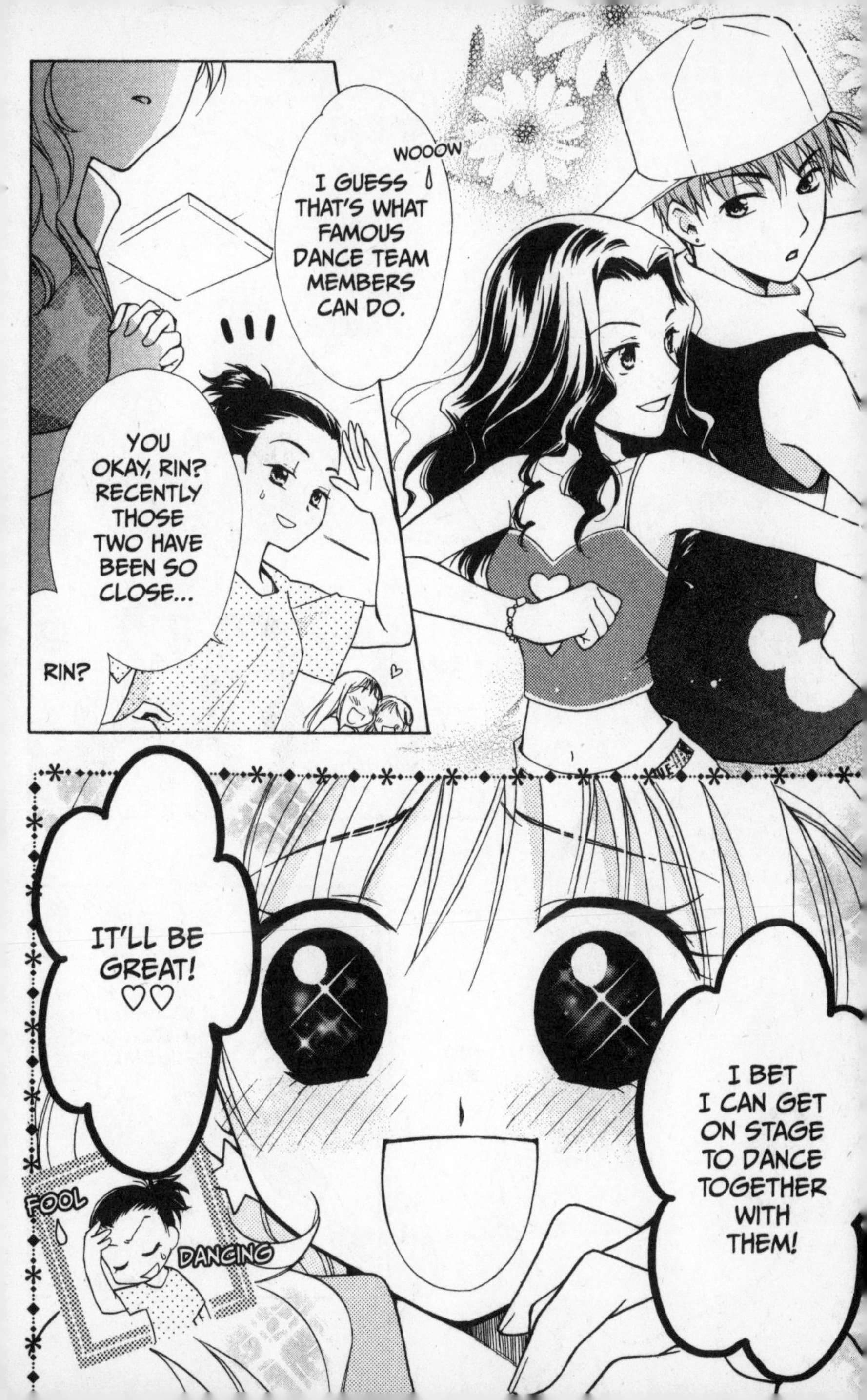
WOOOW
I GUESS THAT'S WHAT FAMOUS DANCE TEAM MEMBERS CAN DO.
YOU OKAY, RIN? RECENTLY THOSE TWO HAVE BEEN SO CLOSE...
RIN?
I BET I CAN GET ON STAGE TO DANCE TOGETHER WITH THEM!
IT'LL BE GREAT! ♡♡
FOOL
DANCING

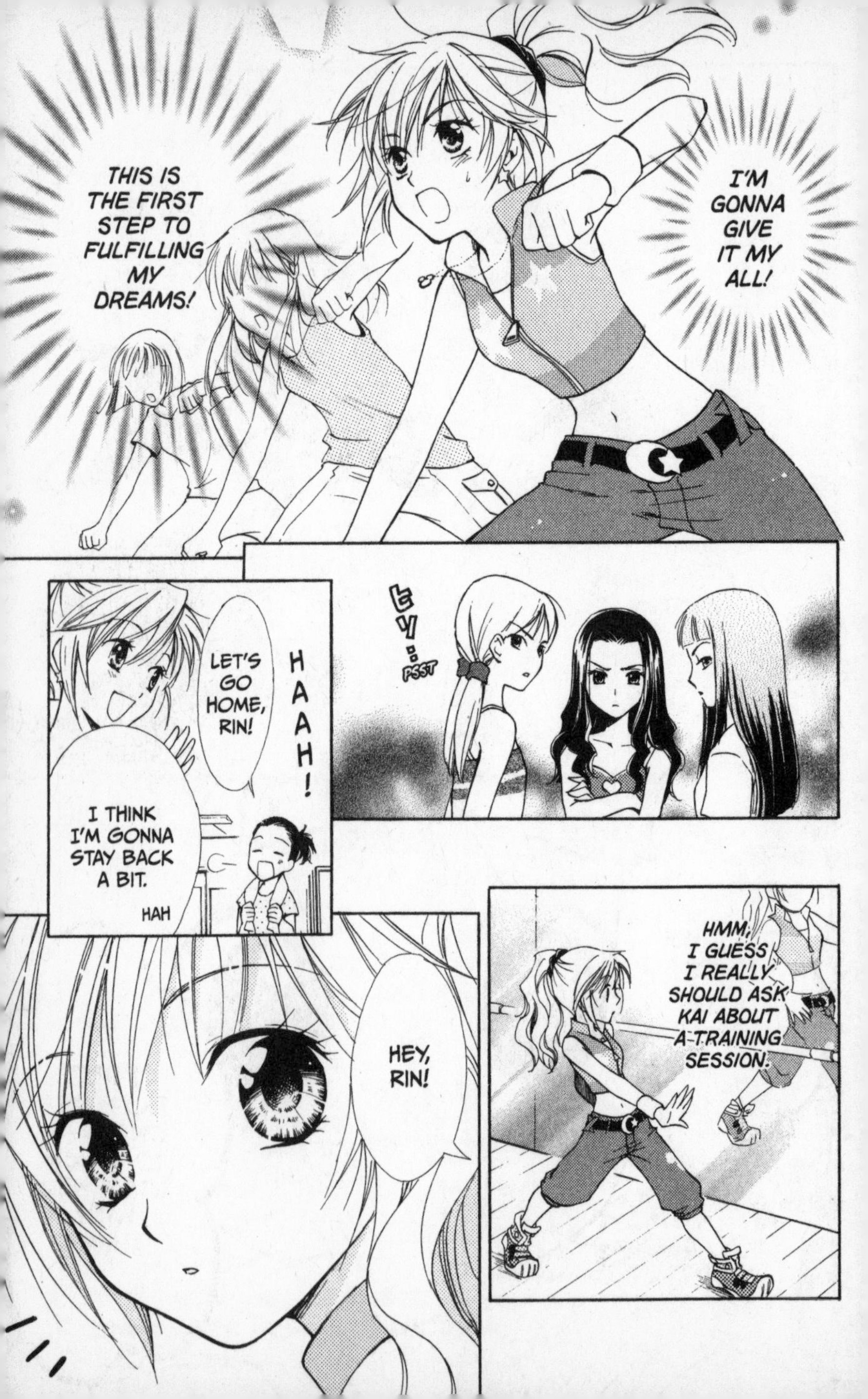
I'M GONNA GIVE IT MY ALL!
THIS IS THE FIRST STEP TO FULFILLING MY DREAMS!
PSST
HAAH!
LET'S GO HOME, RIN!
I THINK I'M GONNA STAY BACK A BIT.
HAH
HMM, I GUESS I REALLY SHOULD ASK KAI ABOUT A TRAINING SESSION.
HEY, RIN!

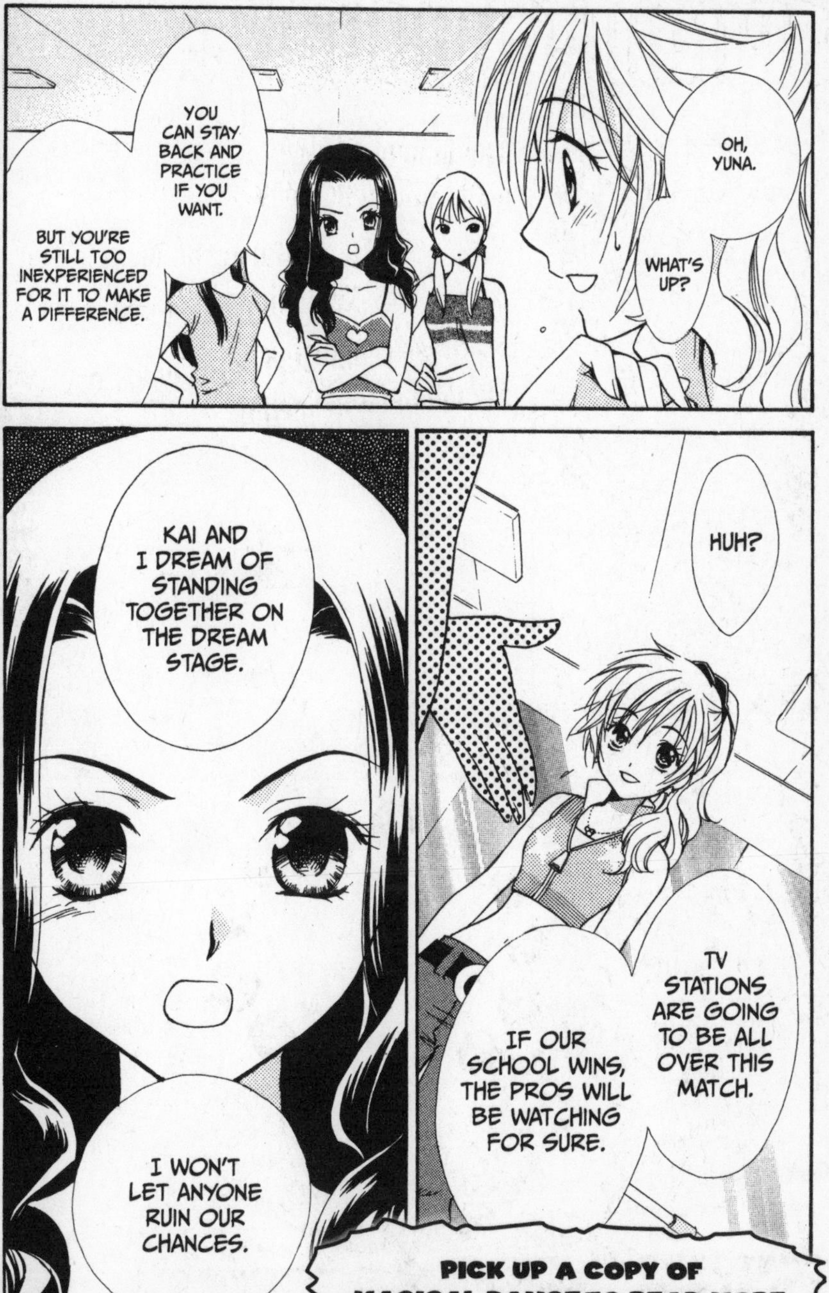
OH, YUNA.
WHAT'S UP?
YOU CAN STAY BACK AND PRACTICE IF YOU WANT.
BUT YOU'RE STILL TOO INEXPERIENCED FOR IT TO MAKE A DIFFERENCE.
HUH?
TV STATIONS ARE GOING TO BE ALL OVER THIS MATCH.
IF OUR SCHOOL WINS, THE PROS WILL BE WATCHING FOR SURE.
KAI AND I DREAM OF STANDING TOGETHER ON THE DREAM STAGE.
I WON'T LET ANYONE RUIN OUR CHANCES.
PICK UP A COPY OF *MAGICAL DANCE* TO READ MORE.

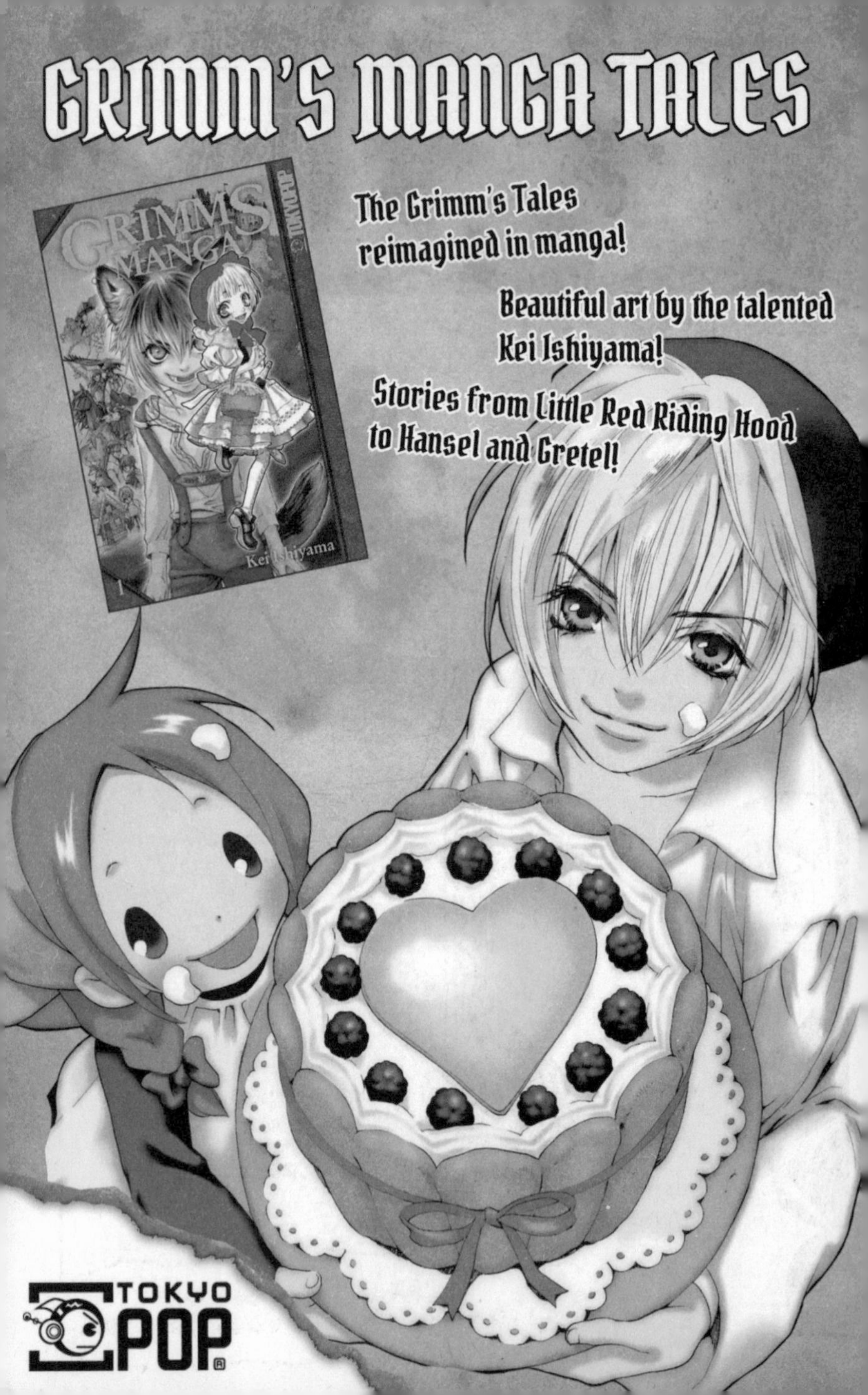

GRIMM'S MANGA TALES

The Grimm's Tales reimagined in manga!

Beautiful art by the talented Kei Ishiyama!

Stories from Little Red Riding Hood to Hansel and Gretel!

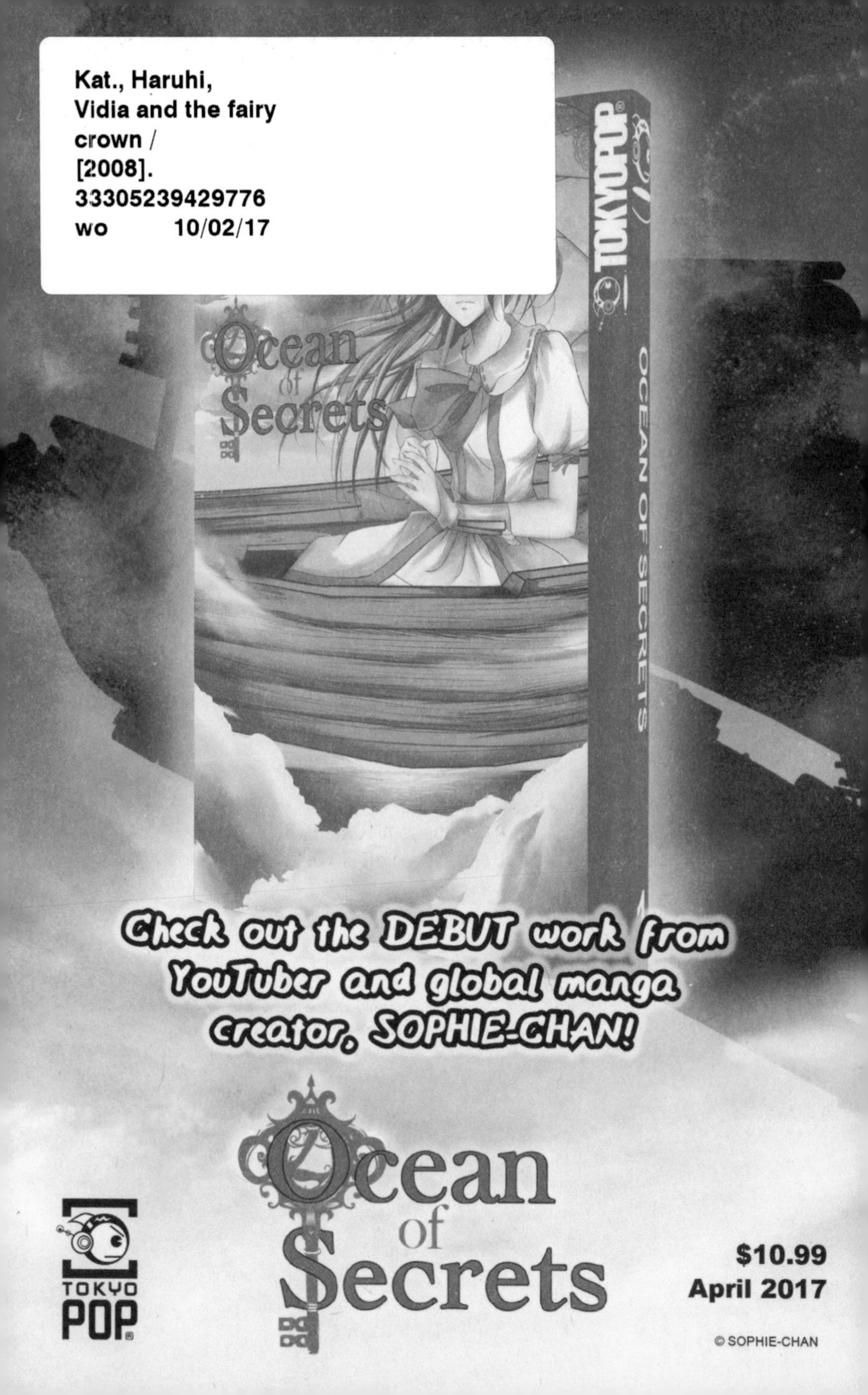
TOKYOPOP
OCEAN OF SECRETS
Ocean of Secrets
Check out the DEBUT work from YouTuber and global manga creator, SOPHIE-CHAN!
Ocean of Secrets
TOKYO POP
$10.99
April 2017
© SOPHIE-CHAN

Disney Fairies: Vidia and the Fairy Crown
Manga by: Haruhi Kato

Publishing Assistant - Janae Young
Marketing Assistant - Kae Winters
Technology and Digital Media Assistant - Phillip Hong
Retouching and Lettering - Vibrraant Publishing Studio
Graphic Designer - Phillip Hong
Copy Editor - Shannon Watters
Editor-in-Chief & Publisher - Stu Levy

A **TOKYOPOP**® Manga

TOKYOPOP and 👁 are trademarks or registered trademarks of TOKYOPOP Inc.

TOKYOPOP inc.
5200 W Century Blvd
Suite 705
Los Angeles, CA 90045 USA

E-mail: info@TOKYOPOP.com
Come visit us online at www.TOKYOPOP.com

f www.facebook.com/TOKYOPOP
🐦 www.twitter.com/TOKYOPOP
▶ www.youtube.com/TOKYOPOPTV
📌 www.pinterest.com/TOKYOPOP
📷 www.instagram.com/TOKYOPOP
t. TOKYOPOP.tumblr.com

ISBN: 978-1-4278-5698-2
First TOKYOPOP Printing: June 2017
10 9 8 7 6 5 4 3 2 1
Printed in CANADA

ST

THIS IS THE BACK OF THE BOOK!

How do you read manga-style? It's simple! To learn, just start in the top right panel and follow the numbers:

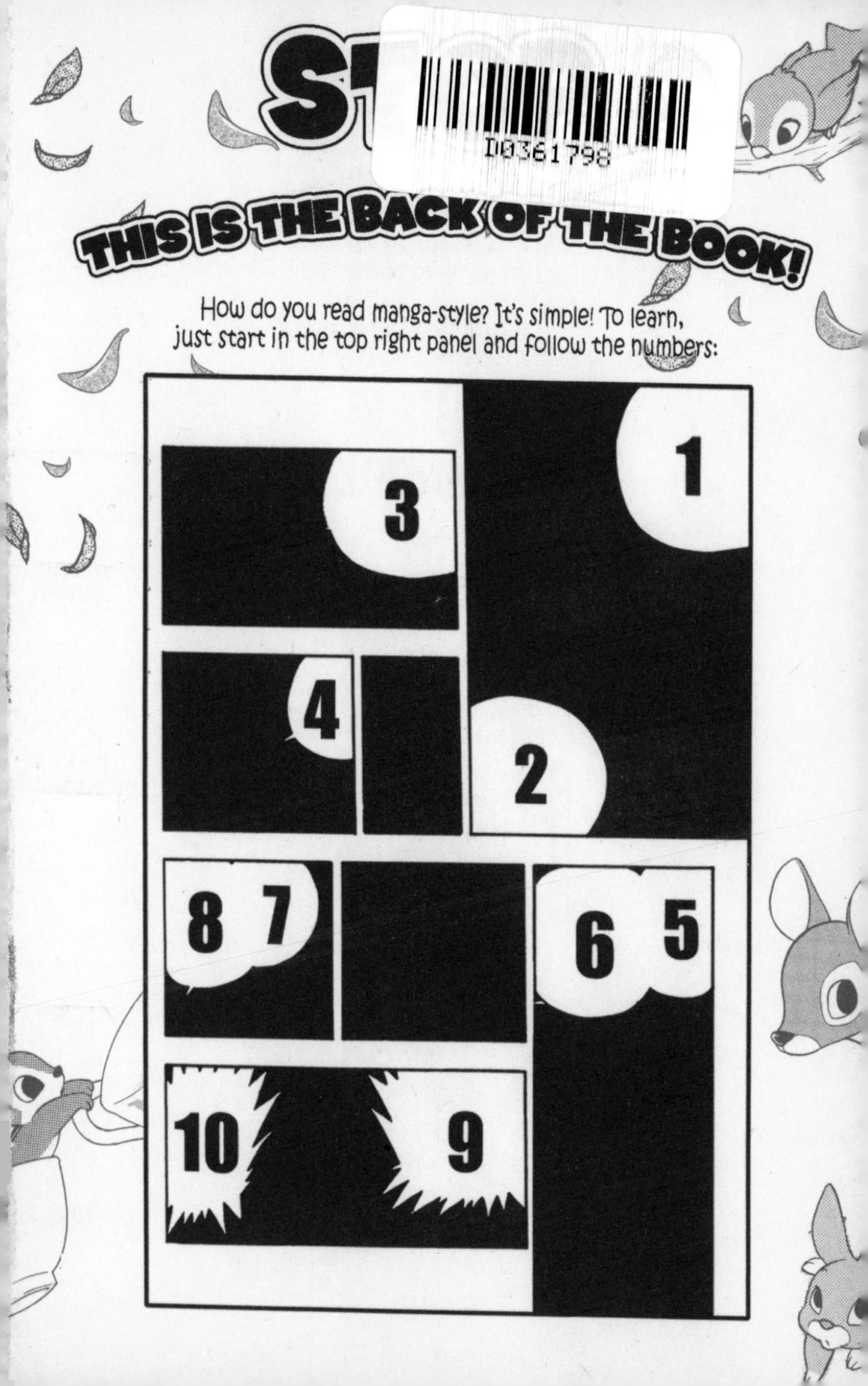
1
2
3
4
5
6
7
8
9
10